The Best Laid Wedding Plans

Lynnette Austin

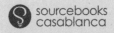

sourcebooks
casablanca

Published by Sourcebooks Casablanca, an imprint of Sourcebooks, Inc.
P.O. Box 4410, Naperville, Illinois 60567-4410
(630) 961-3900
Fax: (630) 961-2168
www.sourcebooks.com

Printed and bound in Canada.
MBP 10 9 8 7 6 5 4 3 2 1

Chapter 1

"To have and to hold, from this day forward…" Jenni Beth Beaumont whispered the age-old vows.

Tiny white lights transformed Savannah's Chateau Rouge's gardens into a magical fairyland. The heavily beaded bridal gown shimmered in their reflected light.

Unfortunately, Jenni Beth was not wearing the gown.

But oh, how she wanted this. Not the wedding itself. No. She wanted to be the driving force behind making a bride's wedding day the most special of her life. Instead of organizing events here at Chateau Rouge, she wanted her own wedding planner business.

Tonight's bride fairly radiated. The groom, Jenni Beth's second cousin, looked so handsome in his dress uniform. He'd just last week come off a tour of duty in the Middle East.

Pain, instant and excruciating, washed over her, left her light-headed. Her brother Wes had been even more handsome in his dress uniform the day he'd graduated from Officer Candidate School, then again the day he'd deployed in his camos. The day she'd kissed him good-bye. The last time she'd seen him alive. Her throat constricted.

She exhaled, forced herself to shake it off. Not tonight. Tonight was a celebration of love. The beginning of a new family. Of dreams come true.

While the bride and groom funneled their guests

through the receiving line, Jenni Beth bolted to a separate section of the garden to make sure the cake, the bubbly, and the band were in place. She did a last-minute check on table settings, place cards, candles—the list was never ending.

The music started, the bridal party wended their way to the area, and the celebration began.

As the evening wore on, Jenni Beth relaxed.

A familiar voice whispered in her ear. "Dance with me."

Cole Bryson. She hadn't seen his name on the guest list.

Shivers raced down her spine, and her heart stuttered. It had been too long, not long enough. "No."

She wouldn't turn around, wouldn't meet those mesmerizing eyes.

His hands settled on her bare arms, and she nearly jumped. As the work-roughened hands moved over her skin, her stomach started a little dance of its own.

"I'm working, Cole."

"Nothin' needs doin' right now. Sean and Sarah are deliriously happy, and everything's runnin' smoothly. Come on, sugar. You don't want to cause a scene."

Knowing she shouldn't, she turned to face him. Mistake. She had always found him irresistible, and that hadn't changed. He'd perfected that slow Southern drawl, had the sound of a true gentleman. But the twinkle in his eyes gave him away. Revealed the bad boy tucked not far below the surface.

Right now, dressed in a dark suit and tie, the man looked like every woman's dream. He appeared smooth and debonair, but beneath lay the wild.

He took her hand, and, God forgive her, she followed him, weak-kneed, onto the portable dance floor, telling herself she didn't want to, that she only did it to keep peace. Knowing she lied.

A full moon shone overhead and candlelight flickered. When he drew her into his arms and pulled her close, she sighed. One hand held hers, the other settled south of her waist.

"You smell good, Jenni Beth. You always do."

His voice, low and husky, sent goose bumps racing up and down her arms. Despite herself, she rested her head against his chest, seduced by the strong, steady beat of his heart, the illusion that he could make everything and anything all right.

One song drifted into another and she stayed in his arms, her mind drifting to what could have been. What should have been. She'd loved this man—or had it simply been a bad case of puppy love?

Whatever. She was over him.

And yet one glance at that face had her insides turning to jelly. She was deceiving herself. Sometimes, late at night, her thoughts still turned to him. The man was drop-dead handsome. All that gorgeous dark, wavy hair, those sexy hazel eyes, and that mouth—capable of making her lose her mind. Her survival instincts.

His feet? Well, they were made for walking, and she'd better darned well remember that.

Still, one night, a dance or two. What could it hurt?

"Your hair looks like molten gold in the moonlight, Jenni Beth." He brushed a hand over it. "Sure wish you'd let me loosen some of these pins and set it free."

Her own hand moved up to the chignon she'd arranged earlier that afternoon, bringing her back to reality. "Sorry, Cole. I'm working, and it's time for me to clock back in."

Before she could change her mind, she stepped out of his arms, felt the slight chill in the air.

She forced herself to stand still, to show no reaction while his eyes traveled the length of her, taking in the slim black sheath, the black pumps, and the understated jewelry. Her work uniform.

Despite herself, she ran her own mental inventory. At six foot, Cole's eight-inch advantage made her feel petite. And every bit of him was muscle. When he held her, she felt protected.

Until he walked away.

And tonight? She needed to be the one to do the walking. For oh, so many reasons.

This would be her last wedding at Chateau Rouge. Earlier today, she and her roommate had packed both her car and a tiny U-Haul to the gills, the day bittersweet. She'd miss Molly, her life here in the city.

She'd be risking everything. No choice. Her parents needed her. And this was her shot at her dream. The old go big or go home. She almost laughed. In her case, she had to go home to go big.

Or she'd go home to fall flat on her face.

Either way, by this time tomorrow, her time in Savannah would be history.

"Good-bye, Cole."

"Good-bye?" He grasped her hand as she took a step away.

"I still have a lot to do here tonight."

"How about later? I don't mind waitin'." He threw her one of those bad-boy looks, the one that made her want to fling herself at him. Made her want to beg for one more minute in his arms, one more kiss.

Stupid, stupid, stupid! She looked away, pretended to check on the wedding crowd.

"That's not a good idea. And after tonight?" Aiming for indifference, she shrugged. "I'm moving home tomorrow, Cole. Back to Magnolia House. So it's not likely we'll be running into each other. You'll be here in Savannah, I'll be in Misty Bottoms."

He frowned. "Thought you liked it here."

"I do."

"But you're goin' home."

"I am."

He leaned toward her.

Her breath caught, but when his lips brushed her forehead, feather light, she let herself relax. Too soon.

With a nearly imperceptible shift, his lips dropped to hers. She fought not to go under as the heat seared her. Battle lost, her hands moved to his shoulders, his hair, and she clung to him.

But sanity returned when his lips slid from hers to taste her neck.

"No, Cole."

He lifted his head, his whiskey-brown eyes heavy-lidded and passion-filled. Wavy brown hair, streaked by the sun, touched his jacket collar in the back.

He winked. "We might be seein' each other sooner than you think, sugar."

With those enigmatic words, he drifted away from the party, into the darkness.

Chapter 2

JENNI BETH WOKE BEFORE DAWN.

Nerves ate at her and left her feeling jittery.

She'd been back in Misty Bottoms, back under her parents' roof for a week now. Between her mother and Charlotte, the family's housekeeper since before Jenni Beth had been born, they'd fixed every single one of her favorite foods, and she hadn't figured out how to tell them to stop without hurting their feelings. So she downed pecan pie, corn pudding, fried chicken and catfish, collard greens, and flaky biscuits spread with homemade peach jam. Then she went to her room and did more sit-ups.

The first couple days, her mother clung to her and dragged out old photo albums. Played old favorite music. But she seldom said Wes's name. "Your brother." "My son." But his name? She avoided it.

Dad canceled his golf games, lunches with friends.

They needed her far more than she'd realized. It shamed her she hadn't come sooner.

By the third day, she'd felt smothered. Claustrophobic. Something had to change, or she'd go nuts.

Over breakfast, she showed them her plans for the house. They'd discussed it at length over the phone, but this was the first she'd sat down with them, showed them her actual drawings.

As gently as she could, she explained she needed

time to work, and they both needed to go back to what they'd been doing before she returned.

And this venture of hers? It would either turn out to be the smartest move she'd ever made or the dumbest in history. Today, the die would be tossed.

As the sky turned pink outside her window, she covered her face with a pillow and mentally role-played this morning's scheduled meeting. So much depended on it.

After showering and dressing, she wandered downstairs in search of coffee. Charlotte, bless her heart, already had a pot brewed. Restless, Jenni Beth drank her first cup and started on her second.

"Why are you pacin' like that, honey? You're wearin' out the floorboards." Charlotte didn't mince words.

"Sorry."

On her fourth pass, Charlotte kicked her out of the kitchen. "If you're not gonna eat, you might as well get out of here and let me work."

Half an hour later, Jenni Beth sat in Dee-Ann's Diner at one of the cute little red-and-white-check-covered tables, annoying Dee-Ann.

"Here." The feisty owner tossed a copy of *The Bottoms' Daily* on her table as she passed, a plate of pancakes in hand. "Maybe it'll take your mind off whatever's makin' you so prickly."

Offended, Jenni Beth sat up straighter. "I'm not prickly."

"Yeah, you are," Jimmy Don said from three tables over.

"Oh, for heaven's sake." Instead of reading the paper, she stared out the diner's window. Main Street, even on this gorgeous day, looked a tad shabby, the quaint brick sidewalk buckled in spots.

Not Dee-Ann's, though. A cheerful red-and-white

awning wished passersby a good day. Ferns and baskets of both red and white petunias lined the front of the building.

At this time of day, the place was nearly deserted. Too late for breakfast, too early for lunch. Her eye caught the Confederate flag in the corner, the tin sign on the back wall that read "American by birth, Southern by choice."

Some nights, when she'd been in Savannah, she'd missed this town to the point of hurting. All she had to do, though, was close her eyes to mentally walk down the uneven brick streets of Misty Bottoms. See Wallet Owens, cranky and eccentric, hunting in the trash bins for aluminum cans, the bougainvillea spilling over the brick wall by the newspaper office. Smell Kitty's hummingbird cake straight out of the oven at her bakery, the gardenias blooming in the town park, the scent of fresh-brewed coffee in the diner. Hear the train depot's noon whistle.

Luanna Connors, order pad at the ready, stopped at her table, pulling her back to the moment. Luanna and Jenni Beth had gone through school together, but when Jenni Beth left for college, Luanna had stayed behind—three months pregnant with Les Connors's baby. Seven years later, she was slinging hash in Dee-Ann's, then going home to Les and three little kids. Through the grapevine Jenni Beth had heard that Les lost another job last week. She'd have to remember to leave a hefty tip, even if it would make her wallet cry.

All things considered, maybe her life wasn't so bad.

"When'd y'all get back into town?" Luanna asked.

"Last week."

"Stayin' long?"

"I've moved back. Permanently." Jenni Beth didn't want to say more. Not yet.

"Really? I heard you had a real good job in Savannah."

"I did. But Mama and Daddy need me here."

"Yeah, they're havin' a rough time, aren't they?"

She nodded at the understatement, felt that quick little jab to her heart.

"What can I get for y'all today?" Her old classmate pulled a pencil stub from behind one ear, loosening a strand of maroon hair from her ponytail.

"Just a big old glass of sweet tea."

"Comin' up."

She picked up the paper and immediately wished she hadn't.

Its headline, "Long-time Misty Bottoms Business Closes Its Doors," spelled disaster for her.

Perched on the worn vinyl chair, Jenni Beth stirred the sweet tea Luanna delivered. She'd worked so hard, had stayed up till the wee hours every night this past week preparing for today's meeting. Everything rode on it. And now this.

Perspiration crept down her back, as much a result of this news as the changing weather. Spring was giving way to summer, the Georgia temperature and humidity rising to meet it. Even this early in the day, the closeness threatened to make a person's clothes cling, despite the overhead ceiling fans that stirred the air. They'd run nonstop from now till late autumn in a futile attempt to cool Dee-Ann's customers.

Jenni Beth gripped the paper and straightened her shoulders. Time to suck it up and remember her heritage. A woman born and raised in the South did not cry uncle. Ever. And by all that was holy, she'd uphold that tradition.

Still, this didn't bode well. Chewing her bottom lip, she concentrated on the story that ran beneath the artist's black-and-white sketch of Misty Bottoms' Main Street.

Her heart sank as she scanned the lead paragraph. Her hometown was dying. People, in search of more variety, shopped online or drove to Savannah, and who could blame them? Most of the mom-and-pop stores were fast giving way to boutiques and trendy gift shops—or boarding up their windows.

Malls were succeeding where Sherman's army had failed.

According to today's news, Darlene Dixon's Quilty Pleasures was the newest victim. Jenni Beth remembered visiting the store as a young girl with her mother. Afterward, they'd stop at the corner drugstore. Mama would buy a new lipstick or some hair spray, then they'd sit at the ice cream parlor and share a chocolate malt.

The ice cream parlor was gone.

Darlene's was closing.

Nobody came to Misty Bottoms anymore.

The timing couldn't be worse. Maybe Richard Thorndike over at Coastal Plains Savings and Trust hadn't read today's newspaper. Maybe he'd slept in. Maybe… She huffed. Maybe pigs *had* learned to fly.

There was a time when the Beaumonts of Misty Bottoms, Georgia, were important. They'd founded the town. Now they were nearly broke.

She had to convince Richard that she could make this work. She knew bone-deep she could. If she had the chance.

Propping her elbows on the table, she rested her chin in her hands. Magnolia House, the antebellum home that had been in her family since the beginning of time—well, before the War of Northern Aggression, anyway—was incredible.

But the old gal needed a face-lift. Badly. Her crown molding was peeling, and fine cracks marred her high plaster ceilings. The oak floors were worn and pitted with age.

The Beaumonts of Misty Bottoms. Held captive by their heritage, one that sucked up the remains of a dwindling bank balance faster than a construction worker downed water on a hot day, they were in dire straits. Too bad she hadn't found a boatload of hundred-dollar bills tucked in the attic's rafters.

But she hadn't. And her stately, badly-in-need-of-renovation family home needed money. Lots of money, if she hoped to make the changes she planned.

First on her list of must-dos? Prove to Richard he should loan her those necessary funds. Her mama and daddy and their mamas and daddies had all done business with Coastal Plains—and so would she.

If Coastal would have her. That ugly finger of doubt poked at her. Left her mouth dry. If not, she'd drive to Savannah and grovel at one of the banks there.

Actually, she'd prefer that. She didn't particularly like Richard, but her father wanted to keep the money in town, wanted to stay with Coastal Plains. That deeply entrenched Southern loyalty, even when it wasn't deserved.

She toyed with the pearls at her neck, the ones Grandma Olivia, her mama's mama, had given her when she turned sixteen. She missed her grandmother and could use her sage advice.

But she was gone, so everything rested on her own slightly unsteady shoulders. She took a long, cool drink of tea.

Wallet, who'd earned the nickname because his seldom opened, came into the diner and headed for his table, the one on the far right.

Dee-Ann shook her head. "Luanna, get Wallet's water and lemon ready."

Her friend delivered both to him. "Gonna have anything to eat today, Wallet?"

"Nope. Wife'll have lunch ready when I get home."

Jenni Beth watched as he squeezed the lemon, then added five heaping spoons of sugar. His no-cost version of lemonade. The man was notoriously tight with his money, not because he had to be but because he chose to be.

The door opened behind her but she ignored it, her mind a jumbled mess.

Seconds later, Cole Bryson slid into the seat across from her, and she groaned. A strand of dark hair curled over his forehead. Sinfully handsome, the man had dimples deep enough to hide in.

He made her mouth water, her temperature spike. She fought the urge to down her iced tea in a single gulp.

A week ago they'd danced under the stars. A bad thing. It had stirred up feelings she'd worked long and hard to tamp down. Cole did things to her... It would be so easy to fall under his spell again, but she wouldn't let that happen. He was dangerous to her. To her plans.

He didn't belong here in Misty Bottoms.

"Whoa, sugar. What's goin' on? You look real good, like a model for *Forbes* magazine."

"Oh, for—" She rolled her eyes. "*You'd* look a whole lot better gone, Cole."

"Your mama taught you better manners than that. You're supposed to say, 'Why don't you join me, Cole?'"

"Seems to me you already did."

"You ran away from me awfully fast at the weddin' last week, Beaumont."

"I was working, Cole. Unlike you, I had things to do. Responsibilities."

"Guess so." He shrugged lazily. "You all settled in?"

"More or less."

His gaze traveled over her, and she hated the quick prayer of thanks rattling around in her head that she'd fussed over her makeup this morning. Had worn her favorite red suit.

"Why are y'all dressed up, Jenni Beth?"

"Cole, don't do this." She heard, and hated, the pleading note in her voice.

"We need to talk, sugar. Clear the air between us."

"I don't want to." Didn't dare was more like it.

He studied her for a minute, then said, "Okay. So, again, why are y'all dressed up?"

"That would come under the heading of none of your business."

Everything was still too up in the air. Her plans might come to nothing. Pride? That figured in, too, though she didn't like to admit it.

Tipping her head, she studied him. Worn denims and a crisp, button-down white shirt, the cuffs rolled to show off those deeply tanned arms. The man looked good enough to eat. Of course she'd cut out her tongue before she so much as hinted at that. That darned pride again.

"Why are you here, Cole? It's a workday. Shouldn't you be in Savannah?"

"Had a couple sales to hit in the area. Thought I'd stop by, see my folks."

"That's nice." For a split second, she envied him. Envied that his family was still intact, still living in the present. Looking forward to the future rather than mourning what could never be again.

"Don't suppose you'd talk your daddy into sellin' Magnolia House to me before it falls in around your ears?"

Her mouth dropped open, and she felt her temper flare. "So not going to happen."

"You know, sugar, I could make us all a fortune from that place."

"No. You tear down the houses you buy. Sell them off piece by piece." She lowered her voice. "You're not getting so much as a nail out of Magnolia House to sell to some yuppie who wants an"—she waggled her fingers to indicate quotation marks—"'authentic piece of history' in his upscale renovated city loft."

"You done?"

"Yes, I am." Hot color warmed her cheeks as she grabbed her purse and dug through it for money to pay her bill.

Cole reached across the table and snatched it from her. "Hold on. No need to get your panties in a twist."

"My panties are none of your business." She all but hissed the words.

"They could be."

Her heart squeezed. There it was again, rearing its

ugly head. That silly crush she'd developed when Cole and her brother had run around together. She'd been so sure Cole was the love of her life.

And later…

Stuff happened and the crush ended.

"In case you've forgotten, you and I, Cole? We're history. Your decision."

Casually, he stretched his legs out in front of him. "Actually, I beg to disagree. I don't think we are. We've reached the end of our prologue, and now it's time you and I start Chapter One. But that's not what I came to discuss."

She stared at him, openmouthed. How could he say something so preposterous, and then just…just table it? Stick it in his back pocket for later? No. She jerked herself back. A head game. Cole Bryson was toying with her.

"Go away, Cole. Please. I have business to attend to, and I need a clear head. My meeting this morning is very, very important."

"I want your house, Jenni Beth."

"And people in hell want ice water."

"I want your house."

"You can't have it," she snapped. "I intend to turn it into a wedding venue. Magnolia Brides." The second the words left her mouth, she wished them back. She hadn't meant to share her dreams—not with anyone outside the family, and certainly not with him. Not yet.

Cole's eyes widened, disbelief flickering across his face. "I don't think I heard you right. I could swear you said you want to start a wedding business. Here." He tapped a finger on the tabletop.

"Yes."

"Do your parents know?"

"Of course they do."

"Is that why you came back?"

"Partly."

He leaned closer, so close the heat of his body nearly singed her. "Have you taken leave of your senses? Do you read the newspaper?" He pointed to the one by her elbow. "Watch anything besides *E! Tonight* on TV?"

"Careful, Cole."

He laughed derisively and shook his head. "Careful? I was beginnin' to think you didn't know that word even existed."

He reached across the table and grabbed her iced tea.

"Hey, that's mine."

"Share and share alike." One sip and his nose wrinkled. "Sweet?"

She shrugged, then called out, "Luanna, will you bring this Neanderthal his own tea? Unsweetened. He's a disgrace to the South."

"Sure will."

"Save the steps, darlin'. I'm good." He took another drink of hers.

She plucked the glass out of his hand.

"Tell me you're not really serious about this."

"Serious as a postal strike on income tax day." She rapped the toe of her favorite black stilettos against the table leg hard enough to rattle the ice in her glass.

He leaned down and looked under the table.

She choked and her fingers involuntarily tugged at the hem of her very short skirt.

He clucked his tongue. "Don't worry, darlin'. I'm not lookin' up that pretty little skirt. I just wanted to know if you had your runnin' shoes on today. 'Cause you'll need them if you're gonna chase this dream."

"You're so juvenile, Cole."

"Yeah." He grinned. "Ain't it great?" He pointed at her shoes. "By the way, I like those. Hot!"

Before she could react, he grabbed her heel and lifted a foot, flicking a finger along the bow at her ankle.

She jerked it away and tucked her feet beneath her chair, ignoring the tingle from his nonchalant touch.

"What are you really doing here, Cole?"

"Here? As in what am I doing in Misty Bottoms? Or as in why am I sharing your table at Dee-Ann's?"

"Take your pick." Ice crystals dripped from the voice she hardly recognized as her own. She'd let him get under her skin, and shame on her for that. Even worse? He'd put a voice to her own self-doubts.

"I'm actually in town nearly every week. The salvaging business has me on the road a lot, scouting out leads on materials. When I'm up this way, I like to stop by and say hey to my folks. Since you haven't been here much, you wouldn't know that, though."

She blinked back the hot sting of guilty tears. She hadn't visited *her* parents every week, hadn't even made it back some months.

At the same time her mind rebelled. Once a week? A tiny bubble of panic formed. She'd see him once a week?

No.

He'd slide into town, visit his folks at the farm, and slip out again without anyone the wiser. He was good at that.

Dee-Ann, coffeepot in one hand, iced tea for Cole in the other, stopped at their table. "Everything okay here?"

"Everything's good." Cole sipped his drink. "Thanks. Not a place in Savannah makes smoother tea."

"Got a notion that tongue of yours is smoother still," Dee-Ann said dryly. "Luanna, your order's up."

As Dee-Ann walked away, Jenni Beth felt Cole's eyes on her. Knew he was assessing her. He dragged out the good-old-boy demeanor when he found it useful, but beneath that? A mind as sharp as any she'd ever known and a memory like a steel trap.

She struggled for composure.

"Sorry about the teasing," Cole said. "You do that well, you know."

"What?"

"I made you mad and, for a few seconds there, you let it out, but then slicker than silk, you slipped right back into the role of prim and proper Southern lady, pearls and all." He brushed a fingertip over the ones at her neck.

She drew back, felt the blush warm her cheeks as that remembered touch stoked a fire deep inside.

"That's not who you are," he drawled.

"Excuse me?"

"You never have been," he continued. "Oh, you can pile on the trappings. Put you on a public stage, and you could fool anyone. But underneath?" His eyes held memories. "You're one hot woman, Jenni Beth, with a temper to match."

She sputtered. Wanted to deny the temper, hated to deny the hot woman part. Ego again.

Calmly, he took another drink, met her eyes over the rim of the glass. "But back to what we were discussin'."

Her head swam. At this point, she wasn't sure she

even knew what that was. He'd made so many U-turns in their conversation, she hadn't a clue where they were headed.

"In case you haven't heard, Beaumont, this isn't exactly the best time to start a new business. The country, hell, the whole world, is workin' to dig itself out of a recession. Oh, the economy's bouncin' back in some places, more so up north and in the big cities. But small towns… It'll be a long time comin', if the recovery comes at all."

He swung an arm to indicate the scene outside the window. "When you walk down Main Street in those killer shoes, have you noticed how many buildings sit empty? How many businesses have been forced to close their doors?"

"Yes, I have. I've also noticed a couple new ones."

He nodded. "And they're strugglin'. There are no jobs around here. No money in Misty Bottoms."

"Exactly," she said.

"Now you're startin' to worry me, sugar, because you're not makin' a lick of sense."

Stubbornly, she planted a hand on her hip. "I most certainly am."

"Did you hear what I said? No money, no jobs."

"Which are both excellent reasons to open Magnolia Brides."

A frown creased his brow.

"If Misty Bottoms has any chance," she continued, "something has to change."

"And you intend to make that happen with this harebrained scheme of yours."

"I intend to help, yes. With my *well-thought-out*

plan. Regardless of the economy, mamas and daddies still spend big money for their little girls' dream weddings, and I intend to be the one to provide that perfect setting. I'll make it the most special day anyone could imagine. And that, Cole Bryson, translates into jobs. Magnolia Brides will need pastries, music, linen, laundry. We'll need a florist and wait staff. A photographer. A caterer."

"And money, Jenni Beth. Lots of it."

Heat rushed to her face. "I'll find it."

"That's why you're all dressed up. What this morning's appointment is about, isn't it?"

Too perceptive by far. She stared him down. "I'm not stupid, Cole. I know I need financial backing along with a whole heck of a lot of hard work—"

"Whoa." He scooted back. "You're actually prepared to roll up those sleeves and get to it? Willin' to risk breaking a nail? Work up a sweat?"

Her eyes shuttered to slits. Determined to keep a check on her temper, she bit back the words that wanted to tumble out.

Pasting on a molasses-sweet smile, she said, "I am. You run along now." She made shushing sounds and swept a hand at him. "Go back to Savannah and play with all those goodies you've confiscated."

"Bought."

"Stole."

His jaw tightened.

She'd hit a nerve. Good. Because the man had trounced on just about every last one of hers.

—∾∾—

Cole realized he'd been hard on Jenni Beth. But, damn, it was for her own good. Wes would haunt him forever if he didn't step in and try to save her from herself. The woman might have graduated at the top of her class with a business degree and organized a bunch of weddings in Savannah, but if she thought she could make a go of some fancy-schmantzy wedding venue here in this town, she wasn't firing on all cylinders.

It had been unfair, though, to imply she didn't work hard. That she was afraid to get dirty. She'd worked her pretty little butt off at Chateau Rouge.

He'd attended a couple of the upscale shindigs they'd hosted, and her second degree in event planning showed. She'd always looked like a million bucks. Confident and in control. More than once, he'd had to rein himself in when guys made moves on her—all of which she declined graciously. The lady could handle herself; she ran a tight ship, and everything went off without a hitch.

Which simply strengthened his resolve to talk her out of this asinine idea. Whatever money she'd sink into the venture had come hard-earned, and he hated to see her throw it away. Pouring money into Magnolia House? Too late for that—as a wedding venue, anyway. Her mother and father hadn't lifted a finger or spent a penny on maintenance since they'd inherited the majestic old plantation house from Jenni Beth's grandfather.

And this last year or so? Forget it. They certainly had.

His mind circled back to Jenni Beth. If she went into this and failed, it would kill her. He couldn't let that happen.

Problem was, once Jenni Beth Beaumont set her mind to something, a locomotive couldn't turn her around. The minute she opened that pretty little mouth, her soft, slow drawl shouted she'd been born south of the Mason-Dixon Line. But all that sugary softness was misleading. She could be stubborn as a weed in his mama's flower bed.

Maybe the bank would deny the loan. No doubt she'd be devastated initially, but it would be for the best in the long run. The Beaumonts, just like Misty Bottoms, couldn't continue as they were. Jenni Beth was right on that account.

If the bank turned her down, he'd make her folks another offer on the place.

He had a plan or two for Magnolia House himself. And, maybe, if he got really lucky, a few plans for Jenni Beth.

Chapter 3

JENNI BETH CROSSED HER LEGS AT THE ANKLES, uncrossed them, and crossed them again. Jeez Louise, this waiting would be the death of her.

More than a few of Misty Bottoms' citizenry had sweated it out in this less-than-comfortable visitor's chair. But her? She'd never actually been in the bank president's office before. Any business done at Coastal Plains Savings and Trust had been done by her parents or grandparents.

As the scent of coffee drifted in from the nearby break room, she smoothed a hand over her skirt and picked off a barely-there speck of lint, a leftover from her napkin at Dee-Ann's.

A phone rang unanswered in the next-door office.

She hated waiting. Hated wasting time. She'd no more than sat down and begun to explain her plan when Richard had been called out to deal with some problem, giving her plenty of time to check out the room. The place was a shrine—to Richard L. Thorndike. Plaques, awards, and pictures of him glad-handing covered the walls, the desk, the étagère shelves.

"Sorry about that." Thorndike steamed through the door, one hand running over his thinning hair, smoothing the comb-over in place. Dropping his bulk into the chair behind his desk, he said, "What you're considering sounds like a pretty big undertaking, Jenni Beth."

"It is."

"Your parents would need to come in and sign off on all this."

"Why?"

He looked taken aback. "Because it's their house."

"And I'm the one borrowing the money and the one who will pay it back. They're behind me one hundred percent."

Her eyes met his. "There's no sense beating around the bush, Richard. We've known each other a long time. Mama and Daddy have their accounts here, so you'd have to be deaf and blind not to be aware their investments have gone down the drain along with so many others'."

Maybe more so, since they'd quit caring.

"Financially, the Beaumonts of Misty Bottoms, Georgia, are in trouble," she admitted.

He nodded, eyes cool.

She hated that. So dispassionate. So calm, while she had so much at stake. He could at least pretend it mattered.

"Bottom line?" she continued. "They can't afford to maintain Magnolia House as a private residence. It's falling down around our ears. I intend to change that."

Tenting his hands beneath his chin, he leaned back, the rich leather chair creaking beneath his weight. "You're right. None of this is news. You're also right about your family's financial status, especially after your father's regrettable gamble last year. And that, in and of itself, makes you a poor candidate for a loan."

Heart lodged in her throat, she leaned in toward him. Insisted he meet her eyes. "I respectfully disagree. My parents are having money trouble. Not me."

He nodded again, slower this time. "Point taken. Run through your plan again. I'm listening."

Satisfied she had his attention this time, she laid out the bare bones of her dream. Shared her vision of Magnolia House as a wedding venue. Told him about the weddings she'd organized at Chateau Rouge. His head bobbed, but his face remained impassive.

"Destination weddings are, and always have been, popular. Savannah is one of the favorite spots, and I think we can capitalize on that."

"Hmmm. Maybe." He rested his hands on his desk, offered no encouragement.

"I'll turn most of the second floor into an apartment for my parents, and I'll live on the third floor." She could see it. Put all that hope into her voice. "Between the first floor, the carriage house, and the guest cottage, we'll have plenty of space to accommodate weddings. And while I intend to cater to the wedding business, we'll host other social events as well."

He merely grunted in response.

Frustration swept through her. Damn him! He wouldn't give an inch. Wouldn't feed her a single kernel of encouragement. Fine.

Forced smile in place, she opened her folder and removed the carefully prepared business plans. Using Richard's massive cherry desk, she laid out several initial drawings of proposed changes to the house, her research on wedding venues, and an estimate of both operating expenses and income. Proudly, she spread out photos from the fabulous weddings she'd organized at Chateau Rouge.

"This is more than a pipe dream, Richard. I've done

my homework, given my vision a great deal of thought, and have the experience. I'm not jumping blindly into this venture."

"I can see that." He pulled one of the sketches closer to study it.

"I need this. Misty Bottoms needs this."

He quirked a brow.

Pompous jerk!

Biting down on her rising temper, she said, "The town needs a shot in the arm. My business, Magnolia Brides, will provide that. It'll open up jobs. During the renovation, I'll put our carpenters, electricians, and plumbers to work. When I get it off the ground and running, there'll be a significant impact on other local businesses—both of Misty Bottoms' hotels, Dee-Ann's, the new flower shop, the pharmacy, and on and on. Everyone will benefit."

Still, Richard sat stoically, saying nothing. She wanted to shout at him. Shake him. She needed this money. For herself. For her parents. She could help bring the community to life again, not turn her back on it like Cole Bryson.

Because her hands wanted to fidget, she clasped them together in her lap and waited.

"How much do you figure you'll need?"

"Two hundred and fifty thousand."

He whistled through his teeth. "That's a lot, Jenni Beth."

"Not really. Not for a business. You've lent that to people to buy a run-of-the-mill house. I'm talking about refurbishing a historic building. Establishing a new enterprise that will bring money into our town. I've got the credentials and the experience. Personally, I think it's the safest loan you've made in quite a while."

"Can you stand to lose that much money?"

Her chin came up. "I won't. I *will* make this work."

Finally, he nudged the drawing away and looked at her. "You know I believe in you, Jenni Beth."

"But?"

He spread his hands wide. "Unfortunately, I have bosses, too. People to whom I have to answer."

Her stomach plunged to her stilettoed toes.

"I can't possibly lend this kind of money without collateral."

Okay, she thought. *Still hope*. "I have some savings."

"The account here at Coastal?"

She nodded. She'd transferred her Savannah account.

"Not enough, I'm afraid. I checked your balance while I was out taking care of the other problem."

She had expected as much. Her eyes focused on a photo of Richard's dad shaking hands with former president Jimmy Carter. A young Richard stood at his elbow. Now or never. Time to play her ace in the hole. "I have a piece of land."

Richard frowned. "Your parents still own—"

"No, this acreage is mine. No one else's name is on the deed."

"Really?" Eyes hooded, the banker rolled a pen between his thumb and index finger.

"My grandfather left it to me."

He used silence again, kept her hanging.

Southern ladies might glisten rather than sweat, but Jenni Beth detected a definite dampness trickle down her back beneath her pretty silk blouse. Richard was supposed to be a friend. While she wouldn't call him hostile, he didn't exactly define affable, either.

But then, she reminded herself, she'd come on business. She hadn't stopped by for a social visit.

"We still own a chunk of land around the house itself, but my folks have sold off parcels of the adjacent land. I'm sure you're aware of that."

"Yes."

"In his will, Grandpa Beaumont deeded a quarter section of bottomland to me. I couldn't sell it till I turned twenty-two. That was three years ago."

She noted Richard's reaction, that small, nearly imperceptible tell.

"Then why not sell it? That would certainly put any money problems to bed. I'm almost certain I can find you a buyer."

"I've had offers on it already, but I don't want to sell the land, and I shouldn't have to."

"Seems to me that would be your smartest move. You should seriously consider it."

"No. I've got dual degrees in business and hospitality and event planning. I can make this work. It's a perfect fit. This is a good loan, Richard, one you shouldn't have any trouble selling to your bosses. That land's worth at least twice what I'm asking to borrow. Do you need an appraisal?"

"No, a similar piece has been appraised recently."

She frowned. "Whose?"

"I can't discuss that." He straightened some papers on his desk. "Give me some time to run the numbers, Jenni Beth. I'll have an answer for you by tomorrow or the next day."

She stood, a glimmer of hope rekindled. Not quite the outcome she'd wanted, but apparently the best she'd get right now.

A chance. That's all she needed.

"Thanks, Richard." She held out a hand, shook his.

"You might want to go over these copies again, show them to your bosses." She pushed the folder with her business plan toward him. "I look forward to hearing from you."

On her way out of the bank, she smiled at the tellers and said good-bye to Gloria, Richard's girl Friday.

She hadn't wanted to bring the land into the deal. Had been afraid she'd have to. Heck, she'd wanted a larger loan but had trimmed it when she'd realized the way the wind was blowing. Less money would mean lots more elbow grease, but she didn't mind that. Sweat equity was a good thing.

The worst of it? The smaller budget almost guaranteed she'd have to ask Cole for help. He was the expert on old houses. Since that moonlit dance, she hadn't been able to roust him from her mind. Last night while she wasn't sleeping, she'd wondered if he'd be willing to help. Her pride and ego would both take a serious hit, but the taste of crow would disappear with Magnolia House's first bride.

After their run-in at the diner, though...

Wedding gowns, bridal bouquets, and smiles. Her own business. She wanted it. All of it. But even more, she needed desperately to save her family home. Her parents could not lose Magnolia House. They wouldn't survive it. If it meant swearing a pact with the devil to make it happen, then so be it.

And speak of the devil.

Cole swung through the door and nearly collided with Jenni Beth. She looked intense and more than a little frustrated.

As she made to walk past, he shot out a hand and caught her arm.

"Everything okay?"

She nodded.

He folded his sunglasses and slipped them into his pocket. He pursed his lips as his eyes moved over her face. "Could have fooled me."

Obviously disgruntled, she ran the fingers of her free hand through all that gorgeous blond hair, giving it a sleep-tousled look. Oh boy! He dragged his wayward thoughts back.

"I take it things didn't go well."

"I don't know."

"Okaaay."

"I despise red tape. I can't stomach other people telling me what's best for me." Those slate-blue eyes, a shade darker than they'd been at Dee-Ann's, flashed with frustration and temper. "And I loathe having to ask for help."

Saying nothing, he noted the racing pulse where his fingers still touched her wrist. "Richard turn you down?"

She shook her head. A strand of silky hair fell over one eye, and she flicked it back. "No. Not yet, anyway. I think he'll come to his senses—eventually."

"If he doesn't—"

"I know. Call you. You'll be more than happy to come tear down my house. Problem solved."

She sounded tired now, her anger sliding into discouragement, and it was all he could do not to wrap her in a hug.

"Actually, I was gonna suggest a partnership of sorts."

Her head tipped slightly to the side. "I take it I'm the fly, and you're the spider?" She paused. "Go ahead. Your turn."

"What are you talkin' about?"

"You're supposed to ask, 'Will you walk into my parlor?'"

"It's not like that."

"Sure. Let me see how things go here. Right now, I've got to run. You have a good day."

With that, she stalked out on those rail-thin heels and left him standing there, hands tucked into the pockets of his worn jeans. Not a bad view!

Offhand, he'd say Thorndike hadn't handled the situation very well. Jenni Beth was one royally pissed lady.

But then, Cole admitted, she usually was around him, too.

And the blame for that? His. Dating back to when he'd been eighteen and stupid. Then again when he'd been twenty-four and even stupider.

Beneath that fierceness, though, was hurt, and he couldn't bear to see that.

Richard popped out of his office. Spotting him, he waved. "How're you doing, Cole?"

"Good."

"In town long?"

"Not sure. I've got a few things in the fire. Some business to take care of."

"Anything I can help you with?"

"Nope, just cashin' a check." Cole walked to one of the tellers' windows.

Richard turned to his secretary. "Gloria, draw up

loan papers for Jenni Beth Beaumont. I'll email you the details in a few minutes."

Well, what do you know? Cole thought. She'd pulled it off. He hoped before she dug herself in any deeper, she'd realize the scope of this project. His own temper on a slow burn, he glanced toward Thorndike's office. Shame on him for stringing her along. For sending her home in a funk to sweat it out.

Power. Thorndike enjoyed wielding it.

Cole finished up his business and walked past Richard's office on the way out. The bank president, phone cradled between his chin and his shoulder, spoke quietly. Still, Cole caught Jenni Beth's name.

None of his business, he told himself firmly. Despite that, he sank onto one of the chairs. Hadn't he promised Wes he'd take care of his baby sister?

"She left not more than five minutes ago. Came in looking for a loan," Richard said into the phone. "I played it cagey. Left things up in the air."

Cole saw red, tipped his head to hear better.

"But," Richard continued, "I think that piece of land we need to close the deal is finally ours. Jenni Beth offered it up as collateral on a scheme that doesn't have a snowball's chance in hell. And, believe me, I intend to give that snowball a little downhill nudge—just in case. A bit of added insurance."

What, exactly, constituted a little nudge? Cole's chest constricted. If Richard harmed so much as a hair on Jenni Beth's head, gave her one second of grief…

Looked like his stay in Misty Bottoms had just been extended.

Chapter 4

JENNI BETH DECIDED TO TAKE THE STILETTOS COLE had mentioned for another walk down Main Street, give herself some much needed cooling-down time. No way could she go home in this temper.

She wasn't sure who she was angrier with: Richard, Cole, or herself.

Could she have done more to prepare for her meeting? Probably not. Should she have downplayed the financial situation at home? No. That would have been stupid. Richard had all that information at his fingertips. He was simply being a jerk. Pulling her chain because he could. She hoped.

And Cole. The nerve of him, asking if she understood the gravity of the town's situation. She'd come back here to live, hadn't she? Not him. The obnoxious oaf.

Yet it appeared he'd spent more time here lately than she had. Maybe he knew something she didn't. Whatever. Too late for second thoughts. She'd left her job, and this was where she needed to be right now.

Realizing she'd actually walked past her target, she slowed and took a deep, calming breath. She couldn't let him get to her like this.

The truth was, Cole Bryson raised her hackles on a good day. Today, when she was stressed to the max and pumped to talk to Richard about her future, running into Cole had been the proverbial last straw. His timing couldn't have been worse. He needed to head back to Savannah.

She'd do fine without him. Better, in fact.

Someone else in town could help her with Magnolia House.

Well, she refused to give him another minute's thought. Time to pull a Scarlett O'Hara. She'd think about all this tomorrow...or later today anyway. Now that the adrenaline rush of the meeting was wearing off, exhaustion hit. She wanted to go home. But first, she needed to check on Darlene.

Retracing her steps to Quilty Pleasures, she studied the buildings that lined Main Street. A couple of the brick ones dated back to the late 1700s. A long time to stand in the hot Georgia sun, but they remained proud, with their bright flower boxes and handblown glass windows.

Misty Bottoms. A micro-Savannah, albeit a little more tired, a little less trendy. But all that quaint charm was here. Grass peeked up between the bricks in the side-walk, and mature trees shaded both people and buildings.

The town's strongest selling point, though? Its people. Misty Bottomers. Most had been born here, attended school here. Would live their entire lives here. And they cared about each other. When someone passed you on the street and asked, "How are you?" it was more than a mumbled nicety. The person actually wanted to know how you were doing.

She sailed through the shop door. The space smelled of citrus and sunshine.

"Darlene? I read the article about your store in today's paper."

"Oh, Jenni Beth. Isn't it awful? I'm so ashamed." Darlene, a reed-thin woman in her sixties, her hair perfectly coiffed, her makeup divine, dropped a quilt square onto the battered counter.

"Ashamed? Whatever for?"

"I'm losin' my business. It's been in the family for just shy of seventy years. Tilly Sorenson, my grandma on my mother's side, opened this shop with her dowry money. My mama worked here as a little girl, then took over for Grandma." She picked up a framed black-and-white photo of the women from the counter. "I've let them down."

Her eyes glistened with unshed tears behind bright purple reading glasses that perched on her nose. Her ankle-length caftan matched the glasses perfectly.

Jenni Beth's heart went out to the shopkeeper. Regret and worry sat heavy on her. Could Cole be right? Was this what she was setting herself up for? No. She'd never failed to meet a goal she'd set, and she wasn't about to start now.

Magnolia Brides would be a success.

"There's no way to save the shop?"

"None that I can think of."

Yapping sounded from the back room, and Darlene opened the door to it. Moonshine and Mint Julep, Darlene's rambunctious Cairn Terriers, peeked around the edge. Seeing Jenni Beth, they skittered out to greet her.

Moonshine sported a purple and green knitted cap, while Mint Julep wore a jaunty bow of the same colors.

"We match," Darlene said as Jenni Beth knelt to scratch the dogs' ears.

"I noticed." She smiled. Everybody in town knew these dogs had more clothes and accessories than any other dogs in the state of Georgia. And regardless of Darlene's outfit, the dogs would be dressed in coordinating colors.

One more thing to love about the South. Crazy aunts—and storekeepers—weren't hidden away but, rather, flaunted proudly.

While Darlene broke a cookie into tiny bites for her fur-babies, Jenni Beth hiked herself onto the edge of the high window ledge. Behind her, sampler quilts in all colors of the rainbow vied with the pink and purple silk azaleas on display.

When Darlene waved to someone outside, Jenni Beth turned her head.

Cole, the weasel, waved back.

Oh, jeez. Her chin dropped to her chest. She couldn't catch a break.

Brazen as a boardinghouse cat, he stuck his head in the door. "Hey, Ms. Darlene. Moonshine, Mint Julep." He knelt to pat the dogs. "I'm doin' a little window-shoppin'. How much for the new mannequin?"

Darlene frowned, and then chuckled.

Jenni Beth stepped down onto the floor. "Ha-ha. Very funny."

"Can we talk?" he asked.

"Not today, Cole." She couldn't. She was too vulnerable for another sparring match. "I have things to do."

He didn't back down. "Nothin' as important as this."

Why wouldn't he go away? "Sure I do. I have to paint my nails, wash my hair—"

"Look, I'm sorry for that comment this mornin'. We both know you work like a dog when you have to. No offense," he said to the terriers.

Jenni Beth turned her head one way, then the other,

and put a hand up to her ear. "Is someone else besides the three of us in the store, Darlene?"

"Nope. Except for my babies." She fed the dogs another piece of cookie.

"Did I really just hear an *I'm sorry* from Cole Bryson?"

His jaw set stubbornly. "Fine. I thought maybe I could save you from makin' a fool of yourself. Guess I was wrong. Excuse me, ladies."

With a tip of his ball cap, he slammed out the door and stormed off down the street.

Darlene gave a soft little whistle. "What on earth has gotten into him? I don't think I've ever seen Cole in a temper like that."

Wide-eyed, Jenni Beth stared at his disappearing backside. Neither had she. Out of sorts? Sarcastic? Goading? Yes. But this went beyond a simple sulk. Did he really have something important to talk to her about—other than convincing her to pressure her parents into selling him their family home?

She seriously doubted it. Maybe Cole had struck out at the bank, too.

And hadn't she promised herself not to think about him anymore? If he'd stay away, it would sure be a heck of a lot easier. The man was exactly what she most didn't want in her life right now. He was like a big dark cloud, and who needed that? Her life already resembled the perfect storm, swirling out of control.

Darlene picked up a feather duster and chased non-existent particles around the counter. "To answer your earlier question, yes, I'm sure. I dreaded makin' the decision, stalled till it simply couldn't be put off anymore. The business is flat broke."

"Do you have enough to stay open another couple months?"

"What good would that do, honey? Circumstances won't be any different sixty days from now. I can't compete with the chain stores and big malls."

Jenni Beth wandered over to the large rack of pattern books. She should be quiet. Anything and everything she told Darlene would be all over town in under an hour.

But, oh, she hated to see another business go down for the count.

"I don't know for certain that anything will change," she said cautiously. "But there might be something coming down the pike that could make a difference."

"You're speaking in riddles."

She sighed. "I know. I really can't tell you anything specific. Not yet. But I'm hoping that, given a little time, things will turn around for Misty Bottoms."

Picking up three skeins of yarn she had no idea what she'd do with, she placed them on the counter.

"You want these?"

Jenni Beth nodded.

"You don't knit."

"No, but…maybe I'll take it up."

Darlene's brow creased, but she rang them up.

Jenni Beth paid, said her good-byes to Moonshine and Mint Julep, and left with the ugliest yarn she'd ever seen tucked under one arm. Maybe her mother could do something with it. Her mood had turned even darker, and there was no bounce in her step as she passed once-thriving businesses. More than a couple had closed up tight, out-of-business signs taped in their windows, for-lease notices posted.

Mixed in with them were a handful of trendy little shops—a deli, a candy store, another selling high-priced art. Good luck with that here.

And yet the town itself? Irresistible. The quilt shop faced a little park, green with trees and bursting with flowers, that ran down the center of Main Street, a little like Savannah's city squares. Alice's gift shop boasted a white picket fence and colorful wooden rockers on its porch. And even though the pharmacy's soda counter had disappeared, Henderson's still sold ice cream and sodas and provided a couple small tables to sit at, relax, and chat.

What wasn't to like about this small town—other than the fact that these wonderful shops and their owners had almost no customers?

The sun scuttled behind a cloud, and a shadow fell over her. Negative Nancy crawled out from some dark recess of her mind and nagged at Jenni Beth. Richard hadn't jumped at her business plan, and she had to return home without an answer. Darlene thought her a total whack-job, although that was a little like the pot calling the kettle black, and Cole Bryson was still in town. The day couldn't possibly get any worse.

Maybe she'd go home, kick off her shoes, toss her suit jacket over the hall banister, and while away the rest of the day on the front porch with a few mint juleps and a good book.

That is, if the porch hadn't collapsed while she was gone. And that wasn't rhetorically speaking. That porch had to be her first priority. She really did need to get some new planking laid and the columns shored up.

She reached the bank parking lot where she'd left her car earlier. Her one true love. Just looking at it made her smile. Unlike a certain somebody who'd been plaguing her the last two days, her '65 'Vette never let her down, never caused her sleepless nights. The car was a thing of beauty. Black with a white ragtop and red leather interior, stick shift on the floor, and a small block with 365 horsepower under the hood.

She should probably sell it. God knew she needed the money. But the car meant so much to her. Her brother had helped her find it, had checked it out for her. She'd taken her first ride in it with Wes beside her.

It was the one thing she'd bought for herself that had sentimental value. And in the grand scheme of things, the money she'd get for it would only be a drop in the bucket compared to what she needed. Still, if things got desperate… Hah, what a joke. Things couldn't get much worse.

So okay. That meant they could only get better, right?

That in mind, she slipped behind the wheel and simply sat for a moment. With this heat, she'd definitely begun to glisten. She dropped the top, but the day was still. Not a leaf stirred. No breeze. It was as if the world held its breath.

She tossed her purse, her suit jacket, and the mustard-yellow yarn on the seat beside her, started the car, and looked both ways. Not another car in sight. What a shame.

Next stop? Tommy's Texaco. Tommy still pumped his customers' gas for them. And her car, while fabulous, guzzled fuel faster than Hollywood celebrities changed spouses.

She pulled under the station's awning and up to the first gas pump.

"Hey, Jenni Beth. What can I do for ya?" Tommy wiped his hands on a grease rag, then tucked it into the hip pocket of his coveralls. He swiped at his forehead with one hand and turned his ball cap backward over a mass of wiry, copper-colored hair.

"Fill it up, Tommy."

"You got it." He unscrewed her gas cap. "You know, y'all ever decide you don't want this car no more, I'll be more than happy to take it off your hands. Give you a fair price for it, too."

"I'll keep that in mind." She slid out and headed inside the Texaco station. Boy, her lucky day. She'd had an offer on both her house and her car, neither of which she had any intention of selling.

But what if she had to? A sick knot settled in the pit of her stomach, and she chewed her bottom lip. Maybe she'd been too hasty in quitting her job. A leave of absence might have made more sense.

She looked over her shoulder, out the window. Tommy ran a hand over her car's fender the way another man, a man like Cole, might caress a woman's leg or shoulder or… Whew! Enough.

With or without Richard's help, she'd find a way to keep her car, her house, and start her business. She could and would have it all.

Failure? Not an option. Darlene might give in and give up, but she couldn't. If she failed, her parents would have nothing. Worry nagged at her.

She opened the cooler door. Water. If the weatherman was right, today's temperature would reach sizzle by noon. She needed to stay hydrated.

Tommy walked in, mopping at his forehead again. "Dang, it's hot enough to fry eggs on the sidewalk."

"Yes, it is. I can't wait to get out of these clothes and into something cooler."

"You look real nice in them, Jenni Beth. That red's a good color on ya."

She smiled. "Thanks, Tommy. I'll take these, too." She set the water bottle and a Three Musketeers candy bar on the counter, then swiped her credit card.

Back in the car, she uncapped the water and took a long, cool drink before nibbling at her creamy chocolate treat. *Mmmm*. Heaven.

On the way home, the wind whipped through her hair and Rascal Flatts serenaded her. For just these few moments, she'd let go, enjoy. Reality could take a short vacation.

Springtime in the Low Country. If she lived to be a hundred, she swore she wouldn't tire of it. She passed houses tucked at the ends of long lanes, a riot of azaleas splashing bright pink, coral, and dark purple through the yards. Flowering dogwoods added their pale pink and white to the palette. Live oaks, dripping Spanish moss, stood guardian.

God, despite everything, she was glad to be alive today.

A vision of Wes, laughing, singing along with the radio, flashed through her mind, and she caught her breath. Would she ever again think of him without pain fogging her brain?

And thoughts of Wes carried right on through to thoughts of his best buddy, Cole.

Way before she reached home, she'd eaten the entire candy bar, licked the melted chocolate from her fingers, and chewed off her remaining lipstick. She probably should have been nicer to Cole today. For two reasons. The first? Guilt. Even though she was inarguably justified in calling him a dog, this constant fighting and bickering made her feel disloyal to her brother.

Second—and she acknowledged this was totally selfish—without a doubt, she'd need Cole's help. Nobody else in town could do what he could.

It galled her, but if they crossed paths again, she'd have to be nicer.

She'd tried that before and where had it gotten her? Dumped. Right before the senior prom.

True, she and Cole had never actually dated. Wes had thought himself in love with Sadie Wilson, whose father wouldn't allow her to single-date. Determined to take her to the prom, Wes had strong-armed Cole into asking his pesky little sister so they could double-date.

Jenni Beth, with her mad crush, had been over the moon.

But Cole, the cad, had reneged the day before the big dance—after she'd bought her dress, her shoes, and told everyone she had a date. That beautiful gown and no guy. Worse, the social disgrace. To a sixteen-year-old it had been the ultimate humiliation. She'd ended up going with Angus Duckworth. The name said it all.

And Cole? As Angus stomped all over her feet, Cole had waltzed in with Kimmie Atherton, Misty High's head cheerleader, on his arm.

Jenni Beth had cried buckets over that.

She downshifted and turned into her lane.

Far worse, though? She hadn't learned a thing. Had been dumb enough to give him a second chance. When she'd been twenty-two—nope, not even going there.

She didn't need that third strike. Two and she'd declared Mr. Cole Bryson out. Definitely out. And who could blame her?

Chapter 5

"MOTHER? DADDY? ANYBODY HOME?"

Jenni Beth bent down and pulled off her shoes, then wiggled her toes. Oh, that felt good. She flung the red jacket that had been so crisp this morning over the newel post.

Charlotte stuck her head around the kitchen door. "Your mama taught you to take care of your things. Get that jacket off there, and hang it up the way you oughta. I'm not gonna be the one to iron it when it's all wrinkled."

"Yes, ma'am." She retrieved the jacket and held it in her hands. "It's really warming up."

"Don't I know it! Thought I'd scrub those patio chairs. Huh! Got one done and called it quits."

Almost afraid to hear the answer, Jenni Beth asked, "Where're Mama and Daddy?"

"If you'd be still a minute, a body could tell you." Her dark brown eyes softened. "They're down by the lake with their coffee."

Uh-oh. Not good.

Her father's go-to plan when her mother unraveled always included a walk down by the lake. The water settled her nerves.

Jenni Beth closed her eyes, sensed the beginnings of a headache. Losing Wes had been difficult for all of them, but her mother was having the hardest time with it. Understandable. Her firstborn. Her only son.

So many families hugged sons and daughters and sent them off to war. Too many never returned. It had happened since the beginning of time, but that didn't make it any easier.

Tears swam in Jenni Beth's eyes, and she blinked them away. She wanted to turn back time. Wanted Wes to come traipsing in with muddy boots, wanted Charlotte to chew him out.

She wanted her parents happy again. It was the ultimate frustration not to be able to help them. She'd never felt so helpless.

"Did something happen to upset Mama?"

"Cole called."

Her mouth dropped open in disbelief. "He called here?"

"He wanted to check on them. Asked if there was anything needed to be done around the house he could help with."

"Oh!" Jenni Beth shook her head. "That underhanded, scheming—"

"Jennifer Elizabeth, you watch that mouth." Her mother's voice cut into her tirade. "That's no way to talk about your brother's friend."

Sue Ellen Beaumont breezed into the foyer. Even her red-rimmed eyes couldn't dim her beauty. Her poise.

"Are you okay?" She moved to her mother and wrapped her arms around her, shocked again at how thin she'd become.

"I'm fine, honey."

She looked over her mother's head, raised her brows at her father. He gave an almost imperceptible nod.

Hands on her mother's shoulders, she said, "Cole Bryson is up to no good, Mama. He wants this house.

He'd like nothing better than to dismantle it and sell it, piece by piece."

"But that's not going to happen, is it?" Her mother smiled and laid a hand on the side of her daughter's face. "Because you have a brilliant plan that will save us and Magnolia House."

"That's a lot of pressure to put on her, Sue Ellen." Her father, always so tall, so handsome and proud, looked stooped from the weight he carried. The worry and sadness.

Jenni Beth hated that and vowed she'd do whatever it took to make things right again.

They'd been scraping along until that unfortunate business deal Richard had mentioned. Her dad, so vulnerable in the months after his son's death, had gotten involved in a scam. He'd invested—and lost—what little savings they had left, including Wes's life insurance. That had been the final straw for her father. It had broken his spirit.

Her mother, normally a fighter, masked her own desolation over their finances rather than hurt her husband with recriminations.

The Beaumonts of Misty Bottoms were dragging butt.

If Jenni Beth hadn't been so busy in Savannah, she might have averted at least that disaster. Twenty-twenty hindsight.

Whether out of compassion or because he didn't want the money leaving his bank, Richard Thorndike had tried to talk her dad out of the risky investment, and that earned him a few points in her book. Coupled with her dad's loyalty, it had been enough for her to go to him today.

"Richard approved the loan, didn't he?" her mother asked. Worry lines creased her forehead. "You didn't run into any problems?"

Not wanting to upset her mother again, Jenni Beth put on a good face. "Everything went fine. Richard will have an answer for me sometime this week."

"Why not today?"

"Because he has bosses to answer to," her father said. "He needs to get approval on something this big."

"It's not all that big, Daddy, but you nailed it. Those are Richard's words, almost to the letter." Her nervous fingers wadded the jacket into a ball. Shoot! She shot a glance at Charlotte and shook it out. "Think I'll run up and change."

"Okay, sweetie," her dad said. "Mom and I thought we'd drive into town and catch a movie. It's a lot cheaper if we hit the matinee."

Not too many years ago, that wouldn't have crossed his mind. Jenni Beth longed for a couple of ibuprofen.

She gave them both a quick kiss and watched the two walk hand-in-hand toward the back of the house. The sun, drifting through the bay window, caught in her mother's hair, and Jenni Beth sighed. That beautiful dark blond hair had turned totally white in the first months after Wes's death.

Charlotte, hands on her ample hips, asked, "You tellin' the truth, little girl?"

"For the most part."

"Uh-huh. That's what I thought. I put a new bottle of headache tablets in your bathroom yesterday. Look like you need them." Without another word, she turned and trudged flat-footed back to the kitchen.

Alone in the foyer, Jenni Beth raised her eyes to the ceiling. A crack ran from the light fixture to the far corner. When had life become so complicated? All through school, she'd been envied as the girl who had it all. The brains, the handsome older brother, the huge house, and great parents.

Even Santa, as good as he was, couldn't deliver a wish list like that.

But somewhere along the line, everything had started to go wrong. She grew up and saw behind the facade. Recognized the peeling paint on the eaves, the crumbling plaster, the water-stained ceilings.

Six months after she'd kissed her brother and sent him off with smiles and promises to write, she'd stood in the Atlanta Airport, tears nearly blinding her. Unsure who'd held up whom, she and her parents had met the plane and Wes's flag-draped coffin.

Nothing had been the same since.

Two steps up the curving stairway, she stopped beside his ornately framed photograph.

"I miss you, big brother. Every single day. You're the first thing I think about in the morning and the last at night." She kissed her fingertips, laid them gently on his cheek. "I wonder. Could you have saved us?"

On leaden feet, she continued up the stairs to her third-floor room. The higher she climbed, the worse the deterioration. But scattered amidst the ruins? Some incredible antiques. She'd collect the best and move it downstairs.

Hand on the railing, she considered the renovation of the first upstairs bedroom. The bridal suite—a dressing room, a hair and makeup area. The perfect photo-op spot with maybe a fainting couch, a huge fern on a stand. In her mind's eye, she saw it, finished and ready.

The groom's room could be downstairs. But the bride and her attendants? They had to be on the second floor. Any bride reciting her vows at Magnolia House would want to walk down this magnificent staircase to her groom. Only natural.

And it would be up to her to make sure all those dreams and wishes came true.

She couldn't wait!

Jenni Beth took her time changing. After all, until Richard approved the loan, there wasn't a lot she could do. Her paltry savings wouldn't make a dent in the necessary renovations. She intended to check out the front porch floor this afternoon to see how many boards could be salvaged, then draw up a list of the supplies she'd need for the job.

Her mother constantly reminded her that a person never got a second chance to make a good first impression. Jenni Beth figured that held true for both women and businesses, so she'd better do this right the first time.

With her parents gone, the time was right to roll up her sleeves and get started. Hopefully, the movie would take their minds off the real world for a couple hours. Maybe they'd have lunch or stop at the bakery afterward. An afternoon out would be good for them.

Since the porch would be hot, sweaty work, Jenni Beth decided on her oldest pair of denim shorts and a pink, well-worn tank top. She pulled her hair into a messy ponytail.

Nobody would see her, so what the heck. No first impressions to make today.

Heading down the stairs, she called out, "Charlotte, do you know where Daddy keeps his work gloves?"

"Humph. I don't know if he actually owns any. But Vernon left his on the back patio by those rosebushes he just pruned. Meant to put them up for him, but guess I forgot, what with the heat and all."

"Okay. Thanks." She slammed out the door to search for them.

After looking all over and back, she finally unearthed the gloves in the greenhouse, neatly placed on a shelf. Charlotte really was getting forgetful. She thought she'd forgotten to put them away, but in truth had forgotten she'd actually put them away.

Jenni Beth shook her head. There was sense to that somewhere. She dug around a bit more and found an old rusty tape measure.

Back inside, she picked up a pad and pencil and, from the faucet, refilled this morning's empty water bottle. Another cutback. Things were bad.

———

Cole turned down the long drive to Magnolia House. Huge oaks on either side formed an overhead canopy, the trees draped with Spanish moss. Sunlight filtered through, forming a pattern of light and dark. It was a little like driving into his past. He and Wes learned to ride their bikes right here, practiced their pitching and tossed around a football. Good memories.

He wished they'd had time to make more.

His conscience gnawed at him along with a deep sorrow. He hadn't visited nearly enough since Wes's funeral. Hadn't been around for his pal's parents, for his sister, but he meant to rectify that. Starting today.

Jenni Beth would be the most problematic. *And whose fault is that, you big doofus?* he asked himself. He had so completely screwed up. He doubted she'd ever forgive him.

The house came into view, and he slowed. Huge magnolias flanked the sides of the once stately plantation home. There'd been a time when this place had been a real beauty. Now? She cried out for a complete makeover. Top to bottom, inside and out.

The porch roof, held up by little more than spit and a promise, sagged in the middle. If a bad storm blew in, they'd be picking up the pieces in this county and the next.

He stopped his vehicle and got out, closing the door quietly. Zeke, the Beaumonts' old yellow Lab, raised his head and opened one eye. Recognizing Cole, he wagged his tail but didn't bother to get up or even bark.

Looking past the dog, Cole's mouth went dry. Jenni Beth knelt on the front porch, her cute little denim-clad tush swinging back and forth to Katy Perry's latest hit.

The stereo, cranked on high, masked his approach. Her mom and dad must not be home because he seriously doubted they'd put up with that volume.

Her back to him, she stood and did a little shimmy. Using the pencil in her hand as a microphone, she belted out a few lines with Katy. Little girl, big voice. He'd always loved listening to her sing. The only time he hadn't put up a fuss about going to church were the Sundays she had a solo in the choir.

Still singing, she reached for a tape measure lying on

the old swing. The same swing where he'd spent lots and lots of summer evenings with Wes, arm wrestling, drinking sodas, and swapping tall tales.

Some nights they'd sneak outside after his parents went to bed and sit on that swing, flashlight in hand, giggling and drooling over the *Playboy* magazine they'd bought from an eighth grader who'd probably snitched it from his old man. They'd both chipped in their entire week's allowance, and it had been worth every penny.

More than once, he'd wondered what it would be like to spend time on that swing with Jenni Beth. They wouldn't arm wrestle. He grinned. Nope. They'd find better ways to keep busy.

She went down on her knees again, her butt still keeping time to the music. Despite himself, he was impressed with her use of the tape measure. After each measurement, she jotted notes on her pad before inspecting the next board. Every two or three planks, she ran the tape.

Yep. She was getting dirty. Doing work she really shouldn't have to do. And, despite his ribbing this morning, that bothered him.

She'd been raised to be a princess.

His Cinderella.

He admired her. Her work ethic, her dedication. *Her*. Period.

The song switched to one of Luke Bryan's first hits, "Country Girl (Shake It for Me)." Luke belted out to shake it for him, and, oh boy, did she ever. Those hips moved to the beat, and her long blond ponytail swayed right along with them. Cole found himself stuffing his hands in his jeans pockets. His fingers itched to undo her hair and bury themselves in those golden strands.

And that wouldn't do. He'd come on business.

He cleared his throat, raised his voice. "Hey, good-lookin'. What are you doin' there?"

She whirled around, a startled expression on her face, blue eyes wide. Just as quickly, they narrowed. "Cole Bryson, are you following me?"

"No, ma'am."

Her brows quirked. "And you're here because…?"

The grin spread. "Honey, believe it or not, I came to talk business." He moved to the porch, stooping long enough to give the yellow Lab's head a scratch.

"How long have you been standing there?"

"Through Katy Perry and well into Luke Bryan. You have eclectic tastes. And some real nice moves."

In her eyes he read the war waging between anger and common sense with just a touch of self-consciousness thrown into the mix.

She flicked off the music. "I'm sure my song choices didn't have you driving all the way out here."

"Nope. Like I said, I came on business."

"We discussed your business already, and I said no."

"Aren't you curious? Don't you want to hear my proposal?"

She wiped a hand down her neck and chest and glanced at her empty water bottle. "It's hot today. Why don't you come in? I'll fix us a glass of tea. You can actually have your own."

He grinned, remembering the glass they'd shared before Dee-Ann came to Jenni Beth's rescue. "Is Charlotte here?"

"She is." She opened the door.

He followed her inside, the temperature a good ten degrees cooler.

"Charlotte? We've got company."

"Who is it?" The housekeeper came around the corner, drying her hands on a tea towel. "Well, if it isn't Mr. Cole Bryson himself."

After a hearty hug, she stepped away. "Where have you been keepin' yourself? A body could die waitin' for you to show up."

"I'm sorry. I've missed you, beautiful." He leaned in again and gave her a peck on the cheek. "The job's been keepin' me busy. I've been spendin' a lot of time in Savannah and Atlanta."

"Hear your business is doin' real good."

"It is," Jenni Beth said. "He gets off on tearing down old houses, then picking their bones to sell the pieces, like a scavenger. He wants to do exactly that to Magnolia House."

Disapproval darkened Charlotte's face. "Jenni Beth, you watch your mouth." Hand on her hip, she rounded on Cole. "You wouldn't do that, would you?"

He felt like a three-year-old caught sticking a paper clip in the electric socket. Dangerous ground here. "Jenni Beth is exaggeratin'."

"Oh really?" Those gray-blue eyes focused like a laser on his own. "Maybe I misheard our conversation this morning."

Cole's mind went to the phone call he'd eavesdropped on at the bank. He definitely hadn't misheard that one-sided conversation. He'd spent most of the drive here trying to decide how to broach it with her.

"Cole? Cat got your tongue?"

"You made some assumptions. Not all of them are correct."

"Well, maybe you can illuminate me now. Which part of our talk did I misunderstand?"

"Didn't you offer me some iced tea?"

"Oh, you're slick, Cole. Nice try, but it won't work."

"I'll get that drink for you," Charlotte said. "You want one, Jenni Beth?"

"Yes, please." She tapped her sandaled foot on the old oak floor. As soon as Charlotte was out of sight, she asked, "So?"

As much as he wanted to, he couldn't do it. He couldn't come totally clean with her. At least not until he knew a bit more. Who had Richard been talking to? And exactly what in the hell had he meant by a "little nudge"?

How badly did the banker want her to fail? What would he be willing to do to make that happen?

Without the answers, along with some alternative plans, Jenni Beth would tell him to go away and mind his own business—something he didn't intend to do.

Without the money Richard would loan her, this place hadn't a chance of surviving. But sure as shooting, if he even hinted at what he'd overheard of the banker's conversation, she'd get her back up and refuse the loan. Everything would be lost at that point.

And it would be his fault. Didn't matter he already thought it was a scatterbrained scheme.

Damned if he wouldn't be the loser either way in this one. If she caught wind of the banker's conspiracy—and that he'd known about it—he'd be dead meat. His plans would go up in smoke right along with hers.

"So nothing," he lied, praying he'd made the right decision.

"I don't like you, Cole Bryson."

"So you say."

"It's true."

He saw the flicker in her eyes, thanked God she wasn't being truthful, either. Still, the words hurt. But he'd play along with her because he'd certainly given her reason to think less than highly of him.

"Okay." He tucked a stray strand behind her ear before she could pull away. "Want me to not like you back? Unfriend you on Facebook?"

She punched his shoulder. "Why are you here?"

"You've got some Herculean plans."

"Dream big," she quipped.

He ignored her. "They'll be expensive and time-consuming."

"And?"

"Don't be naive. At least walk into this project with your eyes open." He pointed a finger at her. "And don't underestimate Richard's motives. The bank is in business to make money."

"I understand that. It's called interest."

"He'll make more if you default on your loan."

"What are you saying?" Jenni Beth came to full alert.

Shoot. He'd stepped into the deep end of the pool, and if he wasn't careful, he'd take in a heck of a lot of water before he resurfaced.

So he went on the offensive. "Nothing you don't already know. Use your head. You go into something like this with the bank, you'd better damn well be sure you can pull it off."

"I can."

"Is there anything I can do to help you?"

She hesitated. "Why would you want to do that?"

He crossed his arms over his chest, quelling the urge to shake her. This woman went beyond infuriating. "What? I can't offer my help without an interrogation?"

"No, I don't think you can. You want to destroy my house, board by board. You said so. Why the hundred-eighty turnabout?"

"You make me crazy."

"Then leave."

His jaw tightened. "No. You want a reason? Because I promised Wes I'd look after you."

Tears misted her eyes, and he swore under his breath. Why in the hell had he said that? Full of regret, he stepped toward her. "I'm sorry."

She held out a hand. "Don't touch me."

He threw up his own hands. "Fine. But if you don't mind, I'd really like to take a look at those porch columns before I leave. Don't know how they're still standing. One strong wind and they'll come tumblin' down."

"You think I don't know that?"

She followed him back outside. Ignoring her, he ran his hands over the columns. Examining them up close, he realized they were worse than he'd suspected. "These posts are rotten clear through. They need to be replaced."

Charlotte, teas in hand, stepped outside. "Here you go. You ought to offer the boy a seat, Jenni Beth." She nodded at the swing. "Either of you want a cookie?"

"Cookies? We're not ten anymore!" Jenni Beth closed her eyes. Shaking her head, she apologized. "I'm sorry, Charlotte. That was rude. I—"

"It's okay. Something's goin' on between the two of you, so I'm goin' to take myself off to a safe zone before things start flyin'."

Neither said anything as she disappeared into the house.

"I miss him, too, Jenni Beth. Wes was my best friend."

Her chin came up. The defiance drained from her. "I know. I'm sorry. Again. It's just—"

"I'm steppin' on your toes."

"No." She shook her head slowly. "It's not that. Not really." Her gaze traveled over the porch, the columns, the windows that were all but falling out. On a half-sob, she said, "Look at this place."

He did exactly that, taking in the decay, the overgrown gardens.

"Will the money you asked for cover materials and labor?"

Bright spots of red colored her cheeks. "No. Not if I hope to have any start-up money."

"Can I help?"

"I don't mean to sound rude—"

She stopped when he snorted. "Whether you believe it or not, I really don't. I know I can't do this alone. But why are you making it so easy for me?" Her voice held suspicion.

"You don't trust me, do you?"

When she remained quiet, he had his answer.

"Show me around."

"Now?" she asked.

"Yeah. Now. I'm here."

Her body language made it clear she wanted to refuse.

"Come on," he urged. "I'm not takin' inventory, sizin' up stock for my store."

"You sure about that?"

He tamped down the pain. "Positive. What can it hurt, sugar? Give me some idea of the size of this project you're bitin' off."

She plunked her glass down on a small white wicker table. "Fine."

Ooo-whee. The lady still hadn't learned to control that temper. He set his glass beside hers and caught the door inches before it slapped shut in his face. Zeke, the old Lab, squeezed past him and plopped down in the hallway. A smart man would hop back in his pickup and head down the highway.

Well, he'd never claimed to be a Rhodes Scholar.

Chapter 6

IT HAD BEEN A LONG TIME SINCE COLE HAD BEEN PAST the first floor in this old house. A long time since he'd had a sleepover here, years since it had been a second home. He and Wes had grown up as close as brothers.

He stopped beside Wes's portrait, his hand on the oak banister. The picture had been taken the year his friend had graduated from college—full of life and ready to take on the world.

Now it hung, a sacred memorial in an ornate gilt frame. Damn!

"I miss this guy."

"Me too."

A moment of shared loss passed between them, their differences forgotten.

"Do you remember what you were doing when you found out we'd lost him?" Her voice was a whisper.

Cole nodded. "Like it was yesterday. I was loadin' a customer's pickup with some green and white tile. My cell rang. When I saw your dad's number on the screen, I knew. Felt like the bottom had dropped out of my world."

She nodded. "I was at a trendy little restaurant in Savannah drinking a cosmopolitan. Discussing wedding plans with a bride and groom." Her lip trembled. "I haven't been back to Adelaide's since. Haven't had a cosmo since."

"I can understand that."

"Can you?"

He nodded.

"I've driven blocks out of my way to avoid the restaurant. Find an excuse to leave if a cosmo is ordered at my table." Her breathing had grown ragged. "Unreasonable, right?"

"No."

"They're triggers. Triggers I can't defeat."

"I can't watch hockey anymore," he said, running a hand up and down her arm. "Without Wes—"

"It's awful, isn't it?"

"Yeah, it is."

"Crazy thing is, I have no idea how I got home from Adelaide's that afternoon. No clue what I told my bride and groom." She leaned into Cole for a moment. "I had a friend finish their wedding plans. I couldn't do that, either."

They stood in silence. A clock in the hallway ticked off the minutes.

"The day of his service? Mixed in with the sympathy cards a friend forwarded from Savannah?"

"Don't. Don't do this, sugar."

"No. I need to. I can't talk to Mama and Daddy."

"Then go ahead. Get it out."

She swiped at the tears that escaped, took a deep breath. "Mixed with the sympathy cards was a letter. From Wes." Her voice broke. "His last to me. He asked about Mama and Daddy. About Charlotte and the dog. Told me not to worry. Other than being sick of eating sand, all was fine."

Cole laid his forehead on hers, held her tightly to him,

and rubbed her back. Felt the waves of pain that washed over her, threatened to swamp her. Acknowledged his own pain. His loss.

He reached out, wrapped his index finger around hers. The smallest of touches, a connection.

God, he was still a mess over this; the wound felt fresh and new. It was being here. Here where Wes had grown up. Where they'd traveled the road from boyhood to manhood.

Releasing her finger, he feathered his own beneath Jenni Beth's chin, tipped it up so their eyes met. "I'm sorry, honey. So damned sorry." His voice grew husky on unshed tears. "You didn't want to hear that from me before, but…"

"I know." She met his gaze unblinkingly, a haze of those same tears in her eyes. "And that was selfish of me. I wanted to believe no one suffered as badly as me. That I had the monopoly on grief. I—" She shrugged. "Well, that doesn't matter."

He believed it did. Whatever she'd been about to say bothered her. A lot. But she'd shut down. Made it clear sharing time had ended. At least on this subject. He could live with that. For now.

"Where's your college picture?"

"Mine?"

"Yeah. Yours. The other kid in the family."

She flushed and waved her hand in the air. "Oh, I don't know. I'm not sure Daddy hung it anywhere."

"Why not?"

Jenni Beth's back stiffened. "It doesn't matter."

But it did. It should. The Beaumonts had two children. One dead, one fighting for the family's heritage.

Both deserved to be celebrated. It irritated him that they took their surviving child for granted.

A couple steps ahead of him, Jenni Beth moved on, and Cole trailed behind her. He reminded himself why he'd come but still found it hard to focus on the house rather than the sweet butt in those short shorts.

He told himself she didn't put that little swivel in her walk to torture him. That it simply came naturally to her. And didn't that make it all that much more dangerous?

He forced his mind to the task at hand.

"You're gonna want to replace the trim along the ceiling here," he drawled, "and on down the hallway, too."

The dog had roused himself enough to join them and poked along, sniffing at everything as he went.

"Expensive?" she asked.

"I think we can find some salvage pieces. Should help. We'll check the house first. Might be able to borrow from some of the rooms that won't be on public display, and then replace it later when some money rolls in."

"I hadn't thought of that. Good idea."

"I've got lots of them." He grinned wickedly, and she rolled her eyes. Better, he thought. Anything that took her mind off the bad. Although he still considered this a fool's dream, the renovation might be good for her, for her parents.

Maybe the family would come back to life along with the house.

At the second-floor landing, the trio—man, woman, and dog—wandered into the first of the bedrooms. "This is the one I'll use for the bridal suite. If we take down the wall between here and the next room, we should have plenty of space to deck it out the way it needs to be."

"You'll need a powder room for your brides." He studied the layout.

"The closet ought to work for that. We can run the plumbing from the bath that's already on this floor."

He nodded. "What all will you want in here?"

"Mirrors. Lots and lots of mirrors. A makeup station. A hair station. Somewhere other than the closet-turned-powder-room to hang clothing and gowns."

"Yeah. You'll need both rooms, then." He opened the closet door and studied the small space. "Should work."

"The study downstairs will be the groom's room."

"Keeping them separated till the last minute, are you?"

"Absolutely. It's bad luck for the groom to see the bride beforehand."

"My guess is that custom started back when marriages were arranged," Cole said. "The bride's parents didn't want the groom to catch a glimpse of what he was getting till it was too late to back out of the deal."

She rolled her eyes again. "Maybe it was so the bride wouldn't run away in fear when she saw her future husband."

"Yeah, there's that side, too." He pointed upward. "You should be able to reproduce that cornice without much sweat—or cost." Casting a sideways glance at her, he stepped back into the hallway. "What'll you do with the rest of this floor?"

"Family area. A private spot for Mama and Daddy. We'll keep the kitchen and dining room downstairs, of course. The parlor and common areas will be shared by clients and their guests and my parents when it's not in use. But I thought I'd give them an apartment on this floor."

"Boy, this will be a big change for them, won't it? Going from the whole house to basically one floor?"

"Yes, it will."

She clasped and unclasped her hands. He fought the urge to take them in his own, calm her.

"They understand the need for it, though."

"I sure hope so." He placed a finger beneath her chin, tipped her head so their eyes met. "What about you?"

She batted away his hand but held his gaze. "I'm a realist, Cole. I understand life doesn't always hand us what we want. I know, too, that if you want something, you'd better be willing to work for it."

For someone who had started life with so much, fate had sure dealt her a tough hand. Yet here she was, determined to ride it out and turn it around. He admired her for that, found it impossible to turn his back on the mess. On her.

"You have paper? A pencil? Think I'd better start writin' some of this down. Heck of a lot more to do than I originally thought. I didn't realize the place had gotten so out-of-hand."

He read the tug-of-war on her face. The pull between truth and family pride. Understood what this cost her.

Truth finally won out.

"Things have been going downhill for quite a while. But before..." She swallowed, cleared her throat. "Before we lost Wes, Mama and Daddy actually made a halfhearted attempt to maintain things. If for no other reason than appearance. Now?" She shrugged. "They simply don't care."

"This house is your inheritance as much as it was Wes's."

"Yeah, well, tell them that."

The same anger that had grabbed him by the throat on the stairs snaked through him again. Why didn't Mr. and Mrs. Beaumont get down on their knees and thank God they still had one child? How could they be so careless with her? He tamped down the mad. It wouldn't do any good. No sense wasting energy on it.

For now. There'd come a time, though, when it could be addressed. Till then, he could show her *he* valued her—if she'd let him.

"Paper? Pencil?" he asked again.

"Sure." She dug a small tablet and the nub of a pencil out of her back pocket.

"How you get anything in those pants besides you is a mystery only Mother Nature could explain."

She threw him a saucy grin, and he instantly felt better. This was the kid sister he knew so well.

Except, hell, she wasn't a kid anymore. And she definitely wasn't his sister. Not by a long shot. And thank God for that! Jenni Beth Beaumont had grown into one incredible woman.

Why hadn't some guy snapped her up by now, claimed her as his? And why did the idea of that happening not sit well with him? Was it because of their history together?

No, it was just his protective side, he argued. Nothing more. Yet when Laurie, his own kid sister, had announced her engagement, he hadn't even flinched.

That was different. He'd known the guy. Sort of. They'd been in a couple classes at college together.

And none of this mattered, did it? He'd help her with the house as much as he could. He'd keep his promise to Wes. Maybe make up for what he'd done to Jenni Beth in Savannah. Get Mr. and Mrs. B. through this. Then he could sleep easy again. End of story.

They went through several more rooms with Jenni Beth chatting about the minimal amount of work needed.

"Since nobody but family will be in this area, I'll pretty much ignore these rooms and concentrate on the public area until I get the business up and running. I want to make the space comfortable for my folks, but I'm hoping to get by with fresh paint and some furniture rearrangement."

Cole nodded. "They can use downstairs for any entertaining they might do."

"Exactly."

One door on the left stood closed. Hand on the jamb, he asked, "What's in here?"

The instant he turned the knob and pushed open the door, he wished he hadn't. It was a punch to the gut.

Wes's room. Looking like a memorial—or a tomb. The drapes were closed, but even in the dim light, Cole made out a pair of boat shoes kicked off haphazardly at the foot of the bed. A pair of worn jeans draped across the back of a desk chair. A room waiting for its owner.

An owner who wouldn't be coming back.

"What the heck?" Pain rushed through him, violent and new. Involuntarily, he took a step back.

She laid a hand on his arm. "I'm sorry. You didn't give me a chance—"

"It's been a year and a half, Jenni Beth. This is insane."

"I know." Tears formed in her eyes, and she blinked at them. "My mother—she can't deal with it. Can't let him go."

"Then somebody else should. This—" He stared

at his friend's room. He wanted to drop to his knees. Wanted to howl with pain.

His breath hitched. How could they live like this? How could Jenni Beth stand to come back here? To walk past this room every day knowing what was behind the door?

"You don't understand. Daddy and I tried to talk to her but finally gave up. She'd never forgive anyone who came in here and disturbed her son's things."

"This isn't healthy." His voice cracked.

"I agree, but—" She shook her head helplessly.

"Her hair's gone white," Cole said. "Last time I ran into her at the Dairy Queen, I was shocked."

"Stress does that sometimes."

When he reached for her hand, she pulled back.

He pretended he hadn't noticed and reined in his emotions. "Why are his things here? In this room? He always had the attic. Boy, did I envy him that space. It was the coolest room ever."

She nodded. "Yeah, he had it until he went away to college. Because I envied him that space, too, I badgered my parents till they let me trade with him. The first Thanksgiving, when he came home for vacation, he begrudgingly helped move his stuff down here and lugged mine up to the attic."

"Guess it made sense."

"It did. I was here, and I needed the space." She toyed with the hem of her tank top, pulled at a loose thread. "By that time we knew he'd never come back home to live. After college he'd move on. None of us thought he'd go into the service, but we understood his plans didn't include returning to Misty Bottoms."

Gently, Cole shut the bedroom door and drew in a

ragged breath. Jenni Beth had gone pale. This was worse than awful.

He jerked his head upward. "What needs to be done up there? In the attic."

"Nothing." She shook her head. "Little by little, I've made it my own. I covered Wes's god-ugly institutional green paint with a fresh coat of pale, pale pink and hung some frilly curtains. When I came back from Savannah last week, I brought my things with me and did some more fussing with the room. I divided it into bed, bath, and work areas. So I'm totally self-contained."

"Mind if I take a peek?"

Her face said yes, she did. But gamely, she shook her head.

"No. Not at all. I've already drawn up some plans for the changes downstairs. They're on my desk. If you've got time, I'd appreciate it if you'd take a quick peek at them. Tell me what you think."

"You already know what I think."

"That I'm crazy. Right. Got that."

"It's just—hell, Jenni Beth, I hate to see you pour time, sweat, and money into a proposition that doesn't have a sliver of a chance of making it." When she opened her mouth, he held up a hand. "It isn't that you're not capable. This is just too big a job for one person. For one pocketbook."

Fire flew from those beautiful blue eyes, and she stomped her foot. "Don't say that again." She pounded a hand on her chest. "I *will* make a go of this. I promise you that."

"Sugar—" He reached for her hand, but she yanked it away.

"Don't 'sugar' me, and don't act all condescending. I

don't want it or need it. I'm more than capable of deciding what I do want and then making it happen. I'm not twelve years old anymore, Cole. I don't need a daddy. I already have one."

"Believe me, I don't want to be your daddy. I don't want to be your surrogate brother." His gaze settled on her mouth, on those full, red lips. "After that night in Savannah—"

Heat bloomed on her cheeks. "I don't want to talk about that."

"One of these days we will," he growled. "Show me the plans." A muscle ticked in his jaw, and he figured he'd just ground off a year's worth of tooth enamel. The woman refused to listen to reason, so he might as well save his breath—and help her. Any way he could.

She motioned for him to take the lead. Since he realized it might be the only time she'd ever do that, he snatched the chance and stomped up the attic stairs.

At the top, one hand on the banister, he stopped. Whistled. Whatever he'd expected, this sure wasn't it. Last time he'd stepped foot in this space, he and Wes had flopped on the bunk beds and discussed whether they had a prayer of making it to second base with their latest squeezes. Wes hadn't held out much hope. At that point, his heart had belonged to Sadie Wilson, and with her strict daddy, it would have taken a lot of convincing to push her over the edge.

An invite to the senior prom had seemed to be the ticket.

And that's how Cole let himself be talked into inviting Jenni Beth to that blasted dance.

But he'd been eighteen and so close to scoring second with Kimmie Atherton. A teenage boy's hormones won out over everything, every time. At the very last minute, he'd been a hound. He'd tossed honor to the curb and took Kimmie to the prom instead of Jenni Beth.

Wes had nearly pounded him into the sidewalk for it. But they'd still double-dated, and since they'd both scored second, all was forgiven—between them.

Not with Jenni Beth, though. Yeah, he got that the prom was a big thing in a young girl's life. And, yeah, Angus Duckworth had trounced all over her feet. Cole had actually found himself wincing. For years, she'd thrown that dance in his face every time they ran into each other as the reason she was so pissed at him—at least until that winter's night in Savannah. He'd been an even bigger dog then.

Still, there was more simmering beneath the surface. Another reason she wouldn't let him close. Another reason for her animosity. Instead of diminishing, it had grown by leaps and bounds this past year.

"What? There a monster in the room? Move." She poked him in the back to nudge him along.

"Sorry. Seeing this space took me back a few years. Although I've gotta say, it never looked like this when Wes and I played up here."

She laughed. "No, it didn't. You guys were pigs."

"That's kind of harsh."

"The truth sometimes is."

He grinned at her over his shoulder. "You're probably right."

Pointing at a stack of boxes in one corner, he asked, "Coming or going?"

"I'm not totally unpacked yet." She sighed. "Six days and I'm suffering withdrawal."

"Withdrawal?"

"No Starbucks. No Ned's Espresso. No Clary's corned beef hash for breakfast. No Saturday morning walks through Forsyth Park. I miss my favorite haunts."

"Guess you would."

"Wouldn't you?"

"Probably. But you chose to come home."

She nodded. "I did. Sort of."

He grunted. "Understood."

He took in the pale blush-colored walls, the pastel flower-covered bedspread on a simple white bed, the antique dresser and mirror. All the little doodads she'd strewn around the place.

But it was the far end that grabbed his interest. Jenni Beth's work area. The rough walls there had been painted the color of expensive French vanilla ice cream, and she'd practically covered them with bulletin boards hidden beneath fabric swatches, paint chips, pencil drawings, and pages torn from decorating and bridal magazines.

Wicker baskets crowded beneath a desk area. A sewing machine hunkered on an old pedestal table.

Here was where she created her dreams—and it fascinated him. The alcove provided a glimpse into her thought process. Into what moved her. Into the real her.

Jenni Beth crossed the room. "I'm working on slip coverings for the dining room chairs right now. With luck, I can find fabric for new drapes."

"Be easier to buy them."

She fingered the material on her table. "Yes, it would be. A whole lot easier. And a whole lot more expensive."

"True."

"I'm trying to decide whether to spend the extra money to pool them."

"They'll just gather more dust puddling on the floor."

"I know, but to be authentic…" She trailed off. "Our ancestors did it to show their wealth, you know. To flaunt the fact they had enough money to waste it." She pulled a face. "I don't. Of course, the extra fabric did double duty as a flycatcher, too, but with air-conditioning, we don't have the windows open all that much." She sighed. "Decisions, decisions."

He joined her at her desk. "Show me your plans."

She slid a notebook and a file from a pile on the corner of her desk. "I have cost estimates, projected income, everything in here."

He breathed in her fresh scent, the faint smell of flowers, then opened the file and sank onto the chair. She'd been thorough, had done her homework. When she'd worked in Savannah at Chateau Rouge, she'd been good at her job, at taking care of the details. He knew that. But if he needed more proof of her ability, here it was, smack-dab in front of him.

"Is this what you presented to Richard?"

"Yes."

"Did you show him all of this?" He waved a hand over the papers.

"I sure did. And I left him a copy of everything in a nice neat folder."

"And still he didn't give you an answer."

She refused to look at him. "No. No answer."

"He's a prick."

Slowly, she turned her head toward him. "I couldn't agree more."

Cole's focus wavered as those incredible eyes met his own, debated again the wisdom of withholding the phone conversation. Too many variables. If Richard changed his mind, he'd have stirred up a hornet's nest for nothing.

But if Richard didn't have a change of heart, Cole figured he'd stick close, make sure Jenni Beth got her dream with no interference from the banker.

He turned his attention to the file again. This was what Richard had brushed aside. Even after reading through it, he intended to exploit Jenni Beth, insist she use her bottomland, land worth a whole hell of a lot more than the loan, as collateral.

What did the man have up his sleeve? One section alone wouldn't do much. There was more here than met the eye. Richard Thorndike would bear watching.

As he digested her plan, her numbers, he became vaguely aware of her moving behind him.

"Jenni Beth, I'm blown away at the work you've put into this."

"Thank you."

Closing the notebook, he turned to find her cross-legged in the middle of that big old bed. Out-of-bounds reactions assaulted him. Being here alone with her in her bedroom? Bad, bad idea. Appalled at the feelings coursing through him, he fought to curb them.

This is Wes's sister. His kid *sister.* He repeated the words over and over in his head like a mantra. He couldn't mess with her. Yet he'd done exactly that in Savannah. For one night, they'd given in to their feelings, feelings they'd tried to ignore for years. They'd made love. He should be satisfied, but he wasn't. Far from it—he wanted so much more.

But then, he wasn't the marrying kind. She was. It wouldn't be fair to take more. End of story.

His conscience dueled with his libido. Maybe it was this room. He'd reverted to a horny teenager, for pity's sake. Blindly, he turned back to her file and stared at the top sheet. Dug deep for some self-control.

Three strides would take him to her. To her bed. His fantasies. He raised a hand to his forehead and found actual beads of sweat. And they weren't caused by the attic heat. Nope. A window air-conditioning unit had the room's temperature under control.

It was Jenni Beth. It was him. It was an eighteen-year-old's hormones running amok in a twenty-seven-year-old's body. He'd crossed those boundaries once and vowed it would never, ever happen again.

So why now?

That damn little porch dance he'd witnessed, that's why. He'd been on edge ever since. She'd put crazy thoughts in his head. Thoughts that didn't belong, that had no place in there.

Thoughts he needed to blow out of the water.

This sweet little Southern belle was dangerous, and he'd do well to remember that.

Maybe his plan to stay in town a couple days, to keep an eye on her, wasn't such a great idea. If he had a grain of sense, he'd get the heck out of Dodge—or go out and have some fun.

Time to call Beck. The two of them could do the town. He almost snorted aloud. The town. Such as it was. Misty Bottoms used to be enough, though. Yeah, and there used to be more of it.

This whole miserable situation depressed him.

He skimmed another page in her notebook. Hell, she'd need nothing short of a miracle to pull this off.

"I know how important this is to you," he started.

The look she sent him would have put even a mother superior to shame. She scooted off the bed and stood, arms crossed, tapping her pink-tipped toes in those strappy little sandals.

"But?" she prodded.

"Damn it all to hell, girl. If you'd lose those rose-colored glasses for even a few minutes, you'd realize exactly how much you're biting off."

"I'm not a girl. I'm a woman, Cole. You think I don't know how bad the house is?" Angry tears misted those gorgeous blue eyes and made him feel a bigger heel.

"Jenni Beth." He reached for her, but she took a step back.

"Don't Jenni Beth me. And these damn tears. I'm so disgusted."

"What?"

"I knew this house was crumbling, but showing you through it, seeing it through your eyes—" She broke off. "It's humiliating."

"Humiliating?"

"I'm ashamed of what we've let happen to Magnolia House. Grandpa Huxley left her to our safekeeping, and we didn't take care of her."

"Sweetheart, there's no shame here. Look at me." He crossed to her. Cupping her chin in one hand, he drew her close. "Things happen. Your family is sufferin'. I don't want to see you lose even more, and I'm afraid you will if you insist on plowin' ahead with this plan. You're puttin' a lot on the line."

"Yes. My home." He winced and looked about as uncomfortable as she'd ever seen him. "Cole?"

And she knew. Somehow he'd found out she'd put up her land as collateral. She felt the blood drain from her lips, her face. "Richard told you?"

He shook his head.

"But you know." It wasn't a question. The answer was written all over his face. "How?"

He lifted his head, his gold-shot hazel eyes meeting hers. "Does it matter?"

"Yes." Her fists clenched. "Yes, it does. I've been betrayed."

"Jenni Beth."

His hands reached out to her, but she drew back. "Don't touch me. I should have known. Small town. Everybody knows everybody else's business. Nothing is private."

"That's not always a bad thing."

"It's my bottomland to do with what I want."

"I won't argue that, but you can be very sure Richard is up to no good."

She shook her head. "He's a businessman. He needs collateral."

"Bullshit." He tossed the notebook he'd scooped up onto the bed. "On a purely business basis, no emotion or nostalgia involved, what you've given him here is enough for the loan."

"But it isn't enough for you."

He raked his fingers through his hair. "This project is a mammoth undertaking. You have no safety net, sugar. Your mom and dad—" He threw up his hands. "I love them, but you can't count on them for any real help."

"Understood."

"I wonder." He studied her until she broke eye contact, toyed with a loose thread on those damned short shorts.

"There's no sense arguing about this, Cole. I'll do whatever it takes to make it work. If that means risking the land, then so be it."

He started to interrupt, but she held up a finger. "Here's the thing, though, and you need to understand this. I don't intend to lose either my home or my land." She picked up her binder and shook it. "I *will* make this work. Come hell or high water, Magnolia House will shine again. Brides will come here from all over for their special day. And I'm fully prepared to make sure it's everything they've dreamed of. The hotels and restaurants in town will boom again. The shops can stay open. Misty Bottoms will be more than a spot on the map."

"Fine." He set his jaw. "I'm helpin'."

Before she could even think about arguing, he silenced her with a finger to those pouty lips. "Don't say anything you'll regret later."

He could almost see the wheels turning inside her head, practically saw the smoke they generated.

"What do you want?" she asked.

"Excuse me?" His forehead creased.

"You heard me. What do you want? There has to be something in this for you."

"Oh for…" He stood and walked to the window, steadied himself. When he turned back, she stood quietly beside the bed. "You're enough to try the patience of a saint."

"Which we both know you most certainly aren't."

He splayed his hands on his hips. "Why can't I

simply do it because I want to? Because I want to help your family?"

"Uh-uh. I've known you too long, Cole."

"Again, I wonder," he said. "Maybe you've never really known me."

Confusion flickered in her eyes.

"Okay. Here's the deal, sugar. I'm not puttin' any money on the table. Not a single cent. That you're gonna have to work out."

She nodded.

"I will, however, offer gallons of sweat equity and toss my vast knowledge at your feet."

Her eyes rolled, and he laughed.

"Seriously, I'm willin' to work like a dog when I can. I do have a business to run, though, so..."

"Yes, you do."

"And I do know a lot about old houses."

"No argument there. No doubt as you're ripping them apart, plank by plank, you get to know them on a very intimate basis."

He decided to ignore that.

"The only thing I'll ask of you in return is that if"— he held up a finger—"*if* your plan fails, I have first option to buy Magnolia House to do with as I choose. No questions, no whinin'."

"Even if my plan fails, I might not want to sell the house."

He shook his head. "You're not being realistic—or your heart is denying what your brain already understands. You and I both know this is a do-or-die situation, sweetheart. If you jump off this cliff, if you sign those papers at Coastal Plains Savings and Trust, there's no goin' back. If your plan fails, you won't be able to afford to keep this place."

She paled and dropped back down onto the bed.

He took a step toward her, but she held up her hand, palm out. "Don't. I'm fine."

That sweet little tongue flicked out, traveled over her lips, and he nearly groaned. He fought to keep his head out of that bed and on business.

"Jenni Beth, have you honestly not considered this aspect of the deal? Not thought about the consequences if it doesn't go your way?"

She met his eyes, and he imagined he could see worlds in them. "You're right. Of course you are, and of course I've thought about it."

Still, she hesitated.

"Jenni Beth?"

"My parents—"

She looked so fragile. So ethereal. Sunlight danced through a window and turned all that golden hair into a halo. He fisted his hands at his side to keep from touching her.

"You have to promise not to tear the house down. No matter what happens."

Since he'd never intended to do that, he agreed. "You've got my word."

"Seriously?"

"Seriously."

"If you do—"

"I won't."

Long minutes passed. She didn't move, didn't speak.

He waited. Watched as the second hand on her bed-side clock swept over the twelve, once, twice.

Finally, she stood again and thrust a hand toward him. "Deal."

He wrapped her hand in his. It felt so small, way too small to handle such a big undertaking. But she'd agreed to let him help. It didn't mean they wouldn't fight every step of the way, but it was a beginning.

Had his offer set wheels in motion that would help... or hurt her? He didn't know. He did know, though, that he needed to leave. The house, the memories. He felt the walls closing in.

The atmosphere inside Magnolia House reminded him of a funereal drape, one that threatened to suffocate everyone inside it. He didn't know how Jenni Beth could stand this day after day after day.

Her parents? Shells of themselves. Living dead. Neither seemed to care about the house, their finances, or the child they still had.

The house, the finances? Whatever. Their loss.

Jenni Beth? She ripped at his heart. She'd not only lost her brother, but, in a very real sense, had been abandoned by her parents. She'd quit her job in Savannah—her extremely lucrative job—to return home. Why? To save her parents. Her heritage. Hell, her town.

Pretty damn big responsibility to dump on such frail shoulders.

And Richard Thorndike stood in the wings, rubbing his hands in gleeful anticipation of her failure.

He tamped down the growl that rumbled in his throat and held out a hand. "Should be a real pleasure workin' with you, sugar. I'll be in touch."

The misery on her face nearly undid him. Without another word, he loped down the stairs and tossed a good-bye to Charlotte over his shoulder. The screen door slapped shut behind him.

A few miles from the house, Cole still struggled with his temper, but he knew he had to set it aside. His strategy? Stay low key and on the sidelines for now.

It would be best for all concerned if Thorndike didn't know she had help. The bastard intended to take advantage of her. Well, Cole would let him continue on with that illusion, at least until the ink was dry on the loan papers.

Then all bets were off. Cole was prepared to do whatever necessary to see Jenni Beth's project to the finish line.

And he refused to think too hard on why that was.

Magnolia House as a wedding venue might or might not be a losing proposition. That outcome was still up in the air. His feelings for Jenni Beth? Nothing would come from them.

Odds were stacked against him on that one.

Chapter 7

HAD SHE MADE A DEAL WITH THE DEVIL?

Jenni Beth leaned forward in the porch swing, elbows propped on her knees, and massaged her temples, hoping to ward off the brewing headache.

So much depended on this project. She'd come back to Misty Bottoms brimming with confidence. Now she felt like a week-old helium balloon. The *oomph* had leaked out of her, her enthusiasm drained.

This place was a mess! When she saw it through an outsider's eyes, the enormity of what she planned to undertake hit her hard.

Except Cole Bryson wasn't really an outsider, was he? He'd been part of their family since he and Wes met the first day of kindergarten. Yet she sure as heck didn't feel brotherly toward him. The man did things to her insides. Things she couldn't control. When those brown eyes of his stared into her own, she couldn't quite catch her breath.

Now she was being fanciful. Stress took her breath away, not Cole.

And why, oh why, had she taken him up to her nest, her only sanctuary? She slapped her forehead. The man was too male, too powerful. He had no place in her private spot. He'd practically sucked all the air out of her pretty little warren. Worse, he'd made her feel...vulnerable, and she didn't like that. Not at all.

More disturbing, though? Until Cole had actually put

into words the downside of her entire plan, she'd refused to truly consider the possibility of it. To seriously contemplate failure and what would happen if she couldn't make her dreams come alive. Queasiness rolled through her.

He'd been wrong, though. Of course, she'd thought about it. After all, she wasn't Wonder Woman. But still, she'd brushed aside the doubts, the what-ifs, and concentrated on what needed to be done. Kept moving forward, putting one foot in front of the other. Walked into Richard Thorndike's office and proposed her plan. Asked for that loan.

What if she couldn't pull it off?

The threatened headache exploded, and she grimaced.

Did those high-flying poker players experience this heart-pounding, dry-mouthed sensation when they pushed their entire pile into the pot?

Because if this didn't work, everything would be gone. Home, job, dreams.

She laid her head back, and with one foot set the old swing moving slowly. Her family couldn't continue as they were, though. Something had to change.

But was her plan the best one? Were there any alternatives? Her chest grew tight as stress plowed through her.

Unable to sit, she jumped up and moved to the planter. Ruthlessly, she ripped out weeds.

Cole wanted the house. But he'd promised not to tear it down. Would he keep that promise?

Richard wanted her bottomland. Maybe. And maybe Cole was making a mountain out of a molehill there. Richard said he needed collateral. Nothing unusual about that. So why did Cole read something sinister into the request?

Did he know something she didn't? Or was he simply trying to cloud her brain, what little she had left? He had the power to do that.

So tired, and she hadn't even started the hard part yet. A big sigh escaped. *Okay. Think. What are your options?*

Her mind whirred, slipped out of gear, and she jerked it back. Try as she might, though, she came up with exactly zero alternatives.

Zip. *Nada*. She lifted her eyes to the heavens, balled her hands into fists. "I will not fail! Whatever it takes."

Time to pull on those big girl panties and make this happen.

Magnolia House. Her family's biggest asset. Her family's biggest liability.

Well, no ifs, ands, or buts. Time to turn this grand old house and its grounds into the best damn wedding venue folks had ever seen. No slipshod job. No lick and a promise. Nope. She'd roll up her sleeves and make this a place her people, her ancestors would be proud to claim.

She dusted her hands and grabbed another sheet of paper. Sitting on the steps, she made two columns. Pros and cons.

Magnolia House had the deepest well with the sweetest water imaginable. Wes had worried about his parents and, at his insistence, the roof, fascia, and gutters had been replaced a couple years ago. As far as furniture went, she'd haul some things from the second floor, some out of storage. She'd be okay in that department. And room? She had plenty.

On the con side? The columns needed to be replaced, and after they repaired some of the siding, soffits, and plaster, everything, inside and out, had to have fresh paint. They'd need to update the kitchen and downstairs bath, plus add the half-bath in the bride's suite.

Another pro? The original oak floors could be sanded and refinished. Huge savings there.

She continued, switching between the columns. The air-conditioning had been retrofitted but would need some work. Porch repair—which she'd started. She'd keep the original glass in the windows but caulk them all. Some of the banister rungs would have to be replaced, which might mean hiring a specialist to re-create copies of the originals. Same with the plaster. Unless she was mistaken, all this was probably only the tip of the iceberg.

Most businesses failed because they were under-capitalized. Because money hadn't been set aside for contingencies. Her contingency fund? Her charge cards.

If only she didn't feel so alone. Cole had offered support, said he'd be there to give her a leg up. He'd promised to help her make it work. But his staying power was questionable, wasn't it?

He'd bailed on her before. Twice. Would he do it again? Probably.

She sat up a little straighter. Well, then, she'd best not count on him. If he showed, if he helped, wonderful. If he didn't? Her jaw tightened. She'd do it alone. Prove to him exactly what she was made of.

After all, this was her dream. Her family's salvation. It would take a Beaumont to make it happen.

—◆◆◆—

Cole had to dislodge Jenni Beth from his mind. She'd taken up permanent residence. This crazy plan of hers was all he could think about. Well, it would *not* be his fault if she failed. The house was a freakin' disaster. Wallpaper and paint, along with some cockamamie wish on the first star of the night, wasn't going to fix Magnolia House.

Despite that, though, he would help. Any way he could. Because he'd promised Wes. No, Wes wasn't the reason. At least, not the whole reason.

It was Jenni Beth herself.

God, he'd missed her. Had actually wrangled invites to events at Chateau Rouge just to catch a glimpse of her.

One of the sexiest little things he'd ever run across, she called to him. There. He'd admitted it—finally. To himself. He couldn't pursue his feelings. Lust, pure and simple, had to be set aside. And wasn't that a kick in the gut?

He'd acted on those feelings once. The biggest mistake of his life. Right now, he was happy with things as they were, content with the status quo. He'd built up a darned good business and had a successful, full life in the city.

When he wanted a woman to share dinner, he had plenty of takers. Sunday afternoons spent with a six-pack in front of the TV with a ball game and his guy pals? The perfect life. He wasn't looking for anything more and didn't want anything more.

Jenni Beth deserved the white picket fence, the two-point-five kids, the happily-forever-after. She wouldn't find it with him—and he sure as heck didn't plan on a quick roll in the hay with her.

Mr. Beaumont, no matter how dispirited he seemed, would have his hide. And rightly so.

Apparently, it had been too long since he'd hooked up with one of his on-again, off-again ladies. In the city, he trod on firm ground. His dates understood there'd be no promises. Savannah wasn't in the cards tonight, though.

He punched in a number on his phone.

"Elliot Construction."

"Hey, Beck."

"Cole? Where the heck are you, buddy?"

"Right here in Misty Bottoms. You busy?"

"For the next couple hours, then I'm free as a bird. I'm finishin' up a job this afternoon. Want to grab some dinner?"

"Sure do," Cole answered. "And drinks. Lots of drinks."

"Duffy's Pub?"

"You got it. Seven work for you?"

"Yep," Beck said. "That'll give me time to wash off the top layer of grime. See you there."

Next, Cole phoned home. When his mother answered, he smiled. A boy never got too old to find comfort in his mom's voice. "How's my best girl?"

"Cole, sweetie! Where are you?"

"I'm in town."

"Dad and I saw you'd been here, but we weren't quite sure when you'd come or how long you planned to stay."

Chagrin tugged at his conscience. He really should have stopped in to say hello, to share a cup of coffee. After he'd run into Jenni Beth…

"I got in late last night, took an early run this morning, then had breakfast in town."

"That's what we figured. Will you have time to stop by before you head back to the city?"

"Sure will. Actually, I'm gonna stay a couple days."

"Oh, your dad will be so happy. He's missed you."

"And you?" he teased.

She laughed. "Okay, you caught me. I miss you something terrible. I've been naggin' your dad to take a trip into Savannah to visit you."

"Well, now you won't need to."

"Here on business?"

"Yeah. I had some banking to do. Could have done that over the computer, but there were a couple estate sales close by I wanted to check out. I ended up buying a few things. As long as I'm here, I figure why not take a day or two at home."

"Anything you need me to do?"

"Nope. I left the windows open to air out the place." Renovating the old barn on his parents' acreage had been one of the smartest things he'd ever done. As much as he loved them, they were all better off with their own space.

"How about I leave some homemade caramel creams in your fridge?"

"Did I tell you how much I love you? That you're the best mom ever?"

"You might have mentioned it a couple times. I know you have lots going on, but can you join us for dinner tonight? I'm makin' fried chicken, some greens, and my homemade biscuits."

A sliver of guilt—along with a huge hunger for his mom's cooking—arrowed through him, and he waffled. He really wanted to talk to Beck tonight, though, needed his take on this Jenni Beth thing. Nobody knew the inner workings of Misty Bottoms better than Beck.

He went with his gut.

"How about breakfast, Mom? I'm gonna be kind of

busy the rest of today, and Beck and I thought we'd hook up for dinner. Catch up a little bit."

"Oh, that sounds wonderful, honey. You boys don't get to see each other often enough anymore. Go out and play with your friend, then come on over for waffles in the mornin'."

"I'll look forward to them. Not sure when I'll get home tonight, so don't stay up watchin' for my headlights."

She chuckled. "I won't. I *will* stick some leftovers in your fridge, though. Just in case you want a midnight snack."

"Again, you're the best. Love you."

"Love you, too, Son."

He ended the call, wondering what he'd do for the rest of the day. He'd fibbed to his mom when he'd said he had plans. He didn't.

Actually, he wanted badly to spend the afternoon with Jenni Beth, and, because he wanted it so much, he wouldn't. Tomorrow would be soon enough to start squabbling with her over what she could and couldn't do. No doubt they'd butt heads.

Too bad the circumstances weren't different. He'd like to make contact with more than that hard head of hers.

Nothing said he couldn't take a quick trip over to the salvage yard in Springfield, though. Last time he'd been there they'd had some humdinger columns. The Beaumonts needed four to redo the front of their place. If Jenni Beth thought she'd be able to fix the ones on her porch, she was fooling herself. Way beyond fixing, the columns absolutely had to be replaced.

He could drive to Springfield, check out what they had, and still be back in time to meet Beck. Good thing he'd left a trailer at his folks' place. He wouldn't take it this trip. If he found what he needed, he'd run back, pick up the trailer, then present the columns to Jenni Beth, deed done. Or maybe he'd take her to look at them first. Either way, the two of them working together should have the porch up and running in two, three days at the most.

Enough lollygagging, Jenni Beth decided. If…no, damn it, *when* Richard came through with that loan, time would literally be money. Every day it took to get this place up and running was a day she'd be spending rather than making money. Time. A luxury she couldn't afford.

Picking up her tape measure and notepad, she tackled the job she'd been doing when Cole interrupted her. A lot of the floorboards could be salvaged with a few nails and some sanding. But the task of evaluating and measuring was downright tedious.

When she finished the last board, she checked her watch. Still enough time to run into town. She'd order the wood she needed, cut to length, from Beck's lumberyard, then stop by the flower shop and introduce herself to the new owner.

And how strange was that? Brenda Freedman had run the only flower shop in town since time began. But a few months ago, she'd decided to retire and sold her shop to a Yankee. Then she'd bought herself a condo in Florida and was right now, no doubt, splashing around in the ocean.

Too bad. It sure wouldn't be the same without her. But when Jenni Beth opened the doors to Magnolia House, she'd need a florist, one who'd work with her.

And that meant touching base—and making a personal connection—with Pia D'Amato at Bella Fiore. Both the owner's and the shop's names sounded too foreign for Misty Bottoms, but nothing remained the same forever. And wasn't that, sometimes, a good thing?

Fortunately, the new owner had decided to keep the garden center, too. Like Brenda, she'd sell plants as well as floral arrangements. The town needed that. The nearest nursery was more than twenty miles away.

If things went well, Jenni Beth might even have time to stop by the bakery, check off another item on her to-do list. Kitty was barely out of high school when she'd baked Jenni Beth's parents' wedding cake. Still in business, she continued feeding the sweet tooth of Misty Bottom's population. How much longer would she want to do that? Be able to do it?

Fingers crossed, Jenni Beth hoped it would be long enough. A bride absolutely could not have a wedding without that special cake. And God knew neither she nor her mother had inherited any baking genes. She could plan one heck of a menu and even design the cake, but she couldn't make them happen. Nor could Charlotte, though there'd been a time when her cakes were some of the finest in the county.

There'd been a time when Magnolia House was the finest in the county, too. There'd been a time when her brother had been here with her, had shared the responsibilities, the fun, the laughter.

That time was no more.

And wasn't she turning maudlin?

Enough.

Taking the stairs at a fast clip, she headed to the

shower. Running grimy fingers through her hair, she cringed. Cobwebs. Yeech.

She hit the last step and stopped. Cole. She could smell him here in her room. He might be gone, but the essence of him remained.

It had been a huge mistake to let that man into her bedroom.

Chapter 8

CONVERTIBLE TOP DOWN, DUST FLYING BEHIND HER, and a swingy little sundress boosting her confidence, Jenni Beth shot into the lumberyard's dirt parking lot. She refused to ruin the beautiful spring day by dwelling on the negatives. Instead, now that she'd set the plans in motion to turn her dream into reality, impatience ate at her.

She parked and flipped up the car's top. No sense coming out to find her leather seats dirty. Slinging her purse over a shoulder, she headed into Elliot's Lumber and Hardware, Misty Bottoms' small-town hybrid of Lowe's and Home Depot. Better than both because it was a mom-and-pop enterprise. If a person had any kind of construction project in the works, he could find what he needed here.

Beck's grandpa had established the family business, then handed the reins to his son. Now the day-to-day rested as much on Beck's shoulders as on his dad's. Beck also ran Elliot's Construction Company from here. Not a slacker's bone in that well-muscled body.

He was doing well, but it had cost him. Big time. Jenni Beth's thoughts turned to her best friend, Tansy Calhoun. She and Beck had been so in love all through high school. But when Tansy went off to college, Beck stayed behind to help his family with the business. Still single, he seemed determined to stay that way.

Tansy, on the other hand, was a married woman with the sweetest little girl ever to inhabit this Earth. Jenni Beth smiled every time she thought about little Gracie. She hoped Tansy would visit soon, but the chances of that happening were pretty slim. Since her marriage, Tansy had pulled away from everything Misty Bottoms. Her hoity-toity husband didn't encourage ties with the past.

Halfway across the lot, she spotted Beck by his truck. He and another guy were unloading tools from the back.

"Hey, Beck."

"Hey yourself, beautiful," he drawled. "How the heck are you?"

She moved in to give him a hug, but he held his arms in the air. "Don't get too close, sweetheart. That's one cute little dress you're wearin', and I'm dirty as all get out. Been puttin' up a new shed for Teddy Higgins out on Old Coffee Road."

"I don't care." She went in for the hug, heedless of a little sweat and dirt. The cotton dress could be tossed in the washer.

The man felt good. Solid. A little leaner than Cole, maybe an inch taller. While Cole's hair was a dark, sun-streaked brown, Beck's was a golden blond and tended to curl. Cole's? His swept back in mouthwatering waves.

And why was she thinking about Cole again? Face hidden against Beck's chest, certain he couldn't see her, she rolled her eyes.

"You know, Beck, you look more like Dierks Bentley than Dierks Bentley."

"That's what all the girls tell me."

"Then what's wrong with you? Go get one."

"I've been waitin' for you, darlin'."

"Yeah, right."

He bussed her on the cheek. "Hear you've got a project goin' on out at the homestead."

"I sure do, and I'm up to my neck in it. I went to see Richard at the bank this morning." She crossed her fingers. "I'm hoping he'll bankroll the renovation and start-up. Cole says I'm crazy, but I can do this."

"If anybody can, it's you. So what brings you to my place? How can I help?"

"I came to drop off an order for some lumber. It's either fix that porch floor or tear the whole darn thing off."

"Yeah, I noticed last time I visited your folks it looked kind of rough. I meant to get back, but…" He spread his hands. "I got busy. Just not enough hours in the day."

"Don't I know it. But that's okay. I'm taking care of it."

"You need some help?"

She shook her head. "I can manage."

"Yourself?" He held her at arm's distance and studied her.

"Hey." She made a muscle. "I can swing a hammer. Nothing wrong with my arm."

He wrapped a hand around her upper arm, pretended to be impressed. "You're right. My mistake."

"Your guys will cut the lumber to length before they deliver it, right? That's the tricky part."

"Yep, they'll do that. You get into trouble, though, despite all that muscle"—he gave her upper arm another squeeze—"you give me a call."

When she opened her mouth, he said, "No need to get your back up. Just makin' a friendly offer of help."

She took a deep breath. "Then thank you. Cole

actually offered to help, too." Going for nonchalance, she said, "He's in town."

"Yeah, we're gonna hit Duffy's Pub a little later for dinner and a couple beers." He hesitated for a fraction of a second. "Want to join us?"

She laughed, knowing full well why he'd been reluctant to invite her. This was guys' night out. Still, he'd been willing to sacrifice, and that meant a lot. "No, that's okay. I've got more than enough to keep me busy."

"Why'd you come home, Jenni Beth?"

"Ah, and there's the million-dollar question, isn't it?"

"Let's go on back to my office. Sit down for a few minutes. Think I've got a couple cold sodas in my fridge."

She followed him through the store, waited while he answered a couple questions tossed at him by an employee, then dropped onto the sagging sofa in his cluttered office.

"Here, let me get some of that." He scooped up a book of wallpaper samples and piled it on the floor by the carpet swatches. Some paperwork ended up in the same heap.

"You need a bookkeeper…and a cleaning lady."

"Got both. But I rarely let them in here." He grinned. "They'd screw up my organizational system."

"Right. I can see that. A place for everything and everything in its place."

"Something like that." He grabbed a Coke from the mini-fridge and handed it to her, then retrieved a second for himself. Settling onto his office chair, he kicked back, booted feet on his desktop.

"So, what are you really doing back in Misty Bottoms?"

She took a long cold drink of her soda, then filled him in on her plan.

"What do you think?" she finally asked.

"Honestly? I believe you've got your work cut out for you. If you can pull it off? Huge win. For you, your parents, and the town."

She nodded slowly. "I thought long and hard before I turned in my resignation at the Chateau Rouge Resort. I loved that job, but my folks need me here."

Beck nodded vaguely. "I see them around town once in a while. Mostly your dad. Your mother—well, they've both aged, haven't they?"

She raised her gaze to the ceiling. Fought back another round of unwanted tears. "Oh, Beck, I should have come back sooner. I figured they had each other. That they were okay. They're not. My mom's barely holding on."

She met his worried gaze and fought for a smile. "So, here I am. And as soon as Richard gives me the go-ahead, I'll tear into the old place. Until then, I'll start on the porch. That's something I can tackle myself, physically and financially."

"My offer of help stands."

"I know." She tossed her empty soda can into his recycling container and dug the itemized list out of her purse.

Beck plucked the notepaper from her and scanned it. "Looks pretty thorough. You're sure of the measurements?"

The arched-brow look she sent him said it all.

"Okay then. Let's get this order placed."

As they stepped from his office, he glanced again at her notes. "Everything's in stock. It'll take my guys some time to get your lumber cut and the rest of the things pulled together. We should be able to deliver it sometime tomorrow. Will that work?"

"It sure will."

"Don't suppose you have a nail gun?"

"Nope. I plan to use a hammer and do it the old-fashioned way."

Walking over to a bin, he scooped up a handful of nails. "You'll want to use this kind, this size." He held one up. "It'll sink deeper and hold better. I'll send some out with your lumber."

"Thanks."

"You gonna paint or stain the wood?"

"The porch has always been white. Think I'll stay with that."

"Let me show you the best."

When she grimaced, he said, "Jenni Beth, you know I'm gonna give you the family discount on everything, don't you?"

"I can't ask you to do that, Beck."

"You don't need to ask. I offered."

"Then again, I'll say thank you." Because quick tears heated her eyes and threatened to embarrass them both, she said, "Lead the way."

She followed him to the paint department.

"When we deliver the lumber tomorrow, I'll match up the color, figure out how much the job will take, and order it for you," he said.

Beck pointed out a couple other things she'd need. She dutifully made note of them, then made her escape, stopping a few times to speak to a former teacher, the pastor at her parents' church, a neighbor. Everyone wanted to know how she was doing—that veiled reference to her brother.

Once in her car, she blew out a huge breath.

She felt shaky. Memories assaulted her.

Being home should be easier. It wasn't. In Savannah she could pretend her brother hadn't been killed. That he was still alive and well and doing his own thing while she did hers.

But here in Misty Bottoms? Wes, his friends, and his memory surrounded her.

She could hide in a dark hole, but that wouldn't solve anything. And Wes would expect more from her. Nevertheless, Jenni Beth took a moment, settled herself before starting the car. She adjusted the vents so cool air blew across her, hit the power button on the stereo, and laid her head back against the seat. Chris Young, in all his sexiness, serenaded her.

A little steadier after a few minutes, she checked the dashboard clock. What was Cole doing? She laughed. Not sitting around wondering what *she* was doing, that's for sure.

Time to get back to business. Everything would still be open for another couple hours. Kitty would be her next stop. The familiar versus the unknown. While she was there, and since she'd skipped lunch, Jenni Beth decided she'd treat herself.

Like a carrot dangling on a string, the idea of a sweet treat provided the motivation needed to get her butt in gear. Once in town, the 'Vette bumped along Anderson's Alley, one of only three cobblestone streets left in town.

Kitty's Kakes and Bakery hadn't changed one iota over the years. The pink and green awning shaded the street and front window. Inside that window, behind the shop's stenciled name, trays of goodies lined the shelves and tempted even a saint to stop and indulge.

Jenni Beth definitely wasn't a saint.

She'd barely made it through the door when Kitty let out a squeal. Wiping her hands on the stained white apron tied around her thick waist, she stepped out from behind the counter to wrap Jenni Beth in a warm hug.

"I heard you were home."

"I am. And I'm staying."

"Your dad told me that. He and your mom stopped in for coffee and a donut." Kitty backed up and held Jenni Beth away from her. Studied her. "How are you, honey? You look a little tired."

"I'm good, and I have some rather ambitious plans. Plans I'm hoping you'll want to be a part of."

Curiosity burned in the baker's eyes. "Oh yeah? Nobody's here. Sit. We'll talk." She waved at a small table jammed into the corner. "It's time for my break, anyway. Want coffee?"

"I'd love a cup—and a chocolate éclair. It's been way too long since I've had one—and nobody makes them better than you!"

"You've got it." Over her shoulder, she said, "Cole Bryson stopped by for a couple of these earlier today. He's in town, too."

Jenni Beth's heart raced. She couldn't seem to get away from the man. "Yes, I talked to him."

"He's sure a good-lookin' devil, isn't he?" Kitty moved behind the counter, efficiently plated Jenni Beth's treat and poured two coffees.

Jenni Beth said nothing, assuming Kitty didn't really need or expect an answer.

Carrying the coffees and pastry to the table, Kitty asked, "So, what's up?"

Jenni Beth took one bite of the éclair and closed her eyes. "Oh boy. A moment of silence, please." She chewed and smiled. "I've missed these."

Reluctantly, she returned the pastry to her plate and shared her plan.

The shopkeeper listened quietly, then softly whistled. "You're takin' on an awful lot, sweetie."

"Yes, I am, but I know I can do this. My brides, Magnolia Brides, will need cakes and pastries, and they'll want the best. Yours. Will you help?"

The woman met her eyes. "I planned to retire, you know." Nervous fingers shredded a paper napkin. "When Harvey got sick, we decided I'd better hang on a little bit longer. Insurance and doctor bills can run you into the ground, eat up everything you've worked for."

"I'm sorry." Jenni Beth laid her hand over the older woman's. "How's Harvey doing?"

"Better. Much better." She smiled. "A few more treatments and we're out of the woods."

"I'm so glad."

"I hope you can make this wedding venue work. As for me?" She breathed deeply, then her face split in a grin. "Oh hell. I've always been a sucker for fairy tales and crazy-assed dreams. Count me in. Besides, weddings are such joy-filled events, aren't they?"

"They are! Thank you, Kitty!"

She patted her hand. "Just tell me what you need and when, and I'll have it ready for you. Keep in mind I'm not one of those fancy Atlanta or New York City pastry chefs, though."

"You don't need to be. I've seen—and tasted—enough

of your cakes to know you're exactly what Magnolia Brides will want."

Jenni Beth couldn't stop smiling as she finished off her éclair and coffee. "I have one more stop to make. The new florist."

Kitty made a face. "She's not one of us, you know. She's a Yankee."

A laugh bubbled out of Jenni Beth before she could stop it. "I've worked with lots of Yankees in Savannah. They're good, hardworking people."

A blush reddened Kitty's face. "Guess the War of Northern Aggression's well behind us, isn't it?"

"Yes, and thank heavens for that." She carried her plate and cup to the counter. "Wish me luck."

Back in her car, Jenni Beth turned onto Church Street. Halfway down the block, she spotted the faded green railroad car that Brenda Sue had converted into a flower shop over twenty years ago.

A new sign hung by the short flight of wrought-iron stairs. Brenda Sue's Flowers had become Bella Fiore. Italian for pretty flower. Kind of ritzy for Misty Bottoms, but maybe the town needed more ritzy to draw people from Savannah.

Jenni Beth parked and marched up the steps. One foot inside the door, she stopped dead, her hand still on the knob. God-awful gaudy. The decor hit her like, well, like a runaway train. Reams of gold ribbon, cherubs, and red velvet—in May! Belle Watson had come to Misty Bottoms. The place practically screamed bordello.

Bella Fiore. One hundred eighty degrees from Brenda Sue's down-home style with its gingham bows and sunflowers.

This was Low Country. Late spring, heading into summer. Where were the pastels, the lilacs and peaches? The spring and summer flowers?

Panic slammed her. Could she work with this woman? Let her anywhere near her brides?

"Can I help you?"

The minute the new shop owner opened her mouth, Jenni Beth heard Fran Drescher, from *The Nanny* reruns she and her mother sometimes watched. She even looked like Fran with all that thick black hair.

Jenni Beth swallowed hard and extended her hand. "I hope so. Are you Pia D'Amato?"

"Yep, that's me."

"I'm Jenni Beth Beaumont."

"From Magnolia House."

"Yes."

"Come on in and get off those feet." She waved her hand in a come-here gesture.

Jenni Beth peeked at her own practical sandals, then gazed longingly at the expensive Hermès espa-drilles Pia wore. Mentally, she wished the woman well. Unless she had a sugar daddy or was a trust-fund baby, she seriously doubted Ms. D'Amato would be able to afford any more designer shoes. Not on the profits from Bella Fiore.

Although that played right into the reason she'd come. "I have a proposal to run by you, Ms. D'Amato. One I hope will benefit both of us."

"Really?" Pia's perfectly penciled brows rose as she dragged out the word. "You want some coffee? I just made a fresh pot."

It was on the tip of her tongue to decline another

cup so soon after leaving Kitty's, but politically, that wouldn't be smart. "I'd love one."

Twenty minutes later, feeling hopeful, Jenni Beth left the little shop. This relationship could work. With a little collaboration, she and Pia should be able to provide Magnolia House brides with flowers. She'd have to keep a close eye on the taste level of Pia's designs, though. Roses and baby's breath. Dogwoods, magnolias, camellias, and Spanish moss. Bouquets and boutonnieres. Another piece of the puzzle that made up her dream snapped into place.

As she slid into her car, Jenni Beth looked over her shoulder. Pia D'Amato was on the phone—and very animated. Good. Maybe she was already sharing their plans with her backer. Jenni Beth didn't know who it was, but felt certain she had one. She sure didn't seem strapped for cash.

No. That would be Jenni Beth herself who filled *those* shoes.

Chapter 9

COLE'S THUMBS DRUMMED ON THE STEERING WHEEL in time to One Republic's "Counting Stars." It had been a good scouting expedition, and he'd found the perfect columns for Magnolia House, assuming Jenni Beth didn't get her back up and dismiss them out of hand. And he'd made it back in time for dinner with Beck. He needed time with his pal, wanted his take on some of the changes going down.

He adjusted the rearview mirror and took a quick look at himself, ran a hand over his jaw. Not good, but not too bad. If he was meeting Jenni Beth, which, unfortunately, he wasn't, he'd need a shower and shave. Since his dinner date was Beck, he could probably forget both.

But Beck mentioned running home to clean up after he finished his job, so he'd better, too. Besides, his mom wouldn't appreciate him running around town looking like some ragamuffin.

Cole turned onto Whiskey Road. If he hustled, he could shower, toss on some fresh clothes, and not be more than ten minutes late.

When he rushed into the house, he spotted a note on the kitchen counter. His mom had put clean sheets on his bed and fresh towels in his bath. Checking the fridge, he found the homemade caramels, downed two, and closed his eyes to savor them. Nobody made caramels like his mom. She'd left him a quart of milk, some fresh bread, cold cuts, and leftover fried chicken—in case he got hungry.

That was his mom. When it came to family, he'd won the lottery.

———

What the heck? Monday night and the parking lot at Duffy's Pub was bursting at the seams. Football season had ended a couple months ago so that wasn't the draw. Must be Meghan's cooking. He sure hoped she had some of her shrimp and grits left. While Savannah boasted more than one top-notch chef, nobody came close to Meghan's down-home cooking.

Stuffing his truck key into his jeans pocket, he pushed through the front door and felt he'd come home. Music played, glasses clinked, conversations drifted over and around others.

Beck waved at him from a side booth. "Get yourself in here. You're already one behind." He lifted the nearly empty bottle and wagged it at him.

"He's drinkin' Bud. You havin' the same?" Binnie asked from behind the bar.

Cole leaned across the counter and pulled the waitress into a big hug. "You still puttin' up with Duffy and all the lowlifes who come draggin' in here, Binnie?"

She laughed. "I'm waitin' on my Prince Charming to ride in and rescue me from all this, but, darn, he's sure takin' his time about it."

"You've got my number," Cole said.

"Yep, I sure do. Just like another hundred or so women."

"Ouch." He laid a hand over his heart.

"So you drinkin' Bud tonight?"

"Is it cold?"

"Duffy's chippin' the ice off it as we speak."

"That'll do then." He slid into the worn wooden seat across from Beck.

"So what brings you to Misty Bottoms, pal?" Beck asked.

"Work. Hit a couple sales, did some banking. Odds and ends." He took the beer Binnie offered and thanked her for the bowl of peanuts.

"You guys gonna eat or just drink your way through the night?"

"Eat," Beck said. "I skipped lunch today. Had a visit from a pretty little gal when I got back to the shop."

"Let me guess," Cole said. "Jenni Beth."

"Yep. She came in to order some lumber for her front porch." He grimaced. "She plans to do the work herself."

"She does. I drove over there today while she was measurin'. That's what I want to talk about."

Binnie propped her tray on one hip. "You want me to come back?"

"No, I'm ready to order." Cole looked at Beck. "How about you?"

"I'm havin' Duffy's fish and chips. With tartar sauce. Gallons of Meghan's homemade tartar sauce."

"Have any shrimp and grits tonight?" Cole asked.

"Sure do. And there should be a pan of homemade rolls comin' out of the oven any minute now."

"Then I'm good," Cole said.

Binnie headed to the kitchen to place their orders, and Cole leaned in toward Beck. "Did Jenni Beth tell you what she's plannin'?"

"Yeah, she did."

Cole stared down at his coaster, his thoughts drifting back to last week at Chateau Rouge, when she'd danced with him in the moonlight. That soft skin, those sexy, bedroom eyes. She felt so good, so right in his arms. Heat rushed through him. He'd hoped…

Beck cleared his throat.

"Sorry." Cole shook his head to clear it. "Woolgathering."

"She wants to make a few repairs to the house."

"More than a few. You been in that house lately?"

"No."

"She walked me through it today." He whistled. "That place is rough! Far worse than I thought." He took a drink of his beer, enjoyed the bite of the ice-cold brew. "Did she tell you she quit her job in Savannah?"

"Yeah." Beck leaned against the booth's scarred back. "I wish she'd taken a leave instead."

Cole shook his head. "That's Jenni Beth. Never does anything halfway."

"Thought she liked it in Savannah."

"She did, but her family comes first, and they're in rougher shape than I thought, too."

"Yeah, I got that."

If anyone understood that kind of loyalty, it was Beck. Hadn't he basically done the same? Given up his dreams for the family business?

Cole hesitated. Should he tell Beck about Richard's call and what he'd overheard? Beck would be in town 24–7. *He* wouldn't be. Couldn't be.

Despite Jenni Beth's arguments, she needed somebody to watch her back. He'd known Richard all his life and found it hard to believe he'd actually do anything to derail her plans. Still…money and greed did strange things to people.

Cole wasn't willing to risk Jenni Beth's safety—or her happiness.

Twirling his beer on the coaster, he jumped in. "I need to swear you to secrecy, pal."

Beck set down his beer, sat up a little straighter.

Binnie showed up right at that moment with their food. "Anything else I can get for you, boys?"

"Not a thing," Cole said. "Looks great."

"I'm good," Beck agreed.

The minute Binnie was out of earshot, Beck looked at Cole. "My lips are sealed. What's goin' on?"

Cole dropped his voice, the morning's anger rushing back. In quick bursts, he filled Beck in on the details of Jenni Beth's plans. "She knows what she's doing. Her plans are sound. But—"

He went on to tell him about Richard's demand for collateral and the phone conversation he'd overheard.

"You think Thorndike would actually try something?" Beck asked.

"That land's worth at least half a million dollars."

Beck dropped back against the booth. "We might have ourselves a problem." He slathered tartar sauce on a bite of fish. "I've gotta ask something first, Cole, and I guess, if you want, you can tell me to mind my own business. You and Jenni Beth." He forked another bite of his fish, chewed. "There something goin' on between the two of you?"

Cole's jaw tightened. "Why would you ask that?"

"It's just, well, there's always tension when you two are together. I need to know what I'm steppin' into."

Cole picked up his beer, set it back down without taking a drink. How in the hell did he answer that? Did he say he wished, but the lady'd shot him down? Close but no cigar?

"Nothing's goin' on, Beck. A friend's in trouble. We need to help her. End of story."

"You say so." But the look he sent Cole was skeptical.

Feeling like a heel, hating all the half-truths he'd been handing out, Cole tapped his beer against his friend's. "To us. We've both got our own businesses, our own homes. We haven't done badly, pal."

"I'll drink to that." Beck raised his drink. Then, head bent, staring at his plate, he asked, "Do you ever miss havin' somebody beside you when you go to bed at night?"

Where'd that come from? He frowned. "As in someone permanent? The same body beside me every night?"

Beck nodded.

"Somebody like Tansy?"

"That's never gonna happen." Beck shrugged. "In general, you know?"

"Gotcha." He pulled on his ear. "My parents have had a good marriage, set a good example. But I'm happy with life as it is. You?"

"I'm good with things."

Cole had an uneasy moment, suspecting they might both be lying to themselves and each other. *Nah*. He shoved the thought aside. He did like his life. He was satisfied.

Dropping his fork onto his plate, Beck flagged down their waitress. "Binnie, how about another round here. Cole and I are gonna play some darts. He might get thirsty, and I don't want him to have any excuses when I win."

Cole laughed. "Oh really? Last time, I beat the pants off you."

His friend waggled his brows. "Ah, but while you've been off tending to business in the real world, I've been practicin'."

"Beck Elliot, no amount of practice is gonna save you."

"We'll see."

They made small talk while Binnie cleared their plates. After they settled their bill, they moved into the back room.

Two games later, Cole had to concede that his friend had indeed been practicing. And *he* was rusty. Very rusty. He'd won the first, but barely. Beck had taken the second.

"Uh-oh," Beck muttered. "Couple things we didn't get a chance to talk about during dinner, bro."

"Save your breath. It won't work."

"What won't?"

"This game's the tiebreaker. You're tryin' to distract me. You can't." He stopped, arm cocked, ready to release.

A high-pitched giggle drifted from the front room. He hung his head. "Kimmie Atherton's back?"

Beck nodded. "And newly divorced. Second time, too. She's on the hunt, friend, and you and she have a history."

"History is right. All in the past."

"Cole!" Like fingernails on a chalkboard, the excited shriek sent shudders rippling through him.

He winced and braced himself just in time. She took one leap and plastered herself to him like Saran Wrap on a bowl of his mama's leftovers. Her legs embraced his hips, and she planted a kiss on him that, in days past, would have had him making up any excuse to get the two of them outside and horizontal on the backseat of his car.

But that was then.

Tonight he wanted nothing to do with her.

He caught the grin on Beck's face and heard the hoots of laughter from several others in the bar.

Throwing his arms wide, Cole looked to Beck for help. He half-hoped that without his arms holding her up, Kimmie would fall free. She didn't. Like a suction cup, she held fast, a stranglehold around his neck.

Setting his beer on a nearby table, Cole reached for her arms. "Kimmie, how 'bout you let go of me for a second here? Step back so I can get a good look at you."

He seared Beck with an I-dare-you-to-laugh-again look.

Kimmie giggled and loosened her hold, dropping her feet to the floor. With a flourish, she extended her arms out to her sides and sent him a blindingly white grin.

Red cowboy boots added a bit of panache to faded denim shorts cut so high they barely covered her butt cheeks and a rhinestone-covered T-shirt slit nearly to her navel. Her heavy perfume clung to him.

"Like what you see, Cole? You sure used to." Seductively, she moved in toward him. He took a step back, then a second and a third.

"You've grown up real nice, honey, but I was just leavin'. I've got a big day tomorrow." He aimed the dart in his hand, arched it toward the board, and pumped his fist when it stuck dead-center in the bull's-eye.

"But, Cole—" Kimmie whined.

"Nope." He checked his watch. "I can't stay. Beck might have time to play a game or two with you."

The expression on Beck's face changed from cat-ate-the-canary to man-smelled-skunk. He shook his head.

"Uh-uh. No can do. My crew starts at daybreak tomorrow. Time for me to head home, too."

Together they beat tracks to the back door.

Behind them, Cole heard Kimmie's booted foot thump the floor at the same time an angry oath exploded from her mouth.

"Her mother would wash her mouth out with soap if she heard that," Cole muttered.

Beck shook his head. "Between you and me, I think her mama's given up on her."

Once in the parking lot, he and Beck caught each other's eyes and laughed like loons.

"Why the hell didn't you warn me?" Cole asked.

"I meant to, but with Jenni Beth's problems and all, guess I forgot. Anyway, I sure didn't think Kimmie would come bouncin' in to Duffy's tonight."

Cole shook his head. "What did I ever see in her?"

"You honestly can't remember?" Beck raised cupped hands to his chest.

Chuckling, Cole said, "Yeah, okay, there was that. Good thing I outgrew them, huh?"

"As if." Beck swatted him with his baseball cap, and the two walked to their respective trucks.

"You'll keep an eye on Jenni Beth when I'm in Savannah?" Cole called across the lot.

"Absolutely," his friend answered.

Cole headed home, the darkness thick after spending so much time in the city. But the stars overhead were magnificent. What had he been thinking? Seriously, Kimmie Atherton? Overt sex. She flaunted it, pushed it right out there in a guy's face. And that's probably one of the reasons Jenni Beth hadn't forgiven him.

He probably could have been a little less conspicuous in his prom choice.

Add in Angus Duckworth, and he was surprised she hadn't hired a hit man to take him out.

He couldn't help the belly laugh that forced its way out. He felt better than he had all day.

Chapter 10

COLE TUCKED AN ARM BENEATH HIS HEAD. TOO early to be awake. The sun had barely peeked above the trees on the far side of the pastureland. He'd left the windows open last night, and a cool morning breeze stirred the air. Tugging the covers higher to ward off the slight chill, he imagined Jenni Beth curled up beside him. The two of them could heat up a room till a man thought he'd die from the fire they created. But he'd sure as heck die with a grin on his face.

This morning, though, Jenni Beth wasn't here.

He loved this old barn and didn't regret for an instant the hours and hours he'd spent turning it into his Misty Bottoms home.

His folks were the best, and he loved them, tried to spend time with them at least once a week. But no getting around it. They all needed their own space. The instant he stepped foot inside his mom's house, he lost his adult status and became her little boy. Sometimes, he was okay with that, enjoyed the pampering, the favorite foods. Other times, he found it annoying. He wasn't used to having to account for his time, for his whereabouts. He'd been on his own too long to check in on the hour.

With this setup, he had the best of both worlds. Since the barn was on their property, he could be close without being underfoot. A two-minute walk landed him in his mom's kitchen for a hug, a cup of coffee, and, when he was really lucky, a homemade meal. But that same two-minute walk took him right back to his own place where he could sprawl on the sofa in his boxers with a football game or the music cranked up, and nobody nagged him to turn down the volume or pick up the socks he'd dropped in the middle of the floor.

This morning, though, he had more on his mind. Jenni Beth. Richard Thorndike. Both caused a tight little stress knot in his stomach, though not for the same reason.

A glance at the clock told him it was only a few minutes past six. His folks would probably be up but not ready for breakfast yet. Throwing back the covers, he reached for a pair of the freshly laundered jeans his mom had left neatly folded on his dresser.

Time to take a ride down by the river. He brushed his teeth, ran a quick comb through his bed hair, and decided he'd shave later. Stuffing his feet into a pair of scuffed work boots, he buttoned up an old denim shirt and headed for the door.

On the way to his truck, he decided on a short detour.

A quick rap on the old wooden screen door and he walked into the kitchen of his childhood. His mom, her short hair still a golden auburn, stood at the sink. She turned, a fast smile on her face, and he wrapped her in a hug.

"The waffles aren't started yet."

"I know, but—" He sniffed the air. "The coffee is."

He released her and moved to a cupboard. Pulling out a mug, he asked, "You need one?"

"Already have mine." She held up her cup. "In fact, I'm on my second. Doc Hawkins keeps nagging me. He tells me I should probably think of changing to decaf, but I'm fighting it."

Coffee poured, he sipped gratefully.

"You're up early," his mother said.

"I know. Bad habit."

"Nothing wrong with that. It gives you a jump start on the day."

"Speaking of," he said. "I've got something I need to take care of. I'll be back inside an hour, though, for those waffles."

She laughed. "I'm sure you will. You bringing any friends with you?"

"Nope. Just me. But I'm hungry as a bear, so make plenty. Is Laurie here?"

"No, your sister and Nick are in Charleston."

"You let her go out of town with him?"

"Honey, they're engaged."

"Still—"

"Still nothing." She arched her brow at him. "You'd do best to stay out of it. Your sister's a grown woman."

"Is this the same Emma Bryson who raised me?"

"Times change."

"Yeah, they sure do." After another quick, one-arm hug, he saluted her with his mug. "You brew the best coffee. Ever. Anywhere."

"Better than those fancy Savannah restaurants?"

He grinned. "Much better."

Roscoe, the family's old beagle, waited for him on the porch. Kneeling, he rubbed the dog's back. "Wanna go for a ride?"

If the dog's tail whipped any faster, he'd have been airborne.

"Roscoe's ridin' shotgun with me, Mom," he called through the screen.

"Okay. Don't let him run the rabbits, though. He'll come home a mess, and I don't have time today to give him a bath. He had one yesterday—after a chase that took him through the creek down back."

Cole stared at the dog. "You've been warned, Roscoe."

The dog grinned and followed him to the truck.

The beagle's head hung out the window, ears flopping, as the two set off toward the Savannah River and Jenni Beth's bottomland.

He should stay out of this. He really should.

Every time they ran into each other, he felt, well, disconcerted. She threw him off stride, did something to him. Something way too dangerous.

One single time, he'd given in to that feeling. Once. A huge mistake, and one he absolutely couldn't make again.

As he and Roscoe bumped along the dirt track, he thought of her yesterday in that hot, red suit, the fabric showcasing that tight little body. Pushed aside the urge he'd had to haul her to his place and remove that suit, the fancy silk blouse, and find out what she wore beneath.

And if that hadn't been enough, he'd driven over to her house and found her there on the porch, wiggling her hips in those skimpy shorts and that body-hugging tank top. When she'd toyed with the shorts' frazzled ends, he found himself holding his breath. If any more of the fabric unraveled, well, he'd have been undone.

He swiped a hand over his forehead. The temperature inside his Ford pickup had spiked a good ten degrees. He cranked up the air.

Rounding another corner, he hit the brakes and whistled. Did she realize what she had here? What she'd offered to Richard as collateral?

He opened the truck door and called for Roscoe to join him. The dog jumped out, nose working the air.

"No hunting, boy. This is a reconnaissance trip. You get filthy, Mom will have both our heads." He slapped a hand on his jean-clad thigh. "Stay right here with me."

The dog blinked once, then rubbed his head against Cole's leg.

"Good boy."

The sun had yet to burn through the fog, and it shimmered around him, dampened his face and hair. Misty Bottoms. The town's name couldn't be more apropos. Cole took a minute and simply breathed in the feel of the place. No sound. No movement. He and Roscoe could have been the only living creatures on the planet.

"Let's go." They set off through the high grass. The Savannah drifted by, slow and calm this far down the river. In the 1700s, they'd have grown rice on this land. His brow furrowed. What plans did Richard have for it?

The bottomland hardwoods stood tall and proud. Twenty minutes later, the sun finally peeked through the clouds, turning the water golden. A couple ducks splashed down, and Roscoe started beside him.

Grabbing the dog by his collar, Cole warned, "Don't even think about it."

Hand shading his eyes, he studied the area and tried to remember exactly where Jenni Beth's land ended. And then he knew. A "No Trespassing" sign had been nailed to several of the trees on the north side.

Hurrying, he walked closer, Roscoe zipping around him, barking, obviously picking up on his sense of urgency. Disappointment crept in, though, as Cole realized the sign wouldn't give him any more information, wouldn't tell him who'd posted the land. Just a cheap plastic, generic hardware store sign.

Determined now, he walked the edge of the property. He'd be late for breakfast, but it couldn't be helped.

Roscoe stopped for a drink. "Watch out for snakes, buddy." The dog barked once and ran back to his side.

Before he even got to the far boundary, he saw another sign. The land on this side was posted, too. The same cheap, black-and-orange sign. No doubt Richard Thorndike had some whopping plans for Jenni Beth's acreage.

But who was the banker in bed with? Because sure as shootin', this land was way too rich for Richard's blood. Over five hundred grand for Jenni Beth's piece, then add the land on both sides into the mix? He smelled an even bigger rat than he had yesterday. Something was in the works here, and Magnolia House had been anteed up without Jenni Beth fully understanding the stakes.

Time for them to have another talk.

After waffles with his mom and dad.

Richard Thorndike knotted his tie and checked the mirror one last time. He slid into his jacket and shot his cuffs. By this time next year, he wouldn't be wearing off-the-rack suits. No, sir. His would be custom tailored.

Halfway downstairs for a much-needed cup of coffee, he glanced at the wall clock and revised his plans. He had plenty of time, and his wife had already left for her office. Instead of making his call from the bank, he'd do it here where he had complete privacy. No snooping ears. The whole town was a bunch of busybodies.

When the phone was answered on the second ring, he said, "Things are under way."

"What time is it?"

"Time for you to be up."

"I am up, and I have been for quite a while already."

"Fine. I'll slap a gold star on your forehead next time I see you."

"Don't get all sarcastic on me. You need us more than we need you."

"Understood. But did you hear what I told you?" Richard asked. "Everything is in place."

"I know. I've talked to Jenni Beth."

"I'd rather we not use names over the phone." Even to himself he sounded prim, but a person couldn't be too careful. Not with this much at stake.

"Oh, come on. Loosen up. We're in Misty Bottoms, for heaven's sake, not in the bowels of some espionage pit. You honestly think your phone or mine is being tapped—just in case?"

"Laugh if you want, but stranger things have happened."

"How about I call you a little later?"

"No. I don't want you calling me at the bank."

"Fine."

"If we intend to get hold of that land—"

"I understand what I need to do. Doesn't mean I have to like it, though."

"No, it doesn't. You can feel sorry as all hell for the Beaumonts and their plight. You can feel sorry for yourself that you're involved in this. I don't care. The only thing I *do* care about is that the loan she signs, the one with her bottomland as collateral, is defaulted on and we end up with the land. Period. And you'll do well to keep that in mind."

———

Jenni Beth wondered if Richard would call today or if he intended to keep her cooling her heels for a while longer. She stood by what she'd told him. As far as a business loan went, this was one of the best he'd had in front of him in a long time.

What she hadn't mentioned were her own fears. As she wandered slowly down the stairs, the bright early morning sun spotlighted and intensified all the old house's flaws. Every water stain, every cracked and chipped baseboard glared at her, taunted her.

Could she pull this off? Or would her efforts be as futile as sticking a cork in the *Titanic*, hoping to stop the leak?

Cole had offered to help. She reminded herself, though, that he'd shown up out of a sense of responsibility. Nothing more. If she failed, he'd no doubt suffer a little remorse, but it wouldn't be the end of life as he knew it. For her, for her parents, it would be.

She struggled to recapture some of yesterday's anger, but it seemed to have evaporated. All she could dredge up was gratitude for his offer to help her—even if his motives were suspect.

As for the rest of it? He and Wes had been best pals; she'd been the tagalong baby sister. That sexual zing yesterday? The result of a stressful situation. Nothing more.

Today? She had a lot to do.

Vernon, the family gardener, had long ago passed his prime, so she'd hired a couple of teens to help him. Jeeters, one of Beck's guys, had come in with a huge mower and knocked down the worst of the high grass and weeds. The boys had done the trimming and hauling.

She carried her coffee outside to the patio table and sat down with Vernon. "Let me show you the plans I've sketched out for the gardens." She spread out her drawings, the different areas numbered according to priority.

"I plan to start small and work my way through this as money comes in. We'll tackle the most visible parts first."

"I'm real sorry everything's such a mess, Ms. Jenni Beth. The grounds got ahead of me."

"It's not your fault." She laid a hand on his gnarled one. "Things have gotten away from all of us. And you used to have help," she soothed.

He pointed at one of the flower beds. "Caught a coon in there this morning diggin' things up. Animal was as big as a bushel basket."

"They can be real rascals." She rolled up the plans and rubber banded them. "Why don't you keep this set? I have another copy if these get torn or misplaced."

Nodding, Vernon stood slowly. "No wind right now, so I'm gonna burn that pile of branches the boys hauled out back."

"Sounds good, but keep your eyes on it. Thought I'd work in the rose garden before it gets any hotter. I need a great shot of it for the website I'm designing."

As she watched him amble away, she remembered the days he'd pitched to Wes and his friends for batting practice. The time he'd climbed the tree to rescue her cat.

Then her mind got busy figuring photo shots and angles. Some bride, somewhere would pull up her site, see the rose garden, and realize it was her perfect wedding destination.

Right now? The garden had disintegrated to nothing much more than a jumble of overgrown roses and weeds. And it was up to her to restore it.

She sighed and ran upstairs to her bedroom. As she hit the top landing, she huffed out her breath. Who needed a pricey gym membership when you could hike up two flights of stairs twenty times a day?

In the corner, by the oversized rattan chair, she'd hung her collection of straw hats, everything from big brimmed ones with fancy decorations to cowboy hats to well-worn plain Janes. She made good use of them. After all, a Southern lady always, always protected her skin.

And her family.

Chapter 11

COLE DASHED INTO HIS PLACE FOR A QUICK SHOWER. If he intended to have it out with Richard, he should probably look a bit more presentable. Though what difference a shave would make in the grand scheme of things he couldn't say.

The shower felt good. He should have sneaked one in before breakfast with his parents. He patted his stomach. The waffles had been excellent as always. His mom was a first-rate country cook. Nothing fancy, although she could lay out a Sunday brunch that would put anybody to shame.

Drying off, he caught a glimpse of himself in the mirror. He leaned into the old watering trough he'd salvaged. After he'd welded legs on it, he'd added funky old faucets, then plunked granite countertops on both sides. He liked it. It made one heck of a bathroom vanity.

He ran a hand over his chin, his cheeks. Heck with it. No shaving this morning. If Richard didn't like it, too damn bad. In fact, it might be better if he didn't. He opened his closet door, and there hung laundered and ironed shirts. His mom. Bless her heart.

Most were the white dress shirts he liked to wear with his jeans. Two minutes, and he was dressed and ready to go. He grabbed his keys from the bowl on his nightstand and headed downstairs.

A slow burn simmered through him as he drove into

town. Richard knew exactly what Jenni Beth and her family had been through these past eighteen months. Only low-down scum would try to take advantage of that. He'd always figured Misty Bottoms took care of its own. Apparently things had changed.

An empty parking spot beckoned directly in front of the bank, and Cole nabbed it. Striding through the doors, he perched his sunglasses on top of his head and nodded at Gloria. "Mornin', beautiful. Is your boss in?"

"He is." She sent him a warm smile. "Let me tell him you're here."

When she reached for the intercom button, he put a hand over hers, stopping her. "That's okay. I'll surprise him."

A frown wrinkled her brow. "But…"

He didn't hang around to listen.

Richard's head jerked up when Cole walked in unannounced, closing the door firmly behind him. Instantly, reflexively, Richard shut down his monitor. "Cole. What can I do for you? I didn't realize we had an appointment."

"We don't." A muscle worked in Cole's jaw, reminding him how close to the surface his anger boiled. Willing himself to calm down, he dropped into the chair in front of the expensive desk chosen to pay homage to Richard's own sense of self-importance.

Cole realized, crossing his feet at the ankles, that he'd never really liked the guy all that much. The present situation simply magnified that sentiment.

"Okay." Richard picked up a pen, rolled it between his fingers, and then tossed it onto the desk. "What's on your mind?"

"Magnolia House."

Richard never even blinked.

Oh, he's good, Cole thought.

"I don't see how the Beaumont plantation is any of your business."

"I'm makin' it my business." Cole met the banker's eyes. "What's goin' on?"

"I'm sure I don't know what you mean."

Cole leaned in toward the man, rested the palms of his hands flat on the shiny cherry surface. "Oh, I think you do."

"I like you, Cole. So I'm telling you as a friend that Magnolia House isn't any of your concern."

"We're not friends, Thorndike."

The heat that raced across the older man's face gave Cole a sense of satisfaction. Good. Might as well be two of them pissed off.

"Cole, I'll ignore that remark. Your mother would be appalled by your rudeness."

Cole shrugged. "Magnolia House?" he repeated.

"I suggest you stay out of things there," Richard said. "I know you and Wes were good friends, but that has no bearing any longer."

Cole flinched at that. At the idea of Richard or anyone else putting him and Wes in the past. At the notion their friendship no longer counted for anything. Pain tore at him. Damn, he missed his pal. And he *would* do right by him.

Like a bulldog with a bone clenched between his teeth, Cole refused to back down. "What's the deal with Jenni Beth and her bottomland?"

Richard leaned back in his leather chair and clasped his hands together over his stomach. "Afraid I can't discuss that with you. It's confidential."

"What? You add an MD to the end of your name now?" Cole asked.

A muscle in the banker's jaw tightened. "I answer to the stockholders, not you."

"Do they know about this?"

"This what? What exactly are you insinuating?" Red bloomed on his cheeks.

Anger or guilt? Cole wondered.

"I have another appointment. You'll have to excuse me."

"Sure thing." Cole backed off. He'd probably already put his foot in it. Jenni Beth needed the loan. He couldn't screw that up for her. Still he raised two fingers to his eyes, motioned from himself to Richard in an I'll-be-watching-you gesture.

Without another word, he left. But he stopped in the doorway to stare pointedly at the god-awful uncomfortable plastic chairs outside Richard's office. The *empty* chairs. No next appointment waited. He turned, threw Richard a mocking salute.

"Don't go making trouble, boy," Richard warned.

"Don't think I need to. Seems it's arrived without any help from me."

Back in the sunshine, in the heat of the day, Cole stood on the sidewalk and swore under his breath. That had gained nothing, had turned out to be little more than two buckets of testosterone tossed at each other. If Jenni Beth got wind of it, his testosterone would probably dry up after she castrated him for messing in her business.

Still, it had to be done.

Frustrated, Cole detoured across the street, through the pretty little park, and into Henderson's Pharmacy.

He needed a cold drink, needed to give himself some cooling-down time before he throttled Thorndike, and Sheriff Jimmy Don ended up tossing him in a cell.

"Hey, Sheryl." He plopped onto one of the old, faded-red leather seats that showed generations of wear.

Sheryl Brooks grinned. "Haven't seen you in a coon's age, Cole Bryson. Heard you're pretty busy down there in Savannah. Your mom's real proud of you."

"I'm stayin' out of trouble." *Liar, liar!* his conscience taunted. He rubbed at the bridge of his nose.

Sheryl and his mother had gone to school together and still did a movie night once a month with some of their classmates. He didn't doubt for a second Sheryl had been kept up to date on all his business.

"What can I get you?"

"I'd like a big, ice-cold tea. To go."

"You got it." She moved across the room to draw his drink. "Unsweetened?"

"Yes, please."

"Lemon?"

"No, thanks." His fingers drummed on the tabletop.

"Heard you and Jenni Beth had breakfast together yesterday." Sheryl glanced over her shoulder at him.

"Um, not exactly." Dang, he should have known. Small town. "I ran into her at Dee-Ann's."

"Yeah. Ran into her again at Darlene's shop."

She'd caught him flat-footed. He removed his ball cap, then clamped it back on his head. "Coincidence. Both times."

"Sure. Them things happen."

He bit back a chuckle and wondered how she managed to talk with that tongue tucked in her cheek like that. Best not to say anything else. Kind of like pleading the fifth on the witness stand.

"Heard she had an appointment with Thorndike," Sheryl continued. "My guess is she needs some money if she's gonna fix up that house of hers. Damn shame they've let it go to ruin. Guess they lost interest after what happened to Wes. Then her daddy got himself in a financial pickle."

She set his drink in front of him, and he paid her for it. Still, she waited.

A heck of a fisherman, he thought. She'd thrown her line in the water and waited patiently for a bite. Well, he'd be darned if he'd swallow that hook or spill the beans. Since it seemed the whole town knew he and Jenni Beth had been together at Dee-Ann's, there wasn't a prayer in hell that the whole town didn't also know what Jenni Beth had planned. But he wouldn't be the one to verify.

"I can't tell you much, Sheryl. I've been out of town these last few weeks. Jenni Beth doesn't exactly confide in me."

"Too bad. If she's plannin' on renovatin' that place, you could be a lot of help, what with your business and all."

"Yeah, well." He shrugged and stood. "Gotta go."

"You stayin' in town for a bit?"

"A few days."

"Good. Your mama's been missin' you."

"I know." He grinned. "She tells me every day."

As he walked the block to his car, he took note again of all the businesses in need of help. He couldn't take them all on, but he sure could help Wes's little sister.

If she'd let him.

Still sipping on his iced tea, Cole surprised himself when he turned the big black Ford dually into the long drive to Magnolia House. He hadn't actually meant to come here.

Now that he was, though, he decided it was a good thing. Time he and Jenni Beth had a heart-to-heart. Time she understood the way the real world worked.

Good might always defeat evil in the Disney films she and her friends used to watch at the movies, but in real life? Happily-ever-after wasn't guaranteed. Sometimes the beast turned out to be…well, just that. A beast.

He found her in the side yard in what used to be the house's crowning glory, the now thoroughly run-down rose garden.

"You need some help with this," he growled as he watched a thorn grab hold of the tender flesh of her arm. He leaned down and untangled her from the tenacious hold the branch had on her. Nearly kissed the small tear before he caught himself.

"Really? I never considered that." She planted a hand in the small of her back and arched into it.

Cole pulled at some weeds to keep his hands busy. To keep them off that sweet body.

Instead, his voice gruff, he asked, "When's the last time you visited your bottomland?"

She stared at him. "Boy, somebody's grouchy. What are you so upset about?"

"Answer the question, Jenni Beth."

"I don't think—"

"When?" he snapped.

"Okay. Jeez. Who took a bite out of your butt today?"

She scowled. "I haven't actually been there in a while. Why would I?"

"Well, maybe you ought to head down there right now."

"I'm working."

"I can see that. And you're doin' a damn fine job. But that can wait. This can't."

Glancing down at her feet, he spotted the scar on her ankle. She'd been tagging along and Wes had warned her to go home. When she wouldn't, he'd shot her there with an arrow—the tip not sharp enough to actually pierce, but enough to break the skin and leave a permanent mark.

They'd have been grounded for a month, but Jenni Beth hadn't ratted them out. She'd lied for them, made up a story about a limb jabbing her ankle while she climbed a tree.

She'd earned his respect that day, the scar a constant testament to her loyalty. Today, in those sexy, totally impractical sandals, it was on full display, as though she was reminding him.

"You got a pair of sneakers?" he asked.

"Of course I do."

"Put them on."

"Cole—"

"Go get them, Jenni Beth."

Surprisingly enough, she did. She ducked into the house and came back minutes later wearing a pair of beat-up gym shoes. He ignored the skimpy excuse for a pair of shorts. They'd do. He put a hand on her shoulders and turned her to face his truck. "Get in."

"Cole, what is wrong with you?"

Instead of answering, he thrust a can of insect repellent at her. "Here. Spray some of this on all that exposed flesh."

"Are you out of your mind?"

"Not yet. But I think you might be."

Shaking her head, she covered herself in insect repellent and crawled into his truck. She stared out the window as they drove in silence to her bottomland. When he turned onto the rutted road, she finally looked at him again.

"Why are we here? What are you doing?"

"Tryin' to wake you up. Help you come to your senses."

"My faculties are in full working order, I promise."

"I disagree. When we get out, just follow me."

"There are snakes."

"That's why you're wearin' those." He nodded toward her sneakers. "Besides, I was here earlier today and didn't see any."

"They were hiding. Waiting till you dragged me down here."

One brow shot up. "Seriously?"

"Seriously."

He snorted and brought the truck to a stop. When she made no move to get out, he walked around to her side and opened the door. He took her hand, instantly sorry. Heat flared inside him both from her touch and the sight of those sleek, bare legs. Would one touch send him to hell?

Yes. One of his own making. Tamping down the desire, he helped her out, his hand lingering at her waist a tad longer than necessary. A wide expanse of marsh grass stretched in front of them. The high-pitched cries of tiny tree frogs filled the air.

Her nose wrinkled. "It smells musty."

He breathed in the pungent, slightly salty smell. "That's the rain we've had. It's left things a little soggy."

With her in tow, he marched to the edge of her land and arrowed off toward the sign. When they got close enough, he pointed to the trees with the "No Trespassing" posts.

"Do you know anything about this?"

"No." She walked up to the trees, ran her fingers over the sign. "Who owns this land? It's never been closed to the public."

"No, it hasn't." He shook his head. "The same signs are on the boundary line of the property to the south."

"Why?" she asked.

"That's what I asked myself. Why post the land?"

"What does all this have to do with me?"

Exasperated, he shoveled his fingers through his hair. "You're a bright woman, Jenni Beth."

Her chin came up. "I like to think so."

He pointed north, then south. "Both the properties touching on yours are posted. Both, apparently, have the same owner."

"So?"

"Argh. Do you have any idea what this soggy land we're sloshin' around in is worth?"

"Somewhere around half a million dollars."

"Exactly. So you do know that. I was beginnin' to wonder."

"I still don't understand—"

"Jenni Beth, stay with me here. Let's say you owned two pieces of property, very expensive property, and wanted to do something with it. Build on it. Develop it. Whatever. Problem is somebody else owns the piece between your two."

She closed her eyes. "Somebody wants to squeeze me out."

"Bingo." He threw his arm up in the air. "And you just gave them the green light."

"Did not."

"Did too."

"Why would you even say that?"

Cole kicked at a clump of grass.

"I'm a businesswoman, Cole, with the credentials, the experience to make my plan work. I don't intend to lose my land, and I don't need my hand held."

In a flash, his temper boiled to the surface. "Maybe not, but you damn well need somebody to stand for you."

"To stand for me? What does that even mean?"

"Richard's up to something. I don't know what, but Wes would clean my clock if I simply stood back and let him steal your land. Together we have a chance to make your dream work. I know you agreed to let me help, but I also know it was done begrudgingly."

When she said nothing, he asked, "Once I'm back in Savannah, are you gonna forget your promise and try to go it alone?"

"I can do it," she said quietly.

"I don't doubt that you can. I never have doubted you. But I can make it easier for you." His voice dropped.

"Why? Why are you so dead-set on helping me?"

"Because I want to. You've been pissed at me for years—and rightly so. I'd like to make amends."

"You don't need to do that. You didn't force me into anything I didn't want."

She looked at the ground, her eyes not meeting his, and he felt lower than scum. Hell, he *was* scum. But she chose to take the higher ground. Another point for Jennifer Elizabeth Beaumont.

"I'll be damned if I'm simply gonna walk away again." He jammed his hands into his pockets. "How about we try this? How about because I want to help my friend. If you were a guy, there wouldn't be all this quibblin'. I'd offer my help, you'd accept it, and thank me. When I'd need help, you'd step in and give me a hand. *Quid pro quo*. Why do women have to make everything so damn hard? Wrap emotion in and around everything?"

She narrowed her eyes, and he held up a hand. "Sorry. Again. Tell you what, I eat any more crow today, and I'm gonna have to turn down my mom's invitation to dinner tonight."

He took her hand, so small and soft. He should pull away, couldn't bring himself to do that.

She bit her lip.

"Promise you'll let me help you."

"Cole—"

"Jenni Beth."

She stared off toward the "No Trespassing" sign. A bird, high in a snag, screeched, breaking the silence.

"Okay. I need help, you offered it. I told you yesterday I'd accept it. Despite my misgivings, I'll honor that. Thank you."

He had to laugh.

"What?" She turned angry eyes on him.

"I'm sorry," he said, still grinning. "But that had to be the least gracious acceptance of an offer I've ever heard."

She scowled.

"Hop in. Let me get you back to that rose garden. You can take your mad out on those weeds."

On the way home, Cole's grin faded. He chastised himself. She'd given him the perfect opening to tell her about the overheard phone call. But she'd been so angry. Knowing her, she'd have driven into town, flew into the bank, and ripped into Richard.

And coming on top of his visit that would have had major consequences.

The papers weren't signed yet, and Jenni Beth couldn't afford to lose the loan. Problem was she sure as heck couldn't afford to lose that piece of land, either. He worried. After everything she'd been through, how she could still own a pair of rose-colored glasses was beyond him. But she did. And she refused, at times, to remove them.

Working with her would be a challenge. It would also be a little slice of heaven. Or hell. He truly wasn't sure if he could stand being around her day after day without the right to touch once in a while.

He'd planned to stay in town for a couple of days, but it might be better if he left tomorrow for Savannah. After all, he had a business to run. But he'd miss her—and that was part of the consequences *he* had to live with.

He'd leave Beck as watchdog.

Before he had time to think it through, he asked, "Why don't you drive down to Savannah in a few days? We can dig through my warehouse. See what you can use."

"I'd planned to buy things cheap at flea markets and estate sales."

"Check out my place first. It'll be fun. And we can hit some great sales in Savannah."

"I didn't invite you to shop with me."

"I've got contacts," he argued.

She held out her hand and rubbed her thumb and fore-finger together. "It still comes down to money."

He shrugged. "We'll work that out."

A surprised laugh bubbled out. "Really?"

"Yeah. I know the boss at Traditions." He grinned. "Think I can probably get everything at cost."

"Hmmm. That would certainly help."

He nudged. "We can have breakfast at Clary's. Your favorite. I'll even pony up for a couple plates of their famous corned beef hash." His lips turned up in a grin. "I can almost see your mouth waterin'."

"How do you know that's where I eat? What I order?"

"You told me when we were in your bedroom yesterday. You said you were missin' that and your Starbucks. Besides, anybody with brains orders Clary's hash." He shrugged. "I saw your car parked outside the place a few times."

"Were you stalking me? Jeez, Cole."

"Hell no, I didn't stalk you. My place is only two blocks over. I pass there on my way to work. To work! While you relaxed over a lazy breakfast, I worked."

He saw her mind circling.

"I'm not sure whether to buy that explanation." She chewed her lip, and he fought back a surge of pure lust. "The alternative is too spooky, though, so for now I'll let it go."

She went still, then twisted on the seat to face him. "Did you send reports to Wes? Did he have you watching me?"

"No," he bit out.

"You're lying."

Through clenched teeth, he said, "I don't lie. I might have mentioned in some of my emails that I'd seen you, but no detailed reports, sugar. I've been too busy for that."

"I'll just bet. With your bevy of beauties."

"Don't you just have that right." He pulled in front of her house and leaned across the seat to open her door. "Let me know what you decide about Savannah."

She jumped out, and without another word he slammed her door and drove away. *A liar?*

Somebody in the town of Misty Bottoms was a liar, but it sure as heck wasn't him.

—⁓—

It had been a long, tiring day. After her field trip with Cole, she'd ripped into the gardens again, taking out her frustration on the weeds. She hated that she'd fought with Cole.

Now, on top of everything else, the attic's window shaker wasn't keeping up with the Georgia heat. It had to be ninety degrees up here, making it impossible to sleep. She tossed off the sheet and thought longingly of her air-conditioned apartment in Savannah.

Guiltily, she pushed that thought aside and willed herself not to think about it or dwell on the gargantuan task ahead of her. The clock on her nightstand read 12:33 a.m.

She must have fallen asleep, though, because sometime later, her sleep-fogged brain registered the sound of erratic footsteps on the attic stairs. Sitting up, she heard a mumbled curse, the sound of an elbow or knee striking the wall.

Her mother?

Reaching for the bedside lamp, she clicked it on.

"Turn that off." The words sounded slurred. A hiccup followed.

Jenni Beth sat on the side of the bed, the light still on. "Mom?"

Her mother reached the landing, her robe belted sloppily, her hair disheveled. She swayed ever so slightly, and the smell of cigarette smoke battled with the scent of alcohol. Tears streaked her face.

Jenni Beth had never seen her mother like this.

Sue Ellen dropped onto the bed and wrapped her arms around her daughter.

"What happened?"

"I miss him." Her chin quivered.

"I know you do." She ran a hand over her mother's hair, down her back.

"I decided to have a drink—out on the back patio. One turned to two, to, well, a few more. I think I'm in—inebri—oh hell, I'm drunk, honey."

Jenni Beth closed her eyes. "Yes, Mom, I think you are."

Her mother's tears slowed, and she grew quiet.

"Are you still awake?"

She nodded.

"Did you start smoking again, Mom?"

"Don't tell your dad," she whispered.

"I won't."

"I'm tired, honey."

Jenni Beth slid over, held up the sheet, and her mother slid in beside her. In minutes, she was fast asleep.

Jenni Beth wasn't that lucky.

At some point, though, as she drifted in and out of sleep, she realized her mother had left. She was sorry about that. It had been a long time since she'd last crawled into her parents' bed in the middle of the night seeking reassurance and protection.

This time, the tables had been turned.

Her mom had needed her.

Chapter 12

THE NEXT MORNING, COLE OPENED THE OLD SCREEN door and leaned in.

Charlotte, dust cloth in hand, motioned him in. "Get yourself out of that heat."

Stepping inside, he asked, "Is Jenni Beth here?"

"Sure is. She's up in that room of hers, tucked away with her plannin'."

"Okay if I go up?"

"Fine with me, but don't you go walkin' in on her unannounced." She gave him the stink eye over the top of her glasses.

"No, ma'am. Wouldn't think of it."

"Humph. Go on now. I've got work to do."

He took the stairs two at a time. He should be on his way to Savannah. He wasn't. After tossing around in bed half the night, he'd decided too much was still up in the air here. So he'd called Mickey, his assistant, who'd assured him Traditions could get along without its owner and master for another day.

At the bottom of the attic stairs, Cole knocked on the banister.

"Come on up," Jenni Beth called.

His heart knocked against his chest. *Think of it as her office, not her bedroom.*

She was working at the computer, all that silky blond hair scooped up in a messy knot on her head.

It struck him how incredibly gorgeous she was, how exactly right with all the clutter of building and planning around her.

Himself? Definitely out of place. A male lost in an ultra-feminine space. He drew in a deep breath, smelled the faint scent of wisteria that clung to her. He sniffed again. Did he smell cigarette smoke?

"Were you smokin' up here?"

She blushed. "No, of course not."

Again, he sniffed. His imagination? Probably, although Jenni Beth sure did look guilty. He'd never known her to smoke, though.

"You busy?"

She laughed. "Always."

"Still mad at me?"

"A little miffed maybe."

"And that's better than mad?"

"By a hair of a degree."

"I'll take it." He nodded toward her computer. "What are you up to today?"

She hit save and swiveled to look at him. "I'm working on the layout for my website. Have to get that up." She pulled a face. "I kind of cheated. I picked a couple areas to make beautiful…and finished. That way I can include some initial photos."

"The rose garden?"

"Yeah, that's one."

"That's not cheatin'. It's smart."

"Maybe." She shrugged. "I've made a few calls to some of the bridal magazines, too. The cost makes me cringe, but I have to run ads. The money worries me, but I think it'll be dollars well spent. Without the marketing, all the other work…" She shrugged. "Well, if nobody knows we're here, everything else will all be for nothing, won't it?"

"Yep. That old 'you've got to spend money to make money.'"

"I only wish I had it to spend."

A frown creased her forehead, and he found himself wishing he had the right to take her in his arms and kiss it away.

And wasn't that the stupidest thing. He and Jenni Beth Beaumont would never, ever reach that point. Nor did he actually want to. It had been a flight of fancy. Charlotte was right. It was damned hot outside. Made a man goofy.

"How about a cup of coffee? Or a glass of lemonade?" Jenni Beth asked.

"Good idea." Anything to give him an excuse to escape her space without losing his dignity.

But he didn't make it. She started past him, and he lost the battle. Reaching out, he caught her hand, turned her into him, and brought his lips down on hers.

She melted into him, and he pulled her closer still, lost himself in the taste of her, the feel of her. The tiny sigh that escaped her sent a shaft of lust ripping through him.

And then she stepped away.

Before she could speak, he shook his head. "No. Don't say anything. I know."

She surprised him by simply nodding, those slate-blue eyes wide, then heading toward the stairs.

Heart racing, he followed her, bound and determined to keep things light. "Do you plan to keep your office in the attic, Jenni Beth? I've been thinkin' about that, and it might prove kind of awkward. You're bound to have parents or grandparents who will have trouble with all these stairs. Have you considered settin' up a different spot to meet with your clients?"

"Already taken care of. I'll use the carriage house. Since you pass it on the way to the main house, it'll be easy for everyone to find."

"Yeah, the location's good."

"A couple years ago, Charlotte decided to move into it, so Dad had the whole place rewired and put in the plumbing and a wall for a small bath. Then she changed her mind. Finish the bath, and I think with a bit of TLC and some decorating, it'll suit me nicely as a client office."

"Sounds like a plan."

"I told you I've thought a lot about this, Cole. This isn't some spur-of-the-moment whim."

"I know—and I believe you."

They wandered into the kitchen, and she poured them both coffees. Wondering how her mother was doing this morning, she added cream to her own coffee, handed Cole his black.

Charlotte had all the doors and windows open, so they heard Beck when he came up the drive with a loaded trailer and a small crew.

Jenni Beth stepped onto the porch, coffee in hand. "Hey! Good morning."

"Hey yourself, beautiful. I understand you need a little work done."

"I needed some lumber cut to measurement," she protested. "The work I planned to do myself."

"Mornin', Cole. Didn't know you'd be here, but an extra hand is always welcome."

"I can do this myself," she said again, but Beck simply rolled over her objections and he, Cole, and his men went to work unloading supplies and setting up their work stations. As Cole and Beck bent over a box of supplies, she smiled. Beck and Cole. One light, one dark. White hat, black hat syndrome? One a good guy, one bad…for her, anyway? She traced a fingertip over her still tingling lips and guessed time would tell.

Cole had caught her off-guard, had unnerved her with the ease with which he'd had her totally under his spell. That wicked mouth of his was a miracle worker.

As she watched them work, she knew the two men's differences went deeper than appearances. While Cole was open and friendly, Beck could, at times, close in on himself. Had he always been like that? Or had he changed after Tansy deserted him and broke his heart?

Since she couldn't change the past, she picked up a sack containing tubes of caulk and a caulking gun and hauled it to the porch.

Her dad stuck his head outside a few minutes later and helped with some of the toting until her mother, with a quickly mouthed "thank you" to Jenni Beth, called him inside. She was sorry about that. It would be good for him to get involved. To spend time with Cole and Beck. Almost like it used to be.

Apparently, though, her parents had some sort of event on their calendar today. She was glad. Her mom needed to keep busy. Her late-night visit would be their little secret. No doubt her mother would just as soon forget it ever happened.

Jenni Beth wished with all her heart she could make that huge hurt go away.

As she watched the men heft huge loads and sweat over them, she felt overwhelmed. The generosity, the friendship. In Savannah, tucked away in her tidy urban apartment, she'd been reluctant to leave the city and return home. To be Jennifer Elizabeth Beaumont of Magnolia House again.

Just yesterday, she'd felt smothered by the small-town mentality and the fact that everyone knew every-body else's business.

As the men carried lumber—for her dream—she realized this was the flip side of that. Everyone pitch-ing in to help when it was needed. Lifelong friendships. People who knew her and her family and wanted to help.

Beck set a couple boxes of nails on the top step. "I thought the guys and I could at least get you started. We'll take care of the porch repair. You've got some siding issues, too. Most of it can be saved, but we'll need to replace some sections." Hands on his hips, he studied the front of the house. "It really could stand some paint, couldn't it?"

"That's an understatement."

"Well, here you go." He handed her a scraper. "You can start with this."

"Oh, lucky me."

"Yeah. That's what all the girls say. There's just somethin' about tools."

She laughed.

Cole sidled up to them. "Hate to ruin the moment, but I need to borrow your lackey."

"Fine with me." Beck threw Jenni Beth a wink. "But it's comin' out of your salary."

"As if," she said.

"I won't keep her long." Cole nudged her back inside. "I drew up some plans for the kitchen area last night, and I want you to take a peek at them. See what you think."

They moved back to the kitchen and Cole, after pushing aside some canisters, unrolled a length of paper on the counter. "I know you don't plan to do any caterin' yourself, but you'll need room for food storage. And cleanup."

She studied what he'd done. "This is good. Better than my idea."

He bowed. "You'll need new appliances."

"You think?" Her gaze traveled to the well-used fridge and stove.

"I do, but we can salvage those. Somebody might be able to use them."

"All right, consider them yours."

"Your best bet? Buy your appliances from a restaurant depot. Should be able to get a great deal on some used ones. Far better than you could afford otherwise."

"I want to include two dishwashers and a second fridge. To separate family and event food."

"Good idea. How about we put the second one, the wedding one, in the pantry? You can store your party platters, glassware, and whatever else you're gonna need in there, too."

They bent over the drawing as he made the changes.

"Mama's helping with this part of it. We're not cooking here, but you never can tell. We might do something small. So, just in case, we're stocking the kitchen with every platter, bowl, and serving piece we can scrounge up in the house. She's digging around in storage, too.

Dad's helping her with some eBay shopping for things we don't have."

His eyes met hers. "That's good. Get her involved in this."

"She needs something to take her mind off, well, you know."

"I do."

"And this is her house, her home. To make it work, she needs a say in it."

"You're a good daughter." He saw the cloud pass over her eyes. "You are."

He thought again of the single portrait that hung in the stairway and wondered how her parents could be so thoughtless, so careless with their surviving child.

Rolling up his sketch, he asked, "What do you say we go outside and give Beck a hand?"

Jenni Beth picked up her scraper. "Let's do it."

While Cole pried off damaged siding, his mind stayed as busy as his hands. Despite what Jenni Beth believed, he'd never had any plans to tear down Magnolia House. Hell, he loved the place almost as much she did. This place had been his second home.

No. His plans didn't include destroying the beautiful old home to sell it off piece by piece. Instead, he'd hoped to save it, too. To keep Wes's folks in their home—and provide them a business if he could talk them into it.

Oh, it would have meant a huge change in their lifestyle. And probably a big blow to their pride. But after hearing Jenni Beth's plan—well, if they were willing to go along with that…

So much of what he'd planned ran along a similar vein. A lot of tourists, especially Northerners, loved the idea of spending a night or two in a real Southern plantation. The romance of it, the history struck a chord in so many.

He'd thought to turn Magnolia House into one of those fancy B&Bs.

Like Jenni Beth, he'd planned on a second-floor apartment for Mr. and Mrs. Beaumont to give them some private space. Unlike her, he'd turn a couple bedrooms into guest rooms along with some of the outbuildings.

He'd figured he'd hire help because he certainly didn't expect Mr. and Mrs. B. to run a bed-and-breakfast themselves. And Charlotte? Years ago, she could have handled it with one hand tied behind her back. Now? She'd aged. The time for her to retire had come and gone. But the Beaumonts were her family, and so she stayed on with them. Ditto for Vernon, their gardener.

A couple years ago, Wes and Jenni Beth had put their feet down and insisted their parents hire part-time help. A couple women from town came in now and did the heavy cleaning one day a week, and Charlie's teenage son and a friend did the heavy outside work.

Glancing around, Cole realized they needed more. The two boys hadn't been able to keep up with the place on a one-day-a-week basis. The magnolias were in bloom and, while they were gorgeous, they were also unbelievably messy.

The red Georgia brick along the foundation needed some work, too.

Jenni Beth had bitten off quite a chunk.

And darned if some tiny part of him hadn't begun to think she just might manage it—with a lot of help from her friends.

He whistled an off-key tune and hunkered down to

work, the sun beating down on him, the sound of hammering and sawing singing around him. Jenni Beth scraped the old boards to his left. Cole couldn't remember the last time things had felt so right.

Half an hour later, Jenni Beth stopped scraping. "Answer a question for me?"

"Sure. If I can."

"You want this house. You've made no bones about that. So why are you helping me fix it up? You're just going to tear it down if I fail."

Without missing a beat, he said, "You're a friend. Friends help each other."

She made a disbelieving sound that he ignored.

His conscience pricked. He should probably come clean about his plan, too. He was holding on to too many secrets. Instead, he'd let her continue to think he was the villain. For now. Yeah, he'd have to put up with some anger short-term, but it would let her keep some of her pride.

If he explained his own plans, she might start to second-guess her decision. She'd wonder if she should let him have his way. At this particular point in time, he didn't think that was the answer. Like her parents, she needed something positive to concentrate on, something to divert her mind from her family's loss. This wedding venue would give all of them exactly that. This was what she wanted, and he'd do what he could to help.

He'd always felt—what? A soft spot for Jenni Beth? More, much more. She'd called him a liar, and he'd denied it. But if he denied his feelings for her? Then he was lying to himself.

Bottom line, she was Wes's baby sister, and as much as he had fun flirting, there was a line there.

Or was there?

If Wes was still alive, would he feel he needed to keep his hands off her?

For one night, he hadn't. One glorious night—that had led to him running like a scared rabbit. The biggest screwup of his life.

He wished it had never happened.

He thanked God it had.

Cole wiped the sweat from his brow.

Those eyes, that pouty mouth. All that beautiful silky blond hair. His fingers itched to loosen that elastic band and bury themselves in it.

And that body. Remembering that tiny little excuse for a pair of shorts, that damn pink tank top, he bit back a groan.

Right now, she didn't have on much more, and he couldn't blame her. This was hot work. Still, he'd eat a skunk if there was a single man among Beck's crew, married or not, who hadn't checked her out up there on her ladder in those skimpy red shorts and that little white tee.

Jenni Beth didn't need designer clothes and a wheelbarrow full of makeup to look good. Nope. It didn't much matter what she wore. She was a natural beauty with the body of a siren.

A brain, too, he admitted. And he loved that about her.

Magnolia House as a B&B would have brought some much needed help to Misty Bottoms. Jenni Beth's wedding venue would bring far more.

—⁓—

By the time Beck's crew called it quits and cleaned up for the day, Jenni Beth's arms felt like rubber. She doubted she'd even be able to pick up a glass of sweet iced tea.

Leaning against the old oak tree in the front yard, she watched the trail of dust swallow up the last of the men's pickups.

She turned to the house and grinned. Oh, it was still pretty much a disaster, but the difference one day, ten guys, and a whole lot of hard work and determination had made was phenomenal. She could hardly believe the changes.

The porch floor was whole again. The new, unpainted siding stood out like a harlequin pattern on the house, but it was being repaired.

On the porch steps, Beck and Cole sprawled, a bottle of water in each of their hands. Only the three of them were left, survivors in the midst of what had practically been a battle. They'd won today's skirmish.

Walking over, she wiggled down between the men. Her brother's friends. Her friends.

Nothing smelled quite like a man who'd worked hard all day. Both radiated heat. Jenni Beth found it sexy on a very elemental level.

She had two men, one on either side of her. One slightly urban, at home whether in the city or the country. The other? Country all the way. Both handsome, rugged males. Yet Beck, with all his good looks, didn't affect her sexually. Didn't make her want to drag him upstairs to her bed. Cole? Whew. Different story altogether. She practically had to sit on her hands to keep them from touching him, from running over his body. And she hated that. Hadn't she learned her lesson?

"Why don't you stay for dinner?"

"With your family? Smellin' like this?" Beck asked.

"If you want, you can take a quick shower."

"We'd have to jump right back into these sweaty clothes, Jenni Beth."

"Fine. Just wash up. Mama and Daddy won't care, and I'm sure I don't smell any better than you guys."

The look Cole sent her told her she smelled just fine. For a split second, she wondered if he'd been sharing her thoughts about taking that shower—together. She groaned mentally. *Get real, Jenni Beth. You're not his type.*

But dang it all to purgatory and back, she knew exactly what Cole Bryson hid beneath that sweaty T-shirt, those worn, torn jeans. It didn't matter, she reminded herself. What he did or didn't have beneath those clothes no longer had anything to do with her.

"Charlotte made potato salad today and one of her blue-ribbon, county-fair-winning chocolate sheet cakes."

"And I'll grill some burgers." Her dad stepped out onto the porch. "It's the least we can do for you boys after what you did here today. We've missed havin' you here." He cleared his throat. "Sue Ellen made me promise you'd stay. Don't make me look bad."

The two exchanged a look, and within no time, they were out on the back patio with her dad at the grill, cold drinks in hand. Jenni Beth, her mom, and Charlotte set the outside table.

"Like old times, ain't it?" Charlotte asked.

Her mother nodded, a sheen to her eyes.

Jenni Beth gave her a hug.

"I'm okay, sweetie. Just, well…" She shook her head, changed the subject. "There seems to be an awful lot of smoke." Napkins in hand, Sue Ellen turned to her husband. "Are you sure you know what you're doing?"

"The burgers keep catching on fire." Her dad slapped at the grill as another flame shot skyward.

"Why don't you let me do that, Mr. Beaumont?" Cole jumped up from the hammock he'd been sprawled in.

Her dad handed over the spatula without any argument.

"Thank you," Jenni Beth mouthed to Cole. He grinned and nodded, bided his time till she went inside to help Charlotte.

"I walked through the house yesterday with Jenni Beth," he said. "I see you've got Wes's college picture in the stairway."

Grief clouded Todd Beaumont's face, and he nodded. "Nice picture, isn't it?"

"It is." Cole hesitated. Probably not his business, but if not his, then whose? He decided to go for it. "That really wasn't my point, though, sir."

Todd's expression turned quizzical. "Your point? I don't understand."

"No, I don't guess you do. Thing is, Mr. Beaumont, you've got two children but I only saw one portrait."

"I don't think—"

As if Todd hadn't even spoken, Cole pointed the spatula in his hand toward Jenni Beth, who stepped through the back door, a large plate in hand, and lowered his voice. "And that one's workin' her ass off—pardon my French—to save this place."

Todd stared at his daughter then glanced at his wife, who sat at the patio table, sipping tea and chatting with Beck.

Ashen-faced, he looked back at Cole. "Point taken."

After she deposited her appetizer tray on the table, Jenni Beth walked over to them.

"Charlotte put some of your favorite cheese on there, Dad." She tipped her head toward the platter.

"I'd better have some, hadn't I? Don't want to get on her bad side."

A look passed between him and Cole.

After he walked away, Jenni Beth asked, "What's going on? Dad looked—funny."

"Just guys talkin' sports over a grill."

Her expression cried *liar* again.

"You and my dad planning something I should know about?"

"Nope."

"Richard still hasn't called."

"He will."

"From your lips to God's ears." She sighed.

Worry hazed those incredible blue eyes, and Cole wanted to punch Richard's lights out for putting it there.

"He'll call."

"You can't know that."

Unease settled in Cole's belly. "Yeah. I do know."

"Hmmph."

He felt like a heel. He felt…untruthful. Like that liar she'd called him. Yet he couldn't tell her about Richard's implied threat or his trip to the banker's office. Not yet.

He'd missed his chance earlier. Now, it would have to wait. It weighed him down.

—⁂—

Jenni Beth dropped onto an old Adirondack chair. Why did Cole sound so certain? And yet, at the same time he prowled, uneasy.

She studied her nails, wondering if there was even the slightest chance of resurrecting them. Helen at Frenchie's Beauty Parlor would probably kick her out if she dared darken her door with this mess.

She smiled. It had been too long since she'd visited pink-haired Helen and her *Grease*-themed shop. Maybe she'd call tomorrow, if only to talk for a minute. If she intended to live in Misty Bottoms, she needed to reestablish herself. And who knew? She and Helen might be able to work up a package for brides and their attendants. They'd need someone to make them beautiful for their special day. Why not Helen and her staff?

She'd need to contact the two local hotels, too, to see if she could finagle some kind of discount rate or group package for overnight wedding guests. Guests who would spend money in town.

Her cell rang. Surprised, she nearly spilled the soft drink in her hand.

Caller ID showed it was Richard. Her stomach fluttered. He quite literally held her—and her family's—future in his hands.

"Hello?"

She glanced up, saw Cole's full attention trained on her. Shifting in her chair, she turned her back on him.

She could handle this. Cole had started Traditions, his own business. Now it was time for her to start hers.

"Sorry for calling so late," Richard said, "but I wanted to clear a few things off my desk before I head home."

"No problem." A lie she prayed would be forgiven. Inwardly, she could gladly have wrung his neck for stringing her along these past couple days on what was a sound business proposal. He was a bully—a small-minded, arrogant bully. She felt sorry for his wife.

"Will you be in town tomorrow?"

"I can be."

"Good, good. Listen, why don't you stop in and we can finish that paperwork. I'll have everything ready for you to sign."

Jenni Beth closed her eyes in a quick prayer of thanks. "Any special time?" she asked.

"Whenever you get here is good. Gloria will have everything drawn up."

She hesitated, almost afraid to ask, but needing to know. One deep breath and she plowed in. "Were you able to give me the full amount?"

"Almost. We'll talk about it tomorrow."

She turned off her cell, understanding what he hadn't said.

Well, she'd deal with that later. Right now, she intended to enjoy dinner with her family and friends. Lightness and life. The old house needed this. Her parents needed this. Beck and Cole had brought a much-needed shot of energy to Magnolia House.

She glanced at her mother, saw a smile on her face. A matching one sat on her father's. Warmth spread through her. The burgers, thanks to Cole, were wonderful—juicy and perfectly cooked. The conversation flew from one to the other, and there was laughter at the table. All in all, the evening was perfect.

While Charlotte and her mother cleared, Jenni Beth walked with Beck to the front yard.

"I know you're the guy with all the connections," she said. "And I understand your own men are already booked up with projects you have scheduled. But I'll need workmen to plaster, to sheetrock, to do some plumbing and electrical work. Are there people in town who can do this, or will I need to bring in some outside help? I'd really like to put Misty Bottoms people to work if at all possible."

"Give me a couple days to do some checkin', and I'll get back to you. I'm sure we can handle this job with local people. Things have been slow here, and the guys will be glad for the work."

"That's what I was hoping. Thanks, Beck, for everything." She stood on tiptoe and kissed his cheek, wondering again why she couldn't feel anything but brotherly love for him. Maybe because Tansy had loved him. Jenni Beth had never understood how her best friend could have married someone else. Could have hurt Beck so badly.

As he walked to his truck, she stood, her arms wrapped around her waist. Everything was starting to fall into place. She waved as he disappeared down the drive.

When she turned, Cole stood behind her.

No noise, no chatter came from the back of the house. Her parents had gone inside. Beck was on his way home. Charlotte was in the kitchen cleaning up. Only Cole remained. In the dim summer light she stared at him, a nervous laugh playing through her mind.

He looked like a dark angel. But his eyes? A rogue's eyes, full of mischief and devilment. How did a woman resist that combination?

No brotherly feelings here. Nope. But feelings? Emotions churned inside her, every bit as chaotic and dangerous as the running of the bulls at Pamplona. Why couldn't she get this man out of her system? He'd let her down too many times. Had broken her heart.

And still, she wanted him.

He took a step toward her, the pale moonlight shining on him, silvering the light streaks in his dark hair. Her pulse kicked up a few notches, and she couldn't help but wonder if he heard the thunder of her heart.

"I have no right to ask, but I'm gonna," he said quietly. "Will you grant me one favor, Jenni Beth?"

"Grant you a favor? You make me sound like a princess or a queen." She laughed. "We both know I'm neither of those."

"No. Thank God, you're a flesh-and-blood woman."

Her breath caught, and she steeled herself for what might be coming.

"Now that your porch is rebuilt and is no longer in danger of fallin' in, will you sit with me on the swing?"

"What?"

"For a few minutes. I need to go to Savannah in the morning, had planned to go back today. I'm only askin' for a couple minutes of your time. No complications, I promise. No kissin', no hand-holdin'. I just want to sit with you."

"Cole Bryson, I swear you're a brick shy of a full load."

"Probably." He stuffed his hands in his back pockets. "So will you?"

"Sit on the porch swing with you?"

"Yes."

She smiled warily at him. "Despite everything, you're a good friend, and you worked darned hard today. You've earned some porch-sittin' time."

He walked toward her. The peepers and crickets sang their song. Somewhere off in the trees, an owl hooted. The summer night air wrapped itself around her, and Jenni Beth wondered if the fireflies truly were magical. If they didn't spill a little fairy dust around when they blinked on and off.

When he reached for her hand, she nearly drew it away. Nearly reminded him of his no-hand-holding promise. Deciding against it, she took that warm, calloused hand in her own.

And almost sighed aloud.

Together, they walked to the porch, through the patches of grass that still needed to be mowed. Past the stacks of lumber pieces left from today's work. They climbed the stairs that needed more than a fresh coat of paint to make them safe and moved to the swing.

He held it as she sat, then dropped beside her. She swore his heat could generate enough electricity to run all of Atlanta for a good week or so. And despite his earlier labors, he smelled good. He smelled sexy.

Despite herself, she laid her head on his shoulder and set the swing moving with the tip of her toes.

Neither spoke.

His arm came around her, drew her closer. Her hand splayed across his chest. Oh boy, did he feel good. So strong, so muscular. And he smelled so male. She wanted to move closer, cuddle till midnight. And beyond.

Knew she didn't dare.

The moon moved higher in the sky. The cicadas added their rasping, buzzing call to the night sounds. Inside, the house was quiet. A faint light in the hallway spilled onto the porch.

How long they sat like that, she couldn't have said.

But when he turned, laid one hand on her cheek, and dipped his head, the warning system she'd so carefully erected around her heart failed.

She opened her mouth and met his kiss head-on. Everything, everyone else disappeared. The world shrunk to the two of them, and she didn't want the moment to ever end. One kiss led to two, then three.

Slowly he drew away and straightened.

"Damn, you taste good. I should probably apologize for that, after my promise and all, but I'm not gonna. Instead, I'll say thank you. Good luck tomorrow. If things don't work out with Beck's guys, give me a call. We'll see what we can do. Good night, sugar."

"'Night, Cole."

When he turned his back to her, she laid a finger on her lips. Even his kiss was full of confidence. So Cole. Whatever he did, he gave it one hundred percent.

Oh yeah. His kisses rang her bell.

She sat there while the lights came on in that big black truck of his, the gold lettering advertising Traditions, his salvaging company, glowing in the moonlight. Watched as he idled down the long drive. Watched as his taillights disappeared from view.

Laying her head back, she stared into the inky sky. Stars spilled across it like so much confetti. Trembling fingers traced her still-burning lips, lips that already missed Cole's. What did he want?

Her or her house?

Maybe it was a moot point. In the morning, he'd drive back to Savannah.

Would he return? She doubted it. His history was that of hit and run. It made sense he'd follow pattern.

Chapter 13

WHAT DID A PERSON WEAR TO SIGN HER LIFE AWAY? Jenni Beth wondered as she rifled through her closet. She shouldn't be this nervous. Richard had already told her she had the loan. Problem was he hadn't approved the full amount.

Why was he being such a tightwad?

Argh! She should have saved more, been more careful with her money in Savannah. She could have eaten at home more, could have stopped at Starbucks less often. Waited for movies to come out on DVD instead of hitting the theater to see them with her friends.

And, she admitted, even with all that she'd still have needed this loan.

She hadn't slept well, had woken periodically to stare at the ceiling, worries chasing around her mind. Because of that, she needed something vibrant for this morning. Something that would give her some color. More confidence.

Her fingers stalled at an aqua skirt and jacket. Nope. No more suits. Misty Bottoms, even in late March, was way too warm. She'd keep a few to wear at client meetings, but maybe she could sell the rest at the new consignment shop on Market Street.

And this wasn't resolving her dilemma.

Her fingers landed on a fun sundress in black with splashes of orange, blue, and yellow. Its flirty little skirt, along with her orange short-sleeve cardigan, would send a casual, you-can't-keep-me-down message. Perfect. Problem solved.

Standing at the kitchen counter, too wired to sit, she wolfed down a cup of coffee and a piece of toast. If she ate more, her nervous stomach might rebel.

"You'll do fine, honey." Charlotte patted her cheek, the way she had when Jenni Beth was ten and worried about a spelling test.

"Thanks, Charlotte. I'm trying my best."

"I know you are. And your mama and daddy are real proud of you."

"Are they both still sleeping?"

"Your mama is, but your daddy went into town to have breakfast with some of his friends. Now quit frettin'."

"I'll give it my best shot. Maybe I'll run into Daddy when I'm done." She picked up her purse, gave Charlotte a hug, and headed into the already humid morning. The bank didn't open till nine, but come hell or high water, she'd be Richard's first customer today. No more time in those uncomfortable chairs than necessary.

Had her great-great-granddaddy Beaumont felt like this when he'd faced Sherman? A skirmish was a given. The only two things in question—which side would be victorious and how bad would the casualties be?

One quick look in her rearview mirror showed she at least still had some lipstick on. No sense going into battle completely unarmed. She put the 'Vette in gear and headed out to face down her enemy.

Because of her lead foot, the drive didn't take nearly long enough. The bank wasn't open yet. Pulling out her little spiral notepad, she jotted down items on her must-do list. Fifteen minutes later, she tucked it into her purse, checked her hair, and sailed through the front doors of the bank.

"Morning, Gloria. Richard in yet?"

"He sure is." She picked up a file from her desk. "I've got all your paperwork right here. Why don't you come with me?"

"Thanks." She followed in Gloria's wake, picked up the scent of musk and vanilla. Gloria had worked for Richard as long as she could remember. Jenni Beth wondered if she liked her job, if working for the jerk made her happy.

Well, not her concern, she supposed.

Gloria knocked on the doorjamb before she peeked her head into Richard's office. "Jenni Beth's here. I have the file."

Not wanting to get stuck outside cooling her heels, Jenni Beth squeezed past Gloria and walked right in, uninvited.

Richard, ensconced in his big leather chair, a cup of coffee steaming on his desk, looked up in surprise.

He pointed at his coffee. "Want a cup?"

"No, thanks, I had some at home."

He took the paperwork from Gloria and nodded. Apparently that was her unspoken signal to leave because, with a smile toward Jenni Beth, she backed out of the door and closed it behind her.

Richard opened the file and flipped through the papers as if seeing them for the first time. He took his time, made no attempt to hurry. In fact, he acted as though he didn't even remember she sat there.

But he did, and she knew it. All part of his game. She

disliked Richard Thorndike more with every tick of the second hand. A playground bully in an adult setting.

Covertly, she wiped her palms on the skirt of her sundress. "Is everything in order?"

"Oh yes. It is." He straightened the papers. "I'm afraid, though, that rather than the full two hundred fifty thousand you requested, you only qualified for two hundred thousand. Not that big a difference, really."

He had the gall to send her a condescending smile.

Her stomach clenched. Fifty thousand less? Not a big difference? Get real! It was huge! A fifth less!

She stirred uneasily in the chair.

Even with her collateral, the bank wouldn't loan her the full amount? Come on! The land was worth double the amount she needed.

She paused, forced herself to think before she responded. Cole's odd statement from yesterday replayed in her head. He'd been dead-on right. Richard was already squeezing her. He had his fingers on her pulse. Worse. Had them on her purse. And he'd decided to pull the strings tightly enough to choke her.

Well, he could think again. She refused to play his game of chicken.

Her grandfather wouldn't have stood for this, and neither would she.

"Two hundred thousand won't work, Richard. At two-fifty, I've cut my budget to bare bones, and you know it." She leaned back in her chair, forced herself to relax.

"You, of all people, know what a huge job I'm tackling. In order to pull it off, I need the full loan. Nothing less." She met his gaze levelly. "You wouldn't try to

sabotage me, would you? To take my land? We both
know it's extremely valuable, and it seems others do, too.
The property on both sides of mine has been sold and
marked with 'no trespassing' signs. Did you know that?"

He hesitated, ever so slightly, and she understood.
Cole had been right. Richard Thorndike wanted what was
hers. But how had Cole known? A good guess? Hmmm.

Richard's face reddened. "I hope you're not implying—"

"Oh, but I am." Heart in her throat, she said, "I'm
afraid the loan has to be for the entire amount."

When he still hesitated, she picked up her purse from
his desk and stood. "I'll take my business to Savannah."

"Sit down," he said. "Fine. I'll clear the check for the
entire amount, but my bosses aren't going to be very
happy with me."

Hah! she thought. Who was the poker player extraor-
dinaire now? The bluff had worked.

Struggling to keep her expression bland, she settled back on her chair and laid her purse in her lap.
"Thank you."

Oh, she wanted to say so much more. Really rip into
him. Bottom line? She had to have the money. Period.
So she bit her tongue till it bled.

She understood, too, that she had to make the business a success. Because if she didn't, Richard would
swoop down faster than a Yankee carpetbagger to take
her home from her.

There'd be no negotiations.

Her father had already left Dee-Ann's when Jenni
Beth stopped in, so she ordered a sweet tea to go and
headed home.

Halfway down the lane to her house, she hit the

brakes, flabbergasted. Three men worked at the side of her house with saws and nail guns.

Slowly, she drove the rest of the way and stared at Beck, who walked over to meet her, his tool belt riding low.

"Beck, why are you here? I don't—"

"You're welcome, Jenni Beth, one friend to another."

Getting out of the car, she wrapped her arms around him, overwhelmed by his generosity. He smelled of heat, sawdust, and man. "I love you."

"I know you do, and I love you right back." He drew away and swiped a finger down her nose. "Charlotte said you were in town. With Richard."

"Yes. It's done." She met Beck's gaze. "The dirty vulture actually tried to short me. He wanted to cut the loan by fifty thousand."

"That would have made it pretty tough, wouldn't it?"

"Impossible. I told him I couldn't do the renovations with that amount. That I needed the full loan. I said I thought he was trying to make certain I failed." Her chin came up, and she took a deep breath, still wondering where she'd found the nerve to confront Richard.

"You honestly think he'd do that?"

She debated with herself, took another fortifying breath. This was Beck. He deserved to know what he was getting into if he decided to help. "Yes. He wants my bottomland, wants to collect on my collateral."

Jenni Beth watched her friend closely. His reaction wasn't quite what she'd anticipated. She'd expected consternation, maybe distress. Instead, she saw previous knowledge.

"But you'd already guessed that, hadn't you?"

This big strong guy actually squirmed in front of her,

and she was torn between anger and resigned laughter. Again, small towns equaled no secrets. She might need to have that equation tattooed on her forehead where she could see it every time she looked in a mirror.

"Cole told you."

"Jenni Beth—"

She held up a hand. "No. Don't lie, and don't make any excuses. I should have known."

"He's watchin' out for you."

"Understood. But I've been taking care of myself for quite a while now. It'll take a bit before I get back into the small town swing of things where everybody knows everybody else's business. Y'all need to cut me a break. Give me some space while I adapt."

His expression turned indignant, and she hurried on, upset that she'd hurt his feelings. "There's nothing wrong with helping each other, with watching out for friends and family. I've just forgotten how tight the net-work is. I'm good with it, though." She squelched the urge to cross her fingers behind her back. "I swear to God, Beck, Richard Thorndike will not get my house or my land. I fully intend to make this work."

Relief smoothed out the lines on her friend's face. "Did he back down on the money?"

"He did." She sent him a half-smile. "I got the full amount. Begrudgingly, but I got it. Which means he had authorization for it all along, and that makes me sad." She rubbed at the ache in her chest. "I thought he was a friend."

"It's business, Jenni Beth."

"Understood. But business should be carried out with integrity. When you stuff your morals in your back pocket and forget about them, you've sold your soul."

"I couldn't agree more." He gave her shoulder a pat, then stepped away. "Well, then, by damn, we'll have to work that much harder to make sure he doesn't get what he wants."

"Yes, we will." Determination flooded her, nearly choked her. "I need to draw up a budget, a really tight budget. Prioritize where the money goes."

"You do, yes. Cole can probably give you a hand with that. Or I can."

"I can manage it, but I might need some help figuring material and labor cost."

"I'm here. Any time. Call, text, or email. Or stop in— whether I'm in the office, out on a job site, or at home. Whatever works."

"Thanks."

He pulled a hammer from that low-riding tool belt. "I can work today, but after that I'm gonna have to move to another job I've got under way. The plasterers will be here tomorrow, along with a couple guys to start the actual carpentry work." He tipped his head. "I told them you'd pay their going rate. Hope that's okay."

"That's good. Thank you so much."

"No thanks needed. *My* morals are right here in my shirt pocket where I can get at them any time I need to."

She grinned. "You're a good man."

"Some people would agree with that, some wouldn't." He tapped the hammerhead lightly on his palm.

Jenni Beth knew he meant Tansy Calhoun and that slick talker she'd met in college.

"Beck…"

"Nah. Let's not get into any of that. Some things are best left buried like an old stew bone." He took her by the hand and led her to the side of the house. "Watch where you step. There's gonna be nails and scrap out here for a while. It might be best if you and your mama wore something other than those cute little sandals for now."

"Okay."

"Wanted to show you what we're doin' here. You've got an almost new roof, which is a real blessing."

"Wes had that done before he shipped out."

"I remember." He squeezed her hand. "That will save you a bundle of money. We've redone the porch floor and braced up those posts. Cole said he'd take care of replacing them."

"He did, did he?"

"Yeah, he did." Beck studied her. "You know, I'm not sure exactly where you two buried that hatchet in each other, but it's time you pulled it out and stuck it somewhere else. It's not doin' either one of you any good."

Jenni Beth swiped one of those sandals he'd warned her about over the mashed-down grass. "I know."

She thought of last night, the peace of sitting with him in the dark. How good it had felt to rest her head on his shoulder. "We're working on it."

"Good. Now…" He pointed to the house, one arm slung around her shoulder. "The siding's a mammoth job on a house this size. We're removing the pieces that are absolutely no good, sanding others, doing some patchin'. When we finish that, we can slap a fresh coat of paint on this baby, and from the outside at least, it'll look real good."

"Kind of like a movie facade?"

He laughed. "A little, I guess. But we'll get the rest pulled together, too. The electricity and plumbing are both in good shape. I had a couple of my guys check those first thing."

"Again, my thanks."

"None needed. I should have been out here before, takin' care of all this. I promised Wes…"

The tension poured off him and slapped at her. A reminder she wasn't the only one mourning her brother.

"We all did. And we all fell asleep on the job," she said. "You're here now, and I, for one, am eternally grateful." She switched gears. "Anyway, the deed's done, the papers signed. I have my money, but I'll have to be frugal. Decide where every penny will do the most good."

"I'll help however I can."

"You do know, despite your promise to my brother, this truly isn't your responsibility."

"Hey, what am I missin'?" Cole came around the building, took in the two, Beck's arm hugging Jenni Beth to his side.

She stepped aside guiltily, then swore under her breath. "I thought you'd left for Savannah."

"Mickey has things under control at the shop, so I decided to stay one more day. I was out back workin' on the siding. You get your bankin' done?"

"I did."

"He didn't shortchange you, did he?"

"Despite giving it his best college try, no. I've already deposited a check for the full amount in my account."

"What're your plans now?"

"As in right now, today?"

He nodded.

"Um, I intended to ask Beck if he'd give me a minute to change, then have him look at the carriage house with me. See if he thinks I can turn it into my client meeting room for under five thousand." She pulled her hair up and away from her face before letting it drop again. Was it the weather or Cole that spiked her hot-o-meter? "That seems like a lot when I have so many other places to put the money, but first impressions are crucial. Since that's where I'll meet prospective brides, grooms, and soon-to-be mothers-in-law for the first time, it's essential the carriage house speak well of Magnolia Brides."

"I couldn't agree more," Cole said. "And although I really hate to see you lose that short little dress, sugar, you're right. You do need to change. Pick out something a little more suitable for a motorcycle ride."

"What?" Confused, she faced Cole. "I can't ask these guys to work while I take off with you."

"Sure you can. First of all, you're payin' them to do a job. They'll put in the time, do good work for you, and you'll cut them a check. Second, this isn't a frivolous playtime ride. We're goin' over to a little salvage place west of here. I found some columns that are perfect for the front of the house. I want you to look at them, give them your stamp of approval."

"Oh. Okay." Still, she stood in place and looked at Beck. Excitement at the idea of finding replacement columns warred with her work ethics.

"Do it," he said. "The sooner those go up, the sooner we can get some paint on this place."

She nodded. "That would be good. I need some pictures, and even with a lens filter, I can't hide the peeling paint."

"While you're gone," Beck said, "I'll poke around your carriage house. I've got a pretty good idea what you want to do out there, so by the time you get back, I'll have a cost estimate drawn up."

———∿∿∿———

Cole watched as she picked her way around the construction and crew. She disappeared inside, and he turned to find Beck studying him.

"What?"

"Exactly my question, pal."

Cole frowned.

"I asked at the pub, but I don't think I got the right answer. Let's try it again. What's up with you and Jenni Beth?"

Startled, Cole said, "I told you. Nothin'."

"Bull! I see the way you look at her."

"What are you talkin' about?"

Beck jabbed his friend's arm. "That innocent face might fool some. Not me. I might not have that fancy college diploma framed on my wall, but I've known you too long, Bryson. A starvin' man, when a big, juicy burger's set down in front of him, wears the same expression you do when Jenni Beth shows up. That one that crosses his face right before he devours the burger."

"You're crazy, Beck."

"I don't think so." He leaned against the side of the house, arms crossed. "What are your plans for today?"

"Like I said, I found some columns for the porch. I want Jenni Beth to see them before I buy them and trailer them here, though. It's her house, her decision."

Beck threw an arm around Cole's shoulders. "Friend, you are in so much trouble. I almost feel sorry for you."

Half an hour later, Jenni Beth closed the door on the carriage house. Despite Cole's impatience, she'd insisted on walking Beck through it. She shared her ideas for the transformation from a mostly unused storage area to an office where she could meet clients and plan weddings. Could see, so clearly, the finished space…and she was in love with it!

Now, dressed in jeans and a red and white University of Georgia T-shirt, she hopped on the Harley behind Cole. On so many levels and for so many reasons, this was a bad idea. But he'd been on his best behavior today. Had helped so much. She leaned into him and wrapped her arms around those washboard abs. A girl could have an orgasm right here and now, she thought, because on top of everything else, the man, as always, smelled heavenly. His body? Hard and hot.

He glanced at her in his rearview mirror and grinned wickedly. He switched on the key, pressed a button, and the motor roared to life. With a twist of his right wrist, he gunned the engine and had the machine thrumming under them.

Oh yeah, he knew how affected she was, and he was enjoying this. Well, let him, because she was, too. Her grin exploded. Another minute and they turned onto the main road, the warm wind caressing her body.

She'd forgotten all this. Had gotten so caught up in city life, in trying to outdo herself with every assignment, in just day-to-day living, that she'd forgotten how much fun the simple things were.

Did she need to go back later and scrape paint? Yep,

till her hands bled, but right now? She'd enjoy the moment, the freedom.

The big bike ate up the highway. Cole handled the Harley with ease. She leaned with him into the corners, smiled as they accelerated on the straight stretches, and turned her face skyward as the sun beat down on them.

The miles flew by too quickly and, way before she was ready, Cole turned off the main road and onto a smaller one.

Random Salvage. The building stood a couple hundred yards off the road, shielded by a copse of hardwoods. A ramshackle metal structure, it looked ready to fall down.

But even before she got off the bike, excitement raced through her. All kinds of goodies crammed the windows and spilled across the parking lot and around the side to the back. Jenni Beth could hardly wait to start poking through the junk to find the buried treasures.

Cole set the kickstand and she removed her helmet. He hopped off, reached for her hand, and helped her dismount.

She laughed. "Thank you."

"For what?" he asked.

"For reminding me what beautiful spring days are for."

He took off his dark glasses and perched them on his head. A grin spread slowly over his face. "You're more than welcome."

As they started across the unpaved parking lot, he warned, "We're here to look at columns for the front of your house."

"I know, but, wow! I need a chandelier for my new office. I'll bet he has something here."

"I'll bet I have a nicer one in Savannah. When you come visit, we'll choose one."

"But, Cole—"

"Nope. Columns only today."

When he opened the door, she had to bite her tongue not to beg for more. She stood just inside for a minute, taking it all in. "This is a salvage yard?" she whispered.

"Yep."

"And yours is like this?"

"Bigger, but basically, yeah."

"Maybe I owe you an apology, Cole. Sort of."

He laughed. "Sort of?"

"Well, yes." Thoughtfully, she pulled the band from her hair. "I had no idea. All these wonderful old hinges and doors and windows would have ended up in the dump, wouldn't they?"

"Most of them, yeah."

"So you really are in the rescue business, aren't you? You find homes for unwanted gems."

"Guess you could say that." He tugged at her hand. "Come on back this way. Let me show you what I found."

"Cole, you son of a gun, you come back for those columns?"

Startled, Jenni Beth turned to see a human tank step out from behind a wall of storm doors.

"Hey, Dinky, I brought my friend to take a peek at them. She's the one doin' the reno, so the decision's hers. Jenni Beth Beaumont, meet Dinky Tubbs."

Dinky, as wide as he was tall, had a belly that completely obscured his belt buckle. Nothing soft about him, though. His arms bulged with muscle.

Even with the welcoming smile, this was not a man she'd want to meet on a deserted street at night.

Cole watched as Jenni Beth, true to her breeding, crossed the pitted concrete floor to shake Dinky's hand. The sun shone through a skylight and turned her hair into a golden halo, those eyes of her into deep, dark pools of blue.

Damn him! Beck was right. Like a riptide, his feelings for Jenni Beth were pulling him under. Time to get out of Dodge. He found her way too attractive for the good of either of them and was riding straight into the open jaws of the beast.

"Pleasure to meet you, ma'am."

Dinky took her hand and, for just an instant, Cole truly believed the guy meant to raise it to his lips for a kiss. And that would have been too bad. He liked Dinky, but the green-eyed monster coming to life inside him would have insisted he stomp him to dust if he had.

"Come on, Jenni Beth." His voice deeper than usual, he nearly growled the words. "What we're lookin' for is in the back."

Without waiting for her response, he headed toward the columns and was relieved when he heard her footsteps following.

"Your place is great, Dinky," she said.

"Thanks. Hope you find somethin' that works. Holler if ya need me."

"I thought he was your friend," she hissed when she reached him.

"He is," he bit back.

"You were rude."

"He was slobberin' all over you."

"What?" She stopped, hands on her hips.

When he didn't stop, she stayed put, forcing him to turn around.

"What is wrong with you?" she demanded.

"Not a damn thing. Come on. Let's get this done."

She muttered something he couldn't quite make out, but he didn't figure he wanted to ask her to repeat it. Sometimes, a body was better off not knowing what others said about him.

He led her to the right section, then just stood back. He watched her examine the columns, one at a time, running her hands over them, and admitted he wanted those slim, soft hands on him.

Since that wasn't in the cards, he pushed the thought away.

Hands in his back pockets, he waited quietly till she got to the ones he'd found the day before. He said nothing. Didn't want to influence her—yet, anyway.

"These are almost identical to what're on the house," she said. "And there are enough of them."

"That's what I thought. They're the same ones that caught my eye. They're good and solid," he said. "They've been taken care of and are tougher than woodpecker's lips."

"Such a way with words, Cole."

He shrugged. "Want them?"

She nodded.

"Let's go dicker."

When they left Random Salvage, she had her new, old porch columns and six crystal dresser pulls she'd assured him would be perfect on a secretary she intended to move downstairs.

She threw a leg over the Harley. "I'm starved."

"Really?" He tossed her a glance.

"I practically skipped breakfast. Nerves. You kid-napped me before I had a chance to grab lunch."

"I didn't kidnap you. I invited you to come with me to check out material for your renovation." He pointed a finger at her. "And you enjoyed it. You said so yourself."

"I did." She smiled and lifted a brow. "And now I'm hungry."

"How about the best burger and homemade fries this side of the Mississippi? Will that do?"

"Do they sell chocolate malts?"

"Made with hand-dipped ice cream."

"What are we waiting for? Get a move on, cowboy."

He laughed. That smile of hers? Unmatched. "I have to warn you, though. The place isn't fancy. In fact, it could be plastered in the dictionary beside the definition for greasy spoon."

"My favorite kind of place."

"You're lying and you know it."

She rolled her eyes. "Sometimes it is. Depends on my mood. And today's a jeans-and-T-shirt, Harley-riding, greasy-spoon-eatin' kind of day, Cole." She slid on her sunglasses.

"Well, when you put it that way…" He climbed on in front of her. "Hold on."

She did. Those arms of hers slid around his waist and she scooted up close. For two heartbeats he simply enjoyed her, the feel of her, the sweet, sexy smell of her.

Then reminded himself the lady was off-limits.

Checking his mirror to make sure she had her helmet

buckled, he started the bike, his sights set on Wimpey's Burger Basket.

Grease floated in the air right along with the oxygen molecules. Jenni Beth didn't complain about that or the beat-up tables and chairs. Standing at the order window, she read through the menu written in grease pencil on a white board.

"I want cheese and mayo on my burger, Cole," she finally said. "Lots of fries and that chocolate malt."

"You got it. While I put in our order, how about you run out and save us a picnic table?"

"Sure." She slipped her sunglasses back in place and left.

He watched her go. So did, he noticed, a couple teenage boys sitting in the corner. Jenni Beth drew attention. It didn't matter if she was all dolled-up or dressed-down. She made a fellow want to be with her just by being.

And what was he going to do about that?

In no time, his food came up, and he carried it outside.

Handing her a wad of napkins, he slid onto the bench beside her, close enough his leg rubbed against hers. She didn't pull away. He smiled and nudged a hair closer.

Inside, Wimpey's Burger Basket was a disaster. Out here? A little slice of paradise. A small stream ran along the property's edge and gurgled as it passed over worn river rock. High in a tree, a bird serenaded them with his happy song. Sun filtered through their table umbrella. A great burger, fries, a chocolate malt, and Jenni Beth Beaumont. It could make a grown man cry from the sheer pleasure of it.

Jenni Beth made a sound of pure, simple bliss as she bit into her sandwich. "This is so good."

He dipped his plastic spoon in the whipped cream on his malt, held it up to her mouth. She closed those luscious lips around it and rolled her eyes.

"Mmm. Good."

A tiny dollop stuck to her lip. He swiped at it with his finger, then popped it in his mouth. Watched her slate-blue eyes darken.

"Yeah, it sure is," he agreed.

For a couple minutes, neither of them said anything.

She rested her chin on her fist. "Can I ask you something, Cole?"

"Sure."

"Why did you decide to go into the architectural salvaging business? I mean, that's not, like, something most little boys dream of."

His eyes met hers, steady and unblinking. "To honor the past."

"Right." She made a small sound of disbelief.

He shrugged. "You said it yourself at Dinky's. Without my business, a lot of our history would end up in the city dumps. I reclaim it. See that it's used and loved again." He took a bite of his burger, chewed while he studied her, tried to decipher the intense look on her face. "And you don't believe a word I said."

"Strangely enough, I do. While we were at Random Salvage, I saw a different side of you. And I realized that, after all these years, you're a stranger to me."

She wiped her hand on a napkin and extended it toward him. "Hello, I'm Jenni Beth Beaumont."

He nearly choked on his unswallowed bite. But the earnest expression in her eyes had him reaching out to shake her hand. "Cole Bryson."

"So, tell me five interesting things about yourself, Cole Bryson."

"Whew. Seriously?"

"Five things."

He held up a hand and ticked them off as he went. "I love my mama and daddy, my grandmother."

She nodded.

"My Harley." He flicked his chin at the big black motorcycle. "That baby's my pride and joy. I love to take Sunday afternoon rides on her."

"So far, you haven't told me any secrets. Everybody in town knows all this," she prodded.

"Ah, but you and I have just met, remember? I like to sleep exactly as I was born. Buck-naked."

She blushed, and he laughed.

"Women have always been a mystery to me. Secret and wonderful. I love them. The look of them, the feel, the scent." His gaze met and held hers. He held up a fifth finger. "And I'm desperately sorry for what I did to you in Savannah."

"Not now, Cole."

"Figured you'd say that. Your turn."

"What?"

"Your turn." He wiggled the fingers of one hand. "Five things."

"Oh. Well, my family means everything to me." She held up a finger. "I have the sweetest little '65 'Vette. A ragtop. That thing sails down the highway."

"Huh-uh. Secrets, Jenni Beth. I want the dirt."

She laughed. "I don't think I actually have any dirt."

"We all have dirt. Some of us have just hidden it better."

"I desperately want to be a wedding planner." She

held up a fourth finger. "I love Cheetos and mocha frappuccinos."

Before he could open his mouth, she said, "And I don't actually hate the jerk that stood me up for my senior prom. I do hate that he took Kimmie Atherton, though."

"Ahhh." Dunking a fry into some ketchup, he asked, "Can we be friends again, Jenni Beth?"

"We were never friends."

"Yeah, we were." He popped the fry in his mouth and chewed.

She shook her head. "No. As a kid, I annoyed you, then, for one night, I didn't."

"About that night—" He cleared his throat.

"Not now," she repeated.

"Why?"

"Because I don't want to talk about it."

"I do."

She shrugged. "You lose. Want to share a dessert?"

He rested his elbow on the table and sent her an exasperated look. "You're still annoying."

With a grin, she said, "Thanks." She pointed to the menu. "How about banana pudding?"

"The malt wasn't dessert?"

She shook her head. "Banana pudding," she repeated.

"Nah, if we're gonna do it, I insist on a hot fudge sundae—with a cherry and more whipped cream on top."

She narrowed her eyes for a fraction of a second. "I can handle that."

"I'll bet you can." He went back inside to order.

Chapter 14

SEX. IT WAS ON JENNI BETH'S MIND WAY TOO MUCH.

She'd let her guard down, and Cole had crept in. The day they'd ridden the Harley to Random Salvage, then stopped for lunch had been too intimate, too enjoyable. They'd laughed and shared a fun day.

When she was with him, she could forget what a snake in the grass he could be. It was only later, when she was alone again, that she'd pull out her memories. Remember why she couldn't allow him to get too close.

And, if she was totally truthful with herself, mourn that fact.

But he'd returned to Savannah on Friday, and she'd returned to sanity. When he'd dropped her off late the afternoon of their ride, he and Beck held a powwow. She didn't doubt for a minute she was the main topic.

It should upset her. The self-reliant, take-charge woman inside was slightly offended that it didn't, but Jenni Beth decided she could keep that part of herself under control. Bottom line? She couldn't handle this project alone. Cole wanted to help, and she had to swallow her pride and let him.

He'd left Magnolia House insisting she'd be okay, that Beck would keep an eye on things.

She told him she'd keep an eye on things herself.

Cocky as ever, he'd winked and slid his sunglasses

in place. Putting the big bike in gear, he'd left her standing in the drive.

Without him, the house felt hollow. And that *did* offend her.

The men she'd hired had the weekend off, but she'd kept busy stripping baseboards, scraping paint, and working on the ad layouts.

She worried about the timing. It was imperative to get her ads out there, but she had to be absolutely certain that when the first call came in, she could deliver. Had to be sure she'd have enough done for the old girl to show well. Since most brides planned their weddings with plenty of lead time, she'd be able to finish her renovation even after someone booked a date. But the bait— the house and grounds—had to be far enough along for them to bite.

Today, the workers had shown up at eight o'clock and hadn't left till after five. The progress was amazing. Everywhere she looked, though, she saw another project.

Everyone else had long since gone to bed. The house, silent except for its comforting night sounds, still seemed to thrum from the day's activities and energy. Construction tools spread throughout the rooms. Partially completed projects waited impatiently for the next workday.

After doing physical labor all day, she ought to drop like a stone, but tonight, like so many others, she couldn't sleep. Instead of shutting off, her mind continually added to her mental list of things to do. She wandered downstairs for a cup of tea as she had last night and the night before and the night before that, carefully avoiding the stairs that creaked the loudest. She carried her mug out to the back porch and sat in the dim light from the kitchen. Sipping her tea, she stared into the star-strewn sky and dreamed.

Almost an hour later, finally ready for sleep, she stumbled up to bed. At the second floor landing, she stopped. Someone was crying.

Her mother.

Jenni Beth tiptoed to her brother's room.

"Mama?" The door stood ajar, and she pushed it open. Her mother stood in the center of the room, her hair a mess, an old robe hanging on her, holding a pillow to her face.

"Sometimes I think I can still smell him." Tears ran down her face.

"Oh, Mama." Jenni Beth started toward her, arms outstretched.

She lifted a hand. "No. Don't." More tears streamed. "Yes, do. Please." She opened her own arms. "I can't bear this."

Neither spoke for the longest time.

"He's gone." Tears waterfalled down her mother's makeup-free face, and she looked older than she had just this afternoon.

Jenni Beth's throat constricted. "Yes, he is."

"All the changes—I realized—" Her mother dropped to the side of the bed, the pillow cradled in her lap. "When Wes came home on leave, I told him not to bother picking up. To leave everything, that I'd take care of it. After we came back from Atlanta, from the airport, I came up here to do exactly that."

She swiped at her eyes, and Jenni Beth dug a tissue from her pocket and handed it to her.

"I couldn't do it, Jenni Beth." She sniffed into the hankie. "If I touched anything, he wouldn't come back. Leaving his room the way he left it would keep him safe. Bring him home."

Her face caved with sorrow, and Jenni Beth fought for breath in a chest gone tighter still.

"Mama—"

On a sob, her mother said, "But I did. I did. It was my fault!"

"No, oh, no. Listen to me, Mama."

She shook her head vehemently. "He'd brought a glass of milk and some of Charlotte's cookies upstairs that last night." A ghost of a smile played over her lips before her face crumbled again. "Oh, your brother ate every cookie, every morsel, but he didn't finish his milk." She sobbed. "He never did. He always left that last drink."

Blindly, she reached for Jenni Beth's hand. "Don't you see? I took that glass downstairs and washed it." Her tears rained heavier. "I killed him," she whispered.

Understanding and grief slashed through Jenni Beth. All this time, and her mother hadn't said a word, hadn't let on that she blamed herself for Wes's death. Irrational, yes, but that made it no less formidable, no less real to her.

Sitting down beside her, she buried her face in her mother's hair. "Mama, the snipers that ambushed his platoon killed him. Not you. Not you," she repeated.

"If I'd left that—"

Jenni Beth sat up straighter, put a hand on either side of her mother's face. "Look at me. If you'd left that glass here till the milk curdled and turned solid, Wes would still be dead. You have to understand that."

Her mother's cries turned into the sounds of a wounded animal. Jenni Beth, her own face wet with tears, held her, let her cry. It was way past time. They both needed this. They'd all been too careful, too afraid to vent their emotions.

Afraid that if they started to cry, they'd never stop.

Finally, her mother pulled away. "You're right. I know you're right." Her words caught on another sob.

"Let's do this, Mama. Right now. Tonight. Let's clean up this place. Give Wes some peace."

Her mother chewed at her lip, then nodded.

Even though it was dark, Jenni Beth moved to the window, stepping over her brother's shoes, and threw open the drapes. Moonlight filtered through the window for the first time in a year and a half.

"Where's Daddy?"

"Fast asleep. I talked him into taking a sleeping pill tonight. It's been so long since he's had a night's sleep."

"And you?"

"I'm okay."

"I love you, Mama." She ran down the hall to the bridal suite for some boxes to hold what remained of her brother's life.

Coming back into the room, she pushed up her sleeves. Her mother turned from the window and nodded at her.

It wasn't easy. Everything they touched brought fresh memories, fresh pain. His high school ring, the one he'd given Sadie on prom night, the one she'd given him back three months later. A couple Little League trophies. A crumpled receipt for gas and a bag of chips from Tommy's Texaco.

Jenni Beth stripped the bed and stuffed the linens

into a garbage bag. No one would have sweet dreams on them.

Her mom folded each and every item of clothing carefully and placed them in the boxes as though Wes would wear them soon. The clothes, minus her brother's ratty Atlanta Braves jersey, would go to a shelter in Savannah. Neither wanted to walk down Main Street and see one of his shirts walking toward them. Cole would handle that for them.

The old jersey? She'd keep it, couldn't bear to part with it.

Many tears and much hand-holding later, the room had been cleared of all but the furniture. The boxes had been marked for storage or donation.

"I have a headache." Her mother rubbed the base of her neck.

Jenni Beth felt like a drum had taken up permanent residence in her own head. She looked at her mother. She was pale, and tear tracks streaked her face.

"Go take a nice long shower, Mama, and slip into a clean nightie. I'll fix you a cup of chamomile tea." She laid a hand on her mom's cheek. "Then you should lie down for a bit. Try to sleep."

Her mother raised a hand and placed it over her daughter's. "I believe I will." She drew her close. "I couldn't have done this without you. You're my rock. Mine and your father's." Fresh tears started. "Don't think for a minute that I don't know how much tonight has cost you, too. I'm sorry."

"Don't be." Over her mother's shoulder, Jenni Beth studied the room. Her chin quivered. She closed her eyes, bit back the cry, and said good-bye to her brother.

—◊◊◊—

"Mama? Daddy?" Shocked and more than a little tired after a nearly sleepless night, Jenni Beth walked into the chaos that was now their kitchen to grab a quick breakfast. "What are you two doing up?"

"Good morning to you, too, daughter of mine." Though she'd applied her makeup carefully this morning, her mother's eyes were still red from last night's tears. Healing tears.

"Morning." Jenni Beth leaned in and gave both of her parents a quick kiss and a hug. "You're up so early. I thought you'd sleep longer."

"With all the noise, sleep's impossible," her dad said. "Besides, we've decided it's time for us to step up. It's our house. We can certainly lend a hand."

"Okay." She drew out the word, but her heart raced.

"Your dad and I had a long talk this morning, honey. I told him what we did last night."

She turned to her father.

"It's good. Way past time." He nodded toward the far wall where Wes's picture leaned. "I took that down while they plastered and painted. There's another behind it that needs to be hung when they've finished."

Tears welled in Jenni Beth's eyes. Her graduation picture peeked from behind her brother's.

Her father cleared his throat, a muscle in his jaw working. "We haven't done right by you, honey, and I apologize for that." His eyes misted. "Cole made a comment last week about us not valuing the child we still have." He reached for his wife's hand, then hers. "We do, baby."

"But we need to tell you more often," her mother said quietly, a tear trailing down her cheek. "And we will. Starting right now."

Charlotte, wiping away tears of her own, ambled over to the table, coffeepot in hand. "Now that that's done, let's have some breakfast so I can get cleaned up before the horde of good-lookin' construction workers hits the front door."

They all laughed, and the tension dissipated.

The four of them ate, talked, and drank coffee. There'd be more storms, more dark days, but Jenni Beth understood they'd turned a corner. Taken some big steps. And Cole Bryson had played an important part in that.

"Your dad's helping in the bathroom upstairs today. Charlie promised to teach him how to lay tile."

Jenni Beth stared at her father, who wore a sheepish grin.

"I can't wait to get started. Your mom watches a lot of HGTV, and I've always admired men and women who can get in there and get it done. Today"—he pointed at himself—"that's going to be me."

Jenni Beth high-fived him.

She turned to her mother. "You watch HGTV?"

"I do."

"When she isn't reading." Her father stirred more sugar into his coffee.

"Why shouldn't I read? All you do is play those stupid computer games, day and night." Her mom shot her husband an accusatory look, then turned to Jenni Beth. "He's up half the night sometimes."

"I can't sleep," her dad groused.

"Jeez, if I'd have known that," Jenni Beth said, "we could've been keeping each other company at three in the morning. I've been sitting on the back porch alone."

"You're not sleeping either?" Her mother laid a hand over hers.

Jenni Beth shook her head. "Too much going on. I can't shut it down."

"How about if we go into town this morning, sweetheart?" her mom asked her. "Beck's team can get along without you for a few hours. Besides, your dad will be here in your stead."

About to say no, Jenni Beth stopped. It would be good for her dad to feel important, to be needed, and she and her mother could use some time alone, some fun time.

They were making an effort. She needed to foster that.

"I'd love to, Mama."

Her mother waved her coffee mug toward Jenni Beth. "You'll need to wear something other than those shorts and that ratty top, though." She quirked a brow and grinned. "After all, you are a Beaumont."

They all laughed, and it felt so good. It had been a long, long time since this kitchen had heard the sound. Charlotte stood at the sink, a grin as big as the moon on her face, tears in her eyes. The wound was, at long last, starting to mend.

She took the last drink of her coffee before racing to the attic to change. Her mother, as usual, looked ready for anything. Again, Jenni Beth wondered how she'd fallen so far from the family tree. Casual suited her just fine. Her mom? Dresses and pearls.

Well, today she'd make her mama proud. A quick

shower, some makeup, and her new sundress, her last Savannah purchase.

By the time she stepped out of the shower, she heard cars and trucks out front, the buzz of a saw, the raised voices of the workers.

Another day had begun.

On the drive into town, her mother chatted up a storm. A heavy weight had been lifted from her. During a break in the conversation, Jenni Beth's mind wandered back to Cole. What was he doing today? What would he do tonight?

And with that, her mind skidded to a halt. *Oh my gosh!* Was he involved with someone in Savannah? He was bound to have a girlfriend, wasn't he? Anybody who looked like him... Why hadn't she thought of that? But would he have kissed her the way he had if that was the case?

She almost laughed. Of course he would. He was Cole Bryson. Love 'em and leave 'em.

Her mother had her face tipped to the sun, eyes closed behind her Jackie O sunglasses. Wouldn't Mrs. Bryson have mentioned something about it to her mom during their every-other-week game night?

Then again, maybe her mother had quit attending Wednesday night ladies' poker.

"Does Cole have a, um, girlfriend in Savannah?"

Her mom swiveled toward her. "I honestly don't know." The smile disappeared, and her mouth trembled.

She'd screwed up. Taken that sliver of tranquillity from her mom. Her stomach plummeted to her toes. What had she said? "What's wrong?"

Her mother shook her head. "How awful is that?

I don't even know what's happening in Wes's best friend's life anymore. I've lost him, too."

"Mama." Jenni Beth reached for her mother's hand. "I'm sorry. I shouldn't have asked. It doesn't matter."

Her mother's expression turned to one of affront. "It most certainly does! And it seems to matter a great deal to you. Anything I should know?"

"No. Absolutely not." She quickly swung the conversation around to the paint colors under consideration for the bridal suite.

They made a fast stop at Elliot's Lumberyard to pick up a couple samples. From there, they decided to stop by Quilty Pleasures. Her mother wanted a new pattern.

They parked and, walking arm in arm, were halfway to the pharmacy when the door swung open. Emma Bryson stepped out, and Jenni Beth stood back while her mom and Cole's mom hugged.

"Jenni Beth asked this morning if Cole had a girlfriend tucked away in Savannah."

She gasped. When had her mother developed such loose lips? Emma sent Jenni Beth an all-too-knowing smile. "None that we know of. His dad and I keep hoping he'll find some cute little gal right here in Misty Bottoms, settle down, and make us some grandbabies."

Mortified, Jenni Beth wanted to drop into that proverbial sidewalk crack—and stay there. She couldn't stop the blush that heated her face. Emma laughed. "Cole's been tellin' us about your dream, honey."

And that did it. That he'd used that word when talking to his parents turned her to mush. Her dream. Darn it all, why did Cole make it so hard to hold a grudge?

"I'd love to see what y'all are doin'."

"Come on over," Sue Ellen said. "I'll give you a tour, show you how hard Beck and his crew, along with my daughter and your son, have been working."

After another couple minutes, they said their good-byes, and Jenni Beth and her mom moved on to the yarn store.

"Mom, why did you ask her that?"

Her mother stopped. "Why ever not? You wanted to know. Emma's been my friend forever, so why shouldn't I ask her?"

Jenni Beth said nothing, simply shook her head and kept walking.

While her mother and Darlene, dressed today in chrome-yellow and black, bent their heads over a pattern book, Jenni Beth poked around the other merchandise. Moonshine and Mint Julep, both wearing knitted bumblebee sweaters, trailed behind her.

"What's this?" Jenni Beth asked, picking up a small pouch.

"It's a crocheted dream pocket. See the opening on the side? You write your dream or your wish on a piece of paper, slip it in there, and sleep on it."

"Clever." Sue Ellen picked up another of the small pockets. "These would make great little gifts."

"I agree." Jenni Beth contemplated the small squares. "For the bride and her attendants. Can you get them in other colors, Darlene?"

"Absolutely. Ms. Hattie makes them and brings them in on consignment."

"Ms. Hattie? See, Mama?" she said excitedly. "Local talent. So once I know a bride's colors, she could match them, Darlene?"

"She sure could, and Ms. Hattie can certainly use the money. She's barely getting by. Her house." Darlene shook her head. "It's in such disrepair."

"I haven't seen her since I've been back."

"She doesn't go out as much as she used to."

Jenni Beth nodded. Time to pay her a visit, then, and check on her. She picked out several in different colors. "I'll start with these and use them as bridal gifts. I'll display some in my office for sale. Brides will like the idea of a homemade dream pocket. It's romantic."

"By the way," Darlene said, "I've thought about what you said before. About trying to hang on a little while longer. This is what you were talking about, isn't it? This big dream of yours."

"Yes. But everything was so tentative—"

"I understand. I've decided to give things here a little more time. Who knows? Once Misty Bottoms becomes a famous wedding destination, my business, heck, the whole town, might boom."

Jenni Beth's heart swelled with hope. "From your lips to God's ears, Darlene."

"I love weddings." Darlene's huge hoop earrings swayed as she clapped her hands and sighed deeply. "They're so romantic and so happy."

"Yes, they are." She had just finished paying for her dream pockets when Darlene's door opened. "Daddy?"

"Todd? I thought you were tiling," her mother said.

"I am. But we needed some more spacers, so Charlie sent me into town to pick them up. I wondered if maybe my best girl wanted to ride back with me."

Her mother looked at Jenni Beth, almost as if asking permission.

"Go," Jenni Beth said. Her dad radiated happiness. He felt busy. Necessary.

Relief filled her. Yes, the project was a godsend for them all.

"I've got a couple more stops to make," she added. "After that I'll be home to give the guys a hand."

"You're sure?"

"Totally. Now go. Both of you." She handed her mother the bag of dream pillows. "Take these, will you? That'll save me having to tote them around."

After they left, she and Darlene talked a bit about her parents and the renovations at Magnolia House.

"I didn't want to say too much until I knew for sure it was going to work." She sighed. "Truth be told, I'm still not positive, but…" She shrugged.

"I think it's wonderful, honey. And you're right. It will be very good for this tired town. It might prove to be the jump start Misty Bottoms needs to fire its engines."

She left Darlene's feeling free as a bird. Since her mom had gone home with her dad and they didn't expect her back at the house yet, she decided to stop at the Dairy Queen for a quick treat. It was that kind of day, meant for playing hooky, for leaving work an hour early.

Normally, she considered the fast-food place off-limits, worried about the calories. But with the way she'd been working this past week, she deserved a Blizzard. The biggest one they sold.

When young Carrie Sue Peterson handed her the decadent chocolate indulgence, Jenni Beth reverently carried it to a shady picnic table. One bite and she nearly swooned.

Two teens sat at a nearby table, totally wrapped up

in each other. She didn't recognize them and wondered who their mamas and daddies were. She'd been away long enough to have lost track.

They held hands and, from the sound of it, were wallowing in teen angst. The boy was apparently having trouble with a friend and his girlfriend had decided to act as intermediary.

"So Keith told me you never want to do anything."

"That's not true, Sara. Keith is the one who never shows up when he says he will, never does what he's supposed to. I don't know if I can trust him anymore."

"Pinky-promise you'll try," Sara said.

Jenni Beth toyed with her ice cream. Was that her problem? Did she really have trust issues like Cole said?

After the boy promised, Sara moved on to her own problem. "Melissa's driving me nuts. She tries to dominate everything. She chooses what we're doing, where we'll do it, and when. And worse, she flirts with everybody else's boyfriends."

Oh, I so don't want to be fifteen again, Jenni Beth thought.

"My mom was talking about moving last night." Sara drew doodles in the condensation on her Coke glass. "She thinks she might lose her job. There's not enough traffic in and out of the hotel. And if she loses it, there's nowhere else in town for her to work."

And right there was reason enough to push on with her project for Magnolia House. Jenni Beth prayed her plans would help Sara and her mother. Would bring guests to the hotel.

The teens' grip tightened.

Her heart broke for them. She remembered that feeling,

that almost desperate urgency to touch, to be touched. The pain of young love. Hadn't she felt it for Cole? Hated Kimmie, who not only won Cole but lorded it over her? Where was Kimmie now? She'd have to ask her mother, then pray she didn't get on the phone and call Kimmie's mom. Sue Ellen Beaumont deserved a good butt-chewing for this morning's stunt with Emma Bryson.

A fortyish man pulled up to the curb and waved at the teens. The boy nearly spilled his soda in his hurry to stand. "Hello, Mr. Mahoney."

The guy dipped his head to look out the passenger window. "Hello, Trey."

Sara and her boyfriend exchanged a hasty, awkward hug. Both stepped back, and Sara opened the car door.

"Why are you driving Kelsey's car?"

"Because I can," he answered. "Your sister's grounded. She got home late last night."

As they drove away, Jenni Beth watched Sara's friend. His gaze stayed focused on the disappearing car, and he sighed when it rounded the corner. Ah, yes. Young love. Her own heartstrings tugged. Just a little. When Cole had left, he'd taken a piece of her heart.

And he would again. Despite anything and everything he said, she needed to keep that in mind. If she had a trust issue, he'd caused it.

Jenni Beth scraped her paper cup to capture the last drop of ice cream before she tossed it into the waste can. Time to head home.

On the way to her car, she nearly bumped into Ms. Effie, who'd been the town librarian since time began.

"Hey, Ms. Effie. I planned on visiting the library tomorrow."

"Oh?"

"Do you have any books on restoring old houses?"

"You stop by, and I'll have something for you. In fact, I have a brand-new book you might like. Came in last week, and I haven't shelved it yet."

"Oh, thank you."

"So, young lady, tell me about these big plans of yours."

Jenni Beth did, knowing full well every person in town would hear every shared detail by the end of the day.

Ten minutes later, she excused herself. Time to get the kitchen appliances ordered. She'd considered going the route Cole had suggested, all too aware of the huge bite new ones would take out of her budget, but if she was going to do this, she wanted new. And she wanted to keep her business local.

An air-conditioned blast hit her as she walked into the only store in town that carried what she needed. Moose Jansen, former Misty High defensive lineman and big as a Humvee, gave her a welcoming pat on the back, hard enough that, had she not been planted firmly, it would have sent her sprawling on the well-worn indoor/outdoor carpeting.

"How ya doin', Jenni Beth?"

"I'm great, Moose." She laughed. "Heard you and Denise have two beautiful baby boys."

"We sure do." He dug a wallet out of his back pocket and flipped it open to a Sears special. "Aren't they the cutest things you ever did see?"

"They are." She said it honestly. Both boys had their mother's faces with the exception of the chin, and that, squared off and solid, was pure Moose. Sturdy little legs and powerful bodies were dressed in the red and white

Misty Bottoms High School colors. "You and Denise must be ecstatic."

"We are. Bet your mama and daddy are glad to have you back home, huh?"

She nodded. "I suppose you've heard what we're doing at Magnolia House."

He grinned. "Heck yeah. It's the talk of the town."

She just bet it was. "I thought I'd stop by to see what you have in the way of kitchen appliances. We need some new ones."

"Okay, but—" He swiped a size fourteen shoe over the carpet and stared down at it. "It's only right you know that Richard came by to see us."

"Richard Thorndike?" Her palms grew sweaty. This had bad written all over it.

Moose wet his lips and looked for all the world like he was readying for a humdinger of a dress-down from the coach. "Thing is, he suggested we get half or so of every order up front, money being tight and all. But it don't seem right to do that without tellin' you why."

Jenni Beth felt sick. The Blizzard she'd just devoured didn't want to stay down. "I don't understand."

"Actually, Richard said we should get all our money before we ordered anything for you." The big hulk shifted uneasily from foot to foot. "I'm really sorry, Jenni Beth."

Fury ripped through her. The chickenhearted backstabber! Work had been held up a couple times, and, unless she ordered through Beck, they'd never seemed to have enough materials. She'd chalked it up to circumstances. Now, though, it took on a different tenor.

Richard knew she had the money. He'd lent it to her, for heaven's sake.

Well, she'd show him!

Rage boiled through her blood, but she coolly walked around the store. "I want this"—she pointed at a range and cooktop—"and two of these and one of these."

Moose made notations on a little notepad.

Heading for the door, she said, "Order them, Moose. All of them. Take care of the paperwork and get a total for me. I'll be back in thirty minutes or less to pay you, in full, up front. I have to take care of something first."

Outside, she threw her car into reverse and backed onto the street. The 'Vette ate up the short distance to the bank way before she'd cooled off even a fraction of a degree.

She stormed into Coastal Plains Savings and Trust, slammed past Gloria, and marched into Richard's office.

Jasper Nolan, her high school biology teacher, sat in the chair opposite Richard.

He looked up in surprise, then tipped his worn ball cap. "Jenni Beth, nice to—" He hesitated, a wary look coming into his eyes. "Um, it's real nice to see you."

"Mr. Nolan, y'all are going to want to leave for a few minutes." She spoke through gritted teeth.

His head swiveling from one to the other, Jasper stood.

"Nonsense." Richard waved him back into the chair. "Jenni Beth, I'm in the middle of something."

"You sure as hell are."

Jasper's eyes went wide. "Jenni Beth? Everything okay?"

Without so much as a glance at him, her eyes fixed on the banker, she answered, "No. It's not. But it will be. Close the door on your way out, please, Mr. Nolan."

"Yes, ma'am." Jasper's gaze settled on Richard, then Jenni Beth one more time. Without another word, he left, shutting the door softly behind him.

"Your parents would be very disappointed in your behavior, Jenni Beth Beaumont."

She squinted as though giving it some thought before she shook her head. "No, I don't think they would be."

"Have a seat."

"I don't want to have a seat, you low-down, back-stabbing—" She cut herself off. "What are you doing?"

Richard tugged at the knot in his tie. "Watch your mouth, young lady." He folded his hands on top of his desk. "I have no idea what you're talking about."

"Is that right? I just came from the appliance store. Seems they need full payment in advance. Someone suggested I might not be good for the money. Any idea who that someone would be?" Moving to his desk, she placed her palms on the shiny surface he was so proud of and leaned toward him.

He rolled his chair back an inch.

Her lips curved. "You're a coward to boot, aren't you?"

"If this is the kind of aggressive, unladylike behavior you've learned in the city, I have to tell you it's not at all becoming."

She said nothing, simply stared at him.

"It's time for you to leave." He hit the intercom button. "Gloria, Jenni Beth Beaumont is leaving now. Would you send Walter in to escort her out?"

"You've got to be kidding." She straightened. "You're going to sic the bank guard on me? Old Walter?"

The guard had to be in his late seventies, and she prayed to God the bank never actually needed security.

If Walter ever drew that gun of his, he'd be bound to shoot off his own toes.

"I don't understand," Gloria fumbled, her voice tinny through the sound system.

"You don't need to understand," he bellowed. "Send Walter in here."

"Don't bother, Gloria," Jenni Beth said. "I was just on my way out." She rounded on him again, eyes narrowed to slits. "Mr. Richard Too-Arrogant-for-Your-Own-Good Thorndike, you're going to be really, really sorry you messed around with me and mine."

"Did you hear that, Gloria? Ms. Beaumont threatened me."

Beyond furious, Jenni Beth said, "No, sir, I did not. I made a promise."

Head high, she walked to the door and opened it. Turning back to Richard, she added, "And I *always* keep my promises. You can take that to the bank."

Once outside, she stumbled to her car on legs so rubbery they barely held her. Laying her head on the steering wheel, she felt sick to her stomach again. Talk about losing her temper! But, to be honest, she didn't regret confronting him—and would do it again under the same circumstances. Still, random thoughts ricocheted inside her brain. At the forefront was the realization she could very well have destroyed her chance to make this venture work.

But he'd already given her the loan. He couldn't take it back, could he? And it seemed to her the rat was already doing everything in his power to make things difficult for her. What more could he do?

An adrenaline headache burned behind her eyes.

Time to go home and lick her wounds—after she dropped off a check for Moose.

That done, she headed toward Magnolia House. A quarter mile out of town, still hot under the collar, she stopped at Tomato Annie's roadside vegetable stand. It would give her a little more time to detox, and some fresh tomatoes and cucumbers would be nice tonight at dinner.

"Hey, Annie."

"Hey yourself, girl. I heard you were in town. Doing some fixin' up at your place, huh?"

"Yes, I am."

"True you gonna hold weddings at Magnolia House?"

"That's what I'm hoping."

"Good for you. 'Bout time somethin' new was happenin' in this town."

Jenni Beth filled a container with her veggies and fished money from her purse.

"You seen Ms. Hattie lately?"

"No. Darlene told me she's having some problems," Jenni Beth replied.

"Money. All comes down to money. Her windows are all but fallin' out of her house, and she ain't got no money and no family but that nephew up in New York state to help her. Don't think she's honest with him about her situation. I buy some of my produce from her, bein' local grown and all. Pay her a little more because she sure does need it."

"Thanks, Annie." Jenni Beth picked up her bag of produce. "I'll see if there's anything I can do for her."

"That would be real good of you. I don't think she's eatin' right, neither. Since her sister died, I'm not sure she cares. Those two never spent a day apart."

Jenni Beth recognized the expression that settled on Annie's face. The realization she'd mentioned the loss of a sibling. She'd seen it so many times this past year. "I'm sorry, honey," Annie said.

"It's okay."

"You tell your mama and daddy and Ms. Charlotte I said hello. Enjoy those 'maters, now."

"I will." Jenni Beth drove away with a heavy heart. Ms. Hattie, in her time, had done for most of the population of the town in one way or the other. When she and her sister Dorothy ran their little country store, Jenni Beth was certain they'd provided lots of credit to families, monies that undoubtedly weren't always repaid.

Two people in one day worrying about her? Definitely time for a visit. She decided to stop by Beck's again and talk to him.

"Is Beck here, Jeeters?"

"Believe he's back in his office, fiddlin' with that computer."

"Okay, thanks." She strolled through the store, noticing things that before last week would have bored her silly. Now she studied hinges and doors, wondering if any of them would work for her renovation. Would Cole have something more authentic at Traditions?

Reaching Beck's office, she knocked.

"It's open," he barked.

When she peeked around the doorjamb, he stood. "Hey, didn't expect to see you today. You don't look very happy. Problem at the house?"

"No. Nothing at Magnolia House. Everything there is phenomenal."

"But?"

"I had a fight with Richard."

"About?"

She explained briefly her chat with Moose, her spat with the banker.

"Jenni Beth, you need to be careful around him."

"I know."

"I'm not sure you do."

"What's that supposed to mean?"

"Exactly that. Keep your wits about you when you deal with him."

She twisted the chain at her neck nervously. "That's not the reason I stopped to see you, though."

"Oh?"

"Ms. Hattie apparently needs new windows. I'll take a ride out there, see for myself, but both Darlene and Tomato Annie mentioned that she's got some real problems. It doesn't seem any of her people are stepping up to help her."

Beck dropped into his chair and motioned for her to sit across from him. "What are you thinkin'?"

"First of all, let me say that I know without your help and Cole's, I wouldn't have a prayer of fixing up Magnolia House or getting my business started. Maybe, even with your help, I'll sink."

Beck shook his head. "Not gonna happen."

"That's what I'm thinking." She grinned. "I'm also thinking a little pay-it-forward is needed."

He opened his mouth, but she held up a hand. "Wait. Hear me out. I mentally reworked my budget between

Annie's and here. If I faux paint the ballroom for now instead of putting up wallpaper, skimped a little bit a few other places, I might be able to swing windows for her."

"Why would you do that?"

"How can I not?"

"Windows are expensive, Jenni Beth."

"I know. But—" She bit her lip. "Could you measure them for me? Price them out? Then, well, we'll see."

He rubbed his jaw. Said nothing.

"Come on, Beck. Work with me."

He sighed. "Okay, call me crazy. I can get out there tomorrow. Give me a couple days to work it up, though."

"Thanks." She leaned across the desk and kissed his cheek.

"This is what you two call workin'?"

Chapter 15

Startled, Jenni Beth swiveled quickly, heard Beck chuckle. She faced a raised-brow Cole.

Oh boy. Her temperature shot sky-high, and her tongue darted out to lick her lips. The man was gorgeous—and he had to know it. Crisp white shirt tucked into snug, well-worn jeans, the sleeves rolled up to show off tanned arms, hair slightly mussed as if he'd been running his fingers through it. The man looked good enough to eat.

"You hungry?" he asked.

Her hand flew to her mouth. Had she said that out loud? No. She peeked at the wall clock. One o'clock. Lunch time. A reasonable assumption.

"Hey, anybody home?" Cole waved a nicked and scarred hand in front of her face. "You want to have lunch? I'm flat-out starvin', and we should talk about a couple things." He held up a file. "Figured we might as well make good use of our time. Eat and talk."

"Oh, sure. Business." *Pop*. Her pretty little balloon deflated.

"If it makes it easier to say yes, then, yeah, you could call it a business lunch." He looked at Beck. "Want to join us?"

His friend glanced from one to the other. "Nah. Think you two will do fine without me playin' third thumb."

"It's not like that," she said quickly.

"Maybe. Maybe not. Still, think I'll stay right here."

"You'll follow up on those windows?"

"Yep."

"Promise?"

"Yes, I do. Get her out of here, Cole, before she comes up with somethin' else for me to do."

"I'm on that." Hand at her back, Cole opened the door and herded her through the store and out into the heat.

"Why are you in Misty Bottoms?"

"Had a delivery for Dinky. I had some tile a customer of his needed, and shippin' it would have cost a fortune."

"Oh."

On the other side of the road, a train clattered past, whistle blowing. The land stretched out in front of her, and for one second she felt torn between her two worlds. Longed for the air-conditioned coolness of Chateau Rouge, wished she could step into a Starbucks and grab an iced coffee.

Cole took her hand, and she forgot Savannah existed.

"Didn't mean to eavesdrop," he said, "but—"

"What did you hear?"

He drew back at the intensity of her reply, and she'd gladly have bitten the end off her tongue if she could take it back.

"I heard you talkin' about Ms. Hattie," he said slowly. "Something else goin' on I should know about?"

"No."

Reaching for her hand, he turned her to face him. "That answer was way too fast, sugar. Let's have it. If you told Beck, you can tell me."

She huffed out her breath.

"I'm gonna find out sooner or later," he coaxed. "Let's make it sooner. What's got you in a tizzy?"

She stared at the railroad tracks. He waited. She studied a fingernail she'd broken that morning. Still, he waited.

"C'mon. Out with it."

"Won't you just go away?" she pleaded.

"Not a chance."

"Fine." She crossed her arms over her chest. Keeping it short and not-so-sweet, right there in the middle of Beck's dusty parking lot, she relayed her run-in with Richard. "He's an ass."

"Yeah, he is."

"Is this why you told me to watch out for him?"

He blinked, and she knew she wouldn't get the whole answer.

"Just so you know, Cole, I can read your tell."

"What are you talkin' about?"

"When you're being evasive or getting ready to skirt an issue, you blink. You blinked when I asked about Richard."

"Blinking is an involuntary response, sugar. Didn't Ms. Turner teach that to you girls in health class?"

She pointed an accusatory finger at him. "And you blinked again."

"Oh, for the love of Mike. You know what? You ask me, you're the expert at evasion. You've turned this whole conversation in on me when you're the one with the tale to tell."

"I already told it."

"Fine. Maybe I should pay Thorndike anoth—a little visit."

"No." She placed her hand on his arm, felt the coiled tension. "Absolutely not." She shook her finger at him. "And that's exactly the reaction I expected. The reason I didn't want to tell you."

"Okay, then." He continued toward his truck. "How about we stop at the store and pick up some lunch? Maybe get an extra sandwich. We'll give Ms. Hattie a call to let her know we're comin' out to visit."

He'd given in way too easy, and it made her exceedingly nervous.

Uneasy, she asked, "You'll go with me?"

"Absolutely."

"Why are you being so nice, Cole?"

His eyes darkened. "I've always been nice."

She snorted.

He shook his head sadly. "I'm so misjudged. Seriously, I like Ms. Hattie. She and her sister were always good to me. We can share lunch and let her know Beck will be comin' out."

She stopped walking. "What if I raise her hopes but can't make the budget work?"

"Between the three of us, you, me, and Beck, we can do some finagling. Some trading maybe."

"I won't take money from you, Cole. I draw the line at that. You, yourself, said right at the start of this that you were willing to offer…" She squinted, trying to remember his exact words. "I believe it was gallons of sweat equity and you'd toss your vast knowledge at my feet. But no money. You were crystal clear about that."

His jaw tightened. "And that still goes. What we're talkin' about here is a totally different kettle of fish. First of all, Ms. Beaumont, it's not you I'm helpin'. This is Ms. Hattie's house needs fixin', not yours.

Second? I'm a big boy, and it seems to me this is my choice, not yours."

"Fine." Her brows drew together fiercely, and her jaw set in a tight line.

"Whew!" He drew back. "If that's the look you wear when everything's fine, I'd sure hate to be on the receivin' end when it wasn't. But then I have been, haven't I?" He grimaced and tugged on her hand. "C'mon. Let's take my truck. I'm not sure what condition Ms. Hattie's road is in. That fancy sports car of yours might scrape bottom."

He opened the door and helped her in, an old-fashioned gesture she realized she enjoyed.

They drove to Bi-Lo, the town's only grocery store. "We can hit the deli," he said. "Martha makes a mean Italian sub."

"I know." She grinned. "I had one last week. And the store's air-conditioned." Exchanging conspiratorial grins, they glanced both ways before they hurried through the parking lot and into the store.

In far too short a time, they stepped back into the heat, lunch in hand. Since they weren't quite sure what Ms. Hattie liked, they'd bought a couple extra sandwiches, some fruit, and a side of mac and cheese. No self-respecting Southerner would turn down mac and cheese.

"We have to be careful not to offend her," Jenni Beth said.

"I know that. I'm not a total country bumpkin."

"I never said you were."

"You implied it." One arm tossed carelessly over the steering wheel, he drove easily. "My mama taught me manners, thank you very much."

She stared out the side window. "Excuse me for insulting your finer sensibilities."

"See?" His hand slapped the steering wheel. "There you go. You yak about *me* not having good manners. I've got a news flash for you, Ms. Beaumont. That sarcastic tongue of yours can cut a fellow off at the knees."

She blushed, instantly contrite. "You're right. I'm sorry. I don't know why, when I'm around you, I'm so—" She waved a hand in the air, searching for the right word.

"Bitchy, Jenni Beth. The word is bitchy."

She gasped. "That's not nice."

"No, don't suppose it is."

"What would your mama think about that?"

"Me callin' you bitchy?"

She nodded.

"Why? You gonna tattle on me?"

She crossed her arms over her chest and said nothing. They rode in silence the rest of the way.

When Ms. Hattie's one-story house came into view, Cole leaned slightly toward Jenni Beth. "Before we pay this fine lady a visit, it'd probably be a good idea for you and me to kiss and make up."

He shot a sideways glance toward her.

"Keep your eyes on the road, Cole."

"C'mon." He tapped a finger on his cheek. "Right here. We'll both feel a whole lot better."

She surprised them both by laughing. "You're impossible." But she leaned across the console and gave him a kiss. One meant for the cheek, till he turned into it, met her lips with his own quick one.

With a laugh, Cole pulled the large Ford pickup into the overgrown dirt drive.

His laugh died, though, as did hers when they took in the small house's condition. The metal roof was brown with rust, the porch stairs listed to one side, and part of the stair railing was missing. Loose, ancient green Astroturf carpeted the top stair and formed a path to the front door. Both Annie and Darlene had been right. Ms. Hattie needed help. Badly.

And the windows. Oh! The bottom half of one had been covered with plywood. Another had several cracked panels. One had been propped open with a mason jar. All of them looked ready to tumble out of their frames.

"Why hasn't someone from town stepped up to help?" Jenni Beth whispered. "It used to be neighbors helped neighbors."

"It used to be," Cole said, "neighbors had jobs. Had the money to help. A lot of people in Misty Bottoms can't take care of themselves anymore, let alone dip into their funds for someone else."

Unbuckling his seat belt, he turned to face her. "You sure you want to try to make a go of a new business here?"

"No, I don't want to try. I intend to do it."

"Damn stubborn fool," he muttered.

No matter that he was upset with her. Good manners had him jogging to her side of the truck, opening the door, and helping her out, lingering a little with her hand in his. When she pulled it free, he reached into the back and grabbed the grocery bags, more glad than ever that Jenni Beth had suggested they add a few extras.

What they'd brought today would feed Hattie the better part of the week.

The inside door stood open, so Jenni Beth knocked on

the screen door. "Ms. Hattie? It's Jenni Beth Beaumont and Cole Bryson. You home?"

"Who?"

The voice sounded older, shakier than Cole remembered. Regret hit, and though he tried to push it away, it refused to budge.

Jenni Beth repeated herself.

"Hold on to your horses. I'll be right there."

The woman who came to the door shocked Cole. Stooped and frail, she barely resembled the spry, smiling woman who'd always had a kind word and a cookie for Beck, Wes, and him as kids. He'd spent a lot of time hanging around her and Dorothy's little store.

His throat clogged, and he didn't have a clue what to say, to do. A quick glance at Jenni Beth showed she battled, too. Her face had gone pale and her smile faltered.

What did he say? "Heard you've been down on your luck lately so we're gonna step in and help"? Wouldn't work. Ms. Hattie might have withered physically, but he'd bet his life's savings her pride hadn't gone anywhere.

"Well, I declare," Ms. Hattie said. "See you finally nabbed this fine-lookin' boy, Jenni Beth. Good for you."

Cole choked on the laugh, managed to swallow it. Jenni Beth rounded on him, nonetheless. The sadness vanished from her eyes, replaced by a look that promised to send him into the fires of hell if he let go with a single chuckle.

"Actually, Ms. Hattie, Cole's been helping me at Magnolia House. He's working for me." She managed to combine smug with scathing. Again promised retribution if he dared deny her claim.

"That so? Heard you'd torn into the place. Fixin' it up so's you can hold weddings there."

"That's right. We've been working hard and decided we deserved an afternoon off." She pointed at the bags Cole held. "It's such a beautiful day, we thought a picnic would be nice. But we bought way too much. Since we were out this way, we thought we'd stop in and share. If you haven't already had lunch."

Hattie's ancient eyes studied Jenni Beth's face, then turned on Cole. He fidgeted beneath the stare. Damn, she was good.

"She ain't tellin' the truth, is she, boy? Somethin' else goin' on."

He tugged at the top button of his shirt. "We wanted to talk to you about somethin', and that's the honest truth."

"Just about to fry up some Spam. Want some?"

"Why don't you save that for later?" He lifted the bags. "We've got plenty here."

"Guess that'll do. Want to eat inside or out back?"

Cole rubbed his chin. "You got a table back there?"

"Sure do."

"Let's do outside."

Cole offered his arm, and she led them slowly around the side of the house, picking her way around overgrown roses and broken stepping-stones. While he settled her into a chair, Jenni Beth set the table with the paper plates and plastic silverware they'd picked up.

Several chickens pecked and clucked around the yard. A rooster ran toward them, and Hattie flapped her apron at it. "Shoo! Go cause trouble elsewhere, Henry, or I swear I'll get that pot boilin' and toss you in, you old coot."

She turned to Cole. "Keep the hens for the eggs, but that old rooster's the meanest thing on two legs."

Cole winked at her. "Ms. Hattie, you must have as hard a time chasin' the beaus away as you do that old rooster. I swear, if I was here in town more often..."

She swatted him. "Get out of here, you young fool. You got a girl like Jenni Beth here, and you want me to believe you'd waste your time on me? Always thought your mama's son was smarter than that."

Reaching for her wizened hand, he kissed the back of it. "I've got a real sweet spot in my heart for you, ma'am, and that's the truth."

He met Jenni Beth's eyes. "Ditto for you," he said.

Blinking rapidly, Jenni Beth handed him a sandwich. "Thanks."

Slowly chewing the mac and cheese Jenni Beth dished up, Ms. Hattie seemed a million miles away. Then she turned those eyes on her. "Is your mama and daddy doin' any better now some time's past?"

"I think so. Mama still has bad days."

"Hard thing, buryin' your child. Ain't no hurt worse."

"No, ma'am."

"How about you? You holdin' up okay? That the reason you came back home?"

"Partially."

"Heard you got a lot ridin' on this new venture of yours."

Jenni Beth's eyes widened in surprise.

"I get around," Hattie said. "I might be old, but my mind's still sharp. People talk, and I listen. You ain't gonna lose that land your grandaddy left you, are you?"

Jenni Beth gaped.

"How did you—" She shook her head. "It doesn't matter."

"She's gonna be fine, Ms. Hattie," Cole said, even as he mentally cursed small-town gossip.

"Why'd you drive all the way out here today in that fancy truck of yours, Cole Bryson? Not just to feed me, that's for danged sure. Although I sure do appreciate it. Martha has a hand with this tuna salad." She took a small bite of her sandwich, then waved a spoon at the mac and cheese. "And this? Delicious. Used to make my own, but I don't do much cookin' anymore. Not since Dorothy died. Don't seem to be much use to go to all that trouble for one person."

Cole was struck by life's injustices. A person spent her entire life working hard, totally engaged, yet ended up like this, alone. Jenni Beth sat across from him, the sun gilding her hair, and for an instant he wondered what it would be like to share his life with a woman he loved.

No. He drew himself up short. Life was good exactly the way he was living it. He didn't want to be responsible for someone else, for another person's happiness. Beck's question over dinner put that thought in his head.

He realized Ms. Hattie was waiting for an answer to her question. Jenni Beth poked at her food, and he was pretty sure that, although this whole plan had been hers, she wanted him to do the explaining. To take the lead. Chicken, he thought. But one heck of a pretty chicken.

He laid down his sandwich and wiped his fingers on a small, stiff paper napkin. "Here's the deal, Ms. Hattie. Jenni Beth and I are up to our eyeballs in construction." He hesitated, still debating how to best approach their plan without poking a hole in this wonderful woman's pride. "We're hopin' that Jenni Beth's gonna help the whole town by bringing in new business. We've been thinkin', though. Why not start smaller? By helpin' individuals. You came to mind."

A wary expression crossed the old woman's face.

"We thought we'd stop by today," Jenni Beth said quickly. "See if there was anything we could do here as long as we already have our hands dirtied."

"You're gonna do some work around here?" Ms. Hattie asked.

"Yes, ma'am. If that's okay with you, that is."

"Why would you do that?"

"Because we want to."

"I can't pay you."

"No, ma'am," Cole said. "We don't expect you to. Consider this payback for all those cookies you fed us boys as kids."

"Hmph. That weren't nothin'." She looked around at her tired old house. "This place looks as bad as I do."

"All right if Beck Elliot comes out tomorrow to take some measurements? We thought we'd replace a few of your windows, fix those steps." Cole watched her, noticed her eyes go a little misty.

"Honey, I should say no, but truth is I'd surely appreciate it."

"Then consider it done."

They stayed awhile longer and chatted. Jenni Beth put away the extra groceries, waving away Ms. Hattie's suggestion they take them home with them.

After hugs all around, Cole helped Jenni Beth into his truck and got behind the wheel. With a last wave, he pulled out of her drive and headed back to town.

He couldn't remember ever feeling quite this good.

"I have another call to make." Jenni Beth pulled out

her cell, made a quick call to her mother, jotted down a number, and dialed it. Inside five minutes, she'd arranged for a local church that delivered meals twice a week to add Ms. Hattie to their route.

She powered off her phone and leaned back. "Done."

"Sweetheart, you're an angel."

Chapter 16

W HEN HE DROPPED HER OFF AT HER CAR, HE SAID, "Wait. Before you go, I've got something to show you."

Her brow furrowed in question.

"You said you wanted a small chandelier for your carriage house, right?"

"I do." Her voice held a note of wistfulness.

"Okay, now, you're under no obligation, but I found something I think will work. If you don't like it, I'll haul it back to Savannah with me. No problem."

"You found a light?"

"I found the *perfect* light. In my humble opinion, of course." He opened his truck's rear door and took out a box. "It's in pieces right now, but you should be able to imagine what it'll look like assembled."

Holding the box in the crook of one arm, he said, "And before you start yammerin' about the price, I bought this from a guy closin' down his shop. Got a whole truckload of stuff for a song. If you like the chandelier, it's my housewarmin' or grand-opening or whatever gift to you."

"Cole—"

"Huh-uh. Don't even start. Take a peek at the thing first. You might hate it. If that's the case, all the arguing would be moot."

Setting the box on the hood of his truck, he said, "It's pretty girlie." He shot her a glance. "Guess that's why I thought of you when I uncovered it."

Emotion flashed through her eyes, across her face. Surprise, happiness, uneasiness? He could usually read her, but not this time. Flipping open the box, he drew out the cream-colored base.

Jenni Beth gasped. "Oh my gosh. Cole." She ran a finger, its nail painted a soft rose color, over a small cherub, his arms and legs wrapped around the center post. Ornate, but understated, five arms flared from the base. "Crystals?"

"A ton of them. Enough to drive any woman over the edge." He reached into the box and unwrapped a handful of them. Pulling out another bubble-wrapped packet, he showed her a crystal bead chain.

"This is beyond perfect, Cole. Since it's a little smaller, it won't overwhelm the room. But it's soft and romantic, kind of shabby chic." Holding up one of the crystals, she made a sound of pure happiness when the sun reflected off it, spewing prisms of color across her fingers.

"Wait." Cole held up a hand and leaned into his truck. "There's more."

"More?"

"Yep." He pulled out another, larger bubble-wrapped package. Stripping the tape from it, he uncovered an ornate, pale pink ceiling medallion. "You can paint it easily enough if you don't like the color, but I thought it would look good with the light."

When she said nothing, he turned to look at her.

"Jenni Beth?"

Catching him off guard, she squealed and threw her arms around him, nearly knocking him off his feet. "I take back every mean thing I've ever said about you."

When she kissed his cheek, he again made a minor adjustment in position, and took her mouth with his. He expected her to pull away; she didn't. Instead she met his kiss, took it deeper. Her tongue met his tentatively, and he had to swallow the groan that bubbled up.

Suddenly, as if remembering herself, she put her hands on his shoulders and stepped away.

He wanted to snatch her back into his arms and kiss her senseless. She left him aching, wanting so much more.

Not here, not now. But he prayed that one day she'd give herself to him again. He vowed he wouldn't be as careless with the gift the second time around.

When she lowered her head, he crooked a finger beneath her chin and raised her face till her eyes met his.

That tongue peeked out again, and he wanted to devour her. Instead, he said, "Thank you."

"I—I didn't mean—"

"Let's leave it at that," he said easily. "No sense over-analyzing a simple kiss."

He curbed the urge to check his nose, see if it had grown with that lie. *Simple?* he thought. Whew, nothing about that kiss came even close to simple. He'd gone hard as a fifteen-year-old boy ogling his first *Playboy* centerfold.

"I'm gonna assume you like the light."

She fingered the chubby, rosy-faced angel again. "I absolutely adore it, and I can't wait to see it in the room."

As she oohed and ahhed over it some more, he tipped his head, hating to spoil the moment, but unable to stop himself. "A wise man would hold his tongue right about now, and I sure don't mean to get your dander up again, but where do you think this fixture came from, Jenni Beth?"

"What?" She frowned at him impatiently. "Savannah, of course. You said so."

"No, I mean where did the little antiques store find it?" he pressed.

"How would I know?"

"You should, if you think about it."

"What is this? A pop quiz, Professor Bryson?"

"That and the medallion both came from an old house scheduled for demolition. A house that had been let go too long. One that couldn't be saved."

"Oh."

"You know why the store had it?"

She shook her head slowly. "No, but I'm fairly certain you're going to change that in the next few seconds."

"You're right. I am. Bruce had it in his shop because a salvager cared enough to rescue it. Rather than this cute little guy being smashed to smithereens by the wrecking ball, you have him now for your office. A piece of history has been preserved."

She stood speechless for all of thirty seconds. Then, looking sad, she asked, "Is that why you brought it to me? To prove your point?"

"Nope." He took the crystal she still held and rewrapped it. "I gave it to you because it *is* pefect for Magnolia House. It belongs in your new office where people can enjoy it instead of hidden in the dusty back room of an antiques store or a salvage yard. I was simply explaining that we architectural salvagers might not be quite the villains you paint us."

"Point taken." Her chin jutted up. "But Magnolia House isn't ready for that wrecking ball yet."

"I tend to agree."

Boy, she was a tough nut. She refused to give an inch more than necessary. He placed both the medallion and the light fixture back inside the truck and covered them carefully with an old blanket.

"The carriage house isn't ready to hang those yet."

"It will be soon."

She made a face. "I want to see how they look now."

"Quit sulking, Ms. Impatient. No pouting allowed, or I'll take them back."

"You wouldn't."

"Try me."

Her gaze flitted from him to the backseat of his pickup, but she held her tongue.

"What's on your agenda for the rest of today?" he asked.

Caught off guard by the quick change of subject, she raised her shoulders, then dropped them. "I'm sanding kitchen cabinets. Beck's guys will give them a fresh coat of paint, and they'll look like new." She bounced her car keys in the palm of her hand. "What about you?"

"I believe I'm sanding kitchen cabinets."

They both worked like dogs. Even after the crew left at five, the two of them hung in there, bound and determined to finish the cabinets before they called it a day.

It was hard, dirty work, and Cole swore the temperature had to be a hundred and ten even though the sun had started its descent.

They finished their last door together.

"We did it." A huge grin on her face, Jenni Beth held up a hand, and Cole gave her a high five.

"Yes, we did. And I'm hungry as a bear. That sandwich we ate at Ms. Hattie's has long ago turned tail and run away. What do you say we grab showers, then I'll pick you up and we can go find ourselves some dinner?"

"I should probably take a pass tonight."

"I'm heading back to Savannah in the mornin'." He hated to beg, hated worse to go home alone.

"Still—"

"Okay. Plan B. How about we skip dinner and make out?" He reached out, wrapped a strand of her hair around his finger, tugged at it.

The sun had dipped low in the sky, and long shadows stretched across the backyard.

Incredulity mixed with…what?…longing passed over her face.

"What is wrong with you?"

"Night's comin'," he said. "It'll be fun. What d'ya say? We can find a hidey-hole here or take a drive in my truck out to the old quarry road."

"To Lover's Lane?" She stared at him as though she'd never seen him before. "Are you serious?"

"Yep."

"No."

"C'mon." He bumped shoulders with her. "It doesn't have to get all hot and heavy. A few kisses, a little tongue. You let me cop a couple feels, you cop a couple." He tossed her a hot smile. "A couple more kisses."

"No." This time, her no wasn't quite as quick nor quite as convincing.

He traced a finger over bare skin, where her T-shirt had drooped off her shoulder, and felt her shiver.

She rubbed at the goose bumps that popped up. "I don't think that's a good idea, Cole."

"Ah, I'm making progress."

She scowled.

"We went from a flat out 'no' to an 'I don't think so.' Tiny steps."

"Yes, well those tiny steps will walk you right off the edge of a cliff if you're not careful," she warned.

"Yeah, they can. Flip side? They can carry you right on up to the mountaintop."

"Not tonight, they won't."

He kissed her forehead, wanted to bury his hands in all that hair. Lose himself in her. But he'd keep it light—even if it killed him. "You're a hard woman, Jenni Beth."

"So you've said. Thanks, Cole. Both for your help here and at Ms. Hattie's today." She paused. "Have a safe trip home."

A sleepless night was what he'd have. That kiss he and Jenni Beth shared today would guaran-damn-tee that, all right.

Chapter 17

JENNI BETH DRAPED AN ARM ACROSS HER EYES. THE morning sun had risen, but she hadn't. Groggy, she blamed Cole for her poor night's sleep. He'd crawled inside her head and messed with it. That shared kiss, her body's traitorous response, their almost make-out session. She groaned. How long since she'd even thought about going parking? Ah, jeez. If he'd had any idea how tempted she'd been. Trouble, trouble, trouble. He was up to something. But then, heck, what was she doing? She'd kissed him by her car like there'd be no tomorrow. Of course, he'd started it, but still. She'd surprised herself with the way she'd answered his kiss, then doubled the ante. They both should have disintegrated from the heat.

On the other hand, she'd been the one in the middle of the drought. It had been a long time since she'd kissed like that, felt that heat. Cole? That man lived in a veritable rain forest of women. She doubted the kiss had affected him the way it had her. No. Not true. She'd felt his arousal against her, felt his need. And that's what had snapped her back to reality.

They weren't kids anymore, and this was a dangerous game they played. Somebody could get hurt. And it wouldn't be Cole.

She sighed. Yesterday, Cole had been so gentle, so patient with Ms. Hattie, coaxing her to eat a little more, to take one more bite. He'd approached their plan so matter-of-factly it never once, not for a single second, smacked of charity. And that allowed Ms. Hattie to maintain her dignity and pride.

The man was a chameleon, one she needed to banish from her mind. They'd ridden the carousel before, and it hadn't worked. Well, not the ride. She huffed out a breath. That had worked finer than fine. It was the aftermath that had been a disaster.

She threw herself into her work, so exhausted she could barely find her bed at night. And still, when she closed her eyes, Cole crept into her mind, into her bed. She'd pull the covers over her head, but she couldn't hide from him.

Late Thursday afternoon, Richard Thorndike showed up, his shiny new Lexus looking totally out of place beside the workers' pickups.

Her stomach rolled, clenched. She took a deep breath. Darned if she'd let the arrogant, deceitful pain in the butt see a single nerve.

"You making house calls?" Jenni Beth wiped her hands on already filthy shorts and stood from where she'd been weeding the flower bed. She suspected she had dirt on her face, too.

Oh well.

"Thought I'd stop by and see how things are progressing." Hands splayed on his hips, he stood beside the Lexus in shirt sleeves and sharply creased dress pants, studying the house from top to bottom. He nodded. "A lot of improvements."

"If you've come looking for an apology, you can hop right back in that car of yours and head into town."

"No. I came to deliver one, actually. I was out of line."

Her brows arched.

"I might not have handled things as well as I could have."

She sent him a saccharine-sweet smile. "You think?"

His ears turned red. "Don't use that tone with me."

"Or what? You'll spread gossip around town?"

He shifted his hands to his pockets.

"That was my biggest complaint, you know. That's why I paid you that visit."

"Paid me a visit? Is that what you call it?" His small eyes drilled her. "Barging in, chasing away customers, and screaming at me?"

"I did not scream at you," she said. "I may have raised my voice, but I most certainly didn't scream."

"Semantics." Richard waved a hand far more manicured than her own grubby ones. "I do, however, apologize for speaking to Moose and the guys at the store. My first allegiance has to be to the people of Misty Bottoms."

Ice flowed through her veins, crept into her voice. "And the Beaumonts aren't citizens of Misty Bottoms?"

"Of course you are. You're being nitpicky."

"I don't think so. You're standing here on my land, in front of my house, insulting me and my family."

His eyes shuttered; his color rose. "As I said, I came to apologize. However, I'm still not totally convinced this idea of yours will be profitable, and I don't want you taking anyone else down with you."

"The good citizens of Misty Bottoms must rest easily at night, knowing you're protecting them from the big, bad monster." She pointed at finger at herself. "Me."

Beck appeared out of nowhere, and Jenni Beth, certain he'd heard the entire conversation, felt a spear of relief.

"Richard." He acknowledged him with a tip of his head.

"You helping out, Beck?"

Her friend nodded, but said nothing.

"Can I take a look inside?"

Jenni Beth glanced at Beck, then back at Richard. The air fairly vibrated with an undercurrent of hostility.

"Richard, I'm sorry, but the house is a construction site. I'm not sure our insurance would cover you if something happened, so I'm going to have to say no."

Beck leveled a well-done look at her, and she almost smiled.

Thorndike stared at her in stony disbelief. No one told him no. What he wanted, he got. Well, not this time.

"We're doing fine," she continued. "We're on track both with the time and our budget. Anything else? Because if not, I have work to do."

He rubbed a hand over his jaw.

Had he really expected her to take him into the parlor? Offer him tea? So not going to happen.

Without a word, he stormed back to his car.

Beck stepped beside her, and she leaned into him. In the shade of the porch, they watched as he drove down the live-oak-lined drive.

"What did he want?"

"I guess he wanted to scratch his curiosity." She shrugged.

"You handled that perfectly. Remember, he's not on your side. He only wins if you lose."

She turned her head slightly. "Now you sound like Cole."

"That's not necessarily a bad thing."

Friday morning, perched on the fourth rung of a ladder, scraping the last stubborn bits of paint from the fascia, Jenni Beth's cell rang. Pulling it from her pocket, she saw it was Duffy at the pub.

"One of my waitresses has a nasty cold and can't make her shift. Friday's a tough night to run short-handed. Wondered if you might want to fill in for her."

"Oh, we're so busy here, Duffy, and I'm a mess. I've been working my butt off all week."

"I'll pay you. I know you're runnin' up lots of bills with that renovation."

"Cash?"

"You bet."

The calculator inside her came to life. A transfusion, no matter how small, would be welcome. Figuring everything at his cost, Beck had worked up an invoice for the absolutely essential repairs at Ms. Hattie's, and Jenni Beth had given him the okay. Whatever Duffy paid her tonight, along with tips, would help offset that tab. If it paid for a single window, it would be worth it. Besides, it had been ages since she'd waited tables at the pub. Might be a nice change of pace.

"What time do you need me?"

—⁓—

Cole's headlights reflected off the Misty Bottoms town limits sign, and he asked himself for the hundredth time what the heck he was doing. Tired and more than a little frazzled, he should be home. In his city condo.

He'd finished up late this afternoon, with no intention of making this drive. Since he'd been spending so much time here, he'd fallen behind in Savannah, both at home and at work. He'd planned to spend the evening taking care of late paperwork, then pick up a few groceries before heading to his condo to straighten up a bit and do some laundry. All the day-to-day stuff.

If he were smart, he'd give both Jenni Beth and Magnolia House a wide berth, tell Mickey to take tomorrow off, and work Traditions himself.

But he hadn't. Like a fly to a honey jar, he'd come barreling in. Chances were good, too, he'd end up in as much of a mess as that honey-lovin' fly.

A glance at his dashboard clock told him it was too late to drive to Jenni Beth's house, too early to go to his place and stare at four walls. As restless as he was, he'd drive himself nuts.

Problem was he was going under and fast—and not at all comfortable with it. He thought about her day and night. She'd even wriggled her way into his dreams.

This wasn't in his plans, wasn't what he wanted.

His stomach growled. His fridge was pretty darn bare, and he didn't want to barge in on his parents. Why not hit Duffy's Pub? He'd eat, play a little pool, drink a couple cold ones, and get his mind off Jenni Beth. It was either that or drive over to her place and climb the ivy to her attic room. That idea? Fraught with all kinds of danger.

By the time he parked his truck, he heard the music rolling out of the restaurant. Friday night. He'd forgotten the pub hired a band on the weekends.

Halfway through the door, he stopped and dropped his head to his chest. He recognized Jenni Beth's laugh from across the room and didn't know whether to laugh at himself or cry. Talk about best laid plans gone awry.

What the heck. A grin split his face. Might as well go with it. He hadn't expected to see her tonight. Now he would. What were the chances Jenni Beth would be here tonight waiting tables? Maybe he should consider it a gift. An opportunity to sit back and drink his fill of her. Or punishment. The grin disappeared. Look, but don't touch.

Didn't Nietzsche say something about what didn't kill you made you stronger?

Guess he'd soon find out.

Muscling his way to the bar, he slid onto a stool and ordered a beer. Settling in, he leaned an elbow on the patinated copper counter and relaxed.

He swiveled on his stool and faced the tables. She wore skintight jeans and a skimpy, white lace halter top. The ankle-length pants showed off simple red flats. Big dangly earrings caught the light and sparkled.

Redder-than-red lipstick, wavy, mussed hair, and smoking hot eyes.

Whooee! Maybe she would kill him.

Leaning toward old Mr. Watkins, she jotted his order on her pad, then said something that had him laughing. She moved to another table with her coffeepot and, chatting, refilled cups. Jenni Beth had her customers eating out of her hand.

Damn. Every male in the place had to be salivating. He sure as hell was. He'd been fighting this attraction for a long while now. Too long. He'd dated his share of women, but none got to him. Yet watching her, so confident and comfortable, spun his system out of control.

Maybe the time had come to throw in the towel and run with whatever was going on between the two of them. He'd dipped his toe in the water earlier this week, throwing out more than a few broad hints, stealing a couple kisses. While she hadn't exactly run with it, she hadn't blown him out of the water, either.

That kiss in the parking lot… Whew. Thinking about it, thinking how she'd felt dancing with him at Chateau Rouge, set his motor running faster still. Made him hotter than hell. Fidgety.

He didn't get it. His taste ran to dark-eyed brunettes, yet this one blond had always been able to work her way beneath his skin. It defied all logic and understanding.

Well, logic be damned. Time to go with his gut.

Slowly, he took another drink of his beer, set down the bottle, and sauntered to the stage. He nodded at Trey, the lead guitarist, indicating he wanted to talk.

When his pal moved to the front edge, Cole leaned in and said, "Do me a favor, bud. You know Eric Clapton's 'Wonderful Tonight'?"

"Sure do. Great song."

"Would you play it? I want to dance with Jenni Beth."

He winked. "You bet."

At the end of the number, Trey struck the first notes of Clapton's hit.

Cole crooked a finger at Jenni Beth, then tugged at her hand when she came close.

Her gaze moved over her tables. "What do you want?"

"Quit scowlin'. You'll scare everybody away. Dance with me."

"Cole, I'm working." She tried to pull away.

"Hey, Duffy," Cole shouted across the noisy bar. "You don't care if Jenni Beth dances with me, do you?"

"Hell no."

Everybody in the pub looked their way, and he watched Jenni Beth's face flush. Somebody in the back whistled.

"Thanks, Duf."

"You're causing a scene, Cole."

"Nope. But you will if you fight me on this."

He laced his fingers with hers and led her onto the miniscule dance floor.

Without giving her even a second to catch her breath or put up more of an argument, he drew her into him, inhaling her sweet scent, a smell so totally and uniquely Jenni Beth. Feminine and delicate with a touch of heat and sizzle.

"You do look wonderful tonight, sugar." He sang along with the song, and she relaxed in his arms.

In one smooth motion, he spun her out, twirled her in a circle. Her quick laugh caused his heart to stumble, proof positive he'd landed himself smack-dab in the middle of some serious trouble.

Dangedest thing about it? He didn't care.

His arm encircled her waist, and he brought her in close as she added her voice to his, singing along with the familiar song. "You've come a long way from that hairbrush microphone in your bedroom."

"What?"

She started to pull away, but he deftly brought her back, her body warm and soft against his.

"Wes and I used to sit on the stairs and listen while you sang to your latest favorites on the radio."

"And laugh your fool heads off, I'm sure."

He grinned. "Sometimes."

She swatted him. "Cole Bryson, you are no gentleman."

"Never claimed to be."

As he twirled her out again, he watched her arrange her expression into that prim and proper Southern lady.

But underneath? He studied her as she gave it up and laughed. In the skintight demins and that sexy-as-sin lace halter top?

One hot woman!

Even at eighteen, in her quiet white debutante gown, the real Jenni Beth had shone through. She had no idea how close he'd come to dragging her away somewhere and devouring her.

And yet it added a layer of excitement when she cloaked that heat and he imagined only he could feel it.

Tonight? She hid nothing. She'd tossed her burning sexuality right out there for anyone and everyone to view.

Again, he fought with himself. He wanted far too badly to toss her in his truck, take her home, and have his way with her. He wanted to make love to her all night long and well into tomorrow.

Problem was, he was scared to death even that wouldn't be enough. He'd had that taste already, hadn't he? And it had only whetted his appetite.

She brought out the beast in him. Always had. And he was beginning to suspect that maybe she always would.

The song ended and, grudgingly, he kissed the top of her head. "Give 'em hell, tiger."

Moving back to his drink, he swung around on his stool and leaned against the bar to watch her. Every once and again, their gazes caught and he damned near stopped breathing.

Good sense dictated he should go home. Catch some shut-eye. He didn't. He ordered dinner and ate, his foot tapping to the band's music. They had a good sound, and Cole found himself wishing Jenni Beth was up there singing with them. The woman had an incredible voice.

At midnight, the band announced their final song, "Hit the Road, Jack." Cole laughed. Perfect ending.

He kept his eye on Jenni Beth as she cleared her last table. Binnie would handle the stragglers.

She caught his eye, and he pointed to a small, empty table in the corner. After a second, she nodded. He held up his beer toward her, and she mouthed, "Yes, please."

Snagging another beer from Binnie, he moved to the table and slid out a chair for Jenni Beth as she made her way to him.

"You handled your tables well."

"Thanks." She took a healthy drink. "Oh, that tastes good. My throat's parched. I haven't played waitress in a long time."

"And you enjoyed it."

"I did." She grinned. "It's nice to mingle. I saw people I haven't talked to in years. And look at this." She reached into her jeans pocket and held up her tip money. "Between this and what Duffy owes me, I earned enough to pay for the materials for Ms. Hattie's new porch stairs."

Didn't that just do it? His heart hit the floor. How was a man supposed to resist a woman like her? She needed that money badly, yet her first thought was Ms. Hattie's steps.

He lov—his mind stumbled over the word—*liked* her. So much he hurt. Dazed, he opened his mouth, but before he could speak, she did. "Jeez, I'm starving." She laid a hand on her stomach. "I didn't get a chance to eat before I left the house."

"What can the kitchen do this late, Binnie?"

"They've shut down the griddle and deep fryer, but the oven's still on."

"I don't want anything heavy. Can they toss together a sandwich?"

"You bet."

Cole stretched his legs out in front of him and watched her devour the club sandwich when it came. Another point for her. He liked a woman who actually ate, one who didn't play with her food. He snagged a couple chips off her plate while they talked about his week, her week. About happenings in town.

"I need to go to bed, Cole."

His wiring short-circuited. To cover it, he laughed and rubbed his hands together. "Okay. Now you're talkin'. I've been waitin' to hear those words from you, sugar."

"Ha-ha. To sleep. Alone. At my house."

"What a tease." As fast as it had come, the laughter left him. He wanted to make her his. Knew deep down what a horrid mistake that would be. Or would it? He didn't know anymore. She scrambled his brains.

Keeping his voice light, he said, "Grab your purse and I'll walk you out."

When they stepped into the Georgia night, the heat and humidity grabbed at him. Overhead, stars scattered across the night sky, winking. The moon frosted Jenni Beth and gave her the appearance of an ice princess.

Because he desperately wanted to wrap his arms around her and kiss her senseless, he stepped to the side, careful not to touch her as he escorted her to her little sports car.

She reached it first and kicked at the front driver's-side tire. "Shoot."

Cole came up behind her. "What's wrong?"

"My tire's flat." She ran fingers through her tangled mass of silvery hair.

Cole knelt and ran a hand over the tire. He moved to the side so he could see it better in the meager light that filtered through the bar's windows. Somebody opened the door and he saw the tire clearly for a few seconds. That was all he needed. Cold fury ripped through him. He took a deep breath to rein in his temper. The tire hadn't gone flat. Somebody had slashed it.

Jenni Beth didn't need to know that. Not tonight.

"I could change this tonight, sugar, but it sure would be easier in the mornin'. We're both tired. Why don't you let me drive you home? When I come into town tomorrow, I'll take care of it." He tugged at his ball cap. "Or later today, I guess, since it's already tomorrow, isn't it?"

"It scares me that I understand that," she said.

Hand on her back, he herded her to his truck, opened her door, tossed a couple files into the back, and helped her in. Heat sizzled through him at the innocent contact.

"There you go."

He walked around the hood of the vehicle and slid in behind the wheel. The truck's cab shrank, grew intimate. The woman smelled so good, so feminine. Lavender. Jasmine. Nighttime.

It felt right to have Jenni Beth here beside him. To drive through the night with her. To pass neighbors' homes with their darkened windows and know they were tucked in for the night.

His head filled with a vision of the two of them heading home to a night together. A dream where she wouldn't have to leave. Where they'd have each other to turn to in the night. Where she'd still curl against him when the sun peeked over the horizon first thing in the morning.

They'd share that first cup of coffee. That first burst of laughter. That first—

She turned on the CD player and pulled back as though burned.

Of all the— He'd been listening to Wes's favorite CD, and Jenni Beth recognized it. Her hands moved to her face.

Quickly he punched the power button and pitched the truck into silence. He swerved onto the road's shoulder and threw the truck in park. When he reached out to her, she pulled away, her breathing ragged.

"Why that CD?"

"It makes me feel close to him, honey. When I'm missin' him, I'll put this in sometimes, turn it up, and go for a ride. I had no idea—"

"I miss him."

"I know."

"And you're crowding me, Cole."

"Crowdin' you?" He turned in his seat and rested his head against the side window, staring at her. "What are you talkin' about?"

"You've wormed your way into my life. Made yourself necessary to me. Made it so that I think about you all the time. I—"

He laid a finger over her lips. "Stop. Don't say whatever it is that's ready to spill from that gorgeous mouth."

"Cole—"

He shook his head. "Please. We can work this out, Jenni Beth."

"I don't think so."

Against his better judgment, he unsnapped both their seat belts and crushed her to him, held her close. Cursed the storage compartment between them.

Her heart raced—or was it his?

He heard the first sob, almost a hiccup. The tears came faster. She shook in his arms, her hot tears wetting his shirt.

He cupped the back of her head and buried his face in her hair. "Oh, sugar, don't. Please. Don't cry." He ran his fingers through her hair.

"You're breaking down my walls," she sobbed. "I swore I'd never let that happen again. After Wes died, I don't seem to be able to invest myself in relationships. I hold back. I can't face that pain again."

"That's understandable."

"No, it's not. I've even wedged that little bit of space between me and my friends, between me and my parents, and I hate it. I'm always preparing, always getting ready to say good-bye."

"I'm not goin' anywhere."

"Not right now, but you will!"

He drew back, rested a finger beneath her chin. "Honey, I'm right here. Always will be."

"No." She jerked away from him. "That's not true, Cole. You know it, and so do I. But I will be. Misty Bottoms is my home. My parents are here. This is where what's left of my heart is. Your niche is in Savannah."

"That's where my business is."

"That's what I said. You belong in Savannah."

"I wonder." He ran his hands up and down her arms. "I'm beginnin' to think my heart is right here. You're doin' something to me, sugar, that I can't fight. That I'm not sure I want to fight."

"Don't say that, Cole."

"Why?"

"Because I can't do this. I can't give you my heart, then watch you walk away. So, please, go now. Before it hurts worse."

Desperation welled in him, and his eyes burned into her. "You're not listenin'. I'm not going anywhere."

"You will." She pushed away. "Take me home."

He did, his jaw clenched so tightly it ached.

The instant the tires stopped turning, she hopped out and walked inside without looking back. When the wooden screen door slapped shut, he swore he heard the sound of his heart breaking. How stupid was that?

He should go. Instead, he sat in the dark, his window down. The sweet smell of roses surrounded him. Crickets chirped. Night birds called. Overhead, the moon shone through the leaves of the live oaks, giving the appearance of a huge lace doily spread across the newly mown yard.

The last light in the house went out, and he was alone.

Time for him to go home, too. Putting the truck in gear, he drove away. Tomorrow would be soon enough to tell Jenni Beth her tire hadn't gone flat. She hadn't run over anything.

Someone had slashed it. Viciously.

And everybody in town knew that Corvette belonged to her.

Chapter 18

COLE KNOCKED SHARPLY AT THE BASE OF THE ATTIC stairs and headed up them two at a time.

"Wake up, sleepyhead. The day's wastin' away."

"What?" Jenni Beth peeked out from beneath the covers and let out a small cry before pulling them over her head. "Get out of here. What do you think you're doing?"

"Kind of grumpy in the morning, aren't you?" He sat down on the edge of her bed, felt it dip beneath his weight.

"Cole!"

"Always wake up this cranky?"

"I'm not cranky!"

"Sure sounds like it to me."

"I was up late."

"Yeah, I know. I was with you, remember? We need to head into town and pick up your car."

"You already changed the tire?" She lowered the covers enough to peer at him.

"Early bird catches the worm."

"Ha-ha." She drew the covers over her head again.

"Actually, I took it to Tommy." He hesitated. "You needed to replace the tire. Now, up." He reached for the spread, and she swatted his hand away.

"You naked under there?" Words meant to be playful had his voice deepening, his heart thumping a little too fast.

"No!"

"Too bad. Maybe this'll help." He handed her a mug.

"Coffee?"

"Yep. Now be a good girl. Get up."

She sat up, pushed the hair out of her eyes, and greedily grabbed the steaming hot coffee.

The morning sun shone on that mass of thick blond hair and she looked just like the angel his mom perched atop the Christmas tree every year. So soft. Her cheeks pink, her hair mussed. She'd never looked more beautiful.

He tore his gaze away. "You don't draw your curtains at night?"

"Why should I? Unless you intend to climb the tree outside my window and play Peeping Tom."

Although he hated himself for it, he had to admit the idea held more than a little appeal.

He covered with, "How can you sleep with all this light?"

"It doesn't bother me. In fact, I was sound asleep— until some idiot came bursting in on me." She made a shooing motion. "Go away. Let me enjoy my coffee."

"God, you're gorgeous in the morning."

Her face flushed. "I'm a mess."

"No, you're not." His words were soft.

"My mother is going to have one heck of a conniption if she catches you up here."

"Sue Ellen's the one who sent me up."

"What?" Jenni Beth bobbled the cup and would have spilled it if he hadn't reached out to steady it.

Their fingers touched, and she drew away. So, he mused, eyes slitting. She felt the zing, too. What he wouldn't give to slip under those covers with her.

"Cole—"

"Jenni Beth." He smiled.

"We skirted around this yesterday, but I have to ask again. What's going on here?" She waved her free hand between them.

"What do you mean?"

"You know exactly what I mean. Don't play dumb." She sipped her coffee and looked at him over the rim, those big, beautiful blue eyes boring into him. "You, me, these kisses you keep stealing. This…thing."

She'd admitted she held people at bay. Well, so did he when it came to women. Usually. He found it safer. It kept him from committing.

He'd never considered actually taking that next step before now. Still, he kept dancing around it, unsure he was ready. One step forward, two back. Enough to confuse anybody, including him.

Not knowing what to say, he shrugged.

"Cole?"

He had no answer, so he said honestly, "Damned if I know."

"When the house is done, will you disappear?"

"Is that what you want?"

"You're really good at this, aren't you?"

"At what?"

"At ducking an issue," she snapped.

He wasn't ready to discuss it, so he did exactly that. He ducked. "Jenni Beth, I care about you."

"But?"

"But," he said, squirming, "I'm happy with my life. At least I was."

"Okay."

"What do you mean?" he asked. "Okay? Just okay and that's it?"

"What do you want me to say?"

The ground turned boggy beneath him. "I don't know, but I thought I meant more than that to you."

Her laugh was sad. "You do, Cole. Now go away."

He didn't move. "Wait. I'm not being fair. Or honest." He raked the fingers of one hand through his hair. "Truth? I wish I understood all this. You. Me. I don't, and it's got me all tangled up. I don't want you to walk away, and, God help me, I can't seem to. How 'bout we play it by ear for a while?"

"Sure. Now go away. I want to sleep." She set the nearly empty coffee mug on her nightstand.

He leaned in, kissed the top of her head. Wanted to lose himself in her. She smelled so good. Felt so warm. Looked so sleep-tousled. He wanted more than anything to crawl into that bed with her and spend the day right there.

But her mom and dad were in the building.

So, instead, he pulled away. "Get some clothes on and meet me downstairs. We've got a lot to do today."

"We?"

"Yeah, we." He pointed a finger first at her, then at himself. "You and me. Don't take too long."

Turning to go, he decided he might as well get the ugly out and done with. On a big sigh, he said, "One more thing."

"What's that?"

"Your tire. It didn't go flat."

"I ran over something?"

"No. Somebody slashed it."

She shook her head. "Nobody in Misty Bottoms would do that."

"You're wrong. Might be a good idea if you don't go out alone after dark."

She gasped and erupted from the bed, dragging the top cover with her.

"Just sayin'."

Cole moseyed back to the kitchen while he waited. He thought he'd find Charlotte there. Instead, Jenni Beth's parents sat at the table sharing coffee and a newspaper.

"Sit down," Todd said. "Knowing my daughter, you've got plenty of time for coffee with Sue Ellen and me." He grabbed a mug and the coffeepot. Back at the table, he handed a steaming mug of coffee to Cole, then refilled his and his wife's cups.

He slid a plate across the table. "Have a cinnamon roll. Charlotte made them this morning. Best in the county."

"Don't mind if I do. Thanks."

Todd peppered him with questions about the renovation, about his business in Savannah. "You've done a good job, Cole. Sue Ellen and I are proud of you."

"Thank you, sir. That means a lot."

"What are you up to today?" Sue Ellen asked.

He licked a bit of frosting from his fingers. Grinning, he said, "I know I should use my napkin, but darned, that frosting's too good to waste."

She laughed. "I know. It's a good thing Charlotte doesn't make these often. I can't resist them."

"Jenni Beth had a flat tire last night." It wasn't a lie, just not the entire truth. The Beaumonts already had enough on their plate and darned if he'd add more. Although maybe her dad... No.

"She didn't tell me," Todd said.

"Understandable. It was pretty late by the time she finished at the pub last night."

"You were there?"

"Pure luck." Cole sipped his coffee. "I drove up from Savannah, decided I was hungry, and stopped by Duffy's in time to have a bite and bring her home."

"Thank you, honey." Sue Ellen patted his hand.

He turned his, grasping hers in a warm grip. This woman had been like a second mother to him, and he'd all but abandoned her when she needed him most. He felt like a heel. Yet neither Todd nor Sue Ellen seemed to notice his neglect. Either that or they were simply too well-bred to mention it.

"No problem. I changed the tire this morning, but her spare's pretty worn. I found the key she'd hidden in the wheel well and drove the car over to Tommy's. He's gonna replace the spare with a new tire. Thought I'd take Jenni Beth to pick it up."

"Wonderful."

"It's a nice day," he said. "She's been workin' hard. Thought maybe we'd take a bike ride, see what trouble we could get into."

Sue Ellen laughed. "Trouble's not something you kids ever had a problem finding."

Whoo, boy. If she had even a clue about the kind of trouble he wanted to get into with her daughter, she and Todd would probably kick him out on his butt.

"You drivin' the same bike?" Todd asked.

"Yes, sir. I keep it at my parents' place. I don't like to drive the Harley in city traffic."

"Don't blame you."

When they stood, Todd wrapped an arm around

Cole's shoulder. "Let's go take a look. Been a couple years since I've seen it."

Wes had one, too, one his parents sold after he'd died. What a shame. It had been Wes's pride and joy. He'd loved that Harley.

But what sense would it make for them to keep it? Cole couldn't, in his wildest imagination, picture Todd and Sue Ellen Beaumont heading down the highway on a motorcycle.

Jenni Beth opened the screen door to see her dad and Cole, heads together, examining something on the big, black Harley. Men and their toys.

Hearing the door slap shut, Cole looked up. "Hey, beautiful. You ready?"

She caught the flicker of surprise on her father's face at Cole's greeting.

"I am."

"Let's go then." He handed her a helmet.

"You always carry an extra?"

He threw her a sheepish grin. "You never know when you'll pick up a hitchhiker."

"I'll bet."

"Did you get breakfast?" her father asked.

"Coffee's good for now. Maybe I can talk Cole into buying me lunch."

"It's a deal."

With a wave at her father, she hopped on the back of the bike, wrapping her arms around Cole's solid form, her palms splayed on his chest. "Bye, Dad."

"Bye, honey. Have fun."

Oh, she would. A Saturday motorcycle ride with Cole Bryson. One of her teenage fantasies. She had to remember, though, to keep those fantasies damped down with a good dose of reality.

When they stopped at the end of her lane, he turned his head. "Thought we'd pick up your car a little later."

"That's fine. Did someone really cut my tire on purpose?"

"Yes. I didn't tell your folks that, though."

"Smart idea."

"Let's forget about that now, though, and just enjoy the day," Cole said.

"I'll second that."

They turned onto the main road, and she grinned so big she was surprised her face didn't hurt from it. Wes had taken her for a ride once in a while, but until she and Cole went to Dinky's the other day, she'd forgotten the sheer pleasure of motorcycles. The wind in her hair, the sun on her face. The freedom. Pure exhilaration.

She didn't have the foggiest idea where they were going, and she didn't care.

He bypassed town and took a little side road to the north.

Ten or twelve miles later, they passed a tumble-down house. Cole slowed and pulled into the next drive.

"I want to check something out." He backed up the big bike and headed in the direction they'd just come from. Idling along, he turned in to what was left of a nearly indiscernible dirt drive, overgrown with grass and weeds.

"Who owns this place?" he asked. "I should know, but I can't remember."

"Ms. Starshine Liberty."

He slapped one hand on his helmet. "How could I forget? Does anybody know her real name?"

"Not that I'm aware of. Apparently she's gone by Starshine since she showed up in town in the sixties. Part of that whole hippie generation."

"*Hmmm*."

"Somebody at the nursing home probably knows. I'd think she'd have used her birth name for Social Security and whatnot."

"She's still alive?"

"Yes, but she's well into her eighties."

He dropped the kickstand, hopped off, and helped her dismount. Wading through the tall grass, he climbed the rickety stairs and stepped lightly onto the sagging porch.

"Any relatives?"

"Why?"

"I want to buy these windows. They're original. See how wavy the glass is? Modern glass is called float glass because it's floated on molten metal. That's why it's a uniform thickness without any distortion to it. These beauties? Not so."

He used an old rag he found to wipe the first three layers of dirt off one of the filthy windows. Cupping a hand over his eyes to shade them, he peered inside.

"Nice molding."

"That's what all the guys say," Jenni Beth quipped dryly.

He laughed. "I want this place."

"Good luck."

"Look at the imperfections in this glass. When the house was built, window glass was mouth blown into cylinders, then flattened by hand into sheets. See here?" He pointed to the bottom. "See how the glass is slightly thicker? That's for stability and to keep water from leaking in. I have to have these windows. This house."

Watching him, she smiled slowly. "You love it, don't you?"

"The glass?"

"The whole thing. Restoration, old houses, salvaging."

"Yeah, I do. It's more than how I make a living. It's my passion." He threw her a sheepish grin. "And that sounds pretty silly, doesn't it?"

"No, it doesn't. It's pretty much how I feel about Magnolia House. My plans for it." She tapped her bottom lip and said nothing else for a minute. Reaching into her pocket, she pulled out her phone.

Cole listened while she talked to her father.

When she ended the call, she said, "Dad says Starshine has a nephew. James Fielding. He's probably in his late sixties, early seventies, so I seriously doubt he's planning to do anything with this place."

Cole nodded. "I want the house. He can keep the land."

"Dad thinks he's moved to Blairsville, but he'll check with Charlotte, see if he can get Fielding's number."

"All right!" Cole grabbed her by the waist and pulled her in for a kiss.

Staggered, she gave in to it.

"Wow," she said when he lifted his head. "I'll try to do a few more favors for you."

"You do that." He ran a fingertip down the length of her nose. "Ready to go?"

"You bet."

"Put your helmet back on, and let's go visit Ms. Hattie. Check the progress there." He reached back and patted his saddlebag. "Your mom sent some of Charlotte's cinnamon rolls for her."

Jenni Beth's heart gave a small, happy lurch. That

distance she'd been holding on to for the last year or so seemed to be melting away. Despite what she'd told Cole, she was finding it harder and harder to stay detached.

That her mom would think to send these to Ms. Hattie? A good sign. Taking care of Wes's room had been difficult, but maybe now her mom could move forward. And her dad? He'd been totally engrossed with Cole this morning and enjoying it. Had been working on some of the small projects around the house.

Hope filled her. Hope that maybe she'd have her parents back soon.

When they pulled up to her house, Ms. Hattie was sitting on the front porch in a rickety old chair. Dressed in a worn blue housedress, an apron tied around her waist, she waved a frail hand at them.

"Hey, Ms. Hattie." Cole removed his helmet. "You look even prettier than the last time we were here."

"*Psst*, boy. You're crazy as a loon." Using the chair arm for leverage, she stood. "But my steps and porch sure do look a sight better."

Jenni Beth slid off the bike, helmet dangling from her fingers, and felt a surge of pride. "Beck and his guys did a nice job, didn't they?"

"Sure did. That Beck Elliot's grown up to be a good man. Handsome, too. Don't know why some young thing hasn't snapped him right up."

Cole bounded up the stairs and kissed her weathered cheek.

"You too." Ms. Hattie patted his cheek. "You're a fine boy. Your mama and daddy have to be real proud of you."

"Thank you, ma'am." He turned to Jenni Beth. "Would you unsnap those bags and get that packet?"

"Sure." When she carried the foil-wrapped package to the porch, she handed it to the older woman. "From my mama."

"A couple of Ms. Charlotte's homemade cinnamon rolls, made fresh this morning," Cole said. "I had one and can swear on a Bible they're the best I've ever eaten."

"You want another?" Hattie held out the packet.

"No thanks. Watching my waistline." He grinned wickedly. "Ms. Beaumont says to warm the rolls five minutes on low, and they'll be as fresh as they were right out of the oven."

"How about a glass of sweet tea?"

Jenni Beth's gaze met Cole's, and he winked. Yes, for Ms. Hattie, he'd drink it sweet and not complain.

Even though she knew Cole wanted to be on his way, he nodded. "Sure thing. Why don't you let me help you? We'll take it out back if that's okay."

He held the door as Hattie entered the house. "Did Beck say how long it would be before he puts in your new windows?"

"He's waitin' for them to be delivered. Said he'd let me know." While she talked, she picked up one of the African violets from her windowsill and placed it in a plastic bag.

"I want you to take this." She thrust the plant at Jenni Beth. "Set it in a sunny window, and when it's thirsty give it room-temperature water. It'll bloom well for you."

"Thank you." She held it almost reverently, prayed she wouldn't kill it.

Then the older woman shuffled into the kitchen. "Baked some cookies yesterday, Cole, in case you dropped by. Why don't I put a few in a container for you?"

"I'd love that. Thank you."

Jennie Beth and Cole looked at each other. She was baking again. Another good sign.

After nearly half an hour, Ms. Hattie's chin drooped and Jenni Beth could see she was tired. She glanced at Cole and nodded toward the woman.

He nodded back. "Sure do hate to leave, Ms. Hattie, but we need to be gettin' back to town."

Reaching for her glass, he said, "Why don't you let me take this in for you? You look comfortable. Stay right here in the sun, maybe take yourself a little catnap."

"I might just do that."

A few minutes later, the glasses rinsed, Ms. Hattie asleep, Jenni Beth tucked the plant carefully into the saddlebag before she hopped on the back of the bike. She hooked her helmet.

"Ready?" Cole asked.

She wrapped her arms around him. "Yes. Thank you."

"For what?"

"You're so good with her."

"I like her. I like you, too, and you sure feel good snuggled up against me like that, sugar."

Not yet ready to admit she agreed, she asked, "Where are we going?"

"Thought we'd take a little ride, then stop at a favorite barbecue spot of mine."

"Sounds great."

They rode leisurely, taking narrow two-lane back roads and detours. Jenni Beth had never seen the area like this. Even in her 'Vette with the top down, things weren't quite so up close and personal as they were on the back of the motorcycle.

She'd had no idea she'd love it this much.

True to his word, Cole idled up to a little tucked-away barbecue joint. Judging by the number of vehicles in the parking lot, she figured that, while it was out of the way, she had to be the only person within a hundred-mile radius not familiar with the place.

She excused herself to go the restroom. When she came out, she found Kimmie Atherton draped over Cole. She froze, and for a few seconds, actually considered running back to the bathroom and hiding.

Nope. Time to meet her nemesis head-on. She'd lost round one in high school, so Kimmie was the one with photos of herself beside Cole at the prom. Kimmie'd also been the one who'd undoubtedly gone to the rock quarry afterward for a make-out session with Cole.

How far had they gone?

It hurt to even think about that. Judging the book by its cover, Jenni Beth didn't figure it was a question worth pondering. Kimmie had never been selfish with that body of hers.

According to Beck, Kimmie, newly divorced, was on the hunt for husband number three.

Cole?

Halfway across the room, Jenni Beth's self-confidence lagged and she stopped short. If Cole actually was interested in Kimmie, did she have the right to interfere? She and Cole had shared a few kisses, done some flirting, but nothing deeper—except for that one time. That one time that had meant so much—to her.

But no claims had been made on either side. Not then, not now.

Thanking God she'd come to her senses before she made a complete idiot of herself, she pulled her Miss Congeniality smile out of her hip pocket and slapped it in place.

"Hey, Kimmie. I'd heard you were back in town."

"Yeah, heard you were here, too." Kimmie obviously didn't possess Jenni Beth's acting ability because she made no attempt at a smile. "What are you doin' here?"

"She's with me," Cole said. He looked about as uncomfortable as a single guy in an obstetrician's office. His gaze flicked from one to the other.

"Want to join us?" Jenni Beth gestured to a chair at the table and rejoiced as a look of pure panic sprung into Cole's eyes.

"Nah. That's okay. I stopped by to pick up a to-go order for my folks." She cracked her gum. "See you later, big boy." Tossing a devil-may-care look toward Jenni Beth, she leaned in and planted a big kiss on Cole.

Jenni Beth had to give him credit. He actually pulled away.

"Tell your folks hello for me, Kimmie," he said.

With his foot, he pushed out the chair by Jenni Beth. "Sit, so we can get ordered, sugar. We've still got lots to do today."

"Bye, Kimmie." She sat down.

"Yeah." A pout on her bright red lips, the other woman stalked toward the counter for her food.

Jenni Beth mentally chalked one point under her column. True, this didn't count for nearly as much as the prom, but she felt proud of herself. Was one step closer to even.

A while later, totally replete, she wiped her fingers on her third napkin. "I have to give it to you, Cole. That was undoubtedly the best pulled pork I've ever eaten, and believe me, I've eaten plenty."

"Next time, you need to try the ribs. Fantastic." He cleaned his hands on the wet wipes their waitress brought and dug some bills out of his pocket for the check. "You ready to go?"

"I am. What's next on the agenda?"

"Thought we'd ride aimlessly for a bit. See where the road takes us. You game?"

"Yes, I'm growing fond of…that bike of yours."

And then, right in front of God and country, he leaned down and kissed her. Not the branding kind of kiss Kimmie had planted on him, but a tender kiss. One that meant so much more. One that had her toes curling.

When he finished, he had a smile on his face. "I'm enjoying today. Enjoying spending time with you."

"The feeling's mutual."

As they walked out, she wondered if there were a few raised brows in the room. One guy, two gals kissing him? No, she thought. She hadn't kissed Cole. He'd kissed her, and that made all the difference in the world.

On her way to the bike, her feet never touched the ground.

Again, he chose winding back roads she'd never been on. They climbed to the top of a lighthouse and stared out over the river of marsh grass, smelled the pungent pluff mud left behind when the tide receded.

They ate ice cream from a small roadside stand and

sang along to Maroon Five's "Moves Like Jagger" that played over the speaker. Licking his cone, Cole stood and did a very Jagger-like dance, with those heavy-lidded bedroom eyes.

Jenni Beth blew out a huge breath. "Whew, be still my heart."

He tugged her up beside him, started moving again.

"You'll get us arrested."

"I seriously doubt that."

Several pairs of female eyes turned their way, and she shook her head. "Behave."

"I am." Looking wounded, he plopped the last bite of cone in his mouth. "Wanna go somewhere private?"

Oh, she did.

Slowly, she nodded.

He leaned in. Their lips met in a kiss that held promises. That made him want more.

"If your parents hadn't been home this mornin'—"

"I can't believe Mom actually sent you up to my room."

"She likes me."

"So do I. Kiss me again."

He did. When she opened her mouth, his tongue slipped inside, danced with hers. The heat grew, and he groaned. "I want you so badly."

She stepped an inch closer. "I believe you."

A laugh escaped him. "I'll just bet you do. Hop on the bike, sugar, and let's get out of here."

She reached for her helmet and slid on behind him. He started the bike, then just sat there.

"What's wrong?"

Shaking his head, Cole turned halfway in his seat. "I don't know where to go."

"What?"

He killed the bike. "Here's the thing. I'm not takin' you to a motel. I think too much of you for that, Jenni Beth. You're not a by-the-hour-room type."

She colored. "No. I'm not."

"My parents are doin' lawn work today," he said. "If we go to my place—"

"They'll know what's up," she finished.

"Yeah."

"And my house…" She smiled regretfully, then held up a hand and ticked off finger after finger. "Mom, Dad, Charlotte, Beck. His crew."

"Not an option," Cole said. "Let me take you to Savannah. Away from here."

"I can't." Frustrated, she sighed. "I'm sorry, but I can't. Not right now. The timing's bad."

He blew out a huge sigh. "How in the hell did things get so complicated? This used to be easy." He threw her a sideways glance.

"Um, have you—I mean, your place here—"

"No woman has ever shared my bed in Misty Bottoms, sugar."

"Oh."

He turned the key and pressed the bike's ignition. "Hold on."

"Where are we going?"

"You'll see."

He drove down the back roads till he found what he'd been looking for. A beautiful open field, huge old oaks spreading shade. Parking beneath a tree, he shut down the motorcycle and held out his hand to help her off.

"Outside?"

"Yep. I have a blanket in my saddlebag."

"But—" She waved a hand. "What if somebody comes by?"

"Ahh, that's part of the thrill, right?"

"Only if nobody actually *comes* by. I'd die if anybody caught us." She laughed. "My mom and dad would ground me."

"You're an adult now."

"And should know better."

His eyes darkened. When he leaned toward her, she closed her own eyes. His lips touched hers, and her mind simply quit working.

His hands were everywhere at once. Liquid heat dripping over her.

God, she was sixteen again. Nothing mattered but this moment. Right now. The two of them coming together. A brass band could have marched down the little dirt road and she wouldn't have cared.

Her hands moved to his buttons, but he brushed them away. His mouth dropped to her breast, and he kissed her through her top, his fingers slipping inside her shorts.

She needed more. Wanted more. Moved against him.

Time melted away.

"I can't take any more," he whispered against her lips. "We need to stop."

"But we didn't—"

"No." His voice was rough. "Not yet. Not today. Not here."

"I thought…"

"I know. Damn!" He pressed his forehead to hers, his breathing ragged. "We're not kids anymore, Jenni Beth.

I can't risk somebody driving past. For me? I don't care.
For you? It matters."

"You're serious, aren't you?"

"Unfortunately, yes."

He flopped to his back, reached for her hand, and
laced their fingers. When he brought her hand to his
lips and kissed every knuckle, she understood for the
first time how a woman might swoon. Her entire body
sizzled. She fought for oxygen.

"Do you think you can climb my trellis tonight?"

He laughed, long and hard. She'd forgotten what a
truly wonderful laugh he had. It had been far too long
since she'd heard it.

"Oh, I wish." He rolled his head to look into her eyes.
"I have to go back to Savannah tonight."

She only nodded.

"You've got me thinkin' crazy things, sugar. These
feelings—they scare me," he admitted.

"And you think you're alone in that?"

That stopped him for a few seconds, but when she
didn't elaborate, he said, "You're like an earworm, Jenni
Beth. You play with my head. You get in there, and I
can't get you out. When we danced after the wedding
at Chateau Rouge, I thought maybe it was holdin' you,
touchin' you after so long."

"Cole—"

"No. Let me finish." His voice deepened. "You. Me.
It scares the hell out of me. But *no* you and me? That
scares me even more."

She stared at him, unblinking.

In one graceful movement, he rose to his feet, then
helped her up, and straightened her top. Some serious

clouds had rolled in. "We'd better get home before it decides to rain."

As he folded the blanket to tuck inside his saddlebag, he fleetingly wondered if he shouldn't have it bronzed as a testament to his willpower. It had taken every single ounce he possessed to stop, to not take what Jenni Beth offered. He wanted her, and he meant to have her. When the time was right.

But damn, that wasn't today.

By the time he dropped her off at Magnolia House, Beck and his crew had quit for the day. Cole kissed her, hopped on his motorcycle, then, swearing, dismounted and kissed her again.

"I'll miss you."

She hugged him tightly. "I'll miss you, too."

His phone rang, and he answered without checking the caller ID.

Standing close to him, Jennie Beth heard a sexy female voice.

"Cole Bryson, why haven't you called? You said you would. I had such a good time on our date—"

Without a word, Jenni Beth turned and rushed inside, leaving one very disconcerted male standing in the middle of her drive.

Chapter 19

IT HAD BEEN A LONG, MISERABLE WEEK SINCE JENNI Beth had seen Cole. He'd phoned every night, but she hadn't answered his calls.

She needed time to pull herself together. To take stock of her emotions. She'd dared to allow herself to start believing and had let Cole in. Opened her heart to him.

And now? She didn't know what to think. In the middle of the night, alone in her bed, she second-guessed herself.

Despite their history, Cole *was* decent.

All his acts of innate goodness. The gentlemanly behavior. The way he treated Ms. Hattie. His dance moves and great butt. His kisses.

Okay. She'd gotten off track.

But had all that blinded her to his faults? Although, to be fair, at Chateau Rouge she and Cole had shared a couple dances and a single kiss. Did that make it wrong for him to date some other woman, a woman whose voice had been pure sex and promises? Jealousy, such an ugly creature, poked its head around the corner.

She couldn't lie to herself. The problem didn't lie at Cole's feet, but at hers. She'd read too much into things. She'd expected too much.

Still, she couldn't help but wonder what the other woman looked like. Couldn't help but wonder exactly when they'd gone on their date.

Well, she had to set that aside. For now. She had work to do.

Things at the house were coming together quickly.

The place looked like an anthill with workers scurrying inside and out, upstairs and down. After the kitchen cabinets had been hung, Beck decided they needed one more coat of paint, so she, her mom, and Charlotte were surrounded by packing boxes and paper. They needed to remove everything inside the cabinets again till the painting was finished.

Her mother held up a silver cake server and gravy ladle. "These are part of the house's original set." She traced a finger along the intricate design on the cake server. "The Beaumont servants wrapped them in heavy felt and buried them in the rose garden in case any Yankees came snooping around."

"We're lucky to have all this history, aren't we?"

Sue Ellen swiped at her forehead before she gently placed the silver pieces in a box. "Most days I think so."

Jenni Beth's heart sang a happy little tune watching her mom. They were up to their armpits in paint samples both for the common areas and for her parents' apartment, in sketches, and furniture arrangements. Even her dad had pitched in. It felt good to have them with her again, to have them smiling again. To hear an occasional laugh.

Sweating, her back beginning to ache, she grinned like a loon. Her home was a madhouse. Guys hollered at each other, a radio blasted out country music, and drills, saws, and hammers added to the din. Very noisy, very happy.

And the smells. She breathed deeply. New sheetrock

and plaster, sawdust, varnish and paint, even the sweat of men laboring. A little slice of heaven.

Over all the chaos, she heard a car pull up out front. A few seconds later, the doorbell rang.

She frowned. None of the workers bothered to knock. Since Magnolia House was now a full-blown construction site, they simply walked in.

Charlotte started to get up to answer the door, but Jenni Beth shook her head. "I'll get it."

Zeke, her yellow Lab, ambled behind her.

Ralph Hawkins, the county building inspector, stood at the door. "Hey, Jenni Beth, your daddy home?"

"No, I'm afraid not. He's gone for a few hours. Why?"

Hawkins scratched his nearly bald head. "I've got to shut you down. Sure am sorry."

"Shut me down? What do you mean?"

"No more work can go on here at Magnolia House. As of right now everything stops."

"Why?"

"No permits."

Her mind raced. So did her heart. This was awful. Hadn't Beck taken care of permits? She was sure he'd told her he'd handle the paperwork with the county. Had he gotten busy and forgotten? She frowned. That wasn't like him. Beck was almost OCD when it came to his job.

"I'm sure we have everything, Ralph."

"Afraid not. The office received an anonymous tip you had all this construction happenin'." He waved his hand, indicating the work around them.

"An anonymous tip?" Exasperated, she said, "I haven't kept any of it a secret. Everything has been right out in the open."

Hawkins rubbed at his head again. "Still, you're out of business until you get the paperwork taken care of. I really am sorry to have to put this on you. I meant to talk it out with your daddy."

"It's fine. I'm the one in charge, Ralph."

His expression remained bland. Without blinking an eye, he put two fingers to his lips and whistled. Around her, everything ground to a halt. No one spoke. No saws, no hammers. Only Chris Young singing his latest over the radio.

"The site's shut down as of right now. Pick up your tools and head home."

"Who is it, honey?" her mother called out.

"It's nothing, Mama. Just a little problem with the job. I'll take care of it." Panic rushed through her, made it nearly impossible to breathe. "You can't do this."

As Hawkins turned toward his car, she grabbed his arm. "Ralph, what are you doing?"

"My job." He shook off her hand and left.

She wished Cole was here—even if he had been a jerk. He'd know what to do. Her lip trembled. On top of everything else, she missed him so much.

Water under the bridge, she reminded herself.

And right now that creek had overflowed. She had a major problem on her hands.

The guys, sweat running down their faces, gathered around her.

"Take a short break," she said. "Drink some water and cool down. Give me a couple minutes to take care of this."

The men wandered off, some to their cars to sit in the air-conditioning, some sprawled in the grass under the oak trees' shade.

She dropped onto the top porch step and called Beck. His voice mail answered. "Can you come over to the house right away? We have a problem. A huge one."

She hung up and sent him a text with the same message.

Not ten minutes later, he pulled into the drive. When he hopped out of his truck, he turned his head one way, then the other, taking in the lounging workers.

"Hey, Jenni Beth, I was already on my way here when I got your message. What's up?" Legs spread, he took in the scene. "Why isn't anyone working? And why do you look like your cat just died?"

"I don't have a cat." She patted Zeke's head, and the Lab's tail thumped on the porch. "Seems I don't have any permits, either. So the work site is temporarily shut down, orders of his royal highness, Ralph Hawkins."

"What?" Beck's face took on an angry set. He ripped off his sunglasses and his eyes flashed fire. "We have all our permits. I posted them out back on the electric pole."

"I didn't know that."

"Maybe not, but Hawkins should have. I took care of them the day you ordered your porch lumber, even though the plans were still in flux at that point."

"Oh." He'd lifted so much of the load. Him and Cole. Again, she pushed Cole to the back of her mind.

"Besides," Beck said, "all he had to do was check with his own office, with the county clerk. Everything's on file."

She told him about the anonymous tip.

"That's a bunch of BS." Plucking his cell from his shirt pocket, he jabbed in a number. His work boots sounded heavy as he strode over to the porch swing.

When the phone was answered, he explained in short, clipped sentences what had happened.

"Yeah. I'll wait."

One look at the set of his jaw, and Jenni Beth was glad she hadn't been the one to rile him. An angry Beck Elliot painted a formidable picture.

After a moment of silence, he said, "You're kiddin' me, right? Put Beulah on the phone. She's the one who filed my paperwork." He paused. "She's on vacation? Well, now, isn't that convenient."

Without another word, he hung up.

"They have no record of our permit."

Her mouth went dry. "What does that mean?"

"Somebody's screwin' with us. Don't worry. I'll take care of it." He leaped off the porch and disappeared around the side of the house.

When he came back, he had several papers in his hand. "Hey, guys," he shouted. "Go home till I call you or head into town for coffee and a donut. But be back here tomorrow mornin', first thing."

She heard the guys grumbling, saw them collect their stuff.

"A wasted day," Beck muttered. "I shouldn't be long, but when you're dealin' with red tape…hard to say."

He strode to his truck, pulled out his cell again, and hit a number. A few seconds later, he said, "It's started. The county inspector shut us down."

Before she could hear anything else, Beck drove off.

Who had he called? And what the heck had he meant by "It's started"? Had he known or suspected this was coming?

Beck was her friend. He'd never do anything to hurt

her. And yet a tiny little kernel of doubt, of dread formed inside her.

He couldn't possibly be working behind her back. She refused to even consider that.

Yet as she started inside to help her mom and Charlotte with the kitchen packing and explain what was happening, her heart felt leaden.

An hour later, as Jenni Beth pondered the fine line of balancing studs and nails with tulle and crystal beads, her phone rang. It was Beck. They were shut down for the next three days.

Somebody had screwed up and entered the wrong name on the computer file. Although that didn't make any sense since his copies had the correct information, nobody could explain it. He suspected it had been changed after the fact.

It didn't much matter, though, because regardless, once the job was red-tagged, they had to fight their way through the tangle of government bureaucracy. No getting around it. Once the guys were allowed back on site, they'd have to hit it hard.

"I left one outraged Beulah Gadsen in my wake— after I called her and told her someone had been fiddling in her files. I suggested she check into it."

"Ooh, I'll bet she's fuming." Beulah Gadsen, when she wasn't sitting on her front porch or tending her African violets, had her fingers in everybody's business. That someone had theirs in hers? That would not sit well.

"Thing is, she's on vacation, and nobody but she can sign off. Typical small-town problem. The minute she steps foot in Misty Bottoms, we'll be back to work."

"She can't take care of it online?"

"Nope, not in this case."

After she thanked him and hung up, she stood in the center of the kitchen, boxes piled around her. One cupboard left. Thank God.

"Go on. Both of you," Charlotte said. "I've got this. You two take care of whatever else you need to do."

"Are you sure?" Jenni Beth asked.

"Wouldn't have said it if I wasn't," Charlotte answered.

"I think I'll take a short nap," her mom said.

"Good." Her mother looked tired. Jenni Beth knew she didn't sleep well. The physical labor today, though, was good for her. "Think I'll work on my brochures a bit. Maybe play around with my website. Or just think. The house is actually quiet."

"Yes, it's been hectic the last couple weeks, hasn't it?" Her mom stepped into the hallway. "The old place is starting to look pretty again."

"She is." She gave her mother a warm hug and vowed to make her eat more. Still too thin.

After her mom went upstairs, Jenni Beth decided the day was far too beautiful to be wasted. She gathered some of her files and went out back to the old swing her father had hung for her and Wes. Despite the circumstances, for the first time in a long time, the yard actually felt peaceful.

Poring through magazines and pictures she'd collected, she imagined the weddings they'd have here. One thing became very clear. Family trees had changed. They'd become relationship trees instead, with a lot of interesting branches.

Jenni Beth wondered if there was such a thing as

a conventional family anymore. Societal changes had made that old Southern question of "who are your people?" a very complicated one to answer.

Smack. A pair of work gloves dropped into her lap and she sat bolt upright.

There stood the man who, for years, had played the role of groom in her own wedding dreams.

Her heart kicked into overdrive. She wasn't ready for him.

"You gonna talk to me ever again, sweetheart?" Cole stood, hand on hips, looking like a fallen angel.

Removing her sunglasses, she studied him. Was that uncertainty in those beautiful hazel eyes? No. Cole Bryson? Never. Still…

It had been a week, eight days in fact, since she'd laid eyes on him, and in his worn jeans and denim shirt with the sleeves rolled up to the elbows, he certainly was a sight for sore eyes. Mentally, she padlocked the shutters she'd placed over her heart.

"This has been the longest week of my life, sugar. I've been missin' you night and day."

She stared up into the live oak and said nothing. Fisted her hands in her lap so she didn't reach up and grab him.

"We need to talk." He squeezed onto the swing beside her. As it groaned, she glanced up, praying the rope would hold their weight.

He overwhelmed her. His heat, his scent, the pull of him. She laid a hand on her belly. Butterflies filled it, fluttered there.

His gaze followed her hand. His eyes darkened, and she nearly forgot to breathe as a need grew in her. She could practically hear that padlock bursting open.

"This swing isn't big enough for two." She wiggled, trying to find space between them.

"Sure it is." He threw his arm over the back, his hand resting on her shoulder. "Truth? I care for you, Jenni Beth. A whole lot. Asking Ava out? A move I made before this thing got started between you and me."

Ava. The name matched the voice.

When she didn't respond, he asked, "Are you listenin'?"

She merely nodded.

"*Mea culpa.*" He clasped his hands in his lap and studied them for a good thirty seconds. "It never crossed my mind to mention my dinner with her because it simply wasn't that big a deal."

He took her hand in his. "You need to help me here. I'm miserable. I can't sleep. I can't eat. I can't stop thinkin' about you."

"Is part of the problem the fact that I'm Wes's baby sister?"

He hesitated, then said, "Yes. It's hard to get past that."

"You didn't seem to have any trouble a couple years ago in Savannah."

"Yeah, actually I did. You've got that figured all wrong. I didn't run away from you that night. I was runnin' from myself. My feelings scared me."

"Seriously?"

"Yeah."

She closed the magazine she'd been scanning and stared at its cover, rather than meet his eyes. "When did you and Ava go out?"

"Weeks ago. It was a couple nights after the wedding at Chateau Rouge."

"After you danced with me? Kissed me?"

"She and I had dinner. Saw a damned movie. It meant nothin'."

She crossed her arms over her chest. "Then why did you do it?"

"Because I'd already asked her out before I ran into you. I considered cancelin', but—" He shrugged. "It didn't seem right."

"Kind of like the prom."

He winced. "The prom. Still a sore spot with you, isn't it?"

She nodded. "Okay, so it seems I overreacted. But I've been thinking."

He groaned. "There you go again with the thinkin'."

"It's who I am." She bit her lower lip. "You're right about Ava. When you took her out, we weren't a thing, as you put it. You had no reason not to take her to dinner."

Relief flooded his face but disappeared as she shook her head.

"Our biggest problem? We're still not a thing. I've never been enough for you, Cole. Not in high school, not—" She stumbled over the words. "Not later. Not now."

"You couldn't be more wrong," he countered. "I've never felt about anyone the way I feel about you." He toyed with her earring. "The way I see it, the problem is that I'm not ready to settle down, and you're not one to trifle with."

"Trifle?" Her forehead creased. "Do you even hear yourself?"

He frowned. "You know what I mean."

"What do you think I am, Cole? Delicate porcelain? I'm strong, and I'm my own person. I make my own decisions."

She stood, took a deep breath, and let it out slowly. "I appreciate everything you've done for my family."

Her back felt like it would snap. She held the magazine so tightly it was surprising it didn't spontaneously combust. If she let her guard down for even a second, she'd break apart into shards so tiny she'd never be able to put them back together.

"But?"

She wet her lips, firmed her resolve. "But I think it might be best if you didn't come by anymore."

"What?"

"I said—"

"I heard what you said. My ears work fine. Is this still about Ava? 'Cause if so—"

She shook her head, fighting back tears. "No. It's about me."

"That's crazy."

"Far from it. It's probably the sanest thing I've done lately."

"You're not makin' any sense."

"Probably not. But you need to go. Now."

For the tiniest instant, she thought he would, and she fought the urge to ignore her common sense, to beg him to stay. She wanted this man so badly, but she'd made the right decision. Now she had to stand by it.

"Like hell!"

Even as the gasp escaped her lips, he sprang to his feet, drew her in, and kissed her. Soul-deep and desperate, the kiss lengthened, coiled inside her, and heated her to a fever pitch.

"Don't push me away, sweetheart," he whispered against her lips. "Please don't make me go."

She grabbed a fistful of his shirt. He tasted so good, felt so good. Her resolution wobbled and toppled.

"What am I going to do with you, Cole?"

"I honestly don't know, but don't shut me out."

"I've been miserable this past week, too," she said quietly. "I don't know what's happening between us, but this *thing*, from here on out, needs to be exclusive."

"For both of us," he said.

"For both of us." She dropped her head on his shoulder, and they stood quietly, the birds serenading them.

"You looked a million miles away when I walked back here," Cole said. He glanced at the magazine in her hand.

She blushed, praying he couldn't read her mind. Didn't know she'd been daydreaming about him. "I was imagining what the house and grounds will be like once they're restored. And that'll be soon—with Beck and his men, with the help you've given." She waved a hand. "The brides. The grooms. Happy families created and joined."

He reached out for her hand, then drew her back onto the swing with him. He scuffed his foot on the ground beneath the swing, his eyes not meeting hers. "The garden's startin' to take shape. You've been workin' hard here."

She nodded, accepting the change of subject.

"Yeah. So." He cleared his throat. "I had to drive over to Beaufort this morning to pick up an order for a customer. Figured since I was passin' this close, I'd stop in to see if we could clear the air. If I could help with anything. Hell, that's not the truth. Well, partially, but the thing is…" He raised his hands, palms up. "I couldn't stay away."

"I'm glad you didn't." The words were nearly a whisper. "Today's turned into a quiet day."

"So I heard. I talked to Beck on the phone. He's still pretty pissed."

Oh, she hoped so because that would help banish those tiny fingers of doubt that had crept into her.

"What's wrong?" Cole frowned. "I thought Beck said he'd handled everything. That you'd be back on track in a couple days."

Her face, so easy to read, gave her away. Something wasn't right. Would she try to bluff her way out of it?

But he didn't dare push since he wasn't being totally honest, either. He hadn't yet come clean about Richard. He suspected the banker had been behind the permit fiasco. It would cost Jenni Beth three days with money flooding out and none coming in. He had a hard time chalking it up to coincidence. Only fools blamed chance for their misfortunes.

She shifted on the swing and her hip rubbed along the length of his. He cursed himself for wedging into this small space with her. Far too close. Too intimate. Every time their bodies touched, little zaps of electricity shot through him.

Lust pooled in him, pulled at him.

And he had to ignore it or at least tame it. Right now, things were tenuous at best between them.

Jennifer Elizabeth would never be anybody's floor mat, and he liked that about her. It would make life hell at times, though, living with a woman that strong.

Beside him, all sun-warmed and relaxed, Jenni Beth sure did look kissable. It occurred to him they'd never been out on an actual date. Sure, they'd spent time together but nothing that had been arranged beforehand. Nothing where they'd set time aside for each other intentionally. He had an idea to rectify that, although he wasn't sure it would technically qualify. If not, though, it would come awfully darn close. If she balked at it, he could downplay the date part, deny it if necessary.

"Since you can't do anything else here today, why don't you come over to my place for dinner? Nothing's pressing in the city, so I don't need to rush back tonight. I hadn't planned to show up before closin' anyway, so Mickey doesn't expect me. I finished things up faster than I'd figured, so here I am with time on my hands."

She said nothing, just stared at him.

"Come on. Two friends sharin' dinner."

She opened her mouth, and he laid a finger over her lips.

"I know what you're gonna say. We're not friends." He met her blue eyes, stared directly into them. "You're wrong about that. Whatever else we are, we're friends and have been for a long time. Besides, you've been sayin' you want to see my house. Check out what I did to the old barn."

He picked up her hand, laced his fingers with hers. "We'll keep things light. Promise."

"Will anyone else be there?"

"Nope. Just you and me. Nothin' fancy. Wear your favorite jeans or whatever."

He swore the earth made a complete rotation while she debated.

"It's not that big a deal, Jenni Beth."

"Your parents will see me."

"Undoubtedly."

"You know what conclusion they'll draw."

"That you're sleepin' with me."

Color rushed up her neck, over her face, and he threw back his head and laughed.

She punched him in the arm, and he winced.

"So will you come?"

She eyed him as if weighing the pros and cons. He figured it was the curiosity, not him, that finally won her over.

She threw up her hands. "Call me five kinds of a fool, but okay. What time?"

"Why don't you come over around six? Or do you want me to pick you up?"

She laughed. "It's not a date, remember? Just two old friends getting together to share a meal. I'll drive myself, thanks."

––⁓––

Cole fretted like a spinster about to get laid for the first time. The invitation had been spontaneous. After she'd said yes, he'd driven home full of worry.

He wanted everything to be perfect. He dusted, vacuumed, and cleaned the sinks and toilets.

Giving in to his baser instincts, he changed his sheets. Just in case. He smiled wryly. A guy never knew when he might get lucky. Hands trembling, he checked his dresser drawer. Yep. A box of condoms ready to go. Again, just in case.

He seriously doubted he'd be so lucky a second time.

His mind flew back to that night in Savannah. Wes had asked him to stop by Jenni Beth's, to make sure she was doing okay. They'd ended up watching TV, eating pizza, and making love. He never had been sure exactly how that had happened, but it was, hands down, the best night of his life.

She'd been so incredibly beautiful, and he'd wanted her for so long. She'd been everything he'd imagined and more.

They'd finally fallen asleep in the wee hours of the morning, wrapped around each other. They'd both worn Cheshire grins and nothing else.

It had fallen apart a couple hours later. He'd woken. Light shone through the window, scattered over her. She'd looked so young, so vulnerable. That vulnerability was shared. Deep down, he knew he'd fallen and hard.

He wasn't ready for it.

And so he'd had to leave.

Without a word of good-bye, without a note or a follow-up phone call, he'd crept out and pretended the night had never happened.

But it had, and they'd kicked it under the carpet too long.

Tonight they'd deal with it, one way or another.

He rubbed sweaty palms over his jeans.

Food! He slapped his forehead. If Jenni Beth was coming for dinner, he had to feed her. He'd been so hung up on, well, other possibilities, that he hadn't actually thought about dinner.

A quick check in both fridge and freezer proved fruitless. He'd have to run into town for groceries, come home, and cook! Oh boy. He was in trouble.

He could handle the basics. Heck, he'd been fending for himself for a long time now, but Jenni Beth probably wouldn't look too kindly on a bowl of Cheerios for dinner or a toaster waffle drowned in syrup. A pizza? Nope. After Savannah, that was definitely off the table.

So he did what every self-respecting, independent male did when faced with this kind of a quandary. He headed to his mom's.

And, bless her heart, Emma Bryson didn't skip a beat. No grilling him. No questions he didn't want to answer. Probably *couldn't* answer under threat of death. No reminders, or warnings, or threats.

Instead, she walked to the freezer and withdrew a casserole dish of homemade lasagna along with a loaf of frozen Parmesan garlic bread. Setting them on the counter, she returned to the fridge for a bag of salad and a container of her own Italian dressing.

He thanked her with a smacking kiss. "You're a lifesaver, Mom."

"That's what moms do." She loaded it all into a bag, her eyes twinkling when she looked up at him. "Jenni Beth Beaumont. Honey, I'm so happy."

Wariness crept into him. "Don't read too much into this, Mom. It's only dinner."

"I know." Still, her smile grew bigger. "She's a brilliant girl. A sweet girl."

Was that a warning or simply pleasure? He wasn't sure, and he didn't intend to ask.

"She's been workin' hard over at her place and deserves a night off, a night when somebody takes care of her for a change."

"Surely her mother does that."

He shrugged. "Things are gettin' better, but for a while her mom and dad were both pretty wrapped up in their own misery."

"That's understandable. I can't begin to imagine—and don't want to." A deep sorrow filled his mother's eyes. It hurt him to see it.

"This house renovation's been good for everybody. Sue Ellen and Todd have finally gotten involved in it. It's takin' them out of their grief."

"Thank you for helping them." She patted his cheek.

"I haven't done much."

"You gave Jenni Beth support. You believed in her. That can be priceless." She picked up a notepad. "Let me write down the heating instructions for all this. You can make your own dessert."

He gaped at her. "I can't make dessert."

"Then it's past time you learned. I'll give you a simple recipe and all the ingredients."

When he left his parents, laden down with food and directions, he couldn't help whistling. The tune, "Dream a Little Dream," had been playing in his head these past few days.

Wasn't that what both he and Jenni Beth had been doing? She dreamed of opening her own business, of saving her family home. And him? He dreamed of having her in his life.

On a temporary basis, of course.

Chapter 20

THE EVENING PROMISED TO BE BEAUTIFUL. THE temperature had dropped and the humidity with it. The azaleas in the backyard were nearly done blooming, but they still looked good. A couple fragrant climbing roses spread splashes of pink and white along the barn-red sides of his doorway.

So much rested on tonight. A long overdue apology. A hope for the future.

On a whim, he decided to move the party outside.

After clearing his whitewashed, salvaged table, he hoisted it up and carried it to the side yard. Heading back inside, he grabbed two of the spindle chairs and set them at opposite sides of the table.

He scrounged around till he found the rest of what he needed. A vintage tablecloth, some chunky candles, and his better plates and salt and pepper shakers. Cutting some of the roses, he arranged them in Mason jars. He stepped away to study the scene with a critical eye.

Not bad.

After he convinced himself it would pass muster, he went inside and put together the pineapple-cherry dump cake. It sure did smell good—even before it started baking. Or maybe that was the lasagna. His stomach growled.

Images of Jenni Beth floated through his mind, and he realized he had an appetite for a whole lot more than food.

After he showered, he actually took a few minutes to wipe the glass door dry and hang his towel. If the gods smiled down on him, would he share the shower with Jenni Beth in the morning?

He hesitated to count on it. Tonight he was determined to put the Savannah episode on the table and deal with it. It might turn ugly. Realistically, the prognosis for that outcome? Not good. But without the discussion? They had nothing.

His hair was still damp when he heard the crunch of tires in his driveway. Moving to the doorway, he leaned against the jamb and watched as she pulled in.

She'd done her hair in some sort of long braid that hung over one shoulder. A skirt, not much bigger than a napkin, rode up as she slid from behind the wheel, showing off miles of gorgeous, tanned legs showcased by high-heeled sandals. A slinky little red top designed to make a man's eyes pop out of his head completed her outfit.

So much for casual.

The outfit made him sweat. Made it hard to breathe.

Slowly, he straightened and walked toward her. She smelled like sin.

He bussed her cheek, decided to wait till later to go for seconds. She leaned into her car, causing that skirt to hike up again, and snagged a bottle of wine from the passenger seat.

"It's red." She wet her lips, and he felt so much better. She was nervous, too. "I wasn't sure what we were having."

"Red's perfect." He took the bottle from her and, with his free hand, captured one of hers. "We're having some of Mom's homemade lasagna."

"Is that what I smell?"

"Yep. Along with a cake I made."

She laughed. "You're kidding, right?"

"Nope. And if I do say so myself, it's a culinary masterpiece."

"This I've got to see."

"First, let me show you around the house."

She rubbed her hands together in happy anticipation. "Oh yes. I've been dying to see inside." She eyed the barn. "What a great place."

"I think so." A hand on her back, he herded her toward the door.

With a gasp, she stopped halfway there, staring at the table he'd set up. "For tonight?"

"Thought we'd dine under the stars."

"You constantly surprise me, Mr. Bryson."

He tugged her closer, set the wine on the table. "Am I forgiven, sugar?" His lips dropped to her ear. Nibbled. "Tell me we're good again."

"We're good again." She wrapped both arms around his waist and tipped her head to give him free access to her neck.

He could have sunk to his knees with gratitude. Nipping and kissing, he traveled from her ear to her neck and back again. When he could resist no more, he took her mouth.

Her fingers tunneled through his hair, and she met him, kiss for kiss.

She felt so good. Tasted like more. His hands slid down to her waist, slid beneath the fire-engine-red top. Her sigh nearly undid him. A tiny corner of his brain still functioned, though.

They were outside. And even though they knew he had company, he couldn't rule out his mom or dad crossing the yard to his place. Best they move inside. This moment was private.

"Come on." He took her hand, led her through the doorway.

"Oh, Cole. This is mind-boggling."

"Yes," he said. "You certainly are."

She laughed. "I meant your house."

His eyes darkened. "I meant you. Give me another kiss, sweetheart."

A quizzical smile met him. "What has gotten into you?"

He grew serious. "Lord help me, but I think you have."

"Cole."

———◦◦◦———

Jenni Beth could barely breathe. This attraction, this draw, was what she'd been fighting so long. She couldn't fight it anymore. Didn't want to fight it anymore.

Stepping closer, she melded her body to his. Felt her power as his need pressed against her.

She kissed his cheek. Kissed his strong chin, enjoyed the roughness of the five o' clock shadow, the muscles that played under her hands. Male, female. So different. Thank God!

Ever so slightly, she drew away. He looked magnificent in the black denims that molded themselves to him, the sleeves of his white dress shirt rolled up. Even now, all cleaned up, he fairly shouted *bad boy*, almost convinced her he had it tattooed somewhere on this magnificent body.

Did he have a tattoo? One that didn't show? He hadn't

had one before. Curiosity ate at her, but not enough to get naked with him to find out.

"Don't pull away, sweetheart."

With a soft cry, she found herself cradled in his arms, carried to the sofa. One kiss led to another and another, and, lost to the heat, she forgot her reticence, made no objection when his hand slid under her skirt, up her thigh.

Her fingers danced beneath his shirt, but it wasn't enough. She had to see him. Making quick work of the buttons, she separated the fabric, ran her hand over that muscled chest, kissed it, nipped lightly at his nipples.

He groaned. "Darlin', you're killin' me here. I can't—"

"Don't stop, Cole. I don't want you to stop."

"It shouldn't be like this. Not here. I want it to be perfect for you. I want to do this right. We should at least go upstairs. To my bed."

"No. I want you right here. Right now."

With a growl, he stripped her top over her head, dipped his lips to the top of her bra. He laid her back on the sofa and undid her skirt, slid it down her legs and tossed it to the floor.

She fought the urge to cover herself as he rested his weight on his forearm. His eyes skimmed over her in her red lace bra and panties. She still wore her stilettos.

"Oh, God, sugar, you're staggeringly beautiful."

He fumbled with the snap on his jeans. Reaching down, she said, "Let me."

A snap and the rasp of his zipper and he was freed.

They came together in a rush of hunger.

She had no idea how long it had been since he carried her inside his house, but when the sex-filled haze lifted she was famished. This time her hunger was for food.

"You said you'd feed me, and that lasagna smells incredible."

He rolled onto his side, taking her with him. One more kiss as he ran a hand over her hip, down her leg, setting off fresh shivers of longing. "Guess I'd better keep my promise."

He scooped his boxers from the floor and pulled them on. "Why don't you wander around the house and satisfy your curiosity while I get the garlic bread heated? The powder room is right over there." He pointed to the far corner of the living room.

"Thanks." Staring hungrily at that bare chest, his six-pack, those muscled thighs, she wondered what she'd done to deserve this. To deserve him. She'd been crotchety. Mean. Yet he hadn't given up on her.

"Jenni Beth? You okay?"

She smiled. "Yes. Very."

She gathered her clothes and slid into them, then moved through the cozy area to the bathroom. She noticed a niche with a couple dozen alarm clocks in all shapes and colors. "You collect these?"

"Yeah. I'm fascinated with the old windups. Don't ask me why. I have no idea."

"I like them. They have character."

"They do." His eyes went dark. "So do you."

Face warm, she ducked into the bath.

After she freshened up, she walked slowly through his space. Over the kitchen island, he'd hung old aluminum washtubs converted into lights. She loved the rustic blended with the new.

The glass-paned kitchen cabinets were a nice fresh white. Splashes of aqua complemented the unexpected blue floor tiles.

Vintage produce crates hung over his desk for storage. In them? Books, a model car, an antique globe, and her brother's basketball trophy from his senior year.

Cole came up behind her and wrapped an arm around her waist, resting his chin on the top of her head. "Your mom gave me that."

"I'm glad."

They stood quietly, each filled with memories of Wes.

"Whoops. I smell the bread." He dropped a light kiss on the back of her neck and headed to the kitchen.

She continued her perusal of his space, amazed at what he'd created. This was a man who knew himself. Knew who he was. A battered door with chunky legs and remnants of red paint served as a coffee table. He'd left the knob and hinges. A metal trough had been adapted as his bathroom vanity.

Everywhere she looked she saw touches of Cole and his uniqueness. Saw his love for salvage.

This, his home, held pieces so different from the things he'd brought to her for her renovation. Different tastes, different needs, and she was certain every home he'd a hand in fit its owner.

Cole Bryson surprised her. So much more complex than she'd ever have guessed. And somewhere along the journey of discovery she'd gone from in lust with him to in love with him.

That, though, was a secret she didn't dare share. It would only cause more self-reproach when he left. And he would leave her. Even after their lovemaking tonight, she understood that.

Bound to spell disaster and heartache, she couldn't avoid it. Couldn't deny it. It simply was, as were the consequences that would follow.

But she wouldn't think about that right now. Instead, she'd enjoy the moment. Enjoy him. Life could be very short.

She walked up behind him as he stood at the stove and wrapped her arms around his waist. "Your home is exactly you, Cole. I adore it."

"Does that mean you adore me, too?" He turned and hugged her to his chest.

She felt the rumble of his voice. "You fishing?"

"Maybe."

"Think I'll hold off on the verdict till I've had my dinner."

"Fair enough, and I'd be sweatin' it out, but, thing is, my mom's cookin' is top-notch. Nothin' to worry about there."

She felt freer and lighter than she had in the last year and a half. "What do you want me to carry out?"

He handed her the salad. "Here you go."

She should feel betrayed—by herself. After all the warnings she'd issued, after all the ups and downs, she'd caved. And she'd never been happier.

Tomorrow would just have to take care of itself.

The animals joined them for dinner.

"Do you mind?" he asked. "I can shut them inside."

"Don't even think about it."

Once they sat down, Roscoe, the family beagle, curled at Cole's feet, hoping for a dropped scrap or a sneaked bite. Jenni Beth smiled when Precious, the gray and white cat, sauntered over and dropped right beside him. The old cat rested his head on the dog and fell fast asleep.

Shadow Dancer, a sleek, all-black beauty, decided she'd play diva. Sprawled on the stone patio, a good arm's length away from the table, the cat eyed them condescendingly, her tail switching back and forth. Even Hinzer, the family's newest feline addition, couldn't get Shadow Dancer to play with him. The tiny ball of orange fur finally amused himself by chasing after a leaf that blew across the patio.

"Hinzer's a strange name for a kitten."

"I named him after a really great friend," Cole said.

"Okay. That works." She tossed Roscoe a piece of cheese. "Why'd it take us so long to reach this point?"

"Here's the deal from my point of view." Cole sipped his wine. "Even when you were a pain in the ass, tagging along with us, you were always more than Wes's little sister. It got complicated, though, *because* of the sister thing." He shrugged.

"I'll buy that. For now, anyway. So why doesn't this little pain in the ass run inside and fetch our dessert?"

"Works for me." He smiled as she sashayed through the door and into his home, Roscoe on her heels. That was a sight a man could get used to.

—◦◦◦—

Replete, Cole pushed aside his dessert plate. Danged if his first attempt at a cake hadn't turned out well. He'd have to thank his mom tomorrow. Maybe he'd call Pia whatever-her-name-was and have flowers delivered to her. The bonus? Jenni Beth had settled down nicely. The real dessert had come before dinner. God, she'd felt so good in his arms, beneath him. There couldn't be a sexier woman on the planet. And if there was? He hoped to God he never met her because his heart couldn't stand it.

All his fantasies about the two of them fell short of reality. She moved him. Every taste, every touch, increased his need rather than diminished it. But they still had some old business to put to bed, and it made him nervous as hell.

Tempted to put it off again, he squared his shoulders and jumped in.

"I did you a huge wrong in Savannah."

"I don't want to talk about that."

"Sorry, but I do. We need to air what happened." His throat constricted. He'd always kept it light with women, and now he was about to step off the cliff into unfamiliar territory. This plagued him, though. Kept him awake at night. Shit!

He reached across the table for her hand, laced their fingers.

"Thing is, Jenni Beth, my feelings for you…" He stopped. Huffed out a breath, then gave a half-laugh. "You've got me nervous as hell."

"Cole—"

"No, let me finish. It's like I've got this anchor tied to my leg, holding me back."

The slate blue of her eyes deepened. "Don't go all dark and heavy on me. I've enjoyed tonight, and I want to keep it that way."

"But—"

"No. Tonight has been the best."

"It can be better."

She patted her heart. "I'm not sure I can survive better."

"Oh, yeah, you can. Come here. Let me show you. Again."

And he did.

Chapter 21

JENNI BETH HUMMED AS SHE TUGGED ON THE OLD University of Georgia T-shirt. It had been a week since dinner at Cole's house. He'd called, but it wasn't the same as having him here.

As great as the night had been, though, a huge weight still rested on her shoulders.

He'd been right. They should have had the Savannah discussion. Sooner or later, they had to stop dancing around it and admit he'd been a jerk. That, maybe, she'd expected too much.

She was working on that.

Yes, she and Cole fit together perfectly — in bed. Out of it? She wasn't sure they meshed. They had different goals.

No matter how many times she denied wanting it all, she did. The husband, the kids, the white picket fence.

Cole didn't want any of that.

Which meant he'd walk again.

Downstairs, she and Charlotte got into a tussle over breakfast. She didn't want any; Charlotte insisted she eat. Finally, to restore peace, she ate a piece of toast standing at the counter. When the housekeeper handed her a banana, she sighed and ate it, too.

"We good now?"

"Yes, we are," Charlotte said. "You can go outside and play."

Jenni Beth tried to glower, but the chuckle spoiled

it. Stepping onto the porch, a cup of coffee in hand, she spotted Beck cutting lumber.

"You're here early."

"I am."

"Can I borrow Charlie?" she asked.

"You bet. Charlie! You're workin' with the boss today."

"The boss." She snorted. "As if."

"Mornin', Jenni Beth." Coming around the corner of the house, Charlie, one of the best finish carpenters in the business, tipped his Falcons cap. "Let me gather my tools and we can get started on whatever it is you're wantin' done."

"The carriage house."

She practically danced, couldn't wait to tackle it. While she still planned to use her attic workspace for the real nitty-gritty of the business, the small outbuilding would be her showroom, her official greet-prospective-clients space. There, she'd set her secret decorator's heart free in the carriage house. Romance. Candles. Champagne and crystal flutes. A bridal gown displayed on a bouquet-carrying mannequin.

Everything she'd ever wanted.

No.

Everything a *bride*, a Magnolia House bride, could ever want.

Not her.

Except in her secret heart of hearts.

Charlie ran to his truck to grab a few tools, and she sank to the building's stoop to finish her coffee.

Resting her chin in her palm, she closed her eyes and let the sun warm her. She pushed aside negative thoughts and filled her head with visions of fairies and sugarplums instead.

What in the heck was a sugarplum anyway? It had to be something to eat. Maybe they could list them on the menu.

Somewhere in this big old house there had to be another pretty little chandelier dripping in crystals for the bridal suite's powder room. She'd scour the house later. In the meantime, she couldn't wait to hang the cherub chandelier, with its pink medallion. She'd unpacked it a dozen times just to look at it. Cole had hit a home run.

A couple of the guys had dragged the occasional chairs she'd found on the second floor up to her bedroom. She'd reupholster them in a fun, flowery print that picked up the pink in the medallion.

Hopefully she could order the fabric from Darlene and start pumping money into the town. That it was her dollars seemed almost inconsequential because eventually the cash would return from outsiders.

She couldn't go too far overboard, too feminine, or the grooms wouldn't darken her door. Still, the emphasis had to be on the bride. When it came right down to it, it was her day.

Charlie headed toward her toting a small, heavy-looking metal box. "Got what I need. Let's get to work."

And work they did.

Jenni Beth had made another trip to Dinky Tubbs's salvage yard and unearthed the perfect old pedestal sink with a handcrafted mermaid faucet and handles. After more than a little time and a whole bunch of elbow grease, they shone like new—but better. Charlie, with a hand from Jeeters, installed it, along with a toilet she'd found. A small chair completed the room.

The carriage house's dark wood walls soaked up

the natural light from the large bay window. Since she wanted the illusion of airy and bright, she and Charlie sanded the walls and put an ivory white finish on them. Again with Jeeters's help, they changed out the front door with a pair of French doors she'd found in a shed out back. Charlie added a wide chair rail so she could display items and the brochures she planned to have printed.

Her pièce de résistance? The cherub chandelier, dripping with crystals.

When Charlie finished hanging it, she flipped the switch. "Oh my gosh," she whispered. "It's totally perfect."

"A little girlie for my taste." He tucked his pliers in his back pocket. "But I've got a feeling that's exactly what you want in here. Give those brides of yours that touch of romance, huh?"

"Exactly."

When he stepped off his small ladder, she threw her arms around him. "Thank you, Charlie."

He blushed. "Just doin' my job."

"You're doing more than that. You're bringing new life to this place."

His blush deepened.

"And I've embarrassed you."

"I can live with that." He laughed. "It's not every day a pretty little thing like you gives me a hug. Can't take it too seriously, though, seein' as how you're about the same age as my granddaughter."

—∿∿—

Every muscle in Jenni Beth's body ached. She and Charlie had worked their butts off yesterday, but, oh, was it worth it. Today, though, she'd find a few less strenuous jobs.

Tucked inside a bureau drawer, she uncovered a pair of pewter candlesticks. Her gut insisted they'd be perfect on the small table by the side window. Eager to see how they'd look, she headed for her office.

She'd barely opened the French doors and stepped inside when the phone rang. For an instant, she hesitated. Gathering her wits, she answered, "Magnolia Brides. Let us plan the perfect wedding for you."

She grinned. What the heck. Might as well try it out.

To her surprise, the woman on the other end gave a little squeal of delight. "Is this Jenni Beth Beaumont?"

"Yes, it is."

"My name's Stella Reinhardt, and I am so excited to talk to you."

Jenni Beth dropped onto the window seat, the candlesticks cradled in her lap. "How can I help you, Stella?"

"Lorrie Davis—You know Lorrie Davis, right?"

"I sure do. We went to school together."

Lorrie had, in fact, been a year ahead of Jenni Beth and hell on wheels. Lorrie and Cole might have had something going on for a bit. Actually, Jenni Beth suspected a fairly large percentage of Misty Bottoms High School boys had had something going on with Lorrie.

"She told me you were opening your home as a wedding venue, so I went online and checked out your website. Magnolia House is so beautiful! I have to have my wedding there, Ms. Beaumont!"

Jenni Beth nearly jumped out of her skin. A client! A real, honest-to-goodness client.

She fanned herself, took a few seconds. "When is your wedding?"

"That's the kicker," Stella said. "Two weeks from last Saturday. You're booked, aren't you?"

"Two weeks?" *Yikes.* Jenni Beth wanted to cry. Her very first client, and she had to turn her down. Nothing for it but to tell the truth.

"Actually, Stella, I'm afraid this is that good news, bad news scenario. We're not booked."

She heard a little cry of joy and hurried on. "But…we're not ready for a wedding yet. We're in the middle of a major renovation."

"No!"

"Believe me, I'm so sorry. I feel as badly as you do."

"But I've always dreamed of getting married at a Southern plantation. Is there any way?"

"I don't—"

"How about the rose garden? I saw it on your site, and that's actually where Bear and I want to get married. Outside, with Magnolia House in the background."

"Seriously?"

"Seriously. We're bikers, my fiancé and I. Harley riders. We'd prefer outdoors."

"Bikers?"

"Yep. But we're not rowdy or anything," she added quickly. "I mean, we're not gonna make a mess at your house. Bear and I—" She laughed. "Bear. That's what I call Steve. We just want to get married." Jenni Beth heard the love. The wistfulness. "And I want somewhere gorgeous. I want your rose garden."

Her mind kicked into gear. The garden was still a little rough, but it could be ready.

"If we can have our cake in the garden," Stella said, "maybe our first dance, we'd like to have the reception at Duffy's Pub."

Jenni Beth could have reached through the line and kissed her. "You've been to Misty Bottoms before?"

"Lots of times. We ride through on our way to bike week in Ft. Lauderdale."

"Hmmm. Duffy's Pub. I'm not sure how many—"

"It's a small group. Including us, there'll probably be twelve to fifteen, give or take a couple."

They discussed dressing rooms, what kind of cake she wanted, flowers. Stella would get dressed right here in Jenni Beth's office, then her maid of honor would drive her out to the rose garden on the back of a Harley. The groom would change in the downstairs study.

By the time they hung up, Jenni Beth had pages of scribbled notes. She and Stella could handle the remaining details by email. All the bride had to do was show up. Jenni Beth would see to the details.

Her first booking!

White roses, tulle, and lace. Beaded gowns and champagne. And for this first wedding? Harleys! She wanted to spend the rest of her life up to her neck in this.

A celebration was in order.

———※———

Cole stomped the dirt off his boots and knocked on Magnolia House's front door. It looked like some good stuff happening here. Lots had been accomplished in a very short period of time. Beck had himself a good team of men.

When Mrs. Beaumont answered the door, Cole

snatched off his Atlanta Braves ball cap and raked his fingers through his hat hair. "Evenin', ma'am."

"Oh, Cole." She took him by the hand and led him inside. "Isn't this lovely?" She ran the tip of her shoe over the newly sanded floor. "Beck tells me they'll stain them tomorrow. Thank you for all your help, sweetheart."

He took her proffered kiss and returned it with one on her petal-soft cheek. She smelled of lilacs. Always had. Wes's mom was a lady through and through, born to the Southern way.

His mom was a lady, too, but Emma Bryson didn't go in for quite as much pampering. They'd had livestock when he was younger, and the barn had been a working one. Taking care of cattle was a seven-day-a-week, dawn-to-dusk job. So his mom and dad had labored hard. The Beaumonts and the Brysons didn't run in the same social circles, except on poker night. But that hadn't made a bit of difference to him and Wes, brothers by all but birth.

"Is Jenni Beth here?"

"Oh, she's around somewhere. Honestly, she was down on this floor like a common laborer a couple days ago. After that, she and Charlie Pearce worked all yesterday in the carriage house." Mrs. Beaumont shook her head. "Todd tells me not to stew about it, that things have changed, and our daughter is doing what needs to be done."

She looked up at him with those same slate-blue eyes Jenni Beth saw in the mirror every day. Those eyes that drove him wild. That saw too much, knew too much. Too often hurt too much.

"That's where she is now. Out in the carriage house."

Todd stepped into the hallway, a glass of iced tea in hand. He held it up. "Want a cold drink?"

"No, thanks. I need to run a couple things past your daughter."

Mr. Beaumont slapped Cole on the back. "I want to add my thanks. You and Beck have really pitched in to help Jenni Beth with this crazy idea of hers." He hesitated. "To be perfectly truthful, it's important to all of us. We're taking on water here at Magnolia House. Sue Ellen and I have pretty much made a muddle of things. And shame on us for that."

He reached for his wife's hand, took it in his, and lightly rubbed his thumb over the back of it. "Things weren't great before, but after Wes..." He stopped, cleared his throat.

"I understand," Cole said. "Believe me, I miss your son every morning and every night and a dozen times in between."

Mrs. Beaumont swiped at tears. "You're such a blessing."

"Jenni Beth loves you both."

"We know that," Mr. Beaumont said. "I'm afraid we've let her down, too. We've really screwed up."

"No." Cole shook his head. "You haven't. You simply staggered a little under the weight of it all. This plan of Jenni Beth's? It'll be good for the entire family."

Mr. Beaumont met his gaze. "She thinks she can save the whole town."

Cole chuckled. "And knowin' your daughter? She just might do that."

Todd laughed. "You're right."

Cole reached for the doorknob. "I'm gonna go see if I can find her."

"You'll be surprised at what she's done out there. Looks like a different space all together."

"It's so romantic," Mrs. Beaumont added. "So— weddingish. I helped her choose the wall color."

With a smile, Cole excused himself and headed along the brick path to the carriage house. Jenni Beth had already accomplished one mammoth goal. Her parents were interested in something other than their own grief.

"Well done, sweetheart," he murmured.

Chapter 22

AS THE BUILDING CAME INTO VIEW, COLE NODDED approval for the white sheers at the windows, the wreath on the newly installed red French doors, the crisp white shutters. Large white metal buckets, exploding with color, stood like sentries at the doorway. She'd filled them with red geraniums, green vines, and some kind of white and blue flowers.

The place looked exactly right. Classy but contemporary. Professional but homey.

What she still needed? A sign to hang from a wrought-iron arm. And he knew exactly where to find it.

He smiled, then knocked at the door. Music drifted out to him. Country again. Hmmm. What kind of mood would he find her in?

He'd missed her. It galled him to admit that, even to himself. He admired her. He respected her. He wanted her—so damn badly that he hurt.

He knocked again.

"Come in!"

He turned the knob, took half a step inside, and stopped. If he'd thought she'd done a bang-up job on the exterior, the interior about knocked him off his feet.

Welcoming. And feminine. A guy would have to be very careful in here. Of course, the ones who walked through this door would be head-over-heels in love with the women beside them and more than happy to sit in this female nest and agree with anything they wanted.

And then he spotted Jenni Beth. A glass of champagne in one hand, a piece of chocolate in the other, she sent him a sloppy grin.

"Hi, Cole. I'm having some champagne." She held up a half-empty bottle. Nestled in a chintz easy chair, her legs draped over the arm, she grinned lopsidedly at him. "I have some left."

"I see that."

Well on her way to draining the bottle, she was tipsy, he realized with amusement. Here, in her office, in the middle of the day. And very, very happy.

He doubted she'd be as happy about it later, though, so he'd better step in and save her from herself.

"How about I join you? Help you finish off that bottle." He snagged the champagne, poured himself a flute, and moved the bottle to her desk, well out of reach.

"Is that all you want?" she asked, a sexy little smile on those full, pouty lips. Untangling herself, she stood and wrapped one arm around his neck.

His heart thumped hard enough to fly out of his chest. For a second, he held her close, rested his chin on all that glorious hair, and breathed in the clean, sweet scent of her.

Hands at her waist, he drew back slightly. "What's goin' on, sugar?"

"I booked a wedding!" The smile burst from her.

"What?"

"Stella and Bear, well, Steve." She giggled. "My first bride and groom! I'm celebrating."

She raised her free hand in a salute, the champagne sloshing in her glass.

He groaned.

"Want to help?" she asked.

"Help with what?" His mind had blanked.

"My celebration."

He blew out a huge breath. He'd stepped into deep water and was going under fast.

"You'll regret this tomorrow," he warned.

"I don't think so. And, Cole?"

"Yes?"

"I'll still respect you in the morning."

Before he could come up with anything, she kissed him. Hot and hungry. Demanding.

He let himself go, lost himself in the kiss, the taste of chocolate, champagne, and sexy woman. Tongue danced with tongue, and her body melted into his, her skin soft as rainwater under his workman's hands.

He couldn't get enough.

Her soft moan snapped him out of the trance.

He took a step away, and his hands stilled. "We can't do this, Jenni Beth. Not here, not now."

"'Spose not." She tugged at her shirt, straightened it. The champagne high remained, her lopsided grin back.

"Tell me about your bride."

She laughed. "You won't believe it."

"Oh, you might be surprised."

"Yeah? Magnolia House's first bride is a biker chick."

His brows rose, and she nodded smugly.

"I told you. It's not quite what I imagined for my first, but—" She shrugged. "The bride is ecstatic, and so am I."

—w—

Wandering to the safety of her desk, she explained that Stella was the friend of a friend.

"Lorrie Davis. You remember her."

His ears turned red. "Yeah, I do. She was a year behind me in school."

"That's right." She couldn't help but dig. "If I'm not mistaken, you knew her pretty well."

"We might have gone out a couple times."

"I heard a rumor or two to that effect." She could almost set aside that tiny lick of jealousy as she watched him squirm.

She rambled on, filling him in on what they'd accomplished with the house while he'd been in Savannah. The entire time she talked, her mind raced. Her body tingled. How stupid to have kissed him. Here.

Thank God he'd the good sense to step away. Of course, he hadn't emptied half a bottle of champagne. But could she blame it on that?

Probably not. Shoot.

"When do Stella and Steve plan to hold this wedding?"

"In two weeks."

"You're kiddin'." His smile faded.

She shook her head.

He moved close, stared into her eyes, and placed his palm on her forehead.

"What are you doing?"

"Checkin' to see if you're delusional with fever."

She swatted his hand away.

"Honey, I don't want to be that clichéd wet blanket, but you can't possibly be ready in time."

"Yes, I can. That's the truly fantastic part. The bride wants the ceremony in the rose garden. We won't need the house itself for anything more than a backdrop."

She made another happy sound. "I explained we were renovating, that the bridal suite wouldn't be finished. She doesn't care. She's perfectly okay with using this office as her bride's room and insists the garden area suits her and her groom to a T."

She bit her lip. "This is exactly what I didn't want to do, though. A hodgepodge, put-out-fires type of job. But..." She sighed. "I have a chance to make some money and start a portfolio. How can I turn it down? It's like a little gift from heaven."

Tears welled in her eyes, and she blinked them away. "Maybe this is Wes up there, helping."

Cole nodded, his face a mask. "You're right. You have to do what you have to do. Speaking of which, this place is phenomenal." He turned, taking in her small office.

"It is, isn't it? Look at the chandelier." She flipped the switch, and the crystals glittered.

"Nice."

"Charlie Pearce helped me with the room. And Jeeters." She grinned and swiped at the last of her tears.

"That's what your mother said."

"I pulled it off on a shoestring thanks to Beck and you."

"This isn't my work."

"No, but you've put in some sweaty days. And you gave me this fabulous light. Plus, I found some things at Dinky Tubbs's salvage that worked really well, thanks to you. Come look at the bath."

He followed her, stood with both hands on the door-jamb, and peered inside. "Impeccable." He walked to the sink and turned the water on, then off. "These faucets are great."

"Very upper-crust, don't you think? Dinky said he found them in an old Atlanta hotel."

"I do. You and Dinky hit it off pretty well, huh?"

"We did." Jenni Beth looked at Cole. "He told me his shop was nothing compared to yours."

"Come see it, Jenni Beth. I've asked you before. Savannah's an hour's drive at most, and I've got a lot of great pieces you can use. This place won't self-destruct if you leave for a couple days."

"I don't know, Cole. I'm not sure that's a good idea."

"I'm not invitin' you for an illicit weekend."

Heat raced up her chest, her cheeks. "I didn't say you were."

"But that's what you're thinkin'."

"You don't know that."

"Oh yeah, sugar, I do. And that pretty pink tinge on your cheeks tells me I'm right on the mark."

"After dinner at your house…"

"Don't forget the pre-dinner appetizer. Pretty good, huh?"

"Yes." Despite herself, she broke into a grin, blamed it on the remnants of champagne in her system. "Maybe too good."

"No such thing. We've stepped over that line, sugar, whatever it is." His gaze drilled her. "Why are you runnin' cold again?"

She gave a little half-laugh. "Oh, there's no cold, believe me. But I have a lot to do. Especially now that I have a booking."

"That's not it. It's Savannah, isn't it?"

"Go away, Cole."

"Damn it, Jenni Beth. I was a jerk. A total jackass." He threw his hands in the air. "I admit it, okay? If I could go back—"

"You wouldn't do it any differently," she finished for him.

He stared at her so intensely she could all but feel the burn.

"You're probably right," he said on a sigh. "Under the same circumstances…" He laid a hand on her cheek. "Wes asked me to check on his baby sister. Make sure you were doin' okay. What did I do?" He made a derisive sound. "Took you to bed."

"You weren't alone in that bed," she said quietly. "But I was when I woke up the next morning. You sneaked out like a cat burglar. You didn't call, email, text. Nothing, Cole."

"I couldn't. I couldn't rationalize what happened, what I'd done. I couldn't come up with anything but lame excuses. I wasn't ready to take it to another level, so I did what I thought best. For both of us. I'm sorry, Jenni Beth. I took advantage of your innocence."

"Cut it out, Cole. I'm only two years younger than you. And I wasn't a virgin."

"You damn well should have been."

"Oh, that's rich!" She braced a hand on her hip and stared him down. "And when did you lose your virginity?" She held up her hand, palm out. "No, don't tell me. You were the sage old age of fourteen. Eighteen-year-old Missy Simpkins took you on your first ride in the backseat of her daddy's Chevy."

Cole's mouth opened, then closed. Opened again. "How do you know that?"

Her chin tipped defiantly. "The same way you know about my hairbrush microphone. I can eavesdrop, too. And, boy, some of yours and Wes's conversations were pretty enlightening. I learned a lot."

He had the gall to look indignant. "You listened to us?"

"Heck yes, I did."

"I don't even want to think about what you might have heard."

She laughed.

He realized how much he'd missed that laugh this week, how much he'd missed her. It scared him.

"Tell me you'll come to Savannah, sugar." A thought struck him. "You didn't leave anyone there, did you?"

"What?"

"A guy. Someone who can't wait for you to hit the city again?"

"No." She shook her head and took another sip of her warming champagne. Maybe it was the alcohol, but she said, "Maybe all this time I've been waiting for you."

"Yeah, right." He turned her to face the mirror over the fireplace. "Take a really long, hard look. You're cover-model, drop-dead gorgeous and so darned smart. What would you want with somebody like me? What do I have to offer?"

"You're kidding, right?"

"My God, you have men droppin' like flies. One look and they're goners. I'm not in your class, sweetheart."

"No, you're not. You, Cole Bryson, are far too good for me."

He snorted.

"Without question. You give to everybody. You're the most kindhearted man I know. Except when you're sneaking out of my bedroom in the middle of the night." She hesitated. "I really didn't expect you to come back, you know."

"You lost me."

"From Savannah. When you left last week, I figured so long—again."

"I told you I'd be back."

"Yes, you did. But talk is cheap."

"I'm here."

"You are. Thank you."

She stared out the window for a minute, watched one of the workers hike across the yard with a couple two-by-fours over his shoulder.

"Here are my thoughts for what they're worth. You're right. You *were* a jackass. But we've both changed since then. For better or worse?" She lifted her shoulders. "I guess only time will tell. Speaking for myself, I'm ready to kiss and make up."

Cole couldn't have said which of them moved first. Suddenly he had his arms full of delicious woman, his mouth on hers, tongue dancing in and out, tasting her heat, her fire, her sweetness and desire.

His hand moved to her waist. Bare skin. He all but groaned. Her shirt had ridden up when her arms wrapped around his neck. Smooth as Dee-Ann's homemade ice cream. Soft as his grandma's chenille afghan. And sexy as hell.

The office door opened, and Mrs. Beaumont walked in, waving a printout. "How about these dishes, Jenni Beth? I think they'd be perfect for a summer wedding."

The two staggered away from each other so fast he probably would have fallen had the chair not been directly behind him.

"Oh, hello, Cole," Sue Ellen Beaumont greeted. "I didn't realize you were still here." She patted his cheek.

He met Jenni Beth's gaze. Her mom had to have seen the two of them crawling all over each other through the glass doors. *Awkward* echoed through his brain with guilt nipping at its heels.

Sue Ellen dropped onto the settee and patted the space beside her. "Sit down, dear, and tell me what you think."

Without blinking an eye, Jenni Beth did as told and listened intently while her mother ran over the dishes' pros and their price. Cole was impressed. Both women apparently had a knack for glazing over uncomfortable situations. Then again, they were bred south of the Mason-Dixon Line. Maybe it was in their DNA.

As for himself, he couldn't decide whether to stay or tuck tail and run. Did they expect him to voice his opinion on the dishes—a real find in his mind—or stay out of the discussion and let them work it out?

Survival instincts kicked in, and he knew exactly what he wanted to do. He wanted to run.

"Order them," he heard Jenni Beth say. "The fact that they come with all the serving pieces makes them ideal. With the pink roses in the design, we'll be able to pair them with Grandma Elizabeth's set. A service for twenty-four becomes a service for forty-eight. Any more than that, the bridal party will have to make its own arrangements with the caterer or go with disposable."

Smart, Cole thought again. He had to hand it to her. She had her head on straight and made decisions with that big brain of hers rather than with emotion. But then, she was a businesswoman—or, at least, that was one of the hats she wore.

"Will do, honey." Sue Ellen rose from the love seat. "Okay, children, go back to what you were doing."

Cole felt himself turn crimson from head to toe. A sideways glance at Jenni Beth assured him she shared his embarrassment, ounce for ounce.

Sue Ellen, on the other hand, showed no such reaction. She kissed her daughter's cheek and patted the hand Cole rested on the mantel. "Have fun, but be careful."

He almost swallowed his tongue as the door closed behind her. He and Jenni Beth nearly collapsed with restrained laughter.

"That probably shouldn't have happened," he said.

"No, it shouldn't have," Jenni Beth agreed.

"Never again," he said, just before he drew her into his arms and kissed her again. Once.

Then he turned tail and ran.

Dazed, Jenni Beth dropped into the cozy arm chair, a finger to her lips. She'd thought she'd loved Cole at sixteen. That was nothing compared to what she felt now. A single taste was enough to send her into a tailspin.

Cole. So totally unpredictable. What should she do about him? If only he'd stayed in Savannah where he belonged.

He hadn't been her first. She'd lost her virginity in college. But Cole Bryson *had* been the first—and last—to whom she'd given her heart.

Tansy had tried to warn her.

She rubbed at her forehead.

She'd be okay. She didn't need him or any other man to make her happy. She could do that herself. Her happiness, or lack of it, was her responsibility, not Cole's.

Mocking herself, she laughed wryly. A wedding planner who didn't believe in love?

No. That wasn't the case. She *did* believe in love and marriage. In dreams of forever. And she really, really wanted to be part of a bride and groom's special day. She wanted to make a couple's commitment to each other a celebration they'd remember for a lifetime because, darn it, Magnolia House brides wouldn't get divorced. They would, indeed, be happy forever after.

But those dreams didn't hold true for her.

Chapter 23

COLE HAD RETURNED TO SAVANNAH. RESTLESS, JENNI Beth puttered around helping with some painting and cleaning up for the guys.

"Has anybody seen Beck?"

One of the guys looked up from the tile backsplash he was installing in the kitchen. "Last time I saw him he was working on the gutter system."

"Thanks."

She hurried outside and saw him at the top of a ladder. "Beck?"

"Yeah?"

"I'm going to Savannah. Just an overnighter."

"Excellent. It'll do you good to get away."

"If you need anything—"

"I'll give you a call or talk to your dad."

"Okay, thanks."

"Tell Cole I said hello."

Her head snapped up. "What makes you think—"

"Don't even go there, honey. I've got eyes and ears. Tell him he'd better treat you right, or he'll have me to answer to."

She smiled slowly. "Love you, Beck."

"Love you, too. Now go. Get out of here and have fun."

Within half an hour she was packed and heading down the drive. Because of the upcoming wedding, she couldn't stay more than a single night, but it would be good to see her friends again. And yes, Cole.

She couldn't wait to see Traditions.

Excitement bubbled in her.

Atlanta might be considered the capital of the South, but Savannah was definitely its brightest jewel. Genteel and full of tradition, it soothed the soul.

Founded by General James Oglethorpe in 1733, the city had come within a hairsbreadth of destruction during the Civil War. But even Sherman, after seeing the beauty of the city, had been unable to destroy it. Instead, he'd sent President Lincoln a telegraph presenting him the city as a Christmas gift.

And thank God for that.

Jenni Beth loved Savannah with its uneven brick sidewalks, the Victorian houses, Forsythe Park and its fountain. The Riverside at the Cotton Factor. Pecan pie and all things Southern. As far as she was concerned, Savannah was the center of the universe.

So much had changed since her great-great-great-great-grandfather had made this trip, delivering his bales to the cotton factors at the riverside warehouses before they made their trip downriver.

Money had been no problem for the Beaumonts. Then. It sure as heck was now. Doubt crept in. Again. The renovation was nearly finished, at least the first stage, but the question still remained: would they get enough business to pay for it?

She prayed Stella and Steve's wedding would go off without a hitch. She still needed a tent, though, just in case the old "rain, rain, go away" chant didn't work. If she had to borrow or steal—she'd already begged—she'd find the money for one.

Running a hand over her Corvette's steering wheel, she wondered if maybe she should take Tommy up on his offer to buy the car. The money would go a long way toward finishing the job. Oh, but she hated to part with her beauty. Still, if she had to… She prayed it wouldn't come to that.

Stella and her Bear were a gift. Their wedding would cover the paint job she'd had done on the outside of the house. And, oh, what a difference the fresh coat made! The old house smiled again and would look beautiful in Stella's wedding photos.

With that covered, she could use the loan money she'd earmarked for paint to buy new ballroom drapes and maybe refinish that floor.

Everything had been stretched that little bit tighter to cover Ms. Hattie's repairs, but she'd make it work. One way or another.

Jenni Beth turned onto one of Savannah's side streets. She'd missed the city's hustle and bustle.

While she was here, she fully intended to visit Leopold's for ice cream along with the bakery on her old street for a slice of hummingbird cake, calories be damned.

But she loved Misty Bottoms, too. Two completely different places, different auras. And each held a piece of her heart. After dropping off her overnight bag at the apartment she'd once shared with her friend Molly, she freshened up and drove down streets canopied by live oaks to the small restaurant on East River Street. It felt good to be dressed in city clothes again and doing lunch.

Walking through the door, she found Molly and Hal already there.

While they ate, they caught up on each other's lives. "How's the reno coming along?" Molly asked.

"Great, thanks to a whole lot of help from Cole and Beck."

"Cole Bryson?" Hal fanned himself. "That boy is hot, hot, hot."

"Yes, he is." Jenni Beth grinned at Hal.

"Is he taken?"

She opened her mouth but stumbled, unsure how to answer that. "Um, you know, Cole plays for the other team, Hal."

"You're sure?"

"Very sure."

Hal's eyes narrowed. "You're blushin', sugar."

"No, I'm not."

"You most certainly are. Isn't she, Mol?"

Her friend laughed. "You're beet red."

"Which," Hal pointed out, "leads me to believe you know of what you speak."

"I do." She smiled.

"Is he a good kisser? Those lips…" Hal crossed his hands over his heart.

"He's the absolute best kisser. Ever."

"Now you're gloatin'."

After lunch, her friends went back to work, and Jenni Beth decided the time had come for her maiden voyage to Traditions. Hopefully she'd find something to use on the front porch. Cole had promised to haul anything she bought back to Misty Bottoms on his next trip.

As she turned onto his street, she wondered how she'd missed Traditions when she'd lived here. The building took up half the city block.

Stepping through the ten-foot-tall double doors, she blinked in the dim light. Two stories and a mezzanine, completely filled with treasures, spread out in front of her.

Wow.

Cole stood at the counter, paperwork spread in front of him. At the tinkle of the bell over the door, he looked up, his face lighting with a broad grin.

He needed a shave; he'd never looked better.

"Welcome to Traditions, sugar."

He crossed to her and caught her up in a hug.

"I'm wondering if the appropriate reaction is to bow down to you. I stand in awe."

He laughed. "I'm not one to say I told you so, but I believe I did tell you you'd like my store."

"Like? Such a pathetically weak word to describe what I'm feeling right now. I could spend a week in here and still probably not see everything."

Right inside the front door, Esmeralda, the fortune teller machine, welcomed her. "I love her! She makes me think of *Big*, the Tom Hanks movie." Running a reverent hand over the carved wood, she asked, "Where did you find her?"

"At an estate sale. I'm kind of hopin' she never sells. We've grown rather fond of each other."

"I'll bet."

Everywhere she looked, Jenni Beth saw more treasures. Lights of all shapes and sizes hung from the high ceiling. The second-floor mezzanine begged to be explored. A door leaned against the wall, resplendent with old knockers that had been mounted on it. One in the shape of a yellow rooster called to her, and she knew she'd be taking it home. It might be nice at the bottom of the attic stairs.

Mantels, fireplace inserts, display cases crammed with hinges, keys, and drawer pulls. Doors and windows, tile, newel posts. Brass, copper, and silver. Overwhelming.

"How do you keep track of all this?"

"Computer inventory. We'd be lost without it."

She glanced at the clutter that spilled over the counter and the shelves behind it and didn't doubt that for a second.

"How can you stand it, Cole? Don't you want to build a house around all this?"

"Hah! I already have. I've incorporated a lot of salvaged material in both my places, the one here in the city and the one at home."

Home, she thought. He still called Misty Bottoms home. The place had a way of seeping into the blood.

"Where are you stayin'?"

"With Molly. She hasn't found a new roommate yet, so my old bedroom is empty. I think she's still hoping I'll move back."

"Not much chance of that."

She shook her head. "No. I intend to make my wedding business a success. A huge success."

"Then you will."

His absolute certainty in her humbled her. She covered with, "Can I wander around?"

"You bet. That's what we're all about."

As she headed for the stairs, he said, "I've practically begged you to come and now that you're here, I have to run across town. If you see anything you want, have Mickey tag it. How about I pick you up at six? We can grab a bite, take in a little bit of the city. It's supposed to be a nice night for a stroll."

Oh yes. She'd like that.

—◦◦◦—

Cole rang the doorbell right on the dot of six.

"Molly, can you get that?" Jenni Beth asked.

"You bet."

Even though she'd only brought a couple outfits, she'd managed to change her mind for the third time about what to wear.

She piled her hair into a messy updo and slipped into a little red silk tank dress, long, black flapper-style beaded necklace and earrings, and snake-print pumps. When she stepped into the living room and saw his face, she knew she'd chosen well.

"Every man we run into tonight will envy me." He held out a hand, spun her in a circle. "Yes, ma'am, you look great comin' and goin'."

"You don't look too shabby yourself." In fact, he practically made her salivate. She rarely saw him dressed up. Tonight he wore gray slacks with a black shirt and tie. It would be a real test of discipline to see whether she could keep her hands off him.

Nodding at her shoes, he asked, "Can you walk in those? Thought we might walk along the river."

"I could run a marathon in these."

"Good enough. I don't know how you women do it, but I'm not going to quarrel because the view is spectacular."

His eyes swept up her legs, and she fought the urge to fan herself.

"Come back to my bedroom with me. I want to show you something." She slid her fingers beneath his necktie and led him down the hall.

He gulped. "Ah, is Molly leavin'?"

She shook her head.

One step inside her room, he stopped, puzzled. Nose in the air, he breathed deeply.

"Dang, this room smells good. It smells like you." He walked to her and buried his face in her neck. His hands ran up and down her bare arms and goose bumps popped up.

"Maybe instead of us goin' anywhere, I could give Molly some money. Send *her* out to dinner."

With a laugh, she shook her head and pulled away. "Huh-uh. You promised me a night on the town, Sir Galahad, and I aim to collect."

"So why'd you bring me back here?" His voice had grown husky.

"This." She pointed at an old trunk near the window.

"This is what you wanted to show me?" His gaze drifted from it to the double bed to her face. When their eyes met, his had gone deep and dark. Sleepy and sexy.

She decided her light-headedness could be blamed on a lack of oxygen because she'd totally forgotten to breathe.

"The trunk was my grandma's. It held her trousseau when she moved into Magnolia House as a new bride. I couldn't squeeze it into the miniscule U-Haul I rented, so I left it with Molly. Do you think you could take it to Misty Bottoms on your next trip home?"

The look he sent her was pure male frustration.

"I miss having it with me."

On a half-laugh, he said, "Sure."

Taking her hand in his, he held it up. Studied the pinky. "You've got me pretty much wrapped around this little finger, don't you?"

"No," she said. "But I'm working on it."

He laughed, full-out this time. "You're positive you don't want to stay in and play?"

She nodded.

"Okay, let's go. I made reservations."

Chapter 24

THE AMBIENCE, THE FOOD, THE COMPANY, ALL PERFECT. Total bliss.

Jenni Beth folded her napkin and laid it on the table beside her plate. "Thank you, Cole. I can't tell you how much I enjoyed this. Away from the renovation mess. A little city time. Quiet time with you." She traced a fingertip over the lace tablecloth.

He nodded, wondering if a person could truly get lost in another's eyes. If so, he was in danger because those eyes drew him in and threatened to swallow him.

Reaching across the table, he took her hand in his, wove their fingers together. "The night's not over yet."

"Don't you have to work tomorrow?"

"I'm the boss, remember? If I'm a little late, nobody's gonna dock my pay." He raised their hands to his lips, kissed the back of hers. "Let's go dancin'."

"Dancing?"

He nodded. He loved to dance, and he needed, in the worst way, to get this woman back in his arms. Someone had once told him dancing was like making love when you were with the right woman. He knew from Chateau Rouge that was almost true.

"Remember, we aren't a couple, Cole. We're—" She waved a hand in the air. "We're two friends out to dinner."

"Do you still really believe that?"

Her tongue darted out to wet suddenly dry lips,

and his eyes drank in the movement. He longed to take that mouth in his, wanted his tongue moving over those lips.

"After that night at my house? We've moved way beyond friendship, and you know it," he said quietly.

Panic flared in her eyes, and he actually relaxed. Their history made her reticent, but the heat was there. The knowledge was there.

"I don't know what to say."

"Say yes, sugar."

"Yes, sugar." A mischievous grin lifted the corners of her mouth.

He took care of the bill and held out a hand. "I know a great little place. You'll love it."

A block away, he drew her inside. The club was jumping. Raw energy filled every inch from the carved bar to the band's stage to the tables jam-packed into the space. Still, the maître d' managed to find a table for two in a dark corner.

After placing their drink order, he led her to the dance floor. Holding her close, he nuzzled her neck and said a prayer of thanks when she pressed closer. Working his way to her ear, he whispered, "You know we're gonna do this tonight, don't you? I need you so badly I can hardly think straight."

She nodded, and then turned her head to press a kiss at the base of his neck, a kiss that worked its way right down to his very core.

"I promise it'll be good, darlin'. It'll be slow and easy and hot tonight. I want to touch, to taste every inch of you."

Oh boy. She nearly melted.

"I need to call Molly."

"You do that, and I'll bring the truck around."

As she stood on the sidewalk in front of the nightclub, she placed her call and wondered if she was doing the right thing. He'd crawled into her head, into her heart. Heck, he'd always been there. She'd thought one more taste of him would be enough. Not so. The night at his house had made her hungrier, made her want more.

So she'd take tonight. What could it hurt?

It would be like one more of Kitty's éclairs before she went on a diet.

She snorted. Comparing Cole to a chocolate éclair? As much as she loved chocolate…

Her friend answered.

"Mol? I… Plans have changed." She cleared her throat. "I won't be home tonight."

"Am I supposed to act surprised? I can if you want me to."

"You didn't know," Jenni Beth argued.

"Oh, come on. The air in here practically sizzled when the two of you touched. I half expected my drapes to go up in flames. Considered grabbing the fire extinguisher, just in case. Girl Scout training. Juliette Gordon Low would be proud of me."

"You are so full of it."

"Yeah, maybe. But you two are only fooling yourselves. Nobody else is buying the nothing-real-is-happening-here."

"Blah, blah, blah," Jenni Beth said.

Molly laughed. "So why are you still talking to me? Go jump that man's bones. Enjoy."

She hung up as Cole's big black truck slid to the curb.

He hopped out and came around the front to open her door. Good old Southern courtesy. And no matter how hard she fought for the independent, can-do-anything woman, little things like a man holding a door for a woman still meant a lot.

The streets were dark and nearly deserted, giving an even greater sense of intimacy and urgency. Neither even attempted small talk.

He turned onto his street, and Jenni Beth felt her chest grow tighter. The truck had barely rocked to a stop before he tugged her out. Laughing, they raced up the curved wrought-iron stairs and into the brick building that housed his condo.

"Top floor," he mouthed. "But it's only four stories up."

He never let loose of her hand as they took the stairs. By the third set, she tugged at his. "Hold on. One second." She struggled for air. "I don't consider myself out of shape, but the pace is a little brisk."

"Sorry." He bent and leaned his forehead against hers. His lips captured hers. One kiss led to another.

When he reluctantly pulled away, she said, "I might be more out of breath now than I was before."

"Good!" He laughed. "Want me to carry you up the last flight?"

"Not in this life, buster. I'll make it on my own two feet…or die trying."

It was worth it, she thought, as she stepped into his condo and moved to the window.

"Come here." He led her to another, shorter flight of stairs.

They stepped out onto a large private deck with panoramic views of downtown Savannah. It spread before them, lights twinkling. He wrapped his arms around her from the back, trailed kissed along her neck, her shoulders.

"I can't wait any longer."

"Me neither," she whispered, turning into him.

His hands ran down her arms before moving to capture her silk-covered breasts.

She worked at the buttons on his shirt.

Not sure how he did it, she gasped as her dress slid off, the night breeze caressing her skin as she stood before him in only two small wisps of lace and her heels.

He swallowed as he took her in. "I have no words."

Scooping her up, he followed her onto a chaise.

The moon shadowed them as they lost the last of their clothing, as they explored one another, as they joined and lost themselves.

They fell asleep curled into each other.

His light kiss on the top of her head woke her. Opening her eyes, she smiled sleepily at him. The moon had traveled high overhead, and stars scattered through the heavens.

She sighed and snuggled closer.

"We should probably move inside."

She nodded.

When he kissed her, her head scrambled to catch up to her heart. She gave in and simply let her body go. Again.

An hour later, they made the trek down the stairs.

"Hungry? Thirsty?" he asked.

"Thirsty."

She followed him through the living room with its beautiful old fireplace, took in the high ceilings with their crown molding, the hardwood floors.

Spying the master bedroom, she stuck her head inside the door. Another fireplace, more crown molding, and a grand old four-poster bed.

This place, so unlike his barn in Misty Bottoms, was also totally Cole, though. He belonged in both worlds, suited them equally well.

The kitchen? A dream. Small, but oh, so workable. Stainless steel appliances, a wine chiller, granite countertops. The ultimate bachelor kitchen. Heck, what was she thinking? Any man *or* woman would totally fall in love with every inch of this place.

He opened a bottle of water, guzzled half of it, and handed her the rest.

Leaning against the counter, he slipped an arm around her waist and tugged her against him.

"I can't get enough of you, sugar. Can't keep my hands off you."

"Personally, I can't think of a better problem to have."

"Let's try out the bed this time."

They stumbled from the kitchen and into his bedroom, where they gave the four-poster quite a workout.

―――ᨆᨆ―――

Bright sunlight streamed through the windows when she opened her eyes. She should be tired. She wasn't. Instead an energy she hadn't known she possessed held her in its grip.

Cole snuggled against her, and Jenni Beth grinned. She hadn't imagined him a cuddler. Had actually wondered—momentarily—if she'd wake to find an empty bed. A note. That he'd gone to work or whatever.

But he'd stayed.

Slowly, methodically, his index finger traced along her bare thigh, down, then up, sending frissons of desire through her.

So he was awake, too.

She turned in his arms, her lips meeting his. Nothing better than morning sex.

The kiss deepened, and his hands moved higher.

Her phone rang.

Cole nipped her lip. "Ignore it."

It rang again and again.

She sighed. "I can't."

He flopped onto his back, an arm thrown across his eyes as she reached for her purse and found her phone.

"Tell whoever it is that I hate them," he muttered.

She laughed. "Hello?"

"Jenni Beth? This is Stella."

"Stella?" Glancing at the clock, she sat up, hugging the sheet around herself.

Cole rolled to his side and gave her a questioning look. She shrugged and nearly lost her grip on the sheet. He reached over, tugged at it, and took a quick peek.

Heat rushing through her, she slapped his hand. "Is something wrong, Stella? You sound upset."

"I'm so sorry."

"About what?" Foreboding colored her words.

"Well, you know," Stella said uncertainly. "That the plans have changed."

Warning bells clamored in Jenni Beth's head, and she swung her bare legs over the side of the bed. *No!* "What plans?"

"*Our* plans. To have our wedding in your rose garden. At Magnolia House."

Jenni Beth swore every drop of blood drained from her·face. "I don't understand."

By this time, Cole had pulled on a pair of sweats and dropped onto the side of the bed, studying her. "Problem?"

She nodded, fighting back the panic that unfurled inside her. "Can I ask, Stella, why you've changed your mind?"

"I didn't," the bride answered slowly. "Your assistant called last night and explained what had happened."

"Stella, I don't have an assistant."

Cole's forehead creased, but she held up a finger in a just-a-minute gesture.

"But she called me," Stella insisted. "I would have called last night, but, well, it was so late, and I figured you'd be so upset."

Stomach churning, almost afraid to ask, Jenni Beth forced out the words. "What exactly did my assistant tell you?"

"Well, gee, you know. That your rose garden had been destroyed. Those kids came in and tore out all your bushes. I can't tell you how sorry I am."

Jenni Beth heard a sob on the other end of the line.

"It was so beautiful," Stella cried, "and I wanted to marry my Bear there."

For what seemed a millennium, Jenni Beth's mind simply froze up. She couldn't process what she'd heard. She rubbed at her eyes, her forehead, aware that Cole sat quietly beside her, running an anxious hand over her sheet-covered leg.

Finally, she said quietly, "Stella, it still will be perfect. The rose garden is fine. I don't know who called you, but—" She stopped herself, met Cole's steady gaze, and drew strength from him.

Not wanting to scare her first bride or embroil her in any ugly mess, she crossed her fingers and lied. "My friend likes to play practical jokes. My guess is she's behind this."

"A joke? Honestly? I don't think it was very funny."

"No. It wasn't, and I intend to call her the minute we hang up."

"She told me not to call you."

"I'm sure she did, but I can't tell you how glad I am you didn't listen to her." She tipped her head and stared up at the bedroom ceiling, rubbed again at the beginning of what she was certain would be a massive headache. "Everything will be gorgeous for your wedding. I can't wait."

"Me neither. You know her from college?"

"Who?" She felt like she'd fallen down Alice's rabbit hole.

"Your friend."

"Why would you ask that?"

"Well, I don't mean to stereotype or anything, but she didn't, you know, have that little Southern drawl you have."

"Really?"

"You know. She's got that New Jersey thing happening."

Jenni Beth fought the anger. "Oh. Sure. I've gotten so used to it that I forget sometimes."

Pia D'Amato had made that call. Why? Her headache budded, bloomed.

Tempted to pepper the bride with questions, she fought the urge. Causing the bride stress was just bad business, and airing the dirty laundry that someone was out to sabotage Magnolia House might scare her away. After a few more assurances, she clicked off and tossed her phone on the nightstand.

"I need to go back to Misty Bottoms."

"I gathered that. Grab a quick shower and get dressed. I'll take you to Clary's first."

Shaking her head, she opened her mouth to disagree.

"Huh-uh. I'm not sendin' you home without breakfast. Besides I want all the details, and you can share them with me over a plate of corned-beef hash. Talkin' about it will settle your nerves."

She watched him leave the room, all rumpled and sexy, and prayed he'd gone for coffee. She needed a gallon—for a starter.

Why would Pia do this? She barely knew the woman, had spoken to her once in person and a couple more times over the phone to firm up the flower order for Stella's wedding.

There had to be something more.

But she'd bide her time. Cole was right. She needed a shower and food. Between last night and this morning, they'd worked off a week's supply of calories.

And right now they should be making lazy love in that wonderful bed of his. Instead she was angry and hurt. She wanted to cry. But tears were weak and useless. She'd shed so many this past year and a half, and they'd done no good.

A quick call to Charlotte affirmed all was well at home. She kept it casual, didn't mention Stella's call.

Hanging up, she grabbed the clothes scattered over the floor and headed into the bath.

The shower, with its multiple heads, almost melted her bones. She stood under the spray and let it loosen her tense muscles. Talk about a morning imploding in the blink of an eye.

When she opened the shower door, she smiled like an idiot. Cole stood there, a towel in one hand, a mug of coffee in the other.

"Which would you like first?"

She opted for the coffee.

"Oh, I'm not sure anything has ever tasted this good."

"I can think of something." He dropped the towel to the floor, reached behind her and turned the shower back on. Hand on her hip, he followed her beneath the spray.

When they finally made it to Clary's, the morning rush was over. Seated at a small table, she exhaled deeply. She'd missed this place with its worn brick and dark green walls, its large counter, its down-home feel and friendly people.

Cole had nearly finished his first cup of coffee when he asked, "So what happened, sweetheart?"

She blinked, muscling aside the tears that even now threatened, and told him about Stella's call.

"Pia D'Amato," he said when she mentioned the Jersey accent.

"How did you know?"

"I ordered flowers for Mom, to thank her for the lasagna. Pia doesn't fit in Misty Bottoms. You have to ask yourself what she's doing there."

Jenni Beth toyed with her food, apologized to the waitress, and gladly accepted a to-go box. Later, she might be able to eat. Right now, she needed to be home.

After a quick stop at Molly's for her overnighter, she headed north to Misty Bottoms, straight into the eye of the hurricane.

—⁓—

"Mickey? Can you handle things at the shop for a couple hours?"

"Yeah, sure. It's a slow morning."

Cole hung up. Slow? Not from where he stood. Things were heating up and quickly.

Clary's would have been the time to come clean with Jenni Beth. To tell her about Richard and his suspicions. But all he had were suspicions. He needed more.

Determined to find it, he sat down at his computer. Come hell or high water, he'd get to the bottom of this. Whoever was behind these shenanigans had definitely taken off the gloves.

Well, so had he.

Chapter 25

JENNI BETH SCROLLED THROUGH HER CONTACT LIST, found Pia's number, and called her. She had absolutely no idea how to handle this mess and could come up with no good reason for Pia to have made a move like that.

Still second-guessing herself, she heard Pia answer.

"Bella Fiore."

"Hey, Pia, Jenni Beth here. Um, have you talked to Stella recently?"

"Next week's bride?"

"Yes."

"No, I sure haven't. Has she changed her mind about the flowers?"

"No, she hasn't. You didn't call her yesterday or last night?"

"No, I've never spoken with her. You've been the middleman."

If Pia was lying, she was darned good at it.

"Is there a problem?"

"This is awkward. Somebody called to tell her the rose garden had been destroyed. That we couldn't host her wedding at Magnolia House."

"Oh no, Jenni Beth, I'm so sorry. When did that happen?"

"It didn't."

"But—" Pia hesitated. "I'm confused."

"That makes two of us."

"So, nothing's wrong?"

Jenni Beth wasn't so sure of that, but she said, "No, I guess not. I reassured Stella, and we're good. Everything okay on your end?"

"Absolutely. Her flowers are ordered and my supplier promised them on Thursday, which gives me plenty of time to finish the arrangements."

When she hung up, Jenni Beth was as confused as before. Had Pia made the call to Stella? If so, why? If not, could the accent simply be a coincidence?

She had a hard time swallowing that.

Jenni Beth had enjoyed Savannah, had more than enjoyed her time with Cole. Just thinking about him sent her body into spasms of ecstasy. So easy in his own body, the man had no problem navigating a woman's, either.

And now? Time to see what was going on at home.

The minute she stopped her car in the drive, she hopped out and raced to the rose garden. The scent hit her as she rounded the corner. And there it was in all its glory.

A huge sigh of relief escaped.

A small piece of her had been so afraid the phone call hadn't been a hoax.

But everything was okay.

Hurrying inside, Jenni Beth hugged her mom, dad, and Charlotte before giving them an abridged and carefully edited version of her trip. She left out her sleepover with Cole as well as the phone call that had brought her running home early.

Thanking Charlotte, she accepted a glass of sweet tea and carried it with her to the attic, her mind swirling with everything that had happened and with all the things she still needed to do for Magnolia House's first wedding.

If she'd learned anything from this whole experience, it was that she couldn't do it on her own. She'd gone into this with no partners and no backup. Had risked everything and felt all alone.

Somewhere along the line that had changed. Oh, the ultimate responsibility for the success or failure of Magnolia Brides rested on her shoulders. The decisions were still ultimately hers. But Cole and Beck had stepped up to the plate and helped her make her dream a reality.

Could she have done it by herself? She'd like to think so. Liked to think she could have hired and supervised a crew. Could have made the correct decisions on replacing all or part of the siding, on the best way to sand and stain the hardwood floors.

Truth, though? She didn't know. And because they were such great friends, she hadn't had to find out.

Wandering over to the board for next weekend's wedding, she studied the printout of the photos Stella'd emailed her. Front, back, and side views of her dress. Ideas for flowers, for the cake. Jenni Beth had taped up color chips and fabric swatches to use in the decorations. Pia had sent mock-ups of the flower arrangements.

Lists covered every surface. In longhand, on the computer, and scrawled on Post-its. They were her life and always had been. Carefully she went through them again, making sure nothing had been neglected or forgotten.

By the time she finished, she'd come to the realization she'd need help on the actual day of the wedding. Charlotte had offered, as had her mom, but even with what they could do, she'd need someone else because, although they wouldn't actually be eating here, there would be the cake, champagne, taped music to cue, and on and on. The list boggled her mind.

At Chateau Rouge, she'd had staff already in place. Not so at Chateau Magnolia.

She called Luanna and explained her situation. "I know it's short notice, but do you think Dee-Ann would give you the day off to work the wedding? I'll pay you two times what you make at the diner."

"Two times?"

"Yes." She winced, but it was the price of doing business. "Absolutely. I need you."

"I'm already off Saturday, and the answer is yes. I'm your girl."

"Bless you. I could really use another one or maybe even two more assistants, so if you know anyone—"

"I do."

"Okay, great. Call them, see if they can work, and get back to me. But be sure they understand that if they agree to come in for this, they can't back out. No excuses. No sick babies or cranky husbands. I need to be able to count on them. There're going to be a lot more weddings here at Magnolia House, and I'll need help at every one of them."

With a mouthed "yes" and a fist pump, she checked that item off her to-do list. The cake and flowers were ordered and a couple of Beck's men were constructing a temporary outside dance floor. Even though the reception itself would be held at Duffy's Pub, the couple wanted their first dance as husband and wife to be here.

Jenni Beth wanted that, too.

Sooner or later, they'd need a moveable dance floor

anyway. The guys had decided to make it in sections so that after the wedding it could be torn down and stored till the next time it was needed. Charlie had come up with the design, and it was a humdinger. The man was incredibly talented, and she wondered vaguely if Beck paid him enough. Or if *she* paid him enough.

Her mind switched back to the big picture. Once things got rolling on Saturday, there was one person she'd want beside her, one person she'd want to share the day with—other than Cole.

Tansy Calhoun. A slight problem with that, though. Now Tansy Forbes, she lived a three hours' drive from here.

Bigger problem? *Mr*. Forbes. The biggest jerk Jenni Beth had ever had the displeasure of meeting.

At first, she'd tried to convince herself she disliked him out of loyalty to Beck, but it was more than that. It was the man himself.

Without giving herself any more time to think about it, Jenni Beth called her. "Tanz? Do you think you might be able to come home for a few days? I haven't seen you in forever, and, well, I could really use some help."

"On the house?"

"No, with my first wedding!" Excitedly, she filled Tansy in. "I'd love to have you here to share it."

In the background, Jenni Beth heard the jerk hollering at his wife to get off the phone. He needed a fresh cup of coffee. His had grown cold.

"Jenni Beth, I'd love to help, but things are…unsettled here. I can't make any promises."

"Why do you put up with that?"

"He's my husband."

And she hung up.

Jenni Beth clicked off and wondered what had happened to the Tansy Calhoun she'd grown up with. Like a beaten dog, she cowered at her husband's commands.

The last time she'd seen Tansy, her friend had been stick-thin and grim-faced. None of the spark that used to shine from her golden eyes had survived.

She'd pleaded with her to leave Emerson, to come home. But Tansy was nothing if not loyal. How good could it be, though, to raise a young girl in a home so completely dominated by that man? What kind of warped view of the male/female relationship would it foster in Gracie?

Well, she guessed she could add that to the list of things to keep her awake at night.

But it sure wouldn't tonight. While she'd worried about Tansy, the sky outside had gone completely dark.

Too tired to even go downstairs to raid the refrigerator, she pulled off her clothes and fell into bed. A smile tugged at the corners of her mouth as she remembered exactly why she hadn't gotten much sleep last night.

Too bad she'd woken up to such a mess. Tomorrow had to be better.

Chapter 26

It had been six days since she'd seen Cole, six days since they'd kissed, touched, made love, and she craved him. Still, with the wedding coming up, the time had passed quickly. Even though he hadn't been able to make it home, he'd called every single day and again right at bedtime. A smile spread over her face remembering last night's conversation. The man should be locked up.

The sun barely peeked through her window, and she brushed a strand of hair back from her face. Wanting to catch another hour of sleep, she pulled the covers over her head and added a couple more things to her mental to-do list.

She yawned. They'd wait, though—till the rest of the civilized world woke.

When she finally crawled out of bed nearly two hours later, she wandered into the bath for a quick wake-me-up shower. Tossing on a pair of shorts and an old T-shirt, she slipped her feet into neon pink rubber flip-flops and raced down the stairs and back to the kitchen for the first cup of life-giving coffee.

"You sure look chipper this mornin'," Charlotte said.

"I feel chipper." She slid into a chair at the kitchen table. "I'm exactly where I'm meant to be. Right here at Magnolia House. The trip last week to Savannah did me a lot of good and lunch with my friends was nice, but I'm glad to be home."

She looked up as Charlotte spread peanut butter on toast for her. "You don't need to do that. I'm a big girl. I can make my own toast."

"I know. But I missed you while you were gone. Oh, not last week," she said, those big brown eyes looking sad. "The years you lived in Savannah. The house was empty without you."

"Oh, Charlotte, I love you." She threw her arms around the woman who had always been there to listen to her, to make her feel better no matter how lousy the day had been.

Chewing a bite of her toast, she said, "You and I need to take a trip to Cole's place one of these days. We'll talk Mama into going along and make it a girls' day. You wouldn't believe his shop. It's like wandering into Aladdin's Castle."

"You found some real treasure, huh?"

Whew. Hadn't she just. The best of it hadn't been inside Traditions, though. She blushed and Charlotte laughed.

"You don't need to say any more, little girl."

She cleared her throat. "I'll finish the garden area today. It'll need one final go-through before Saturday, but I can roust most of the weeds and get the bushes trimmed up. If anybody calls or if Mama or Daddy needs me, that's where I'll be."

"Take a bottle of water along. It's gonna be hot, and you need to stay hydrated."

"Yes, ma'am."

She finished her breakfast, then headed out to the shed for her tools. What a fantastic morning. After all the hours she and the guys had put in, she felt more than confident. And with Luanna and a friend or two coming to help?

No worries.

First on her list? Deadheading the roses. Gardening shears in hand, Jenni Beth smiled up at the beautiful blue sky. Wispy white clouds floated across it.

She hugged herself. Although she'd put on a good front, inside she'd been a nervous wreck.

And Cole. She—

"No! No! No!"

The clippers fell to the grass. She closed her eyes, opened them again, her stomach rebelling. Then she simply dropped to her knees.

Every single rosebush had been destroyed, either ripped from the ground and tossed helter-skelter or hacked to pieces. She put a hand to her forehead, the other to her mouth. It couldn't be!

"Why would anyone do this?" Hot tears scalded her cheeks. Message received. The call had been a warning, one she'd ignored. Stella's wedding hadn't been cancelled. The ploy hadn't worked, so someone had taken the next step.

Gasping sobs ripped from her. Slowly, anger seeped in around the edges of pain. Somebody didn't know her very well if they thought she'd simply give in. But damn, damn, and double damn, this hurt. This was personal. Very personal.

This couldn't be fixed with a Band-Aid or a pat on the head.

This was real. Devastating.

She stood and stumbled closer, swiping at the fast-falling tears, her brain rebelling at what she saw. Wanton destruction.

She couldn't let her mother and father see this.

Couldn't let them know someone had come onto their land, their property, and done this while they slept.

Her trembling hand reached into her shorts pocket and, without thought, without debating the wisdom of it, she hit Cole's number.

When he answered, she said, "Where are you? Are you in Savannah?"

"Jenni Beth?"

"I need you."

Fear reached right inside Cole's chest cavity and tightened its fist around his heart. "Are you okay?"

"No." She sobbed. "I mean yes, physically, but… Oh, Cole."

"I'm halfway there already, honey. I drove up after work last night. Give me five minutes."

"Okay. I'm in the garden."

The line went dead.

He tossed his phone on the seat beside him and hit the gas, his heart racing faster than his big black truck as it lapped up the miles.

What had happened to have Jenni Beth calling him in tears? Visions of the worst kind flew in and out of his head. He should have asked about her mom, her dad, Charlotte. If one of them—No, he refused to go there.

He pulled into her drive on a wing and a prayer, his truck sending up a spray of gravel as he stopped. Throwing open the door, he jumped out and raced around the house.

She sat in the grass, her head buried in her arms,

fragile looking. He saw why she'd called and cursed ripely, crossing to her at a fast lope.

"Jenni Beth, I'm here. I'm so sorry. I thought—The phone call. You said—"

Her head lifted and he swore. Stricken. Shattered. "Somebody did this last night." She sniffled, wiped a hand at her tears.

"Any idea who?" He had his own suspicions.

"I don't know. Cole, I can't even think." Her lip quivered, and, blindly, she reached for his hand.

He dropped to the grass beside her and pulled her into his lap. He cradled her as he would a new baby, whispering soothing words and rocking her.

"Grandma Elizabeth planted a lot of these, starting quite a few from her grandmother's clippings. Some were already here when she came as a bride. And now they're gone. All of them. I failed."

"Shhh, it's not your fault."

Cole kissed the top of her head, thumbed away her tears. He hated this, hated not knowing what to say. To do. So he simply drew her closer and held tight.

Five, ten minutes passed before Jenni Beth sighed deeply. "The garden is ruined. Stella's wedding is ruined. Richard wins."

"No." He shook her gently. "Don't say that. Don't even think it."

"We can't host a wedding here. Look at it."

"It'll be fine. Come on." He pulled her to her feet. "We've got work to do."

"What?"

"Do you have any buckets?"

"Buckets?"

"Yes, buckets. Of any kind."

"There're some empty five-gallon paint buckets. Charlie stacked them behind the house."

"Good. I'll get them. You hook up the hose."

"What are you going to do?"

"We'll get as many of these bushes as we can soaking. Keep the roots wet. It's too late for some, but quite a few are salvageable."

She clamped on her wide-brimmed hat and pulled on her leather gloves. Working together, within the hour, they had twenty bushes soaking and, after clipping branches to put in root starter, had hauled the unsalvageable remains to the construction dump area.

"You know who this belongs to?" He whipped a hat out of his back pocket. The well-worn, frayed-edge, olive-green ball cap had "Maudie's Roadkill Restaurant" embroidered on the front.

"I've never seen it before. Why? Where'd you get it?"

"On the ground over there. Figure whoever came to visit last night dropped it." He gripped her arms lightly. "Do you have anything else to do for the wedding?"

"A ton of details to see to, but what difference does any of that make?" Another tear spilled over and trickled down her cheek. "Without a rose garden, there's no wedding, Cole. The best-laid wedding plans. Gone."

"There will be a wedding right here in two days," he said gruffly. "Guests have been invited, flowers and food ordered. Go take a shower and get cleaned up. Do whatever else it is you need to do."

He ran a finger down the side of her face, smudging the dirt that clung there.

"Where are you going?"

"Think I'll take a trip into town. When I come back, we need to talk. Somebody's been trampin' around your bottomland, too."

"What?"

"That's where I was this morning. After that call last week, I thought I'd check it out. Gotta figure it's your new business partner."

"My partner?" Confusion marred her face.

"Richard Thorndike."

If he needed proof she still wasn't firing on all cylinders, he had it when she meekly nodded, and without asking any more questions, headed inside.

Cole rinsed off as best he could with the hose, then walked to the front of the house where he'd left his Ford parked drunkenly at an angle, the driver's door hanging open. He wondered what she'd tell her folks. Thankfully, neither of them was up yet.

Before he drove into town, though, he needed to unload the things he'd brought back from Savannah for Jenni Beth, including the trunk. He laid a hand on top of it. He didn't know what she had stored in it. Maybe bricks.

A truck turned into the lane, and Cole raised a hand to shade his eyes. Beck. Hallelujah. The cavalry had arrived. Crossing his work-booted feet, he leaned against his truck.

"Hey." Beck raised a hand in greeting. "When did you get back into town?"

"Last night. Good thing I did, too. We've got trouble."

"What's goin' on?"

"Did Jenni Beth tell you about the call she got from Stella while she was in Savannah?"

"Yeah." Concern filled Beck's eyes. "But everything was okay."

"Till this mornin'," Cole bit out, his fists bunching. "Somebody destroyed the entire rose garden. We're talkin' vandalism on steroids."

Cole walked back with Beck while he checked out the damage for himself.

Beck gave a low whistle. "You think Richard's behind it?"

"I know he is. But he's got help. No way would he dirty his own hands, and this scheme is too big for that numbskull to handle alone."

"Did you call the cops?"

He shook his head. "Not yet. Ever see this?" Pulling the hat from his pocket, he handed it to Beck.

"Yeah. The Stuckey boy wears it. Why?"

"I found it out in the garden."

"Shoot." Beck kicked at a dirt clod. "Jeremy's dad left town about six months ago, and the kid's gotten into one scrape after another since then. His mom's fit to be tied. Can't seem to do anything with him."

"Ralph Stuckey left?"

"Yep. Moved in with some twenty-three-year-old over in Rincon."

"So now his mama's gonna have new grief to deal with. Damn fool kid. I swear if Richard's behind this, I'm gonna pummel him to dust."

"Really? Want me to visit your mama while she copes with the grief that'll cause *her*? You won't be able to help her or Jenni Beth because you'll be behind bars."

Cole glared at his friend.

Beck shrugged. "Just sayin'. Where's Jenni Beth now?"

"Inside cleanin' up. I'm gonna head into town, see if I can find some new roses or somethin'." He pounded the tailgate. "This pisses me off."

Eyes narrowed, he nodded at the trunk. "Want to help me move this inside? It's Jenni Beth's grandma's, and I don't want to take a chance on scratchin' it up."

"Sure."

Cole's conscience groused at him. His friend had agreed too readily. Wait till he lifted this sucker. He'd be crying uncle in the first five feet.

Sure enough, Cole dropped the tailgate, hopped up in the back, and, grunting, slid the trunk toward the edge. Jumping back to the ground, he said, "I think if we each get a grip on the side—"

Both groaned as they took the full weight.

"What the hell's in here?" Beck spread his feet a bit wider as he settled into the weight.

"Don't have a clue, but it damn well better be worth it."

Jenni Beth came to the screen door, hair wet, and dressed in clean clothes. She held the door open. "You brought my trunk. Can you take it up to my room?"

"To the attic?" Cole blinked.

"Yes."

The two men exchanged horrified glances and moved into the front hall.

"I think," Beck said, "it would look great in the parlor. On the first floor."

Cole studied the room off to their right. "Yep, it would be perfect there."

"Not on your life. Upstairs."

"Might be our lives," Cole mumbled as he took the first stair.

Trunk delivered, Cole climbed into his truck and sat behind the wheel for a minute, rolling his shoulders. That thing weighed a ton. But it had brought a smile to Jenni Beth's face.

The look in her eyes, on her face out in the garden haunted him, and the anger built again. One person in Misty Bottoms wanted her to fail badly enough to stoop to something this low, this underhanded.

Too damn bad he couldn't walk into Coastal Plains Savings and Trust and handle this, once and for all, with Richard Thorndike. Beck was right, though. That would get him nothing but a cell in the local jail.

A night spent there would be worth every second if it weren't for the fact he couldn't help Jenni Beth from there. He'd only add more self-reproach to her pile. And, yes, his mama would be awfully upset.

He slid the truck into gear and headed instead to the only florist in town. Pia D'Amato. The new florist with the Jersey accent. Was she in cahoots with Richard? Misty Bottoms was a small, sleepy town. What the heck was going on?

Well, whatever. Maybe Ms. Pia would have some replacement roses. They wouldn't be Jenni Beth's grandma's, but right now, they'd do to keep the wedding on track.

He drove like a bat out of hell, his temper outweighing his good sense. He needed to fix this for Jenni Beth. Afterward, he'd prove Richard culpable. A siren rent the air, and Cole, swearing a blue streak, slammed his fist against the steering wheel. Could the day get any better?

He slowed and pulled onto the shoulder. Checking his rearview mirror, he watched Jimmy Don slip on his wide-brimmed trooper's hat before he moseyed up beside Cole's truck.

He lowered his window. "Hey, Jimmy Don. How are you doin' today?" He reached into his glove box for his registration.

"Better than you, Cole. What're you doin' back in town?"

"Helpin' Jenni Beth Beaumont, Wes's sister. She's renovatin' Magnolia House."

Jimmy Don took the proffered registration and Cole's license. "Heard she's startin' up a weddin' business."

"Yes, sir, she is."

"So why are you in such an all-fired hurry?"

Cole met the trooper's gaze. "Jenni Beth had some trouble at her place last night, and I'm tryin' my best to help her. She's got a wedding comin' up in a couple days."

Jimmy Don's eyes turned steely. "What happened?"

"Somebody tore out her rose garden."

"What?" The sheriff's eyes went big.

"All her grandma's roses and the ones there before her have been destroyed. A very deliberate move to sabotage Jenni Beth's plans. This weekend's bride requested the rose garden for her wedding. Everything's ordered and on track." He spread his hands. "Now? No rose garden."

"Son of a pup," Jimmy Don said. "Why didn't she call me?"

"She should have. Or I should have. To be honest, neither of us was thinkin' very clearly, I guess. But I did take some pictures with my phone."

He pulled them up and handed his cell to the officer.

"You think kids did this?" Jimmy Don asked as he scrolled through them.

"Maybe." Cole handed him the ball cap. "This was left behind."

"That's Jeremy Stuckey's."

"Yep. He probably did the actual damage, but I seriously doubt he was the mastermind. I've got a pretty good idea who was, but I don't have any proof. Not yet. I will, though."

"Don't go doin' nothin' stupid, Cole."

"I won't. You ought to take a ride out there, talk to Jenni Beth about this yourself. You can write up a report, maybe use the cap as leverage to get the kid to talk. In the meantime, I need to find some rosebushes. As soon as we're done here." He nodded toward the cards Jimmy Don still held.

The trooper handed them back to him. "Go on. Get out of here. But slow down. Consider this your official warnin'."

"Thanks." Cole tucked his license into his wallet and put away his registration.

"I'm headin' out to the Beaumonts right now."

Cole watched as Jimmy Don backed up, turned on his lights, and did a U-turn in the road.

Even with everything that had happened that morning, Cole smiled. Jimmy Don loved those lights and that siren. As it turned out, the stop had been advantageous. He hadn't gotten a ticket, and the vandalism at Magnolia House was on record.

But he still had to find—and buy—an entire damn rose garden.

Chapter 27

DRIVING UP CHURCH STREET, COLE SCOWLED AT THE NEW sign outside the flower shop. It seemed strange to see Bella Fiore where Brenda Sue's name used to be. He reminded himself that nothing stayed the same. Change could be good.

Sometimes.

Last night's change in Jenni Beth's garden sure as hell hadn't been for the better.

Hot under the collar, he parked and slammed out of his pickup. He sure hoped the new owner had what he needed.

When he stormed in, a beautiful woman, long black hair curling around a Madison Avenue face, smiled at him. Whew. Full, pouty lips, enough cleavage to make a man drool, and a short little skirt just about guaranteed that any man who walked in the shop would have a rise in his blood pressure and an open wallet.

And yes, he was human. But he had more pressing matters to deal with. Besides, he found he had a preference for blonds with slate-blue eyes.

"Are you the new owner?" he asked, pushing everything but Jenni Beth to the back of his mind.

"I sure am." Bracelets jingled at her wrist as she extended her hand. "What can I do for you?"

Oh, now there was a loaded question delivered with eyes that promised the world. He decided to tread carefully. "I had some flowers sent to my mother, Emma Bryson, last week. She said they were stunning. Thanks."

"You must be Cole."

"I am."

"I'm glad she liked the bouquet."

"Today I'm shopping for rosebushes. Do you carry any?"

"I do. I have a wonderful selection. They're in the side garden." She opened the door and preceded him down the stairs and around the side. "What kind are you looking for?"

Cole scratched his head. "I don't really know."

"Where did you plan to put them?"

By now, they stood surrounded by rosebushes of all kinds.

"They're not actually for me."

"For your mother?"

"Nope, although now that you mention it, I might pick up an extra one for her."

"That would be nice. You're a good son."

"You from Jersey?" He picked his way down an aisle, leaning in to smell some of the roses as he went.

"I am. See any you like?"

"This one." He pointed to a deep red rose. "And maybe this one."

"Both great choices."

"They're goin' to Magnolia House. My friend, Jenni Beth Beaumont, has a wedding this comin' weekend—in her rose garden."

A guarded look came into Pia's eyes and shoved aside the sultry vixen. "Yes, I know Jenni Beth." Pia fingered a leaf on one of the bushes. "I'm doing the flowers for this weekend's wedding. It's her first."

"Yeah. And it's really important things go off without any hiccups. We've unfortunately run into a massive hiccup. Somebody destroyed her rose garden last night."

He watched her face but other than a quick eye blink, she gave nothing away.

"If I catch the bastard who did it, he, or she, is gonna be one sorry SOB." Cole figured he'd said enough. "Anyway, I'll take everything you have in red."

Pia's expression changed. Cole studied her more carefully. Her color came up, and she looked extremely uncomfortable. Her eyes no longer met his.

"You okay?"

"Yes, it's just that, ah, I didn't realize you needed these right away."

"Is there a problem with that?"

"Actually, um, these roses are sold."

"All of them?" Disbelief crept into his words.

She nodded.

"I don't see any sold tags."

She played with a large silver and turquoise ring. "I'm sorry."

"How about the pink ones, the white or yellow ones?"

"They're all sold."

"Why'd you show them to me?"

"I thought you were planning to order some."

"You're kiddin'."

He waited but she said nothing more.

He raised the stakes. "I'll pay you double whatever the askin' price is."

Pia shook her head. "I can't. They're already paid for. What if they come to pick them up before I can get a new delivery?"

"Okay." Mentally, Cole ran through the problem, searched for possible solutions. He didn't for a minute believe the plants were sold. Maybe if he pushed a bit, she'd give. "Who bought them? I'll call and explain the situation."

"I don't have a name, and I don't know the people here in Misty Bottoms all that well yet."

"A sale this big and you don't know who bought them?" He swept a hand, encompassing her display of roses.

"It was a developer."

"What name was on the check, the credit card?"

"He paid cash." She leaned down and pulled off a dead rose. "Honestly, I'd love to help Jenni Beth, but I can't."

Cole stared at her, but Pia refused to meet his eyes. His jaw tightened. "I hate to come right out and say I don't believe you, but I don't believe you."

Her back stiffened. "I'm sorry you feel that way."

"Are you? I wonder." He stuffed his hands in his jeans pockets. "Well, thanks for nothin'. I hope that developer gets back here soon to pick up this odd assortment of bushes. Strange that he'd go with such a variety."

Pia shrugged. "Everyone has different tastes."

"Isn't that the truth? When you talk to Richard, tell him I'll be around to see him. Soon."

He ignored her surprised gasp and walked around to the front of the shop.

He couldn't remember ever being so angry. He was so furious he actually shook from it. Damned if he'd let them destroy Jenni Beth.

Inside his truck, he picked up his cell and started making calls.

———∿∿∿———

"Slow down, Kitty. You're talking too fast. I can't understand you." Jenni Beth dropped onto her office chair. If it was at all possible, this day had just taken a turn for the worse.

"Oh, honey, I'm sorry. The cake was almost finished. I had the bottom two layers finished, and it looked fantastic. Not like anything I'd ever done before, but nice."

Jenni Beth gritted her teeth. She'd told the baker to slow down, not give her a blow-by-blow.

"Anyway, I left it setting on my worktable while I ran to the post office real quick. My grandson's birthday is this comin' week, and I wanted to pick up a special card for him and get it in the mail."

"Okay," Jenni Beth said patiently. "What happened to the cake?"

"Oh, the cake. It's ruined. While I was gone, Toby came in to wash up the dishes. She brought her two boys with her. Long story short…"

She hesitated and Jenni Beth rolled her eyes. "And?"

"They got to roughhousin', I guess. One of them bumped into the worktable and the cake toppled and fell to the floor."

Jenni Beth pressed her forefingers against her eyes. "Can't you make another? The wedding's not today, Kitty. You've got plenty of time."

"That's the thing. I'd put the cake topper, you know, the special one Stella sent me with the bride and groom on the Harley, on the table beside the cake. It fell off, too, and shattered into a million pieces."

Jenni Beth didn't reply. Apparently the universe was

dead set on derailing her first Magnolia Brides wedding and doing a bang-up job of it. First the venue, her grandmother's rose garden, destroyed, and now the cake and topper.

Her mind raced. "If I find you a topper, can you bake a new cake?" She fought to keep her voice even, to hide her frustration.

"I suppose so, but it would mean stayin' over tonight and workin' late. I have other orders, you know."

"I'm sorry, Kitty, but I have a bride who needs a wedding cake on Saturday. One that's already paid for."

Of course, without a garden maybe this was all a moot point. But Cole had said to let him worry about that. And, oh, jeez, wasn't that unfair? None of this was his problem.

Once again, though, he was stepping up to the plate. Loyalty to Wes? Desire to help her folks? And yet didn't he want her to fail so he could take over her home?

She chewed at her bottom lip. He'd promised not to tear it down, and she had to believe he'd keep his word. So what *would* he do with it?

Nothing. Because she refused to fail.

Things had changed between them. Simply thinking about him made her pulse race. Their night in Savannah—had to be put on the backburner. For now.

Nothing made sense anymore. A massive headache scrambled her brains, and she couldn't think.

"Where you gonna get another cake topper at this late date?"

"I honestly don't know, but you let me worry about that. If we need to, we'll improvise."

"Your bride had her heart set on that one she sent special delivery."

Thank you, Kitty, Jenni Beth thought. "I understand, but you said it can't be repaired."

"No, ma'am."

"Bake and decorate a new cake, and I'll take care of the topper."

After she hung up, she leaned back in her desk chair and fought back tears of frustration. Why had she ever thought she could do this?

Well, she was in it neck-deep at this point. She'd promised Stella and Steve she'd provide the perfect wedding for them. And, by darn, somehow or another she meant to do exactly that.

Five minutes on the computer and another five on the phone and she had an identical topper nailed down.

She phoned her dad who was on the golf course. "I hate to bother you, but I've got a huge problem."

"Something more than the rose garden?"

"Yes."

"What can I do to help, honey? Just a minute." He put his hand over the phone, but she heard him say, "Go ahead. Play this hole without me."

Then he was back to her. "Okay. I'm yours. What do you need?"

And there was the dad she'd always known. Confident. Plugged in. What a difference these past few weeks had made. Thank God!

She explained the problem with the smashed cake and topper and that she'd managed to track down another.

"I don't suppose you could make a trip to Savannah tomorrow?"

"As a matter of fact, I can. Think I'll take your mother along. We can leave early and have lunch at her favorite restaurant, pig out on their fried green tomatoes, crab cakes, and pickled watermelon rinds. It'll do her good. She hasn't been eating enough."

"No, she hasn't been. You sure you don't mind?"

"Absolutely not. It's the least I can do."

"Thank you, Daddy. I'm leery of having it delivered. If it doesn't get here, I'm sunk."

"Understood. This is the smart way to handle it."

She hung up. One problem down, and too many to count still to go.

Jenni Beth tossed and turned, too restless to sleep. Cole had assured her they could fix the rose garden before the wedding. She had serious doubts about that. The garden had been a work in progress for over a hundred and fifty years. How did you restore it in a day?

He'd left here in a huff, and she hadn't heard from him since. Although she did have a visit from Jimmy Don who'd said Cole had sent him. The sheriff took photos, questioned her, and filled out a report.

Flipping back the covers, Jenni Beth moved to the window.

Headlights! Aimed at the rose garden.

The vandal had come back? Well, this time it wouldn't go so well for him. Without thinking, she slipped on the pair of silver sequined flip-flops by her bed and ran down the stairs, through the hallway, and out into the humid night air.

As she rounded the house, the scent of roses, sweet and delicate, wafted to her. Her forehead wrinkled in confusion. She heard the thwump of a shovel striking dirt. What? He'd come back for the roots?

"I've already called the cops," she shouted, "and I've

got a gun. If you know what's good for you, you'll get the hell off my land!"

The digging stopped.

Jenni Beth didn't know which was louder, the humming of the cicadas or the beating of her heart.

Please, she prayed, *just leave*.

Slowly, the shovel dropped to the ground, and the intruder raised his hands.

She held her breath. What if he attacked her? She should have wakened her dad. Should have actually called Jimmy Don and grabbed some kind of weapon for defense. Had she turned into one of those romance novel heroines who was too stupid to live?

Despite the night's heat, she shivered.

When he turned and stared straight at her, the moonlight caught in his hair and highlighted him.

"Evenin', sugar."

"Cole?"

"What in the hell are you doin' out here in your nightgown, Jenni Beth?"

She stared at him, speechless.

"If you do have a gun, sweetheart, put it down slowly before you hurt one of us," Cole said.

"What are you doing?" she asked.

"Plantin' you a rose garden. I had to drive seventy-five miles to round up enough plants, and I've got a blister on my hand and about a dozen thorns in my fingers. So I'm feelin' kind of mean right about now. And here you are, rushin' out in the middle of the night to protect your garden. Don't you have a lick of sense?"

"Of course I do. Do you have any idea what time it is? Why are you here in the dark?"

"Because I just got back into town." He squinted into the dark. "You *don't* have a gun, do you?"

She shook her head. "No."

"And you didn't call the police."

Warned by the edge in his voice, she hesitated. "No."

He swore. "Somebody needs to take you over his knee and give you a good spankin'."

"Well, it won't be you!"

His eyes glittered in the moonlight—anger and something else.

"I wouldn't bet on that, sugar."

He moved toward her, and she took several steps in retreat. "Don't you come near me, Cole Bryson, or so help me I'll scream bloody murder. Daddy *will* have a gun when he comes running out, and he won't hesitate to use it."

"I don't think you're gonna do that, sweetheart."

"Don't sweetheart me."

When he continued toward her, she took another, then another step backward, her heart in her throat. It wasn't only fear, though. It shamed her to admit how much his words had excited her.

Before she understood what he was up to, he reached down and grabbed a hose. "I'm filthy. Let me rinse off the top layer."

She stood impassively while he hosed some of the dirt from his hands.

"Done?" She tapped her flip-flop in the grass.

"Not quite. Think you got a little dirt on you, too. Right about there." He turned the hose on her, hitting her square in the chest.

Shocked, she let out a smothered squeal. She plucked

at her nightgown where it stuck like plastic wrap to her. And, she realized in horror, the white cotton had turned nearly as transparent.

"You imbecile. That water's freezing cold."

Laughing, unguarded, he dropped his hand to his side.

In a flash, she lunged at him and turned the hose full blast on him. He reached for it, her foot slipped in the wet grass, and she went down, dragging him with her.

He somehow managed to twist on the way down, hitting the ground first. She sprawled full-length on top of that gorgeous hard body.

She stopped breathing as his arms moved around her, drew her closer. His warm lips covered hers, his tongue sliding between them to taste her.

She groaned.

How long they laid like that, his large hands moving over her back, her legs, her bottom, she couldn't have said. Totally lost in him, the rest of the world disappeared.

"Jenni Beth, I—" He rested his lips against her neck. "Oh God, as much as I want to stay right here with you like this, as much as I want to tear what's left of that nightgown off you and have my way with you, we need to talk."

"Now?"

"Yeah. Time to get this done." He rubbed a thumb over the back of her hand. "Let's go around front and sit on the swing."

His face had turned serious.

"You're scaring me, Cole."

"I don't mean to, but there are things you need to know."

Even though the Southern night was warm, the slight breeze chilled her, and she shivered.

He stopped by his truck and took out the stadium blanket he kept there. Wrapping it around Jenni Beth, he walked her to the swing.

Settled, his arm thrown over the back and draped around her shoulder, he said, "You're probably not gonna like everything I have to say, but promise you'll hear me out."

"Can it really get worse?" Her stomach pitched, and she rested a hand on it.

"I'm afraid so. First, though, did Jimmy Don visit you today?"

"Yes. We took care of the paperwork. He said, more than likely, Jeremy Stuckey is our culprit." She ran a hand over her damp hair. "I sure hate to be the cause of any more trouble for his mother."

"You didn't cause it. Might actually turn out to be a cheap lesson for him if it turns him around. Right now, though, I'm not overly fond of Jeremy and you shouldn't be, either."

"I'm not, but I like his mom."

"Understood. Okay, here goes." He held her hand while he shared the conversation he'd overheard the day she'd gone in for her loan.

"And you saw no reason to tell me about it." Her voice held a chill.

"I did tell you. Sort of. Remember the trip to the bottomland?"

She stared at him.

"Beck and I—"

Her mouth dropped open. "You told Beck."

"Yes." The lead balloon in his stomach expanded. He'd waited too long.

He let go of her hand and swiped a thumb over the corner of his mouth. "I wanted his take on it, but don't blame him. I made him promise not to say anything to you. It was my decision to keep you in the dark. So if you're gonna be mad at somebody, be mad at me."

"Oh, I am." The chill shifted to a deep freeze.

"I figured that." He held up a finger. "But you promised to hear me out."

"Fine."

"So, anyway, I've been doin' some diggin'. I got a phone call today while I was out chasin' rosebushes that answered most of my questions. One of the pieces of land that borders yours was sold to a company in New Jersey."

"The woman who called Stella had a Jersey accent."

"Right. Richard's wife brokered the deal."

"That makes sense. She's a realtor," Jenni Beth said.

"Also makes things very convenient. I talked to the couple who sold the land. Turns out they'd gone to Richard about a loan. He managed to convince them that sellin' their bottomland, instead, was the right thing to do."

"He tried that with me, too."

"I know he did. Let me tell you, this couple has a real bad case of seller's remorse. My guess is their meeting with Richard was kind of like grabbin' a free lunch with those people who sell time-shares. The only way to ransom yourself is to hand them your checkbook and buy somethin' you don't want and will never use."

"How about the other?" Jenni Beth worried the cuticles on her left hand.

"The owner of that piece got into some gamblin'

trouble. The same Jersey company took him on one of those sponsored trips to Atlantic City. One thing led to another, and he used his bottomland to settle the debt."

"Somebody isn't playing fair."

"No. And unfortunately, by takin' Coastal Plains' money, you're playin' ball with the same people. And you're up to bat."

"But if I fail, the bank owns the land, not Richard."

He toyed with a strand of her wet hair, wrapping it around his finger. "Good thinkin'. But, who's gonna be the first to know you've defaulted?"

"Thorndike."

"Exactly. And since his partner has plenty of money, they'll snatch it right up. Do you have any idea what they can do with that land? The three plots together? A housing development, condos, you name it, all at top dollar."

"And I'll be left with nothing. My family will lose their home. I should have listened to my gut and not gone to Richard. But Daddy and I both wanted to keep everything here in town. Wanted to do business with the same bank we've always dealt with." She sighed. "How can Richard do this?"

"Because he doesn't care, sugar. He has no conscience. To him it's all about the bottom line, how many Judas coins he can line his pockets with."

She struggled to take it all in, to make sense of it. To accept it. "What's the connection between Richard and the Jersey company?"

"I asked myself the same question. The owner of the company? Antonio D'Amato."

"Pia's father? Her husband?"

"Father. Pia's here to keep an eye on things. Daddy buys her a business, something to keep her happy and occupied, and she lets him know if things start going south. Or if Richard suddenly develops a backbone. My guess is that Richard owes D'Amato. That he's up to his eyebrows in something D'Amato is holdin' over him."

"Gambling?"

Cole shrugged. "I have no idea. I haven't found that answer. Not yet, anyway."

"What do we do?"

"I'd considered going by the bank, havin' myself a little come-to-Jesus meetin' with Richard."

"That's not a good idea for so many reasons."

He nodded. "Not smart, I know. D'Amato's a crafty guy, I'd guess, and I doubt very much this is his first shady deal."

She turned to face Cole, felt the heat that poured from him. "I wish you'd told me about this sooner."

"I had suspicions, sugar. Questions. That's all until today. Hell, we still have no real evidence. Except that filthy ball cap."

"Jeremy Stuckey's."

He nodded. "We'll see what the sheriff can do with him."

"You make me so mad, Cole."

"I know, and I'm sorry."

She rounded on him. "You're always sorry. Till the next time."

"What's that mean?"

"You keep going behind my back. Sticking your fingers where they don't belong, then waltzing out again."

"I didn't want to add to your family's worries if my suspicions turned out to be unfounded."

"And what about Kimmie Atherton? Hmmm? What about her? You went behind my back and asked her to the prom when you already had a date with me."

"Ancient history, Jenni Beth." He sighed. "What's the real reason you're mad at me?"

"You made me go with Angus to the prom."

"No." He held up both hands. "I did not. You chose to do that."

"You let Kimmie kiss you at the barbecue place."

He sent her a sidelong glance. "I'm not even gonna dignify that with an argument."

"Wes enlisted."

"He did."

"Why?" She hated the plaintive sound in her voice. "You two were supposed to room together at college, then go into business together. Why didn't you? Why did you open your business without him?"

Cole leaned back against the swing. Moonlight shone on Jenni Beth's face, highlighted the anger and sorrow.

Finally, she'd voiced the real reason for her on-again, off-again antagonism. Obviously, she blamed him, on some level, for her brother's death, and that hurt. Deeply.

"Wes changed his mind, sugar."

"Why didn't you change it back?"

"I wish I had an answer for that. It keeps me awake at night."

A tear dripped off her chin, and Cole started to reach for her but pulled back, not sure she wanted his touch.

"Everything fell apart the day he died. Nothing will ever be the same." She swiped angrily at another renegade tear and turned her back to him. "Go away."

"No."

"You did before."

"Yes, I did," he admitted.

"So did I." She spoke quietly. "I went back to Savannah after the funeral and left my parents to cope with things alone."

Oh God. How did he deal with this? What could he say to make it better? He hurt. For her. For her parents. For himself. And, most of all, for Wes.

"Your mom and dad are adults, honey. They had each other."

"They needed me. They needed Wes to come home."

This time, he didn't hesitate. He put his hand on her shoulder, turned her into him, and wrapped his arms around her. Her body shook with tears and more than a few of his own wet that beautiful blond hair of hers.

Both of them hurt, the pain soul-deep.

"You blame me for your brother's death." He spoke the words into her hair.

"No." She burrowed deeper, clutched his shirt in her fists, and wept.

Each fresh tear dug a new furrow in his heart. He placed a hand under her chin and raised her face until she met his eyes.

"Jenni Beth."

"All right. Yes, I do." Her eyes misted again and a sob escaped. "But I don't. Not really." She bit her lip. "It's just—Oh God, it still hurts so badly."

"It always will." He kissed the top of her head. "I'm sorry, baby. I'd give anything to change what happened, but I can't."

"I know." She tapped the side of her head. "Up here, I understand. But I keep thinking that if I just wish hard enough, I can undo it. Bring Wes back. Make things like they used to be."

Shakily, she got to her feet. "It's late. Thank you so much for all your work in the garden." With that, she handed him his blanket and disappeared inside the house.

He stood alone on the porch and swore. Damned if he'd leave yet. He still had roses to plant.

With every shovelful of red Georgia clay, he cursed the fates. Wanted to throw his head back and howl at the moon like the wounded animal he was. Every time he thought he and Jenni Beth had a fighting chance, every time they took a step forward, fate knocked them back two.

He was tired of it.

After he'd finished planting the bushes he'd bought, he toted all the injured ones, the ones they'd stored in buckets of water, to her new office. There, beside the carriage house, he set out a little ICU nursery. That way, if any survived, Jenni Beth could still enjoy her grandmother's roses. Maybe she'd think of him when their rich scent drifted through an open window.

Finished, Cole turned and walked away, stiff-backed. Gone was his easy saunter. When he reached his truck, he stuffed his hands in his pockets and stared into the night sky, at the stars that not long ago had seemed so magical.

The magic had died.

Chapter 28

IN AN UGLY MOOD, JENNI BETH SMASHED THE STAPLER with the palm of her hand, once, twice, three times. She'd been so unfair last night. Cole had worked that gorgeous butt of his off, had spent his entire day and half the night trying to right her world, and she'd bitten his head off, piled undeserved blame on him, and sent him home.

Except he hadn't gone home. Instead, while she'd gone to bed, he'd gone back to her garden. Dug more holes. Planted more roses.

If he never spoke to her again, she couldn't fault him.

Her office phone rang and her pulse sped up. Maybe it was him. Maybe he was willing to give her once more chance.

"Magnolia Brides."

"Hey, Jenni Beth, it's Stella. I have a question. Actually it's more of a request, but you can say no if you want to."

Uh-oh. The day before the wedding and the bride wanted to make changes? After the scramble to restore the garden, then browbeating Kitty to make another cake and sending her parents off today to pick up the replacement topper, she wasn't sure she even wanted to hear this.

But she put a smile on her face and in her voice. "What would you like, Stella?"

"The wedding's small. And that's okay," she added quickly. "It's just that, well, we've been thinking. We're so happy, and we'd like to share our happiness with others. Years from now when I show our kids their parents' wedding pictures, it might be nice to have more people in them, you know? Bear doesn't have any family, and mine lives in Canada. My folks don't want to travel this far, and my sister's eight months pregnant."

"Um, well, a lot of people choose small weddings."

Jenni Beth's mind kicked into emergency mode. How many more did Stella intend to invite? Could she round up enough chairs? How would she rearrange things? What about the cake? It would be big enough for another ten or twelve max.

"Like we did. I know," Stella answered, pulling Jenni Beth back to the conversation. "Bear and I understand what we're asking is a huge imposition, but we were wondering if maybe your family and a few of your friends might share our day with us. It would be, I don't know, more festive."

"My family?" she echoed, caught totally off guard. "I'm sure my parents would love to attend. This is a big moment for them, too. Charlotte, our housekeeper, would enjoy it, although I've got to warn you, she'll cry."

Stella let out a little yip of happiness. "I'd love that. Anybody else? If you'd all like to go to Duffy's with us after we're hitched, we'd love to have you as our guests."

"Let me see what I can do, Stella. I promise to get back to you today." She paused a beat. "Tomorrow's your big day. Excited?"

"Excited, nervous, thrilled, anxious. You name it. Bear? He's just happy."

"That's a good thing."

"Yes, it is."

When Jenni Beth hung up, she immediately started making a list. Besides her parents and Charlotte, she jotted down a few more prospective guests—Cole and his parents, his sister Laurie and her fiancé. *If* any of them were still talking to her.

Outside her window, Beck strolled by, whistling some silly ditty. Aha! She hurried to the front door.

"Beck?"

"Yeah?"

"I have a favor to ask. *Another* favor."

He grimaced. "Why do I have the feelin' I'm not gonna like this one?"

"Actually, I think you will. Stella called a little bit ago."

"Our first bride." He sounded as proud as she felt.

And why wouldn't he? This had been a group project all the way.

She smiled. "Yes. She'd like me to invite a few more guests to her wedding."

"Who?"

"That's for me to decide."

His brow creased in a frown. "Why would she want to do that?"

"So when she and Bear look back on the day, it will feel, I don't know, fuller, I guess."

"Even if the guests are strangers?"

She shrugged. "The bride's always right, and neither she nor Bear have family who can make it."

He squinted at her, propping his ladder against the side of the house. "So what's the favor?"

"Would you be willing to come?"

"To the wedding?"

"No, to Saturday night's dirt track race. Yes, to the wedding, nitwit."

"Nitwit? Name calling's not gonna get you anywhere." He laughed and ruffled her hair. "Yeah, I can come. Do I have to dress up?" He grimaced.

"Nope. They want to keep it casual." She toyed with her bracelet. "Sure wish Tansy was coming."

Beck tensed. "Why would you want that?"

"Support. Help. Most of all? Because she's my best friend."

"You can do better than her," he growled.

She sighed. He'd never gotten over Tansy's desertion. She understood that. Still, he needed to move on with his life.

Studying him carefully, she said, "I think I'll call her again. Try one more time to get her here."

"Don't bother to tell her I said hello, because I didn't."

With that, he grabbed the ladder and strode around to the back of the house.

Whew! A lot of emotion boiling inside that calm exterior.

Back in the main house, standing smack-dab in the center of the bridal suite, Jenni Beth turned in a circle, her grin growing. It had turned out so much better than she'd expected. Beck and his guys had quit working on the room in order to finish up the odds and ends outside for tomorrow's wedding. The bath here wasn't quite finished, so Magnolia House's first bride would still need to use the carriage house, but that was okay.

That's what they'd planned.

Something was missing, though, and she couldn't

quite put her finger on it. Another visual sweep and she knew. Stepping into the room, the bride and her party would have a lace-edged window shot of the live-oak-lined drive. A newly upholstered fainting couch was tucked into the corner and a beautiful oversized fern sat on a mahogany table beside it.

But the wall above needed something. Her mind skipped through the rooms, envisioning what hung on the walls in each, hoping she'd catch on exactly the right photo, the perfect artifact. But she drew a blank.

Then it hit her. With a laugh, she raced to her attic room. The trunk Cole and Beck had struggled with held the answer.

Digging inside, she unearthed an old hatbox that had been her grandmother's. Gently prying off the top, she hit pay dirt. Vintage valentines. The romantic ones from a time when quality trumped quantity. She lost herself in them. In the innocence of bygone years. In the scrawled messages on the backs.

She stood, sighed, and stretched. She needed a frame. Hurrying to the basement, she pulled the string that turned on the overhead light and mentally readied herself for an onslaught of spiders. When she saw none, she breathed a sigh of relief.

Dust covered everything and, poking in corners, she sneezed. Without thinking, she rubbed a hand over her face.

"Oh boy!" There, behind a discarded iron headboard, she spotted exactly what she needed. A stack of old frames. She flipped through them and found an oval one, painted white and gold. Just the thing.

Treasure in hand, she bolted into the first-floor hall and straight into Cole.

He reached out and grabbed her arm to steady her. One finger flicked out, traced down her nose. "You're covered in dust, sugar, and I have to say that, on you, it's a cute look."

She rolled her eyes, then sobered. "Cole, I apologize for last night. I was wrong and spiteful. I don't blame you. For anything."

Instead of shrugging it off, he surprised her by saying, "Understood, but you hurt me last night."

A lump the size of a Georgia peach stuck in her throat. "Forgive me?"

"Always."

"I don't deserve you."

"Probably not." He chuckled. "Just try to get rid of me, though." He nodded toward the frame. "What are you doin'?"

"I needed something to hang in the bridal suite and remembered the box of beautiful old Valentines Grandma had stored in her trunk."

"Valentines? That's what was in there? I'd have sworn it held enough stone to build half the Great Wall of China."

"Funny." She made a face at him. "Anyway, I'll make a collage with them in this frame. Romantic. A touch of the past. A reminder of why the brides are here, what the day is about. Love."

He shifted on his feet. "Yep, and it's unique."

"Yes, that too."

"Your eyes are shinin', Jenni Beth, like stars in the nighttime sky."

"Cole—"

"And I'm standin' here fightin' to keep my hands off you. Think I'll throw the fight. What do you say?"

In answer, she moved to him, offering up a prayer of thanks as his lips covered hers, as his hands ran up and down her back.

His lips slid lower.

"If this is losin'," he murmured against her neck, "bring it on."

Charlotte cleared her throat behind them. "You kids might want to go somewhere a little more private," she said dryly. "Your daddy sees you doin' that, he's gonna have a fit."

"He's in Savannah."

"Don't make no difference."

"I think Daddy suspects I've done this a few times."

"Suspectin' and seein' is two different things. Now go on. Both of you. I have to dust in here. We've got people comin' tomorrow."

"Yes, ma'am." Cole picked up the frame. "Let's take this out on the porch and clean it up."

He held the door for her.

As she cleaned the grime from the wood, Jenni Beth asked, "Did you have some reason for coming by? Other than wanting to hear my apology?"

"I sure did." His finger traced along the ridge of her spine. "Jimmy Don just called."

Her breath caught. "What did he say?"

"He's arrestin' Richard. Thought you might want to be there."

"Honestly?"

He nodded. "Jimmy Don picked up Jeremy late last night. The kid tried to be tough, insisted he knew nothin'. His story was full of holes, and his arms are a mess from his night's work in your garden. Jimmy Don figured an overnighter in a cell might loosen the kid's tongue. It worked. By the time the sun was comin' up, Jeremy spilled his guts. Arlene was there and helped her son work out a deal. He'll trade juvie time for community service in exchange for testifyin'. Hope that's enough for you."

"It is. He's a young, mixed-up kid, and Richard took advantage of that. Hopefully, Jeremy and his mom can turn things around."

"All the paperwork's taken care of and Thorndike's at work."

"What are we waiting for?" Jenni Beth headed to the front door. "Charlotte? I'm going into town."

"I heard." The housekeeper stood just inside the kitchen door. "'Bout time Thorndike got his comeuppance. Always did think he was better'n everybody else."

Cole wasted no time. Before Jenni Beth had time to assimilate everything, he swerved into a parking space in front of the bank.

"We're here, Jimmy Don," Cole said into his cell. He slipped the phone back into his pocket and looked at her. "Now we wait."

In seconds, they heard the siren. Cole shook his head. "I swear he'd quit if the town council took that thing away from him."

Rather than park at the curb, the sheriff stopped in the middle of the street, lights flashing, siren wailing.

Cole sighed.

"Hey," Jenni Beth said. "This is probably the apex of his career. Not much in Misty Bottoms will beat this."

"True."

Hand on his gun, Jimmy Don nodded at them, then

strode into the bank. Quick as two cats, Cole and Jenni Beth were out of the truck and sailing in behind him. Walter, the bank guard, ran a hand through his white hair, listening to Jimmy Don.

"I'm here on official business, Walter. I need you to stay out of it, no matter what Thorndike says."

"Am I gonna lose my job?"

"No. Absolutely not."

"Good. Then do what you need to do." He swept a hand, motioning them in.

Wallet stood at one of the teller's cages. "What's goin' on?"

"Nothin' that concerns you," Jimmy Don assured him.

"Not gonna lose the money in my savings, am I?"

"No, sir, you won't."

"Okay then."

Both tellers, along with Gloria, watched wide-eyed. By now, Richard had come to the door of his office.

"What's going on here?" he demanded. "And why on earth is that siren wailing?"

"Richard Thorndike," Jimmy Don said, his chest puffed up like a robin redbreast, "you have the right to remain silent. Anything—"

"What in the hell do you think you're doing?" Richard yanked his arm free when Jimmy Don reached for it.

"Oh, now that's not gonna do." The sheriff grabbed him again, this time snatching his cuffs and slapping them on the banker's wrists.

"You can't do this!"

Jimmy Don tapped the badge on his shirt. "This right here says I can." Holding a struggling Thorndike, he calmly finished his recitation of the Miranda warning.

Standing just inside the door, Cole leaned toward Jenni Beth. "Remind me never to get Jimmy Don mad at me. He's enjoyin' this."

"Yes, he is," she said. "So am I."

It did her heart good to see Thorndike brought down for what he'd done to her, to Jeremy. She wouldn't be surprised to find out there'd been other abuses of his power. How many Misty Bottomers had been the victims of his shenanigans?

"Do you know who you're messing with, Jimmy Don?"

"I believe I do."

"No, I don't think you do," he snapped. "You're going to be sorry you pulled this little stunt."

Jimmy Don held tight to him, despite his kicking and screaming. "You threatenin' a sworn officer of the law, Richard? I'll make note of that in my report."

Richard's eyes landed on Jenni Beth, and he actually snarled. "I should have known you were behind this."

She felt cold. Goose bumps raced over her arms. No one had ever looked at her with such hatred. When Cole put an arm around her waist, she drew strength from it.

"You did this to yourself, Richard." She met his eyes. "We all make choices, and we all have to live with the consequences, good or bad."

"Miss Goody Two-shoes, aren't you?" He leered at her. "You'd better watch your back."

"Another threat, Thorndike?" Jimmy Don asked. "Guess you're not quite as sharp as I thought you were."

Sawyer Liddell, the only reporter for *The Bottoms' Daily*, rushed through the door as Jimmy Don herded Richard through it. A camera flashed, and Richard shouted obscenities.

Wallet, moving faster than Jenni Beth had ever seen, managed to position himself in time to be included in the next few pictures. Walter did, too, she noticed. Their sixty seconds of fame.

Gloria sat motionless at her desk, white as chalk.

Jenni Beth walked over to her once Richard was gone. "You okay?"

The assistant nodded. "The bank's books should be examined. I think something funny's been going on, but I can't prove it."

"Thanks, Gloria. I'll pass that on to Jimmy Don."

On the way back to Magnolia House, both were quiet.

"I feel sick to my stomach, Cole."

He glanced at her. She'd gone pale. "Want me to pull over?"

She shook her head and rolled down her window. "This kind of thing isn't supposed to happen in Misty Bottoms. Did you see the way Richard looked at me? Like he wanted me dead."

"He can't hurt you, sugar."

"I know. Still—"

"He's a pompous bully. He played with people's lives." He hesitated. "One more thing you should know."

"I'm afraid to ask."

"I went by Pia's shop on my way to your place this mornin'."

"Why?"

"I had a text message from her."

When she simply stared at him, he said, "Bella Fiore is locked up tighter than Fort Knox. I think she's involved in all this clear up to her eyeballs."

"Stella won't have any flowers tomorrow!"

"Yeah, she will. Pia might not be rotten to the core. In fact, I think she's the one who made that call to Stella. She was sendin' you a warnin', hopin' you'd back off."

"She didn't know me very well," Jenni Beth muttered.

"Truer words were never spoken. But I think, in her own warped way, she tried to help. I had Jimmy Don check her house. Nobody home. Nothing personal left behind. This morning's message said that your bride's arrangements are finished and waitin' in the cooler at Bella Fiore. A shop key's under the mat for you."

"I'm thankful for that." Jenni Beth's heartfelt sigh filled the truck. "You think Richard will talk?"

"I honestly don't know."

As they pulled up in front of Magnolia House, Jenni Beth threw her arms around Cole. "You want to go to a wedding?"

Startled, he asked, "What?"

"Stella's. She'd love to have you there."

"Wouldn't miss it for the world."

Chapter 29

Tansy, her auburn hair curling wildly, breezed into Magnolia House an hour later, unannounced.

"I can't believe you came!" Jenni Beth threw herself at her friend.

After a long, heartfelt hug, Tansy said, "I can only stay a couple hours. I promised Emerson I'd be home tonight, but I had to see you, to be part of this in some small way. You have to be so excited."

"I am." Jenni Beth tipped her head and studied her friend. "Do you ever call him anything else?"

"Who?"

"Emerson. It's so formal. Does he have a nickname?"

"Are you kidding?"

She shrugged. "Where's Gracie?"

"I left her with Grandma. The two had big plans for the afternoon."

Tansy's smile didn't quite reach her emerald eyes. When they'd hugged, Jenni Beth swore she felt Tansy's ribs, she was that thin.

"I'm sorry I was short with you on the phone." Tansy shrugged. "It wasn't a good day."

"Tansy, can I do anything to help?"

Her friend stiffened. "I came to help you, not the other way around."

"I know, but…"

She shook her head. "I'm fine."

Liar, liar, pants on fire. Jenni Beth bit her tongue. She couldn't push. If and when her friend wanted to share, she would. Until then, Jenni Beth would have to bide her time. That didn't mean it would be easy, though.

"So what do you need done?"

"Are you up for a little last-minute weeding?"

"You bet."

"I left some gloves on the table out back. I've been after it all week, so this is kind of touch-up. Together we should finish in no time."

"I'll get them," Tansy said.

Jenni Beth picked up the pruners she'd laid down when Tansy had driven up. As she straightened, she saw Beck round the corner of the house and, literally, collide with Tansy.

Uh-oh.

Beck reacted as though he'd been threatened him with a bucket of scalding water. Hands in the air, he backed up. Without a single word, he shot off in the opposite direction.

Tansy stood without moving, but Jenni Beth swore her shoulders sagged.

Jenni Beth closed her eyes. Why couldn't these two, who'd loved each other, at least be friends?

When Tansy returned with the work gloves, they set off for the rose garden. Beck's name didn't come up in their conversation.

Ruthlessly searching out even the smallest weed, Tansy said, "I can hear the questions in your head, Jenni Beth, so let me lay it out there. Emerson and I are still together, but our marriage isn't good. We fight all the time. We haven't slept together in—" She gave a half-laugh. "It's been so long I couldn't even tell you."

"Why don't you leave? Nobody would blame you."

"I—"

The crunch of tires had them both turning.

Tansy rested a hand on her friend's. "Please don't say anything about this to the others."

Jenni Beth crossed her heart.

Cole slid from his truck, and Tansy ran to greet him. He swept her off her feet in a huge bear hug.

"Gosh, it's good to see you, Tanz." He reached behind him and shut the truck door, meeting Jenni Beth's gaze over their friend's head. "I brought that arbor I was tellin' you about, sugar. Why don't you come take a peek and see if it'll work?"

"I wondered where you'd disappeared to." She moved to the back of the truck as he jumped into the bed to lift the white latticed arch.

"It's perfect." She clapped.

He jumped out, and without thinking, she gave him a big kiss. Red-faced, she stepped back.

Tansy sent her a mischievous grin. "So that's the way the wind's blowing."

"It's more of a storm most of the time," Cole said. "Your friend here has a real temper. And, boy, can she hold a grudge."

"That's so not true," Jenni Beth argued.

"Yes, it is," the other two said together.

She stuck out her tongue.

"There's maturity for you," Cole said. "I have somethin' else to show you. If you approve, I'll hang it today."

Jenni Beth watched as he reached into the backseat and withdrew a long, blanket-wrapped bundle. When he uncovered the wood and wrought-iron sign, she simply stared at it. Words deserted her.

Magnolia Brides, in elaborate script, had been engraved into the wood. Magnolia blossoms formed the dots over the i's. The wrought-iron bracket suited it perfectly.

"What d'ya think?"

"Cole, it's incredible. I love it." She launched herself at him. "It's real, isn't it? Magnolia Brides is real."

"It is. You want me to hang it by the carriage house door?"

"Yes. Oh yes!" She laughed, raising her hands to her cheeks.

"First, though, let me get this arbor in place. Tanz, this isn't heavy, but it's kind of awkward. Why don't you grab one end, and we can carry it out to the garden while Jenni Beth admires her new sign."

As they moved off, Beck came back toward the front of the house. "There are a couple small things I'd like to finish. I know you don't want any more mess till after tomorrow's wedding, but I promise to keep out of your way."

"It's fine. The sooner all this is done, the better."

"Anything else you need right now? For tomorrow?" He hitched up his tool belt.

"Nope." She showed him the sign. "Isn't it wonderful?"

"It is. You want me to hang it?"

"No, Cole's going to. It amazes me, but I think we're good. I desperately wanted a tent in case the weather turns bad or someone needs shade, but no matter how I crunch the numbers, I can't find a way to justify the cost."

"Why didn't you say somethin'? I've got one at the lumberyard that should be large enough considering Stella's small group."

She shook her head. "I can't afford it, Beck."

"I'll put it on your tab. When this place is rollin' in dough, we'll settle up."

"Beck—"

"Nope. No arguing with me about it. The thing's packed in a box doing nothin' but takin' up space. Might as well get it out and dust it off."

She grinned and threw herself into his arms, giving him a hug and a big smooch.

Cole felt Tansy tense beside him. He understood her feelings exactly. The sight of his girl in another man's arms didn't go down very well. The fact she hadn't admitted yet that she *was* his girl made no difference.

And Tansy and Beck? Man, those two had themselves some history. How had their lives—all of them—derailed so badly?

Voice carefully neutral, he said, "Doesn't mean anything, Tanz. She does that all the time. With everybody."

"I know. It doesn't matter to me, anyway. I'm a married woman, remember?"

The sadness in those big beautiful eyes just about cut him off at the knees. "Come on, sugar, it's all gonna be okay." A finger beneath her chin, he pleaded, "Don't you dare cry. I can deal with almost anything but a woman's tears. They destroy me."

Her chin quivered, but she sent him a watery smile. "Let's stand this trellis up and see how it looks."

"Deal."

They'd no sooner finished than his phone chirped.

Jimmy Don. Cole listened as he walked back toward Jenni Beth. Finished, he pocketed his cell.

"That was the sheriff," he said.

"Did Richard confess?"

"He's dancin' around it right now. Jimmy Don probably won't be able to charge him with much more than mastermindin' the vandalism, but Thorndike played fast and loose with moral and ethical codes. All things considered, I imagine we can renegotiate that bank loan of yours and have your bottomland removed as collateral."

"He wanted my land even before I went in, didn't he?"

"Yeah. You got sucked into a game of dominoes, sugar. You owned the land, your folks were in financial trouble and always dealt with his bank. Richard knew it was only a matter of time till you came in for a loan. You'd have to give up the one asset you had."

"What if I *hadn't* gone to him?"

"He'd have made it work somehow or another. When the mob's squeezin' you, you do whatever it takes. You threw a wrench into his plans by refusin' to sell him the land outright."

Cole dropped onto a stone bench and pulled her down beside him. He'd already filled Tansy in on their morning, and she sat in the grass beside them.

"How's Pia tied into this?"

"Her dad. Word is he has ties to the family, if you know what I mean. Kind of a Gotti-wannabe. My guess is that Richard's more afraid of D'Amato than of jail time, so I doubt he'll roll on him."

"Why would he get mixed up with someone like that?"

"Jimmy Don's been pokin' into that. Turns out our bank president likes to gamble. He's probably into D'Amato for a huge hunk of change. Following Gloria's hunch, Jimmy Don contacted Coastal Plains' headquarters, and they've already got a team on the way from Savannah."

"Wow."

"Yeah, wow. He probably dipped in the till to stall D'Amato until he got his hands on your land. And *that* might earn him some jail time."

"This will give them something to talk about at Dee-Ann's," Tansy said. "Who said Misty Bottoms was a quiet little town?"

Chapter 30

Stella's wedding day broke bright and sunny.

Jenni Beth had one finishing touch for her office, today's temporary bridal suite. For her first wedding. *Oh please, oh please, let it go well.*

She hated that Tansy hadn't been able to stay but was so thankful they'd had some time together yesterday.

Off to the left of the rose garden, she caught sight of the white tent Beck and Cole had sweated over last night. It glistened in the morning sun, and she crossed her fingers that the day would stay sunny.

"Have you got it, Dad?"

"Sure do."

The two of them made their way slowly across the yard, her grandmother's gilt-edged mirror between them. Maneuvering it through the door, they rested it against the carriage house wall. Beside it, on the window ledge, Ms. Hattie's African violet was lush with deep purple blooms.

Her dad draped an arm around her waist, and together they stared at their reflection. She leaned her head on his shoulder.

The last shard of the ice around her heart melted. For the first time since they'd received word of her brother's death, her heart felt totally open.

Cole had found the key, and this moment put that key in the lock. She was alive. She wanted to feel again, to love again.

"Love you, Daddy."

"I love you, too, sweetheart, and your mother and I are proud of you." He kissed the top of her head. "And I'm so thankful you've come back to us."

"I'm glad I'm here, too."

"Are you?" He took a step away and placed his hands on her shoulders. "You've given up a lot to rescue your mother and me."

"Daddy—"

"No. Let me say this, Jenni Beth." Her dad's mouth worked with emotion. "Your mom and I didn't handle any of this well. Not Wes's death, not the house or our finances, not you. We forgot in our grief over losing one child that we still had another who might need us."

He swiped at a tear, and Jenni Beth had trouble breathing.

"Cole reminded me of that, and I'll be forever grateful." He sniffed. "Thing is, you rode in and rescued us. You shouldn't have had to do that."

"I think maybe we rescued each other."

"Maybe." He patted her back. "I'll go check on your mother. She was fretting about what to wear."

Jenni Beth laughed. "She'll look beautiful. She always does."

He nodded. "I'm a lucky man. I have *two* beautiful women in my life. Two women I love."

With that, he walked out, closing the door softly behind him.

Her heart nearly exploded with emotion. Love, happiness, sadness, thankfulness, regret all raced through her mind, nipping at one another.

She moved back to the mirror, reached out to run a

finger along the edge. She imagined she saw her grand-mother's face staring back at her.

"Thanks for this, Gram," she whispered. "The house will be full of life and love again."

A touch of sadness flitted over her. "I hope you're not upset with what I've done, but it's the only way. For Magnolia House, for the Beaumonts, for Misty Bottoms. I think Great-Great-Great-Great-Grandpa Beaumont's wedding gift to his bride will save us all. It all started with a wedding. We've formed a circle."

Stella and Bear's wedding went off without a hitch.

Her father, who'd insisted on handling the music, hit the power button on cue and "Destiny" by Jim Brickman played over the speakers. As the song ended, Stella rode down the rose-strewn carpet of grass on the back of her Harley. Stunning in a white cocktail-length bridal dress, her short veil flowed behind her and the ribbons in her bouquet fluttered in the breeze.

The second Bear saw her, the hulking six-foot-five groom broke into tears as big as spring raindrops.

When Charlotte joined him in the weeping, Jenni Beth handed her a hanky. Stella glanced at them and grinned.

The service was sentimental, romantic, and funny, and the weather was absolute perfection. Even though the tent hadn't been necessary, Kitty commented that the shade kept the sugar roses from melting and sliding down the sides of the cake. Now there was something to be thankful for.

And Pia's flower arrangements? Jenni Beth had never seen better. And there was a worry. Misty Bottoms no longer had a florist. No florist, no bridal bouquets.

Somebody had mentioned Beck's cousin was a florist. That she was considering opening her own shop. Jenni Beth would have to check that out, see if she could talk her into opening it here in Misty Bottoms. But right now? Today? She'd concentrate on Stella and Bear.

Luanna and her friends served Kitty's impressive cake, its Harley-riding bride and groom topper firmly in place, and uncorked champagne with great aplomb. Toasts made and glasses raised, her father once again moved to his post. There wasn't a dry eye in the house when Stella and Bear hit the floor for their first dance as man and wife to Celine Dion's "Because You Loved Me."

Yes, Jenni Beth thought, this would be a forever marriage. Her heart swelled with happiness. And then her gaze landed on Cole.

She loved the man beyond words.

A heaviness centered in her heart even as pride forced a smile.

———◇◇◇———

At Duffy's Pub, Cole snagged a table for his family and Beck.

"Dance with me, Nick." His sister took her fiancé's hand and dragged him onto the postage-stamp-sized floor.

Cole sipped his beer. Maybe he'd ferret out Jenni Beth and talk her into a celebratory dance. Her first wedding had been flawless—despite Richard and Pia, a destroyed rose garden and wedding cake, a broken cake topper, and, and, and! She had to be one happy woman right about now.

He spotted her across the room, her back to the wall,

swaying to the music and wearing a grin the size of Texas. And he knew what he had to do. This wasn't what he'd planned or the way he'd imagined it, but it felt right.

Making his way to her, he handed her a flute of champagne, tapped his own glass to hers. "You did it, Jenni Beth."

"I did, didn't I? With a whole lot of help from my friends." She sipped at her glass. "None of this would have happened without you, Cole."

He shrugged.

"If I'd failed, you'd have gotten the house."

"Yeah, me or Richard."

"So tell me. I'm dying to know why you worked so hard at losing."

"The house belongs to you and your family. It's meant to be."

"What were your plans, Cole?"

When he looked at her questioningly, she said, "That morning at Dee-Ann's, you told me you had plans for Magnolia House, too."

"I intended to turn it into a B&B."

She looked shocked. "You're kidding."

"Nope. It would have been a huge change for your folks, but I planned to hire help to take care of all the day-to-day work. I didn't expect your mom and dad to do anything except show up for social hour once in a while."

"Why would you do that?"

"So Todd and Sue Ellen could stay in their home. At first, it was for Wes. I'd made him a promise. But somewhere along the line things changed, and it became all about you. You wanted this so badly, sugar, and I wanted you to have it."

"So when I was saying all those mean things to you, none of them were true. You were actually watching out for my family. Helping my brother, my parents, and me."

"Mostly you."

"That's way over and above what you'd promised."

He took a deep breath, his heart pounding, his hands sweating. Now or never. He plunged in. "I did it because I love you, Jenni Beth. A soul-deep, forever love."

She blanched, and he panicked. What if she didn't feel the same for him?

He swallowed, took her hand. "I think we should get married. At Magnolia House."

"Married?"

He nodded. "You. Me. Magnolia House." He spoke slowly, as if to a young child.

She stepped away. "Married?" she repeated. Her tongue flicked out to wet her lips. "Cole—"

Although his heart was breaking, he forced himself to back up. "It's okay, sugar. I'm a patient man. I'll give you time to get used to the idea."

She said nothing.

More nervous than he'd ever thought possible, he plowed on. This was turning out to be a heck of a lot harder than he'd imagined. "Shoot, I know this isn't a Hallmark card proposal. You deserve the works— candles, romance. Heck, a little privacy."

When she continued to stare at him, he said, "I do know a great wedding planner. She's just opened an incredible venue."

He reached for her hand again, stared into those

slate-blue eyes. "I don't have the fancy words, Jenni Beth, but I love you. I want you to be my wife. Mrs. Cole Bryson."

"You mean that?" Her eyes misted. "This is real?"

"Yeah. The feeling, the wish. Both are very real. And, Jenni Beth? Just so you know, I'm not goin' anywhere. I love you, and I'm here to stay. Forever and ever."

With a squeal, she launched herself at him, dribbling champagne down his neck. "Yes, yes, yes! I love you, Cole. I always have, and I always will."

Cole held her close. And that, he thought, was what happened when you dared to dream a little dream. A dream of forever.

Read on for a sneak peek from

Every Bride Has Her Day

Magnolia Brides, Book 2

MOBSTERS, MORONS, AND MOONLIT GARDENS. AN odd trinity.

"Unless you're me," Cricket O'Malley sang, excitement, happiness, and nerves bubbling through her.

She centered her camera on the old railroad car, clicked, and sent the photo via Facebook. Her new shop, the Enchanted Florist! Her parents would love it.

And so did she.

A horn tooted behind her.

"Thought this might be a good time for you to meet Jenni Beth," her cousin Beck called out, "but I just talked to her and she's not gonna be back in town till later tonight."

With the window of his monster truck down, he rested one forearm on the door frame. "You up for a meetin' with her tomorrow?"

"I sure am! My partner in crime! Sort of."

"You might want to be careful who you say that to, considerin' the circumstances." He nodded toward her shop. "Lock up and let's go. I'll take you to dinner."

"Oh yeah?"

"Yeah. Want to ride with me or drive yourself?"

"I'll go with you if that's okay."

"You bet."

"Anybody ever tell you that you look an awful lot like Dierks Bentley?"

"Yep." He grinned and slid a pair of dark glasses into place.

Cricket did a little happy dance as she locked up. She couldn't remember the last time she'd been so excited. It was a whole lot like buying a new notebook for the beginning of the school year. Nothing had been written in it yet, no mistakes made. The pages were waiting to be filled. An exciting new adventure begun. A month ago she'd been out of work and fast running out of hope. One phone call from her cousin had changed all that.

Now, here she was in Misty Bottoms—a very small town in Georgia's Low Country. She'd lived here the first five years of her life before her folks packed up and moved to Blue Ridge in the North Georgia mountains.

She and Beck, with whom she'd shared her first Christmases and Thanksgivings, had kept in touch through social media, and he'd found her a new business and a new house.

He leaned across the seat and opened the door for her. Sliding in, she buckled up, then rolled her shoulders. It had been a busy day, a very physical one. A lot of inventory to unpack.

"You gettin' rid of the ghost of Pia D'Amato?"

"I'm sure tryin'. Hope nobody holds her taste against me." Cricket grinned. "I stripped the place bare and repainted. Pastel blue and green. A lot of work, but the shop looks so much better."

They drove past Kitty's Kakes and Bakery, and Cricket pressed her nose to the window.

"Want to stop?" Beck asked.

"No. So tempting, though. Kitty's sticky pecan rolls. Mmmm."

Beck slowed down.

"Keep movin', cuz. Don't encourage me. I've already indulged too many times this week. So many times that I stopped at the Piggly Wiggly yesterday and stocked my fridge with yogurt. That'll be dinner after tonight."

"I don't know." Hands on the steering wheel, he raised first one, then the other, palms up. "Sticky roll, yogurt."

"Stop it! You're bad." She smacked him, and he laughed.

"Okay, but tonight when you're lyin' in bed salivatin' for one, don't say I didn't warn you."

"Fair enough. Right now, I want a big, juicy cheeseburger and a mountain of greasy fries."

Beck drove down Main Street and parked in front of Dee-Ann's Diner. The old brick sidewalk, the red and white awning, the petunias and ferns in baskets and planters made Cricket smile. The owner obviously had a green thumb.

"We've come to the right place, then," Beck said. "Dee-Ann serves the best artery-clogging fries and burgers in town."

~~~

Later Beck dropped her off in front of her shop, and she gave him a big hug. "Thanks for dinner. And for everything else."

"You are so welcome." He studied her face. "Despite all your happy-happy, you look exhausted, Cricket. You're not gonna work anymore tonight, are you?"

She yawned and stretched. "Nope. Time to head home."

Driving along the quiet streets of Misty Bottoms as the light faded, Cricket tried to look past all the empty stores and concentrate on the prosperous businesses. On the outskirts of town, she waved to some boys playing ball in an empty lot. She wanted so badly to be part of all this. To belong here.

She turned onto Frog Pond Road, the shady little lane she now called home. The light on her front porch welcomed her in the growing dusk.

Georgia's Low Country. She loved it...and the cute little house Beck had found for her. She'd given him the green light to rent it sight unseen. The price was right, and he'd promised it would work fine, at least temporarily. It did. Wisteria twined up the porch banisters, Knock Out roses snuggled against the stone foundation, and a spot out back cried for vegetables and herbs.

A new home. A new shop. A new chapter in her life!

The only smudge on the whole cheerful tapestry? The abandoned house across the lane.

She couldn't actually see much of the two-story house itself. Mother Nature had pretty much claimed it as her own. Cricket wasn't sure what held the place up, unless it was the tall weeds and vines that had overrun the yard. She'd been tempted to head over there with some pruning shears and a lawnmower, but she'd held back. Getting arrested by Sheriff Jimmy Don wasn't exactly at the top of her bucket list. Besides, a person would have to be insane to tackle that place. It had strayed beyond the point of salvation.

And it wasn't her problem, was it? Refusing to think about it anymore, she walked inside her own well-taken-care-of home, kicked off her shoes, and changed into shorts and a tank top. Moving into the kitchen, she poured a glass of iced tea and carried it to the back patio. Even in the heat of the day, it was comfortable in the shade of an old oak. Sprawling on the chaise, she pulled out her phone and thumbed through the photos Jenni Beth had sent of Magnolia House and its first bride.

Cricket had arrived in Misty Bottoms with a mortgage on the flower shop, the tiniest U-Haul the company made, and a promise she'd get all the work for the Magnolia House weddings.

She yawned again. Right now, she wanted only two things. That big, old piece of banana cream pie she'd brought from the diner, then her bed.

Sam DeLuca had never run away from a fight. Until now. And look where it had landed him.

Smack-dab in the middle of nowhere.

"This has to be the stupidest idea I've ever had."

He'd forgotten how dark country nights could be. A thin moon scuttled from cloud to cloud and only a rare star twinkled in the inky sky. His Harley's single headlight cut a narrow swath through the darkness. A dog barked in someone's yard.

Not a solitary light shone from the windows of any of the houses he passed. Was every single person in Misty Bottoms, Georgia asleep?

He checked his GPS. He was close. As he approached an intersection, he idled along, looking for a street sign. And then he spotted it. Frog Pond Road. Thank God.

Twenty years had passed since he'd stepped foot in this town, and he'd been all of ten. Sitting at the crossroads, he couldn't remember if he was supposed to turn right or left. Well, roll the dice and pick one. He could always turn around if his choice proved to be the wrong one. He sure as hell didn't have to worry about traffic.

The clock on his instrument panel read a little after one a.m. He had wanted to arrive in the daylight hours, but between his late start and all the hold-ups of summertime interstate construction…well, it was what it was.

His already sour mood took a further dip. There it was, his great-aunt Gertie's house. Hell, his house now. Or what remained of it.

Sam pulled up in front of the deserted building. He sat on the motorcycle, legs spread, studying it in the nearly nonexistent light. No streetlights. No porch lights. He cursed small towns and rundown houses as the Harley idled smoothly beneath him.

He backed up the big bike and turned so that he sat perpendicular to the house, his headlight spotlighting the tumbledown two-story.

"Nope, not a very well-thought-out plan, bud."

Muttering a curse, he wondered if he shouldn't book a room at some little motel for the night. If he shouldn't turn around right here and head north, back to the city. A person would have to be crazy to even consider doing anything with this place. But then he was, wasn't he? Crazy? Why else would he be here?

Maybe it was karma. Maybe he was meant to move into this dump, as broken down as he, himself, felt.

Maybe the two of them could nurse each other back to health, or at least some semblance of sanity.

Squinting, he studied the place once more before setting his kickstand and climbing off the Harley. Halfway to the house, an owl hooted and he automatically reached for his shoulder-holstered gun—the gun that wasn't there anymore. His rueful laugh sounded loud in the once-again silent night.

Nah. Who was he kidding? He and the house had both passed the point of no return.

About the Author

The luxury of staying home when the weather turns nasty, of working in PJs and bare feet, and the fact that daydreaming is not only permissible but encouraged, are a few of the reasons middle school teacher Lynnette Austin gave up the classroom to write full time. Lynnette grew up in Pennsylvania's Allegheny Mountains, moved to upstate New York, then to the Rockies in Wyoming. Currently, she and her husband divide their time between Southwest Florida's beaches and Georgia's Blue Ridge Mountains. A finalist in RWA's Golden Heart Contest, PASIC's Book of Your Heart Contest, and Georgia Romance Writers' Maggie Contest, she's published five books as Lynnette Hallberg. She's currently writing as Lynnette Austin. *The Best Laid Wedding Plans* is the first in her sparkling new contemporary romance series, Magnolia Brides. Visit Lynnette at www.authorlynnetteaustin.com.

Made for Us

Shaughnessy Brothers #1

by Samantha Chase

New York Times and *USA Today* Bestseller

———————

Can't make time for love?

The Shaughnessy brothers have spent the years since their mother's untimely death taking care of one another and trying to make their father proud. Oldest son Aidan is hardworking, handsome, successful—and still single. Sure, he'd like to have his own family someday, but who has the time?

She'll show him how to find it

Zoe Dalton, a stunning designer Aidan meets on one of his construction jobs, has the beauty and heart to make Aidan realize how much he's been missing. But it's not easy to break down walls you've spent years building up. Now there's a major storm bearing down on the North Carolina coast, and it could be catalyst enough to force Aidan and Zoe into some major decisions of the heart.

———————

"Chase grabs readers by the heartstrings and
reels them right into the antics of the lively
Shaughnessy family." —*Publishers Weekly*

For more Samantha Chase, visit:

www.sourcebooks.com

Not So New In Town

Harmony Homecomings

by Michele Summers

—〰—

You can't go back, and you can't stand still...

Lucy Doolan is a marketing genius. She can sell rain to a frog and snow to a polar bear. Newly single and unemployed, she's lured back to her hometown of Harmony, North Carolina, to help out her pregnant evil stepsister...only to find her former crush, heartthrob Brogan Reese, has returned too, to open a new business in town. To add insult to injury, he's still hot.

If the thunder don't get you, then the lightning will...

Brogan never noticed Lucy much when they were young, but seventeen people have recommended her to help him. She's got his attention now. With her sweet personality, brilliant imagination, and penchant for doing the completely unpredictable, Brogan is finding a whole lot of excuses to spend his days—and nights—with Lucy.

—〰—

Praise for *Find My Way Home*:

"A lot of emotion and off-the-charts sexual tension." —*RT Book Reviews*

For more Michele Summers, visit:

www.sourcebooks.com

I'll Stand By You

by Sharon Sala

New York Times and *USA Today* bestselling author

When no one ever takes your side...

Dori Grant is no stranger to hardship. As a young single mother in the gossip-fueled town of Blessings, Georgia, she's weathered the storm of small-town disapproval most of her life. But when Dori loses everything within the span of an evening, she realizes she has no choice but to turn to her neighbors.

All you need is one person in your corner

Everyone says the Pine boys are no good, but Johnny Pine has been proving the gossips wrong ever since his mother died and he took over raising his brothers. His heart goes out to the young mother and child abandoned by the good people of Blessings. Maybe he can be the one to change all that...

Praise for *The Curl Up and Dye*:

"A delight...I couldn't put it down." *—Fresh Fiction*

"One of those rare treats." *—RT Book Reviews*

"Engaging, heartwarming, funny, sassy, and just plain good." *—Peeking Between the Pages*

For more Sharon Sala, visit:

www.sourcebooks.com

Brave the Heat

The McGuire Brothers

by Sara Humphreys

The only fire he can't put out...

Jordan McKenna is back in town, and Fire Chief Gavin McGuire's feelings when he sees her after all these years are as raw as the day she left. Then he was just a kid wearing his heart on his sleeve. Now he spends every day trying to atone for the tragedy he couldn't prevent.

Is the torch he carries for her

Jordan's life has not exactly worked out the way she expected. A divorced mother of two with a failed acting career, Jordan's biggest concern about coming back to Old Brookfield was seeing her first love. But when a series of suspicious fires breaks out, Jordan and Gavin realize that dealing with the sparks between them may be the least dangerous of their problems.

Praise for Sara Humphreys:

"Sizzling sexual chemistry that is sure to please." —*Yankee Romance Reviewers*

"Steamy love scenes...intriguing plot...the reader will be entertained." —*Fresh Fiction*

For more Sara Humphreys, visit:

www.sourcebooks.com